W9-DIL-837

# The Marriage Masquerade

# The Marriage Masquerade

Cheryl Anne Porter

THE MARRIAGE MASQUERADE



ISBN: 0-7394-2448-3

Printed in the United States of America

Published by St. Martin's Press, 175 Fifth Avenue, New York, NY 10010.

To my mother, Pauline W. Deal, for always being a rich source of inspiration and fun . . . and jewelry.

And to my sister, Paula D. Clark, for her fabulous research on the Pinkertons, for her unfailing support and enthusiasm . . . and for being older than me.

My sincere thanks to Ms. Carol Lillis for sharing with me (and always on short notice) her vast knowledge and expertise regarding the British peerage. Who knew there were that many of them? Your help has been invaluable, Carol, and any mistakes are mine.

I also must thank my favorite British gentleman, Captain Jeremy Steele-Perkins, for his help with my initial question regarding the peers. When I asked him what to call the duke's mother, meaning what would be her title, he replied, "Well, I just call her Mummy."

It was at this point that we (Pattie Steele-Perkins and I) looked at each other and brought Ms. Lillis in.

# Chapter One

**Pinkerton National Detective Agency**
**151 Fifth Avenue, Chicago, Illinois, 1876**

The heavy door to Mr. Allan Pinkerton's wainscoted private office was closed. Inside the well-appointed room, an aura of efficiency and stability emanated from the very furnishings, as well as from the agency owner himself. He sat ensconced behind his rectangular walnut-wood desk as Sarah Margaret "Yancey" Calhoun paced in slow ovals in front of him. She looked every inch the lady, but looks can be deceiving. And Yancey Calhoun was no mere lady.

True, a moss-green hat, similar in color to her eyes, perched atop her upswept auburn curls. And her fashionable street dress of merino wool trimmed in velvet matched the color of her feathered chapeau. She'd drawn off her white kid gloves which now, resembling protectively crossed hands, resided atop her drawstring handbag. In turn, that particularly feminine accessory lounged like an indolent cat on one of two padded leather chairs facing Mr. Pinkerton's desk.

Putting the lie to the lady were her stiff movements and the halting manner of her speech. Neither fear nor illness underlay her behavior. The truth was Yancey Calhoun, sore over every inch of her body, was beat to hell. Her bruised jaw ached fiercely. A headache pounded with each beat of her heart, and her ribs hurt worst of all. But any movement of her bandaged right arm, where the whore's bullet had grazed her skin, kept Yancey sufficiently mindful of her narrow escape from death only two days past.

"The only reason I'm alive, Mr. Pinkerton," she was saying to her employer—a big man with a full beard, piercing deep-set eyes, and a prominent nose—"is I already had my gun at the ready and hidden under my handbag as I sat talking to Clara."

Backed by two large windows between which his desk resided, Mr. Pinkerton's frowning countenance told her that he wasn't the least bit happy with that news. "Are you telling me that you went in there alone, knowing there would be trouble? That's not how I've trained you, Yancey."

"No, sir. It wasn't until I was already seated in the room with the door closed that I realized something was wrong."

"I see. Then, what tipped you off?"

"Clara's behavior. She wasn't acting the same as she had on my previous visits. She kept looking past me to the closed door of her room. Suspicious—and rightly so, it turned out—I secretly slipped my gun out of my handbag." Yancey's next thought had her attempting a grin, but her aching jaw reduced it to a grimace of pain. "You'd think a lady of ill repute would know she could trust an elderly Christian lady who's there to rescue her from a life of sin."

"And that's what concerns me. The disguise, I mean." Mr. Pinkerton tapped a finger against his lips, as if it helped him to think. "You did use a clever disguise, one that's been successful in the past."

"Something's most definitely afoot. This is the third time in as many months that I've been found out. And I know I've been careful and well disguised. I *know* I have."

"I don't doubt you, Yancey. Still, it occurs to me that one of three things has happened." He readied himself to count them out on his fingers. "One, someone in your personal life who, for some reason, may hold a grudge—"

"That can't be it, Mr. Pinkerton. I have no family, as you know. And I'm not keeping company with anybody. So there's no one to—" She'd almost said *care*. "No one to hold a grudge."

"Then we must consider a second possibility. Someone from a past case of yours. Perhaps someone who didn't seem important at the time." He paused, staring pointedly at Yancey, who became increasingly concerned for what might follow. "You should know that I have assigned two senior agents to review the files of your recently closed cases."

Just as she'd feared. Yancey's posture stiffened with this direct hit to her professional pride. "You're placing me under review, Mr. Pinkerton?"

He nodded in the affirmative. "For your own protection and nothing more. Do you understand?"

She could only stare at her employer. The agents would be looking for anything that, through her own carelessness or at least a lack of thoroughness, had rendered her unwittingly vulnerable. If such details were found with any consistency, her job with the agency would be at risk. Yancey swallowed the lump of angry pride clawing at her throat. "Yes, sir, I understand."

"Good. Because I won't sit idly by and have my agents threatened or allow them to come to harm."

"No, sir. I wouldn't expect you to." Neither had she ever expected to find herself the target of a review. After all, she was careful. Calculating, even. She took pride in that. Living up to her code name—the Fox—she knew that she was crafty and sometimes sly. She had to be, if she hoped to stay alive. She'd been trained to approach each of her assigned cases as if it were a game of chess. Such forward-thinking tactics made her a highly successful agent. Or so she'd thought until recently when events began proving otherwise.

When Yancey realized that she'd been quiet overly long, she returned her attention to Mr. Pinkerton, only to see that he'd been watching her. Determined not to appear shaken, though she was, she moved the conversation along. "And the third possibility, sir?"

"Presumes upon the second one, actually. We could be looking for a relative of a criminal you've caught. Someone we knew nothing about. A brother. A widow. A son or a daughter or the like."

Someone she hadn't known existed. This was good, and Yancey perked up. "Yes, you're right. Someone who may have bided his time until now."

Mr. Pinkerton's expression puckered and made him look older than his fifty-seven years. "Well, don't look so happy about it. I fear someone may have put a price on your head."

Yancey bit back a grin of pride. The bigger the bounty placed upon an agent's head, the more respect that agent was accorded among the Pinkerton operatives. "I've thought of that, too, sir."

"I'm certain you have. But it stands to reason. You can't be as good as you are and not make enemies."

Pleased at his acknowledgment of her abilities, Yancey pulled herself up to her full height, which wasn't considerable—or even easy, given her bruised ribs. "Thank you, sir."

Mr. Pinkerton's frown was fierce. "Why are you thanking me? Do you think I'm happy that someone could be out to kill you?"

"No, sir. Not at all. I know you better than that."

"I should hope so." He leaned back in his chair, causing the hinges to squeak, and went on with the subject at hand. "Now, what I need from you, and in detail this time, is another recounting of what happened to you two days ago. I want to make certain I have the details straight in my mind."

"Yes, sir." Still standing in front of her boss's desk, Yancey began. "As I told you, I was up in the red room with Clara. She was telling me about her last visit from Thomas Almont. About that time, a man burst in and shouted at Clara to shut her mouth. Surprised, we both jumped up. My purse and gun fell to the floor. The man told Clara I was a Pinkerton, pointed to my gun as proof, and said the agency is after Almont for that train robbery." Yancey gingerly rubbed her jaw. "Clara certainly has a mean left hook when she's defending her man."

At last—a grin from Mr. Pinkerton. "Looks like it from here, too. Anything familiar to you about the man who burst in?"

Quirking her lips in thought, Yancey considered how best to answer that question. "Yes and no. What I mean is, when he burst in, I had time only to defend myself. Only afterward, when I had time to think, did I realize that I knew of him."

"Let's save that for now. What happened next?"

"Clara hit me and knocked me to the floor, practically atop my gun. And that's the same moment I saw *him* charging. I knew I couldn't fight both him and Clara—or allow a man of his size to get his hands on me. Clara tried to pull me up by my hair, but I twisted around and fired off a shot at him. He had no more than dropped to the floor when Clara let go of me, produced a gun herself from somewhere, and started shooting at *me*. That's when I lit out."

Recalling the chaotic scene, Yancey commented, "I don't mind telling you that some surprised upstairs women and their customers will have a story to tell. There I was, a gray-haired old lady tearing out of there, a smoking gun in her hand and a dead man on the floor."

"I expect you're right about that." Grim of expression, the man known as "the Eye" rubbed his forehead. "I've already talked to the police. As a favor to me and in consideration of your safety, they'll pass this off as just another whorehouse disturbance. So that's good." He tapped a small stack of letters that lay atop his desk. "But now I want to talk about these. Why don't you sit down and quit that pacing? You're making me hurt just watching you limp around like that."

"Yes, sir." Yancey went to the overstuffed, leather-upholstered chair where her white gloves and velvet handbag lay. "Those letters started coming about the same time my cases began going sour."

"Which is why they concern me."

"Me, too." Mindful of her many bruises from her fight with Clara, Yancey gingerly bent over and scooped up her belongings. When she straightened, she met Mr. Pinkerton's concerned gaze. He was a good man whom she respected and admired. He'd taken a chance six years ago on a desperate and untried twenty-year-old girl with a burning in her belly to be an agent. Since then, he'd paid her very well, as he did all his agents, and had been nothing but good to her, much like a father—the one she wished she'd had instead of her own.

A fleeting yet hardened expression claimed Yancey's features at the mere thought of her real father, that hateful man, Emeril Calhoun. He would have been well advised to stay away from his family and the small prairie homestead he'd abandoned years before. But he *had* returned home. And Yancey, an only child, had made him sorry that he had. But not before it had been too late for her mother. The remembrances ached too much. Yancey purposely blanked the long deceased and hateful man from her thoughts and lowered herself onto the chair that fronted her employer's desk.

Mr. Pinkerton again indicated the letters that only today she'd turned over to him. "These letters, taken by themselves, say nothing to me except mistaken identity."

"That was my first conclusion, too." She arranged her gloves and her handbag—heavy with the weight of her gun—atop her lap. "An easy enough mistake to make, I suppose, since the writer doesn't seem to have ever met her own daughter-in-law. Apparently all she had to go by was a name and a city."

Mr. Pinkerton idly fanned the edges of the stacked letters, much as he would a deck of cards. "Very curious, indeed. Four of them. All from England." He was thinking out loud. "All from the same woman saying she needs your help. Or that of someone with your name." Suddenly he focused on Yancey. "When did the first one arrive?"

"Around Christmas. I didn't pay it much mind, knowing this woman had the wrong American woman and thinking she would probably discover her own mistake. But I was wrong. She didn't, and I've received a letter every month since."

Troubling Yancey was the palpable desperation evident in the woman's pleas. *You must find it in your heart,* she'd written in one letter, *to forgive and put your troubles behind you. Please come to England at the earliest possible moment. We need you here more than words can say. I beseech you, Sarah. Please help us. Only you can.*

Mr. Pinkerton hunkered over his desk and leaned toward Yancey, bringing her back to the moment. "Yancey, you are my best female agent since Kate Warne, God rest her soul. And the most experienced. So you should know better than to keep something like this to yourself. Why didn't you tell me before today about these letters?"

"I didn't think them important, not at first, not when I had only the one. But then they kept coming and got more insistent. In that last one, the lady as much as demanded this Sarah's help. She called upon her sense of decency and duty to come to England at once."

He'd been nodding as she talked. "Yes. I read that. And she's British."

"So was the man who accosted me in Clara's room."

His expression sharpened. "Aha. I see. Seemingly unconnected events connected."

"Yes, sir. At first the letters appeared a harmless mistake. Then they continued to come, and my cases started ending badly. So, dismissing coincidence, I came to believe that this woman's thinking I'm her American daughter-in-law could somehow be part of something more."

"Turns out you were probably right, too." Her employer's stare was pointed. "You also made my point regarding the need to inform me immediately of curious happenings such as these."

Yancey felt the warmth blooming on her cheeks. Being chastised by Mr. Pinkerton, who expected such high standards from his operatives, was never pleasant. "I'm sorry, sir."

"All right, well, having said all that . . ." He waved a hand as if to brush away that subject. "Let's look at what we have here. The letters. The complications in your cases. This Englishman who attacked you. And all occurring at roughly the same time. Hmmm." He cocked his head at a questioning angle and frowned at her. "Did you never answer the lady to inform her of her mistake?"

Yancey shook her head. "No, sir. I was working undercover out in the field most of the time. I forgot about the letters. In fact, I didn't even know about letters three and four until yesterday when I was home and could collect my mail." She pointed to the letters as if she were identifying a suspect. "She's a persistent lady, this letter-writer, I'll give her that. You'd think in the face of no replies—here it is April—she'd stop trying."

"Yet she didn't." Mr. Pinkerton eyed her and his brow furrowed. "I have to ask, Yancey. You're *not* actually the wife of this woman's son, are you? You're not the Sarah Margaret Calhoun she's addressing?"

A bit taken aback, Yancey's chuckle was one of denial. "Of course I'm not, Mr. Pinkerton. I thought you knew me better than that."

He shrugged his shoulders. "I'm too much the detective, I suppose. Just being thorough. But that *is* your name?"

Yancey firmed her lips. She'd never go by the name given to her by a father she refused to honor, even after his death. She went by Yancey, her grandmother's maiden name. "Yes, that is my name. But I'm the wrong woman. This dowager Duchess of Somerset has me confused with someone else."

"Apparently. But is there another Sarah Margaret Calhoun in Chicago?"

He knew his agents, he knew Yancey, and he would assume that she'd check. She had. "Yes, sir, there is. Well, there *was*."

"Was?"

"She died last year. In November."

Mr. Pinkerton was quiet for an uncomfortable stretch of time as he held Yancey's gaze. "How unfortunate. How long have you known that?"

Had Yancey been less sore, she might have squirmed. "Since January."

"I see. So you were curious enough three months ago to check, but not enough to inform me of these letters. Or to inform this dowager of her mistake and the other Sarah Calhoun's death? I'm surprised at you, Yancey."

Yancey self-consciously picked at a piece of lint on her skirt before meeting her employer's gaze. "Allow me to explain my reasons, Mr. Pinkerton. You see, this other Sarah was known as 'Miss Calhoun,' and not Mrs. Treyhorne—or whatever her title would be if she were a duchess. And I thought it curious that a duchess would be working as a maid, which is what this other Sarah did. None of that seemed logical. So I could only conclude that she wasn't the duchess. Given that, I saw no reason to further distress this English lady by telling her this other Sarah, who most likely was not her daughter-in-law, was dead."

Mr. Pinkerton rubbed thoughtfully at his chin. "Good points, those. Now, how did this Sarah die?"

"Badly, I'm afraid. Mrs. Palmer—the lady who owns the boardinghouse where this other Sarah worked—said an Englishman came around one day asking for Miss Calhoun, saying he knew her."

"An Englishman? Now we're getting somewhere."

"Yes, sir. And Mrs. Palmer, a very friendly lady who pitied her maid as a woman alone in the world, was delighted to meet someone with a connection to her. So she told him Miss Calhoun was working on the third floor. The man thanked her, tipped his hat, went upstairs"—Yancey drew in a deep breath—"and quietly murdered Sarah Calhoun."

Mr. Pinkerton sat back heavily in his chair. "Murdered? Dear God."

Yancey nodded. "It's very shocking. No one, not Mrs. Palmer or even the other maids, heard a thing. Nor did they see the man leave. He just disappeared. One of the other maids discovered her body later."

"This is most distressing. But how did he do his dirty work so quietly?"

Yancey felt a bit ill just thinking about it. "He . . . slit her throat. He must have come up behind her and surprised her."

Mr. Pinkerton, looking slightly ill himself, ran a hand over his mouth and stared at Yancey.

She knew she had to tell him the rest, but her heart ached with the knowledge she was about to impart. "It's worse than you know, Mr. Pinkerton. The woman was with child. Not greatly so but noticeably."

Mr. Pinkerton's expression fell. He closed his eyes and rubbed at his forehead. "What kind of monster would kill an expectant mother?" he asked, sounding world-weary.

"By all accounts, the same one who attacked me in Clara's room. The description I got of Sarah's murderer matches him . . . as did the accent."

Mr. Pinkerton's expression hardened. "Then I'm glad you killed him. And I don't say that lightly. But tell me, what did Mrs. Palmer know about her maid? What did she tell you? I'm wondering if this man could have been Miss Calhoun's baby's father."

"A good point, sir. But I don't believe so."

"Why not? It makes perfect sense. An unwanted child, an inconvenient mother. Perhaps she was blackmailing him for money."

Yancey nodded. "I would have come to the same conclusions except for the way things ended, sir."

Mr. Pinkerton considered her and then waved a hand at her. "I see you have a theory. Proceed."

"Yes, sir. Mrs. Palmer said Sarah Calhoun just showed up one day at the boardinghouse where she sought employment. She had no belongings and was very quiet. She kept to herself and, when questioned, seemed either confused about her past or secretive. She never spoke of her baby's father and actually seemed unaware at times that she was going to be a mother."

Mr. Pinkerton shook his head. "Very odd."

"Yes. Mrs. Palmer pitied her and gave her work and a room of her own. But despite Mrs. Palmer's friendly overtures, the woman never warmed up. Then, following Miss Calhoun's murder"—Yancey experienced the oddest feeling coupling her own name with death—"the police couldn't find any family to claim the body. So she received a pauper's burial and remains a mystery."

Mr. Pinkerton drummed his fingers on his desktop. "A mystery, indeed. A sad, sad case. And this Englishman who killed her. The man you shot, by all accounts. Hmmm." Without warning, he hit his fist on his desktop, causing Yancey to jump. "You could have been killed."

He was angry because he cared about her. Yancey knew that, but she immediately came to her own defense. "But I wasn't, sir, and when I did put it all together—only yesterday—I came directly to you, Mr. Pinkerton."

He exhaled gustily, appeared a bit mollified, though not happy, and eased his frown somewhat. "Yes, you did. And not a minute too soon, I'll warrant. Give me the rest of it. You don't believe this Englishman was the baby's father?"

"No: Because right before he died, sir, the man I shot said there'd be others who'd come after me. He said this wasn't over, and it wouldn't be until I was dead."

Mr. Pinkerton snapped to. Yancey believed her employer's expression would have been the same had he been slapped with a glove and personally insulted. "Then you *are* a target and this other poor woman was killed by mistake?"

"Either that, or the man I killed meant to kill every Sarah Calhoun he could find in an effort to eliminate the one he'd perhaps been paid to kill."

Fierce of expression, Mr. Pinkerton narrowed his eyes in thought. "Yes, very possible. Obviously he'd been following you. Add to that the fact that this dowager in England has your address. And the man you shot—mortally wounded and with no reason to lie at that point—tells you there will be others after him. This smacks of a mastermind behind these events, Yancey."

It was Yancey's turn to nod. "I agree. But I don't think it's the dowager duchess, sir. Because if she'd hired the killer, she'd have been informed of his success as long ago as last autumn when this other Sarah Calhoun was murdered. She, therefore, would have had no reason to write her letters."

"True. Still, it's important to your well-being that we come up with as many questions and probabilities as we can between us. Only then will we have a direction in which to proceed from here for the answers. We must act before we can again be acted upon."

"Yes, sir." Gripped with the excitement that always seized her when she took on a new case, Yancey sat forward as alertly as her sore muscles would allow.

"Let's start here," Mr. Pinkerton began. "Suppose the murdered Sarah was in truth the runaway duchess this dowager in England is pleading with. Why did she run away? And from what or whom was she hiding—not very well but with good reason as it turns out? We can't simply assume it was the duke or his mother who sought to have her killed. After all, this distraught dowager appears to have been trying to get her to come to England, an act that very well might have saved the woman's life and that of her baby."

"I thought the same thing, sir."

He nodded. "Yes. Would have been most convenient, though, if this dowager had stated what specifically the trouble was. Save us all a lot of bother and worry."

"I can only assume the other Sarah, if she was the runaway duchess, knew what the trouble was, so there was no need to state it in a letter."

"Good point." Mr. Pinkerton was then quiet as he eyed Yancey in a way that warned her she was not going to like one little bit what he had to say next. "I have decided to take you out of the field, Yancey. It's too dangerous for you here right now."

Disbelief shot through her. "But Mr. Pinkerton, you can't do that. My life is always in danger when I work undercover. This is nothing new—"

"But it is. Before now, you've had your disguises to afford you a modicum of anonymity and safety. Recent events have proven that is no longer true. So what I say stands. You will be taken out of the field here. To do otherwise would be irresponsible on my part."

Yancey's eyes widened. He was going to do it. He was going to take away her true identity. The Fox. Top Pinkerton female operative. It was all she had. The agency was her life. It was who she was. She had no one or anything else she cared about. Just her job. And now . . . it too might be snatched away, just as her mother had been. Yancey sat forward, clutching at the edge of his desk. "Please, Mr. Pinkerton, I beg you to reconsider."

He shook his head no. "I won't be talked out of this, Yancey."

Her thumping heart and leaden stomach seemed to switch places as Mr. Pinkerton picked up one of the letters on his desk, opened it, and read it to himself. Then he directed his gaze her way. "Here's the way I see things, Yancey. Right now, you're no good to me here."

His words sent a jolt straight to Yancey's heart. "Please, Mr. Pinkerton, you can't—"

He'd raised a hand, palm toward her, to further forestall her speaking. "You were almost killed, Yancey. And the man you shot warned you that other attempts would follow. That puts not only your life but also our clients' concerns in jeopardy." He paused as if allowing time for his words to sink in. "That being so, I've assigned other operatives to the Almont case, which means you don't have any ongoing investigations. Correct?"

Yancey knew that he knew she didn't. What he wanted was for her to acknowledge his point. What else, then, could she do but agree? "Yes, sir."

"Good. Now, we have a dead and departed Sarah Margaret Calhoun. Killed last November. Maybe the actual American duchess. Maybe not. But in December, you started getting these letters saying there's trouble in England and this duke needs you. Then, over the course of the next months, more letters, more appeals arrive, and your identity and disguises are repeatedly revealed, this last time nearly costing you your life."

Realization dawned on Yancey that perhaps Mr. Pinkerton was pointing her somewhere. She listened now with more curiosity than trepidation. "That's right, yes, sir."

"Exactly. Now, it's not so far-fetched to believe that this dowager Duchess of Somerset, with her money and influence and desperation, could have someone working for her in America. Someone doing her bidding, and I mean shutting off all avenues for you to operate undercover or even to live your private life in order to force you to go to England. Someone like that Englishman you shot."

"I suppose." Just talking about the man had Yancey seeing again, in her mind, the shocked, then horrified, look on the big man's face that said he couldn't believe she'd inflicted on him a mortal wound. She'd seen that same look once before . . . on another man's face. Her father's. She quickly blinked that memory away. "But he murdered the other Sarah. And then tried to kill me. Why would he do that if the dowager wants this Sarah to help her?"

Mr. Pinkerton mulled that one over. "Maybe a double-cross? Maybe the man was playing both ends against the middle for his own gain." He sat up straighter with this new line of reasoning. "Maybe an unknown someone paid him more to kill his quarry than what the duchess would have paid him to get you—or the real duchess—back to England, Yancey."

"It makes sense. It's about the only explanation that does."

"Then it must be true." Still, he made a sound of frustration. "We just don't have all the pieces. That's the only thing I'm certain of right now. And I'm afraid that puts you in even worse danger."

She was used to her life being in danger, but still a hard knot of healthy fear pressed against Yancey's breastbone. "If only I hadn't been forced to kill him. We could have questioned him."

Mr. Pinkerton nodded. "True. But don't blame yourself. The man caused his own death by bursting in like that and charging you. Remember, he knew who you were, so he had to know you'd be armed. I believe he meant to kill you just as he did that other poor woman. After all, if his intention had been merely to kidnap you, he could have waited until you walked out of Clara's room and grabbed you from behind. Or simply have shown up on your doorstep. But he did neither of those things. So he got what he deserved."

"Maybe. But I've never had to do that before. Kill someone, I mean." But she knew she was lying. She had killed someone before. For a split second, she saw his hateful face before her eyes. His remembered scowl alone threatened to drag Yancey back to that day so long ago—

"You did the only thing you could, Yancey." Mr. Pinkerton's understanding words brought Yancey gratefully forward in time. "Something else that's curious here, though, is this same Englishman knew Thomas Almont was your target. And you said that Clara was obviously waiting for someone to rush in. So this man could very well have been a confederate of Almont's and meant to kill you for that reason. We'll question Clara about that. But no matter what, you did what you had to do. It was either him or you." Mr. Pinkerton smiled fondly at her. "And I'll take *you* every time."

"Thank you, sir." High praise, indeed, from Mr. Pinkerton, the founder and owner of the foremost detective agency in America. And she was one of his agents. The best of the best. The Fox. She got the job done. She was experienced and smart and tough and . . . right now, none of those things. Instead, she was beat all to hell, shooting at everything that moved, and not so cocksure about anything anymore. Yancey stared unhappily at her boss. "What's going to happen to me now, sir?"

"Happen? Why, you're going right back to work, of course."

Surprise had Yancey dropping her hand to her lap. "But you just said you were pulling me from the field."

"From the field *here*. While I don't *want* you to work, not while you're so sore and stiff, I think I have a plan—if you're up to it."

Instant excitement seized Yancey. "I'll do whatever you say."

"That's the spirit. Here's how I see it. With the other Sarah Calhoun lost to us, as well as the dead Englishman, we're left with our duchess in *England* as the only thread we can unravel."

Suddenly, Yancey knew where this—and quite possibly *she*—was headed. "Oh, Mr. Pinkerton . . . England?"

"Yes. A lovely country." He folded his hands together atop his desk. "As it turns out, I've been contacted by Scotland Yard regarding some new information on an old case we were working on with them a while back. It's unrelated to this, but it needs our attention. Now, as luck would have it, I don't have an agent in England at the moment."

There it was. That word again. England. Yancey's jaw suddenly throbbed, and her head ached. "How . . . unfortunate, Mr. Pinkerton."

He smiled, clearly pleased with himself. "Yes, isn't it?

However, I think you could do with some rest while you mend. Rest combined with work, that is. Time spent on trains and ships ought to do the trick, don't you think?"

Yancey could only stare miserably at her employer. "I wish I'd never brought those letters to your attention."

"It's a good thing you did because they're your next case. Now, with you safely away, I'll proceed with the investigation here into events surrounding your recent calamities. And you'll be in merry old England answering this dowager's cry for help. Between the two of us, I believe we can find the connection, if there is one, and solve this mystery."

He'd obviously latched onto this intrigue like a child to its mother. Yancey knew when she was defeated. "Yes, sir."

"Don't look so glum, Yancey. You're not being punished. The simple truth is, you're not safe here, not with the criminal element knowing your identity. Why, I'd have to keep you under armed guard around the clock, and I don't think you'd like that. But quite frankly, I can't spare the operatives to watch over you. So it's possible, left unguarded, that you could be killed in your sleep."

Yancey's eyes widened. "Thank you for adding that to my nightmares, sir."

Mr. Pinkerton chuckled. "It's my job to think of every angle. And right now, the angle we need to pursue is our worried duchess in England. On the whole, she doesn't sound the least bit violent, and she clearly needs help. Now, I have every bit of confidence in your ability to protect yourself when you're across the Atlantic, Yancey. But if you like, I can assign another agent to accompany you."

Yancey's spine stiffened with pride. "I work alone, Mr. Pinkerton."

"Knew you'd say that. Very well, then, we'll discuss more of the possibilities so you're totally prepared. And then, it's off to England with you. You'll travel in a new disguise, of course, and under another name. Don't want anyone following you."

Well, she'd walked right into that. There remained only one question. "In what capacity will I be going, sir?"

Mr. Pinkerton folded his hands atop his desk. "How

would you like to be the long-lost and now newly found American Duchess of Somerset?"

"The what?" Dumbfounded, Yancey put a hand to her chest. "May I point out to you, sir, that this duke just might notice that I'm *not* the woman he married?"

"I'm certain he will. But you have the same name and it will at least open the doors to get you inside. And after that? Well, knowing you, my dear, this duke will probably wish you *were* the woman he'd married."

# Chapter Two

**MAY 1876; COUNTY CUMBERLAND, FAR NORTHWEST ENGLAND**

Only wind and rain welcomed Yancey to the imposing and palatial manor house that the coachman assured her was Stonebridge, the ancestral seat of the Duke of Somerset. Yancey sat in the meager but dry comfort of the hired coach and watched the driver pound on the impossibly huge double front doors of the manor. Awaiting an answer, he hurried back to the coach and proceeded to unload her trunks from the boot. Looking around, Yancey exhaled.

"So this is Stonebridge." She was glad to be at the end of her odyssey, and her body assured her that it still felt every jounce and jolt of what had seemed endless weeks of travel in crowded railroad cars to New York City and then the steamship crossing of the North Atlantic. That had culminated in a brief stay in London on Pinkerton business. Following that, she'd then been obliged to endure another round of overland travel by train and finally this hired coach.

"But I made it," she murmured while raking her gaze over the impressive estate situated on the edge of nowhere.

A wry grin quirked her lips. It was certainly that . . . the edge of nowhere. The surprising thing to her was how similar northwest England was to the western states of America. Certainly the vast stretches of green hilly openness now surrounding her reminded her of the leading edges of the prairie states. And the high, forbidding mountains, so close behind the manor house of Stonebridge, brought to mind the great Rocky Mountains. She imagined that winters here were bone-numbingly cold and bleak. Just the thought of them sent an involuntary shiver over her skin, much as if she'd experienced a chill forerunner of a winter's wind. Thank heavens she would be long gone before the snows arrived.

She breathed in the fresh air, heavy with the warm spring rain. Greeting her nose was the distinctive smell of the leather of the coach and the tang of the winded horses. She heard their huffing and blowing as they stamped their hooves, impatient to be on the road again. They would leave soon enough, but she was staying. Yancey concentrated on the manor facing her. Viewed through the rain, the imposing mansion seemed to her to jut confidently from the very ground on which it stood. As if the great stones comprising the ancestral home of the Duke of Somerset had tumbled out of the hulking nearby Cumbrian Mountains, only to arrange themselves, of their own volition, into this structure.

Yancey's roving eye was suddenly captured by a feature of Stonebridge that to her seemed whimsical and defiant in the same breath. Much like a crone in distress, a tall, round stone tower sat imprisoned in the back northwest corner of the manor. From there, the building's bricked façade spread toward the east, as Yancey faced it. On each of the three floors, many equally spaced tall windows kept the occupants' secrets behind their closed draperies. And that had her wondering about the people who lived here.

What would the dowager do, she worried, when faced with her? Even more importantly, what would the duke, her "husband," do? As Yancey had pointed out to Mr. Pinkerton, while his mother didn't seem to know her daughter-in-law, certainly the duke would know Yancey wasn't his wife.

Of particular concern to her was the possibility that the duke could turn out to be the mastermind she sought. What if he had, unknown to his mother, driven his pregnant wife away and then had her killed? If that were true, he certainly would not be happy to have another Sarah Margaret Calhoun from America simply pop up here in England. Another consequence had occurred to her. Wasn't it conceivable that the duke and the dowager duchess could simply think her an opportunist and call the law after her? Well, thank heavens she had in her possession the letters that she'd received from the dowager.

Thinking of the law recalled to Yancey's mind the men of Scotland Yard. They'd proven more than helpful to her in settling the unrelated case—a theft of a valuable piece of art—that Mr. Pinkerton had sent her here to discharge. While at the Yard, Yancey had easily drawn the men out regarding the Treyhorne family. She'd appealed to their masculine compulsion to brag when faced with a pretty, smiling face, a young woman who hung on their every word. That pose worked every time, and it was exactly why Mr. Pinkerton employed women.

Absolutely enchanted to meet a female operative, something new to their experience, the British detectives had been very chatty. She'd been told the Duke of Somerset, along with his family, was not in London for the season. A situation of some note, they assured her, as Parliament was sitting and the duke should have been in attendance. But instead, still proving eager to gossip about their betters, the men had revealed that the family had gained special dispensation from the queen to repair to their ancestral home. Stonebridge, in the northwest of England. A fairly recent family tragedy lay at the root of their absence from society.

The older brother, Geoffrey Charles Treyhorne, had died suddenly and unmarried with no heir. Yancey now wondered if he'd merely *died* . . . or if he'd been *killed* in some subtle way. The man's death left the second and, by all accounts, reluctant son—a man who had spent the last several years in America and had taken an American wife—with the title and the considerable inheritance. Considerable enough to kill for, the men had confided. All very intriguing. And Yancey had written what she'd learned to Mr. Pinkerton and had also apprised him that she would be traveling on to Stonebridge.

And now, here she was, seated in the coach, with the high

humidity sticking her traveling costume to her skin. She admitted she had no clear idea of exactly what it was she was supposed to do or how she should proceed. Very disconcerting. Especially since, back in Chicago, one Sarah Margaret Calhoun was already dead. Yancey greatly preferred that the second one, namely her, not end up the same way. She would be wise to trust no one here, then. Just watch and listen and learn and keep her wits about her.

Yancey squeezed her eyes shut and pinched the bridge of her nose. Taking a deep breath, she remarked out loud, "This could be the death of me."

It was true. Until she'd arrived here and had seen for herself the absolute isolation of Stonebridge, she hadn't fully appreciated how truly alone and at the Treyhornes' mercy she would be. *Well, so be it,* she told herself bravely. She was on her own here and would remain suspicious of everyone. When, since she'd been a girl, had it ever been any different for her? She answered her own question with one word. "Never."

"Looks like the rain's letting up, miss."

Startled, gasping, Yancey put a gloved hand to her throat, where she could feel her pulse racing erratically. Then her mind registered what she was seeing. The coachman, a pleasant, red-faced, paunchy older man named Tom, had appeared at the coach's door, which he'd just opened. "Tom, you scared the life out of me."

"Not quite all of it, I'd say, miss, you being able to talk and all," he answered cheerfully. "Didn't mean to scare you, though. Got your trunks over there under the eave, out of the weather. We may as well get you out, too, while there's this bit of a break in the rain." He opened the narrow door farther and held out a helping hand to her. "Here you go, now. Watch your step, miss. It'll be slick, it will. Mind your skirt and the puddles."

Yancey immediately complied. From being days on the rough and rutted roads with Tom, she knew that he was a man who believed in a schedule and who brooked no delays. Still, gallantly he steadied her with a hand to her elbow as she held up the maroon skirt of her traveling costume and navigated the small step that was mounted just under the stagecoach's passenger door. "Thank you, Tom."

"You're welcome, miss. It's my pleasure."

Though she liked Tom well enough, Yancey was used to keeping her own counsel and seeing to herself. Her passing thought was how irritating it must be to be an actual duchess, to have servants and maids doing your every bidding and performing every small service having to do with your person. A shudder for such intimacy slipped over Yancey's American skin.

Now on the puddled, muddy ground, and smelling the commingled scents of the warm, moist earth and the sweet scent of the air, Yancey—with Tom's ever solicitous help—made her way up a graveled walk to the wide steps that led to the impassive front doors of the manor house. Each step of hers was accompanied by an escalating unease regarding the advisability of her presence here. Her heart thumped dully. Her chest tightened.

She then glanced over at Tom, only to see him casting questioning looks her way. "What is it? Is something wrong?" she demanded.

"Oh no, miss, not with me. But I was just wondering—I mean, the duke and all what lives here . . . he is expecting you, right? You wouldn't come all this way without an invite, now would you? A nice American lady like you would know she doesn't drop in unannounced on her betters, wouldn't she?"

"An American lady, Tom, would not allow the notion that she has 'betters.' "

"I meant no insult. But I will tell you that the people who live here will behave like they're your betters. Be ready for that."

Yancey chose not to argue the point further, because the truth was, she had done exactly as Tom had accused. She'd arrived uninvited. She'd done something that, according to English custom, simply wasn't done. Yet she wasn't about to admit that to her hired coachman and lose status in his eyes. "Thank you for the warning, though," she added. "Or the etiquette lesson, I suppose it was. Still, you can assume that I *do* know better. I am expected. Perhaps the duke just didn't hear your knocks."

Tom raised his bushy eyebrows at her. "Oh, miss, you're going to be in a peck of trouble here, I can already tell. It wouldn't matter if the duke did hear me knocking. He wouldn't be the one coming to the door. That's what servants are for."

Yancey felt her cheeks warming up with embarrassment. "I know what servants are for, Tom. We have them in America, too."

"Yes, miss." That comment brought them to a halt in front of the barrier that was the double wooden doors. To Yancey they looked solid enough to withstand repeated blows from a battering ram. But Tom didn't appear to be daunted by them. "We'll just give it another try then, won't we, miss, with this here brass knocker?"

Yancey waved a gloved hand in permission. "By all means."

Tom banged the lion's-head knocker against its solid plate, creating a great racket that Yancey imagined echoing inside through many grand, high-ceilinged, empty rooms. *What if I've come all this way and no one is here? What then?* This was an angry, not a plaintive, thought. How dare people who weren't expecting her not be home? Hadn't she come all this way because of those letters that begged for her presence here? Well, here she was, so open up. Yancey was all but tapping her foot impatiently.

Then she made the mistake of looking up. She stiffened her leg muscles as if she were still on board a ship and as if she might stagger at any moment with the movement of the sea. Her wondering gaze traveled up and up to the full height of the dizzying three stories that soared over her head. She put a hand over her heart. Overwhelmed, as if a great wave rose before her, threatening to crash down on her and drown her, Yancey only just stopped herself from clutching at Tom's arm for support.

Forcing her gaze downward to eye level, and breathing in deeply for calm, she listened to her detective's instincts, which screamed at her for caution. But overriding that voice was another one, a new voice deep down inside her. *Danger lurks here,* it whispered. Tensing again with premonition, Yancey peered surreptitiously left and right to the wide banks of windows on either side of the doorway. But nothing met her gaze. Not so much as a flutter or a jerk of a drapery to indicate that it had just fallen back in place.

Shaking her head, she convinced herself that she was overwrought, that was all. The journey here had been long and trying. And she was tired. Very tired. Still, never had she felt so small or unequal to a task as she did now, while she waited and Tom knocked over and over. Finally Yancey put her hand on his arm. "That's enough, Tom. Nobody's home. I'm sure they'll be along presently. I'll just wait here for them. You go on."

Clearly he wanted to do just that. He looked from her to the coach and the impatient, stamping horses hitched to it and then again at her. "Well, I don't like it one little bit, miss, leaving a fine lady like yourself here in the rain."

Not for the first time in her life did Yancey wish she were more of a formidable presence than she actually was. It was just her luck to be a slender, small-boned woman like her mother. Of course, her delicate appearance accounted for much of her success in her assignments because men never believed her to be a threat. One look at her, one fluttering of her eyelashes, and they fell apart. But none of that was going to work with Tom, her self-appointed protector. With him, she needed to be imposing. So Yancey drew herself up importantly and spoke with great authority. "I will be fine. I am certain the duke will be along presently. And if not, I can take care of myself, Tom, I assure you."

He was not convinced. Yancey's irritation with him escalated. It was misty and foggy out here. Clammy and sticky. Right now she could barely breathe this soup the English called air. And she wanted him gone because she intended to enter this manor house, if it had to be through a window or door, locked or otherwise. That being so, Tom's gallantry posed the bigger impediment to her plans. "Really, Tom. You may go."

He looked around as if for assistance or guidance. But

none was to be found. So he faced her again, his heavy-featured, weather-reddened face showing his lingering uncertainty. "Well, if you're sure, miss. I do need to be on my way."

"I'm sure. Thank you and goodbye. You've been a wonderful driver and protector." She accompanied this with her best and most winning smile. She knew how to be charming when she needed to be.

Since they'd already settled their account and she'd tipped him generously, Tom was left with no choice, Yancey knew, except to take his leave, which he finally did. Sprinting awkwardly back to his waiting horses, he quickly climbed up onto the seat, settled himself, took up the reins, then waved to Yancey and called out, "Goodbye, miss."

Still smiling and making the effort to look confident standing there small and alone on the front steps of a manor situated against the stark backdrop of high and forbidding mountains, Yancey waved back and watched him drive away. The clatter of the coach and the plodding sounds of the horses' hooves on the muddy drive slowly faded away, leaving Yancey feeling alone. More than alone. Deathly, quietly alone.

She surprised herself by watching the coach, with no small amount of trepidation and longing, until it rounded the far curve of the closest hill and disappeared from view. An unexpected impulse urged her to chase after it and tell Tom she'd changed her mind and she didn't want to be here. Instantly, Yancey tamped down this moment of cowardice. She pulled herself erect, reminding herself that she was the one with the brave plan to gain entry through an act of stealth. And wasn't she also the one who had a revolver, her last line of defense should things go badly, tucked away in her purse? Yes, she was.

Thus fortified, Yancey turned around to face the doors. One of them was opening. Her heart pounded with anticipation, which quickly turned to shock because greeting her from the doorway—and tearing a startled scream from her—was the single largest human being she had ever seen in her life. Yancey stumbled back, a hand over her heart. "Dear

God," she swore, sucking in a huge breath. "You nearly scared the life out of me, man."

If "man" was the right term. This silent, staring creature filled the entire space. Not even good manners could keep Yancey from openly raking her gaze over his large person. Dressed in servant's livery that wasn't quite big enough or broad enough or long enough, the man stood several inches over six feet. Several inches. His hair was light in color and blunt-cut across his forehead. The bones in his face were heavy from generations of some giant peasant stock. And an overhanging brow shaded light gray, almost colorless eyes. His neck was more a thick column, while his body was as rectangular as the doorway. With his hands alone he could have uprooted mature trees.

He said not a word. He just stared at Yancey. Unsmiling. Unblinking.

Recovering, she bit at her lip and tried to think how next to proceed. Of course she'd composed, over the course of the past month on her journey here, a veritable speech to offer. But now, faced with the silent giant before her, the words fled from her mind. She finally settled for, "Good afternoon. I'm Yancey—uh, Miss Sarah Margaret Calhoun."

Nothing. The man did not so much as blink. Yancey couldn't even be sure he was breathing, except for the fact that he stood there. Then she remembered whom she was supposed to introduce herself as and could have pinched herself. Here only five minutes and already she'd made a mistake. Blame it on the startling giant facing her and disconcerting her. "Of course I was born a Calhoun," she quickly added. "But I am now a Treyhorne. In fact, I am the American duchess you're expecting."

Of course they weren't really expecting her. And she wasn't really the duchess at all. The man-mountain seemed to know that because he stepped back inside the foyer and—unbelievably—closed the heavy door in her face.

Standing on the wide, rounded top step, Yancey blinked in astonishment. How very disconcerting. Then she noticed that all around her the day was darkening again. She looked up to the bruised bank of clouds that roiled in upon themselves and seemed to suck up the very air into their many folds. Yancey groaned. More rain was on its way imminently.

That did it. She hadn't come all this way over land, sea, hill, and dale, all at great expense to Mr. Pinkerton and her aching bones, just to stand out here and get soaked because of some rude, oversized butler. Tired, hungry, angry, and with really no other option than to gain entry, Yancey attacked the brass lion's-head knocker with every bit of strength she could muster. Relentlessly she pounded the lion's nose against the base plate, certain that the only thing she was hurting was her arm.

When that got no results, she pounded directly on the door, hitting it with her flattened palm as she yelled, "Open up this door this instant. Do you hear me in there? You can't leave me out here. It's going to rain, and I'm a duchess. I thought you people revered your nobility. Well, let me tell you, I'm as noble as the next son of a—"

A metallic click on the other side had her cutting off her words. Breathing hard, her teeth gritted, Yancey stepped back, waiting. Sure enough, the door opened. The same huge specimen stood there. This time, he reached out a hand and, with his fingers, poked Yancey in her breastbone—hard enough to have her stumbling back down to the second step before she could regain her balance.

"Don't do that," he said in a deep voice that rivaled thunder. He then closed the door in her face again.

Her mouth agape, her fists planted at her hips, Yancey stood frozen in place, not able to make the least bit of sense out of this. She looked all about her as Tom had done earlier. No assistance or explanations were forthcoming for her, any more than they had been for him. Frowning, she faced the door again, her expression one of utter disbelief. She dared to bang on the door again. "Don't do *what,* you big—"

The door opened. The big, big man grabbed Yancey by an arm and, as if she weighed no more than a rag doll and had fewer bones, snatched her inside a marble-tiled grand entrance hall. Black-and-white tiles in a geometric pattern. She had time only for that one impression before the giant released her and closed the door behind her. Her eyes wide, her heart tripping over itself, Yancey turned to face him. All she could think was *finally* she was inside. However, all of a sudden, she wasn't so sure that was a good thing.

The big man pointed a cigar-sized finger at her, right in her face, almost touching the tip of her nose. "Stay here."

The same order one would give a dog. Yancey defiantly raised her chin and pretended not to be terrified as she met his dull gaze. Still, she took a subtle step back, away from that pointing finger. Then she remembered her trunks outside and the threatening rain. She pointed to the closed doors behind her. "My belongings. They're outside. And it's going to rain. Could you—"

"No." With that cryptic word, he turned away from her, making his lumbering way over to a wide sweep of stairs that curved up to the second floor.

"Hold on. Where are you off to?" Yancey took tentative steps forward, her eyes finally sending signals to her brain regarding what she was seeing. Gold-flecked wallpaper. Elaborate light fixtures in sconces upon the walls. A center table upon which resided a huge vase stuffed with fresh spring flowers. And, finally, ornately framed oil paintings of most probably past dukes and duchesses, some with their children and dogs and horses and even, incongruously, a few chickens scattered about in the background. Yancey called out again. "Will you please tell me where you're going?"

Now about three steps up, the huge man turned and faced her. Again he pointed at her. "Stay there."

Yancey was getting sorely tired of this man. She tried duchess-haughty. "You've no right to order me about. What is your name?"

He ignored her, turning around and making his way up the stairs. The man's heavy footsteps echoed like a cannon shot through the space where she stood. She wondered if the creature would come back at all. And if he did, would he have some sort of weapon with him—or, worse, other large beings of his kind? Or both?

Then a most unsettling thought popped into her consciousness. *Dear God, maybe he's the duke.* Yancey had spent a fair amount of time trying to imagine what a duke looked like, but she certainly hadn't pictured this lumbering giant. She shook her head, dismissing the notion that this man could be a peer of the realm. He was the butler, plain and simple, given his livery and the duties he'd performed, such as answering the door and going to announce her to the family . . . if that's actually what he meant to do.

Yancey exhaled. Was she really supposed to just stand here for the rest of her days?

She glanced to her right and to her left. Behind one of these many closed doors had to be a drawing room. Surely the rude man would not begrudge her a chair, Yancey fussed silently, denouncing him as not the least bit hospitable. Of course, she realized that she was the uninvited one here. But it wasn't up to this man to snub her. That was the job of his employers. And what exactly had she envisioned that those people would do? Had she thought the duke would fall on her, crying and thankful? His mother might, she decided. She envisioned a dinner party to introduce her. Perhaps a welcoming-home fete. A soirée.

But then she came back to reality. They'd hardly do any of that. For one thing, they were in mourning for the first-born son. And for another, she was not the second son's actual wife. So their most likely response would be to toss her out. If they tried, she'd tell them who she was, a Pinkerton, and offer them her services. She'd be willing to bet they hadn't anticipated that, much as she hadn't anticipated the daunting servant who'd only now disappeared around an upward swirl of the stairs that led to the upper floors. Who could have anticipated him?

Just then, Yancey became aware of movement to her right. A door was opening quietly, cautiously. She tensed, clutching at her handbag . . . and the gun inside it . . . as she waited to see what would happen next. Slowly a very aged and gnarled hand crept out, its arthritic fingers holding on to the thick wood that comprised the solid door, which stopped just barely ajar. Almost breathless with fear and anticipation—given the appearance of the butler—Yancey raised her eyebrows and her chin, ready to fight or flee, whichever seemed more prudent as events transpired or even stranger beings revealed themselves.

But the hand stayed where it was, clutching at the door only several inches above the polished brass knob. This told Yancey that the owner of the fingers was probably someone of small stature . . . who neither opened the door farther nor presented himself or herself for Yancey's inspection. Which was fine with her. Then, a tiny, tinny voice all but whispered, "Is he gone yet?"

Yancey looked from the fingers . . . to the empty stairs . . . and back to the fingers. "Gone? Do you mean the butler?"

"Shhh! He'll come back and find me."

Yancey frowned, a sudden fierce and protective instinct welling up in her chest for this obviously ancient and perhaps crippled person. "Are you afraid of him? Has he mishandled you?" She could certainly imagine that he had or could.

"Mishandled me? Who? Scotty? I'd like to see him try. No, we were playing hide-and-seek. And he's 'it.' Although I don't believe he actually hunts for me. I think he allows me to hide and then he goes on about his business. That's quite rude, don't you think?"

As insane as the conversation was, Yancey found herself agreeing with the elderly person. "Yes. It is rude. Especially since I think he's done it to me, too. Ignoring me, I mean."

"See? Rude, I tell you."

Nodding her continued agreement and eyeing the stairs, Yancey now feared that she hadn't been dropped off at Stonebridge at all. Instead, she'd been left on the door of an asylum for the mentally infirm. And apparently they were in charge. That was the only explanation that made any sense. No wonder Tom the coachman had been so eager to be off. Yancey berated herself, thinking she should have known. Fine detective instincts she possessed. Such honed skills and keen perceptions. The Fox had been outfoxed.

"You're her, aren't you? The American." This was from the person still behind the door.

Yancey's nerve endings pricked up alertly. "Yes, I am. I'm Sarah Margaret . . . Treyhorne. The Duchess of Somerset." There. She'd gotten it out. "And who are you?"

A pause of several moments' duration passed. Yancey wondered if the person hidden behind the door intended to answer her.

Then . . . that same scratchy, aged voice said, "I'm Sarah Margaret Treyhorne. The Duchess of Somerset."

# Chapter Three

Stuck out in the horse barn while he waited out the downpour, which was finally slacking off, Samuel Isaac Treyhorne, the twelfth Duke of Somerset, stood smoking a cigar as he leaned a shoulder against the rough wood frame of the open oversized doors. The smell of rain freshened the air as a stray tendril of breeze swirled past, carrying away his cigar smoke. Squinting in concentration, Sam marked the hired coach's progress up the curving driveway until the manor house blocked it from his view.

He didn't get much company at his country house. Especially during the season. And especially from persons in hired coaches, immediately identifiable to him by its distinctive coloring. His equals owned their own conveyances. Besides, anyone who would have visited them in their time of mourning had already done so and would now be in London enjoying the mindless rounds of balls and other assorted inane gatherings that marked the upper class's social life.

Sam's smile was sardonic and self-directed. Too much time in America had left him pained by the very notion of such ritualized social expectations. And speaking of such, who dared to visit without an express invitation? In his mind, he could hear his mother saying it simply wasn't done. Now, that bit of etiquette he did like. All a man had to do was not invite anyone to visit, or decline certain invitations, and thus be spared a fair amount of tedious company.

But apparently that rule had been broken by this person or persons in the hired coach. Suddenly he didn't like the feel of this visitation. Whoever it was, he reasoned, had to be the bearer of bad news because that was the only kind he'd had of late. But no matter the reason, he'd know soon enough because Scotty would greet the interlopers, determine the nature of their visit, and then simply toss some hapless young page out the back door and send him running to the barn at risk of life, limb, and general health to tell him that the duke's presence was needed in the manse.

The duke. That got a snort of self-derision out of Sam. He was the duke. That had a nice ring to it, but it sure as hell hadn't been his idea to assume the title. He'd had the good sense to be born the second son and to leave as soon as he'd achieved his majority. He'd gone to America to seek his own fortune and had left all the titled responsibility to Geoffrey Charles, firstborn and a man ideally suited to the task of administering a thriving duchy. Or so Sam and everyone else had thought.

His expression hardened with grief and no small amount of anger. Geoffrey. Tall, strong, capable. Intelligent. A very good man. Compassionate. But secretly and privately troubled. And now . . . dead.

Sam's throat worked. He handled his cigar, tamping the ash before once again clamping the rolled tobacco between his teeth. Squinting now against the rising emotion in his heart that beat painfully in his chest, Sam fixed his gaze on the ancient tower that formed the cornerstone of the grand manor house. His and Geoff's favorite place to play when they'd been small boys. Sam admitted that he missed his older brother more than he would let on to anyone.

"Dammit, Geoff, how did this happen?" His voice was soft, barely above a whisper.

"Did you say something, Your Grace?"

Startled, Sam pivoted around, looking for the speaker.

There stood a work-dirtied stableman who held a pitchfork in his calloused hands. He'd obviously been mucking out the stalls. Standing in the barn's dim interior, the big man bowed and then waited deferentially for Sam to speak. Impatience had Sam quirking his mouth. He'd grown up with this deference, of course, and was used to it. But, again, his years in America, with its brash openness and ideals of equality, had changed him. Taking the cigar from between his lips and exhaling the smoke, Sam searched his mind for the man's name. "Daniel, isn't it?"

"Yes, Your Grace." He appeared pleased that Sam could recall his name.

Sam was, too. He knew that his notice of a servant was outside the norm in most upper-class households where, for the most part and with only a few exceptions—such as the butler, a valet, or a lady's maid—servants remained out of sight of their employers and totally anonymous. "Well, yes, Daniel, I did speak. But it was nothing to concern yourself with."

"Yes, Your Grace." Daniel turned away, going solemnly back to his chores. Hay rustled underfoot as he tramped through it and turned left toward the next row of stalls.

Just as Sam turned back to the open doors and reflected on a life spent mucking out manure and how similar, figuratively speaking, that existence was to his own life of late, a sudden darting movement from up at the manor caught his eye. *What's this?* He tensed, but then he spotted the source of the disturbance and relaxed. Just as he'd predicted. Bursting out of the ornate gardens and tearing down a hill, then across the open meadow, and running with total abandon toward the horse barn, came a young boy splashing—no doubt happily—through puddle after puddle. Indeed, his course zigzagged as if in an effort not to miss a single one.

Sam chuckled, surprising himself that he did. He couldn't remember the last time he'd smiled. And now here he was laughing. That lifted his spirits. Maybe it was the running boy. The exuberance he showed. The freedom and joy. This didn't look like bad news. Or feel like it, either. As he watched the boy coming his way, an air of expectancy seized Sam, all but shutting off his thoughts. Within a few more moments, the joyously soaked boy slid to a halt in front of Sam, who urged him to step inside the barn.

Out of the weather now, the lad stood dripping and silent. Sam half expected the freckled page to shake himself like a dog would. Instead, staring up at Sam, his brown eyes wide with respect, the boy sketched a formal bow. Instead of being annoyed, Sam found it rather amusing under the circumstances. After all, here they were out in the horse barn with the smell of manure all around. The boy's clothes were soaked. And Sam's riding attire—buff breeches, white, open-necked shirt, and Hessians, his favorite pair of tall black boots—was informal, to say the least. Yet manners and rituals would prevail. As would protocol.

"Well? What is it, lad? Speak up," Sam encouraged.

Blinking, with water dripping off his longish brown hair and into his eyes, the page looked up at Sam. "Begging your pardon, Your Grace, but Scotty sent me. He says you're to come to the manor house at once."

"I see." Sam doubted if Scotty had actually said all those words. They would comprise his entire vocabulary. Sam tossed his cigar butt out on the wet gravel. "Were those his actual words?"

"No, Your Grace. What he said was 'Fetch.' "

A word for a dog. Sam raised his eyebrows. "And you assumed he meant me and not perhaps Mr. Marples?"

"No, Your Grace. I mean yes, Your Grace. He meant you, Your Grace." The boy's face colored, further emphasizing his brown freckles. Then his eyes widened, perhaps with a new doubt. "Was I wrong, Your Grace?"

"Probably not. Did Scotty say *why* you were to fetch me?" Of course, he knew why—the visitor in the hired coach. But he thought by questioning this boy he might find out something about what awaited him in the manor.

"Yes, he did, Your Grace. You have a lady visitor."

An unexpected thrill chased through Sam. Not so much a pleasurable one, but certainly one of anticipation. "A lady visitor, is it? That can't be bad." *Or boring.*

"No, Your Grace."

One more *Your Grace* and Sam felt certain his teeth

would itch. Trying to have a meaningful conversation with anyone since he'd assumed the title had become a tedious and protracted chore. "Do we know who the lady is?"

"Yes, Your Grace."

And there it was. Another *Your Grace.* Sam's teeth itched. "Well, lad? Who is she?" He assumed a proper upper-class glower and crossed his arms over his chest.

The boy swiped a hand over his brow to sweep his wet hair to the side. "She says she's the duchess, Your Grace."

"The duchess of what exactly?" Sam needed this narrowed down. England was currently overrun with duchesses. A man couldn't take ten steps without stepping on the toes of one.

The boy swallowed. "Why, the Duchess of Somerset, Your Grace. Your wife. Newly come from America."

Inside the manse, on its third floor, a veritable parade had assembled and now marched along a hallway in the west wing. Yancey followed the housekeeper, Mrs. Edgars, a tall, thin, no-nonsense woman who'd come back with the gruff giant unbelievably named Scotty. He too lumbered in front of Yancey. For her part, her hand was lightly held in the gnarled and knobby little hand of the tiny white-haired woman whose game of hide-and-seek Yancey's untimely appearance had interrupted. At least now Yancey knew the benign reason why the elderly lady had identified herself as the Duchess of Somerset. She tended to repeat word for word what was said to her, but only apparently those words that struck her fancy.

Flanking Yancey and her new friend were three husky young men who handled her traveling trunks. And behind them trailed three imperious longhaired white cats. They must make quite a sight was Yancey's opinion as she proceeded as decorously as possible toward the closed door that she'd been told led to the suite of rooms she would occupy.

Painfully enough, her suite was the one adjoining the duke's—as befitted his wife, she'd been told by Mrs. Edgars.

She'd also informed Yancey that, though she hadn't known when to expect Her Grace's arrival, she'd been told in private by Her Grace Rosamond Sparrow Treyhorne, the duke's mother, to anticipate it. Yancey had accepted this silently, knowing that the housekeeper thought her the actual duchess and not the pretender that she was.

Yancey tucked away two bits of knowledge from this conversation. One, the housekeeper had been told *in private* by the dowager to anticipate her daughter-in-law's arrival. That meant the mother had kept her letter-writing activities a secret from her son, just as Yancey had wondered about with Mr. Pinkerton. And two, no one here doubted for a second that Yancey was who she said she was. Obviously, the duke's household had not ever met the real duchess. Interesting, but in her favor.

Still, surprising her had been the moment of conscience she'd experienced downstairs. Responsibility for her attack of guilt lay with the tiny elderly woman, whose beautifully tailored though overlong skirts now trailed along the polished floors. Her Grace Nana, everyone called her. She was instantly lovable. And she'd seemed so happy to see Yancey—or Sarah Margaret—when she'd introduced herself that Yancey had almost blurted out the truth right there.

How distressing. It was one thing to deceive criminals. It was quite another to lie to honest and accepting people such as these. But lie she must, Yancey felt, in order to see the dowager duchess. Get inside by presenting herself as the woman's daughter-in-law, Mr. Pinkerton had said. Only in that disguise, he'd told her, could she be assured of an audience with the dowager. Any other person could conceivably be turned away. But not the daughter-in-law, the duchess herself.

Yancey glanced over at her companion. The ancient wispy-haired woman kept up a steady stream of chatter about people and places Yancey had never heard of. Even navigating the many stairs up to the third floor hadn't winded the ancient woman. Nor did it seem to bother her that Yancey didn't answer her. She would have been pleased to make polite remarks at appropriate intervals, but her venerable escort had yet to take a breath that would allow Yancey to do so.

At last, Mrs. Edgars and Scotty stopped. Yancey and company did the same. Along with the housekeeper, the giant turned to face her. Glowering, he pointed to a closed door. "Here."

Yancey managed a smile. "Of course. Whatever you say . . . Scotty."

The men with the trunks excused themselves—"Pardon us, Your Grace"—as they pushed around her and followed Mrs. Edgars and Scotty into the room ahead of Yancey, Her Grace Nana, and the three cats. Then Yancey looked again and chuckled. Make that three cats and a dog. Apparently, somewhere along the way they'd picked up a small, fat brown dog to add to the menagerie around her ankles. The terrier stayed a respectful distance from the impassive but watchful cats.

"Well, hello, Mr. Marples, you scamp. And where have you been off to all day, you bad boy?" Cooing, Her Grace Nana bent over to pat the dog's head. Its stubby tail wagged and it jumped up on her, nearly knocking the old woman to the floor. Yancey whipped an arm around the woman's shoulders to steady her.

"Thank you, Sarah Margaret," she said. "Say hello to Mr. Marples. He's a fine young man, despite what Alice and Mary and Jane say." She tugged on Yancey's bodice, pulling her down until Yancey's ear was even with her mouth. She whispered, "Don't listen to them. They're the jealous sort, my dear."

"I'm sure you're right," Yancey whispered back, forced to assume the woman meant the cats.

"I'm sure you're right," Her Grace Nana repeated. "Mrs. Edgars has kept your rooms fresh and aired out for you, Sarah Margaret. We knew you would come. We just knew it."

Knew it—or hoped it? Were they in on the dowager's secret letter-writing campaign? That was what Yancey wanted to know. But faced with such sweet innocence as Her Grace Nana exuded, she knew she would save the hard questions for someone more formidable. To the elderly woman, she replied, "Thank you. I'm sure the room is very lovely."

"The room *is* very lovely." Then Her Grace Nana reached up a gnarled little hand and stroked Yancey's cheek. "You're very beautiful. I can't imagine why Samuel didn't bring you back with him. And why he doesn't want you here. He's not going to be happy to see you, dear."

Just as she'd feared. Yancey straightened up, releasing the richly dressed and stooped older woman. At that moment, her arm was grabbed and she was plucked right through the doorway and into the suite of rooms. Of course, Scotty had a hold of her. Yancey aimed a droll expression the giant's way. "Scotty, you simply must stop handling me like this. You might break something vital."

Still with a viselike grip on her, with his free hand he made a sweeping gesture that indicated the room at large. "Yours."

Yancey had time only to gain a fleeting impression of a large, well-furnished lady's sitting room before Mrs. Edgars very properly and formally said, "I hope you will be comfortable here, Your Grace. And will find everything to your liking."

She didn't mean that. A sudden chill of certainty slipped over Yancey's skin. The housekeeper's tone of voice hadn't matched her sentiments. She'd said it more like *I hope you don't fall into the vat of boiling oil we've placed in a pit under the carpet.*

"It's very lovely. I'm sure I will," Yancey said cautiously, eyeing the woman and thinking that she bore watching.

Before she could do more than store that observation away, the young men who'd handled her trunks again filed past her and out of the room, each of them nodding his head, not quite meeting her gaze, and murmuring either "Your Grace" or "Duchess."

With a regal bob of her head, acting as if she'd been doing this all her life, Yancey acknowledged the servants' show of respect. Only when they were gone could she follow Scotty's impatient gesture and give the rooms their due attention.

She'd intended to behave in an imperial manner, to appear judgmental and slightly bored in her perusal of her accommodations. But that notion fled when the dazzling splendor that met her gaze wrenched a delighted gasp out of her. Yancey stared in awe, a hand to her mouth. Why, this was a room meant for a fairy princess. Or a real duchess.

Apparently satisfied with her response, Scotty released her arm. As if in a trance, Yancey stepped inside and slowly walked around, marveling at what she saw. This was unbelievable. Back in Chicago, she rented a room in a respectable and comfortable women's boardinghouse. But a suite of rooms such as these? Why, she had only been able to envy such luxury—and that from the outside looking in. But now, here she was inside, and this was hers. Or actually the duchess's . . . the real duchess's. The dead duchess's.

Yancey put that thought aside until a later time when she could be alone with her thoughts. For now she wanted to concentrate on the rich display before her. Commanding this small room was a richly upholstered three-piece suite situated conversationally in front of a fireplace. Small tables with chairs arranged to either side reposed against the walls covered in a delicately rose-patterned wallpaper. Tall windows across the way let in the light. Feeling instantly at home in this room with its cozy feeling of intimacy, Yancey realized she was smiling as she crossed the sitting room and stood on the threshold of the bedroom itself.

Her breath left her. A large canopied bed with a thick mattress and many pillows commanded the room. Its coverlet, a wonderful sky-blue shot through with gold thread, appeared to be of a silky material. Yancey walked straight to it, put her handbag atop it, and then ran her hand over the fabric . . . so sleek and soft. She longed to lose herself in its comfort and sleep straight through until tomorrow. Impossible, though, it being not even teatime yet.

She next turned her attention to the huge wardrobes and armoires that stood like sentinels on opposite walls. Her three trunks hunkered like whipped dogs next to the nearer wardrobe. Yancey quirked her mouth in embarrassment. Her painfully few dresses would get lost in even one of those smaller armoires. She next came to a delicately feminine dressing table carved from a light-colored wood. Decorative boxes and glass bottles and a silver-backed comb and brush set awaited her. She imagined herself sitting in front of this vanity and brushing her hair. A sigh for such simple luxury escaped her.

She then moved past the washstand and came face to face with a closed door that stopped her. No doubt, it opened onto the dressing room that joined this bedroom to the duke's room.

A chill of foreboding chased through Yancey. How easy it would be for the duke to slip through that door and kill her in her sleep. And how ironic that Mr. Pinkerton had raised the specter of that happening to her if she remained in Chicago. So he'd sent her here to England for her own safety. Yet here—and going by what Her Grace Nana, who was obviously a family member of some standing, had said—she would not be welcomed by the duke. Especially not if he'd had a hand in his real wife's death, if the other Sarah had indeed been his wife. And if she had and if he had, wouldn't Yancey be a shock to him, then? She told herself she definitely needed the key to this door. She only just stopped short of looking around for a sturdy chair to angle under the doorknob. *Let him come through that.*

Hearing herself, Yancey shook her head. She needed to remember to allow for simple explanations. For all she knew, the duke was a sweet little cherub of a man who never in his whole life had harbored a single hurtful thought. Or perhaps he was a painfully shy and ineffectual man who ran at the sight of his own shadow. Maybe he missed his wife terribly and didn't know she was dead. If she was. After all, Yancey still had only hunches, no evidence. So what if he came rushing in happily, expecting his beloved wife, and found her, Yancey, standing here? How distraught he would be. And how cruel she would feel. Feeling sorry for this imaginary duke's distress, Yancey moved away from the door.

She stepped over to a writing desk and ran her fingers over the polished wood. Very pleasing. Positioned next to the desk was a lovely cheval glass, a full-length mirror for a lady to view her appearance in one exquisite gown after another. Yancey knew she wouldn't be using the mirror for that purpose because she didn't own a single ball gown. Not much call for them in her line of work. Well, except for now. But it was too late to worry about proper clothing. All she'd brought with her were the sensible, serviceable clothes she did own. Nothing of the frivolous lady resided in her trunks. How would she explain that? Well, maybe she didn't look too bad.

She glanced at her reflection in the mirror, and saw staring back at her a tired-looking, rain-dampened, and rumpled woman whose hair was frizzing and coming loose from its pins. Amused and mortified by her appearance, Yancey shook her head, pronouncing herself not fit for an introduction to a duke. Still, it was like a dream, seeing herself here in this room. She tried hard not to feel inadequate or like an interloper. Yet she knew the truth—she was both of those things.

Exhaling, she crossed the room to an enormous marble-framed fireplace where she traced with her fingers the intricate patterns of pink veins that ran throughout the cold stone. Adrift in her own world, forgetting she was attended by six persons and four domestic pets, Yancey turned to the tall windows adjacent to the fireplace. She went to the nearer of the two and, a hand on the heavy folds of sky-blue drapery, peered outside. Her breath caught.

If the window could be thought of as a frame, then this view could be a painting of a country scene of exquisite beauty. Green and rolling hills. Lush meadows wherein fine horseflesh grazed contentedly. In the distance a large herd of cattle milled about, also grazing. Closer to the house, formal gardens of geometric beauty caught the eye. And colorful flowerbeds showed a loving hand in their creation—

"Beautiful, isn't it?"

Gasping in surprise, Yancey whipped around, all but tangling herself in the folds of the draperies. She pulled free of them only to see, standing framed in the bedroom's doorway, the tall and commanding figure of a man in his full prime—and no one else. A thrill of fright coursed through Yancey, leaving her feeling overly hot, yet cold as stone. Tumbling thoughts and instant impressions tussled about in her mind. *Where is Mrs. Edgars? Her Grace Nana? And Scotty? And the young men who carried my trunks up? And the cats, the dog? When did they leave?*

Leave? They hadn't merely left. They'd been dismissed by this man. Since then, he'd been watching her. She knew that as surely as she knew that her hair was red and her eyes were green. Yancey inhaled deeply yet discreetly as she fought to compose herself and meet the challenge in the level stare of the dark-haired man dressed in a white open-necked shirt and buff-colored riding breeches tucked into Hessians.

He offered no further conversation, not even an apology for being alone with her in what was essentially her bedroom. Such a circumstance, even by itself, compromised an unmarried woman. Yancey knew she had every right to demand that he leave. But under the circumstances—her being here under false pretenses—she thought not. Too, she'd sooner be damned than protest and appear to be the squeamish little miss. All the better because, at the moment, she couldn't be entirely sure that she was physically capable of speech.

The man was absolutely stunning. Even as she tried desperately to convince herself that this was her objective opinion as an experienced observer, as well as a usually calm and rational woman, she failed miserably. Virility rolled off him in waves that threatened to sweep her away. And how could this be . . . this soul-deep certainty in Yancey's heart that his hands already knew her body? That his mouth had already hungrily claimed hers on some wild, dark night in a long-ago time? Insane, yes, but the improbability nevertheless held for her the ironclad weight of a factual reality.

Rationally, Yancey knew she had never seen him before. But rationality held no sway here. Instead, her heart insisted that it *knew* this man. Fear teamed with anticipation to dry Yancey's mouth. Such confidence, such daring, he exuded. And such arrogance. No introduction was necessary. This, then, was the duke who lolled languidly against the bedroom door's frame, unmoving and soberly staring back at her . . . waiting.

Finally, but in actual time what was really no more than a passing moment from question to answer, Yancey replied, "Yes. It is very beautiful."

He nodded . . . slowly. "Imagine how happy I am that you agree."

Yancey flinched. He couldn't care less what she thought. Normally that would have rankled her, but this time, with this man, and wisely, she said nothing. She watched him now as he watched her.

With no more than a shrug, he pulled away from the door's frame and strode across the room with a lazy yet powerful grace that had Yancey surreptitiously clutching handfuls of her skirt's material. She called herself a coward. And the closer he came to her, the more she steeled herself to stand her ground. As he drew even with her, Yancey judged him to be tall, about six feet. His coal-black hair was worn a bit longer than was fashionable. And his eyes were a very cool gray. His face boasted high cheekbones, a firm jaw, and full, sensual lips.

Yancey tensed at his nearness, but he ignored her, walking right past her. Immensely relieved, her heart racing, she exhaled as discreetly as she could manage and let go of her skirt. Her next breath, however, was nearly her undoing. Because the air she took into her lungs proved to be redolent with the unique scent of this man, mingled with a remembrance of hay and cigar smoke and cleansing rain. Intoxicating.

And dangerous. That bee sting of a realization brought Yancey sharply back to earth. This man certainly was not the milksop duke she'd imagined. What he was, then, was no one to trifle with. As she turned around to keep him in sight, and with her skirt swishing around her ankles, she knew she must keep her wits about her and remember that he was very probably the enemy here.

With an eye to that, and while his back was to her as he stared out the same window he'd caught her facing, Yancey raked her gaze over him, from his broad, muscled shoulders, down his tapering back to his narrow waist and tight buttocks. His long legs, with their perfect musculature, defined the breeches, giving them shape . . . and elevated her pulse in ways that could all too easily make her forget the threat he was to her.

Suddenly, the duke pivoted his shoulders and turned his head as if he meant to speak to her over his shoulder. Yancey tensed, waiting. He didn't look directly at her, yet she figured that he could see her out of the corner of his eye and was aware of every move she made, every breath she took.

"Who are you?"

His deep growl, as much as his abrupt question, rumbled through Yancey's chest, taking her breath. She wanted to believe that she had no idea what was wrong with her, or why he had this effect on her. But she couldn't lie, not to herself. She knew, all too well, that this was a hungry need, a fierce and unexplainable attraction to him that she was experiencing. So be it. She was no virgin, no stranger to those emotions.

But the rest of it . . . the way she wanted to run, to cry, to get away from him so she could breathe, the feeling of being naked before him, of being overwhelmed and vulnerable . . . she couldn't define or explain. And because she couldn't, she was afraid. Yancey struggled for control. *Resist his pull,* she told herself. *Remember why you're here. You have a part to play, a murder to solve before you're the next victim.* She need only remind herself that she was an experienced Pinkerton undercover operative, she concluded. A smart woman. The Fox. And this game was hers.

Yancey knew all this. But still, she imagined that right now, here in the enthralling presence of the Duke of Somerset, that she couldn't feel less afraid if, instead of him, she had suddenly found herself face to face with a winged angel. A dark and terrible angel.

# Chapter Four

No doubt motivated by her silence, the tall and imposing duke turned away from the window to face Yancey. Against the weight of his unrelenting stare and his physical nearness, she felt very small and unprotected. The duke looked down his patrician nose at her and held her gaze. "Cat got your tongue? Surely you know who you are."

That stung her into speaking. "Of course I know. As do you." Relief swept over her that her voice could sound so calm.

"As do I?" His slanting expression was pointed, sharp, like teeth . . . or fangs.

Swallowing hard, Yancey reminded herself to keep her wits about her. "Yes, you do. I feel certain that whatever servant announced my presence to you informed you of my name, since I did give it."

"Quite so, my little American. And yet I would like to hear *you* speak it."

He'd picked up on her accent and had issued a dare. Even as much as she hated saying her detested name, Yancey was determined to do so without any hesitation in her speech. "Very well. I am Miss Sarah Margaret Calhoun."

His eyes narrowed dangerously. "Not Treyhorne? Not the American Duchess of Somerset? I was told that you presented yourself as such. Which is why you were put in these particular rooms . . . next to mine."

Guilt, as well as heated images of bedrooms and lovers, brought a flush to Yancey's cheeks. She thought it best if she didn't reply.

"I'm waiting," he said. "And let me warn you . . . I am in no mood to be trifled with."

Yancey believed him. She'd thought the same thing about him only moments ago. "I assure you it's not my intention to be trifling. I apologize for the confusion, but I am indeed Sarah Margaret Calhoun." When that got no response from him, Yancey came up with a glib lie. "What I had done, you see, was *ask* if your mother, the Duchess of Somerset, was at home."

He cocked his head at a disbelieving angle. "I see. A simple misunderstanding. But one you did nothing to correct."

Thanking her six years of working undercover that had made her a good actress, Yancey maintained a straight face and an injured air. "Your staff gave me no opportunity. I was swept up by them and carried along, much as if I had fallen into a swift current."

The duke continued to regard her in an assessing manner. Then his lips curved upward. On anyone else, Yancey would have called the expression a smile. "Have it your way, Miss Calhoun," he drawled. "Allow me, then, to answer your inquiry. The duchess is *not* at home."

How well she knew that. The woman was most likely dead and buried back in Chicago. Still acting, Yancey feigned distress. "Oh. I see."

"Do you? What exactly do you see?"

"That there's been a mistake."

"Apparently."

Refusing to succumb to her heart-pounding fear born of his unyielding manner, Yancey assumed the actions and mannerisms of someone whose embarrassment compelled her to be industrious. She set off across the room—away from him. "Well, then, as my trunks are not yet unpacked and as it turns out that I've made a grievous mistake in coming here"—she headed for her handbag on the bed—"and I have obviously upset your household, for which I apologize, perhaps if you would be so kind as to summon your men to help me with my belongings? And if you can see it in your heart to arrange for a hired conveyance for me, I'll take myself away from here and relieve you of the burden of my presence—"

"Stop right there. You're going nowhere."

Victory. Halfway to the bed now, and with her back to him, Yancey allowed herself a covert smile before turning to the duke. Feigning surprise, and with a hand to her bosom, she said, "I beg your pardon?"

His solid body framed by the window at his back, her host had crossed his arms over his impressive chest. "You heard me. You're going nowhere."

"Do I take your meaning correctly? You intend to keep me a prisoner here?" She raised her chin for effect. "Perhaps, then, I should take myself off to the tower I saw from the coach and wrap myself in chains?"

The duke's sober expression remained so. "I assure you that such dramatics are not necessary. I simply meant I have more questions to ask you, *Miss Calhoun*. And if I don't like your answers, you will be leaving. Very soon."

It wasn't exactly the invitation to stay that she'd hoped to wangle. But apparently she wasn't to be tossed out on her nose, either. At least, not just yet. All she knew was that her continuing proximity to the duke could be very dangerous. And for more than one reason. Yancey adopted an expression of innocence, widening her eyes in a way that she knew from experience could disarm men. Most men. "Well, I can now say I understand the rules. But, my goodness, you make this all sound like a mystery."

"I think it is. And the mystery is you."

Yancey's abrupt chuckle reflected practiced disbelief. "I assure you that there is nothing of the mysterious surrounding me. I am indeed Sarah Margaret Calhoun."

"So you say. Yet I have only your word for that."

"You have no reason to assume that I would lie to you."

"In fact, I have every reason to assume that you would."

Only too aware that she was suddenly more excited by this dangerous game of words than it was wise to be, Yancey nevertheless upped the stakes. "Meaning, I take it, *Your Grace,*" she said pointedly, finally using his title despite his not having introduced himself to her, "that I am *not* the Sarah Margaret Calhoun you *expected* me to be?"

The man's gray eyes blazed. Had his stare been a weapon, Yancey figured she would already be dead on the floor. "I *expected* no one. But what I *suspect* is that you are fully aware of that, too."

Yancey matched the duke—a more than worthy adversary—stare for stare and word for word. "You assign me many motives, sir. I assure you that I am a simple woman who—"

"The one thing you are *not* is a simple woman. I would be disappointed if you were." Having said that, he relaxed his posture, rubbing his chin with his thumb. "Now, allow me to begin my questioning, keeping in mind that if I don't like your answers, you and your baggage will be set on the side of the road."

What could she say? "Fair enough. Begin."

"Thank you," he said with exaggerated grace. "Tell me, Miss Calhoun, how did it come about that you presented yourself on my doorstep? As far-flung as Stonebridge is, I hardly think you acted on whim or caprice."

Just listening to him talk, to hear how he used words, excited Yancey beyond anything she'd ever felt before. She fought to stay in character, that of an aloof woman. "Neither caprice nor whim, as you stated. Instead, I arrived here only after considerable direction and planning."

Yancey's reward was the look of surprise that crossed his features. "How so? What are you saying?"

"I'm saying I was asked to come here."

He straightened up. His was no longer a casual pose. "By whom were you asked?"

With a smile, Yancey played her ace. "By the Duchess of Somerset, Her Grace Rosamond Sparrow Treyhorne."

Again, surprise flitted across the duke's features, raising his eyebrows. "My mother?" He quickly followed this with a scoffing sound that dismissed Yancey and her answer. "I find it hard to believe that my mother would ask you, a virtual stranger, to Stonebridge."

He'd called her a liar, which at the moment and on this score she wasn't. Not really. Behaving as if insulted, Yancey raised her chin a notch. "I can see how that would be hard to believe. But do you suppose I merely pulled your mother's name out of the air—and all the way from America?"

"No, I do not. My surprise and disbelief, however, arise from the fact that my mother is the *dowager* duchess, not the *titled* duchess. That honor is reserved for my wife, who is in no condition or position to invite anyone anywhere. So whoever invited you here—"

"The 'whoever' was your mother. She invited me. Forgive me my mistake in thinking her the titled duchess instead of the . . . dowager, did you say?"

"Yes. Put simply, a duchess becomes a dowager when her husband dies and the title passes to her son. His wife then carries the title of duchess."

"I see. Thank you for that lesson." Of course, she knew what a dowager was, and she knew that the woman who'd written to her was the dowager. It just better suited the half-true story she was telling him to pretend otherwise. "I plead being an American not fully versed in the protocol of the British peerage."

He said nothing, only silently considered her. His gray eyes moved restlessly, as if in time with his rapidly developing thoughts.

Forced to await his conclusions, Yancey watched him, only belatedly realizing that her gaze had slipped to the dark, crisp, and curling hair on his muscled chest that his shirt, open at the neck, revealed. She forced her gaze upward to his face and her mind back to his answers. Specifically, he had spoken of his wife in the present tense. So either the duke believed his wife to be alive, or wanted Yancey to think he did. Yancey realized she hoped it was the former. Why? Was it because she didn't want him to be guilty of murder?

"Then she wrote to you, I presume? My mother, I mean."

He spoke so suddenly that Yancey blinked, having to first

replay in her mind his question before she could answer him. "Yes. Of course."

"Then you have with you the letters from her?"

"Her letters?" A sudden alarm sounded in Yancey's head. Lightning-quick conclusions flitted through her mind, one after the other. He hadn't known until just now that his mother had written to his American wife. As Yancey had already suspected, this confirmed that the dowager had kept her letter-writing a secret from her son. Was he dangerous? What if he was the mastermind behind the events in America that had seen one woman dead and her own self attacked? What if his mother hadn't known that?

But all that aside, how could Yancey let him read one, given their contents—the dowager's desperate pleadings and the unfavorable allusions to her son? There was no telling what sort of response that might spark in the man. The truth was the dowager had written secretly for some good reason. Yancey concluded that she too should keep the woman's secret until she could speak with her.

When Yancey spoke, it was with a show of sincere regret. "Oh, I am so sorry. Having no idea I would be required to defend myself like this, I didn't keep the letters your mother sent me."

Yancey barely kept her guilty gaze away from her handbag on the bed. The letters were in the handbag. Mere feet away. So was her gun.

"I do apologize, Miss Calhoun, for causing you to feel a need to defend yourself. But you have to admit that this is a most unusual circumstance."

"Unusual? In what way?"

"Please don't play at ignorance. It's insulting to us both. For one thing—and as I suspect you well know—you bear the same name as my wife, if that is truly your name. And for another, you say my mother wrote to you. If she did, it's obvious her letters were somehow misdirected. Otherwise, how exactly would *my* mother know someone like *you*?"

Offended by his last statement, and ignoring his other correct conclusions, Yancey narrowed her eyes. "Someone like me? You mean an American? Or the fact that I'm what you would call a commoner?"

His smile broadened into an absolutely treacherous grin that had nothing to do with humor. "Both . . . of course."

The insult only increased. Yancey felt her cheeks growing warm. "If nothing else, I do applaud your honesty. How difficult this must be for you to have to deal directly with someone so far beneath your usual notice."

He shrugged his magnificent shoulders. "It's not as dire as all that."

"It isn't? Well . . . lovely, then. Still, I don't see why we need letters. If you could simply ask your mother if I may have an audience with her, I feel certain she can verify my invitation to come to Stonebridge. After all, it was her I came to see. And her I asked for when I arrived."

Yancey meant to reveal to his mother, in private, that she was a Pinkerton agent. She would then question the dowager to ascertain what the trouble here was and if she, the dowager, was in any danger from her son.

But the duke ended that hope. "Like you, I would like nothing better than to question my mother. However, she is presently not in residence, and I don't expect her to be for two to three more days."

Yancey frowned, worrying that the duke may have already done away with his own mother, too. "Oh, dear. Well, that does make things awkward, then, doesn't it? Perhaps you could send a message to her apprising her of my arrival?"

"I could. But it would be pointless. She is visiting her sister, a trip of two or more days, depending on the weather. As luck would have it, she planned to be starting for home at about this time. So, you see, a messenger from me would merely meet her on the road."

Yancey pronounced herself heartened by the amount of detail in his narrative. His mother was alive. The details he'd offered lent truth to her conclusion. Or maybe the duke knew that, too, and was as accomplished a liar as she was. Yancey smiled and, knowing they were at a pivotal juncture, looked directly into the duke's eyes. "I see. Then I find I don't know how to proceed from here."

"Luckily, I do. I will endeavor to get to the bottom of your presence here, *Miss Calhoun*. And at the end of my inquiries, I think it is safe to say that I *will* be sending you away." He narrowed his eyes. "And you can count yourself lucky if that is all I do."

His open threat charged the air between them. Yancey half expected to hear thunder roll and to see lightning blaze across the room and strike her dead. As it was, she found it hard to breathe. With her heart in her throat, she was unable to give him an answer . . . not that one was required.

"However, in the meantime," he said, with a mercurial change in demeanor and tone of voice, "and as you are, to all appearances, an invited guest of my mother's, I will honor her invitation and welcome you to Stonebridge. A lady's maid will be up presently to assist you in settling in to your room. When you are refreshed, I ask that you attend me in my study in one hour. Is that clear?"

Yancey's gaze narrowed, and her jaw tightened. He had a funny way of asking. But what this man, this powerful duke, didn't know was that those things that scared her only made her more determined to see her way past them—a lesson her father had finally and fatally learned. Yancey nodded. "It is perfectly clear."

Pushed back in his chair, with his feet up on his desk and his legs crossed at the ankles, Sam sat brooding in his first-floor study. He hadn't changed his attire from an hour ago when he'd left the lady upstairs. That didn't make him much of a gentleman, he supposed. But then again, he hadn't ever been accused of being one. No, he was not one to stand on ceremony, much to his mother's chagrin, since he'd returned from America. A smile hovered at the corners of Sam's mouth. America. His taste of independence while there remained sweet on his tongue. He'd embraced the freedom offered him, the freedom to live out his life as he chose instead of being a slave to his birthright.

His birthright? No. Not his. Geoffrey's. Sam's smile faded and he shied away from that recent hurt. Instead, holding a crystal glass of whisky in his hand, he focused his gaze across the way at the floor-to-ceiling bookshelves and gave free rein to his wayward thoughts of his unexpected guest.

She was very intelligent. And no innocent. Everything about her said she had her own secrets and harbored those of others, as well. She was also too damned beautiful by half to be anything but dangerous. Never before had Sam seen such green flashing eyes. Never before had he seen hair the color of hers . . . a rich, deep red shot through with burnished gold. Beyond that, he hadn't the skill to do her crowning glory justice. Only an artist with an extensive palette of colors stood a chance of that.

Still, Sam tried to imagine her hair unbound, with sunlight glinting off it. The vision shortened his breathing. He slowly shook his head in sensual wonder, recalling now how he'd found her peering out the window. *Magnificent.* The truth was she excited him beyond measure, even as his senses warned him away from her, telling him that she was danger personified. After all, she had presented herself here using his wife's name. That told him she was up to no good. Perhaps she was an opportunist bent on extracting money from him for her silence. Maybe somehow she knew about his wife and what he'd done.

Sam frowned. Who was she really, this woman ensconced upstairs in the rooms next to his? Not for the first time since he'd come downstairs did Sam remind himself that it was the specious story behind the American's appearance here that deserved his attention. And not her womanly attributes . . . which she indeed had in good measure. Very good measure. Not too tall but shapely—not lushly so, slender yet curvaceous.

*There. I've done it again.* Exasperated with his mind's masculine though thoroughly understandable wanderings, given the heady subject, Sam exhaled, shaking his head as if that would rid his mind of lascivious thoughts of the woman going by the name of Miss Sarah Margaret Calhoun.

Instant guilt tightened Sam's chest. That name. Sarah Margaret Calhoun. His wife's name. He closed his eyes against the memories of her, even pinching the bridge of his nose in hopes of expelling the images in his mind. *Poor Sarah. You left me no choice but to do what I did, what I had to do.*

When that old and familiar ache threatened to tear at him, Sam muttered a curse and sipped at the strong spirits in his glass, concentrating on the whisky's pleasant burn as it slid down his throat and warmed his stomach. He glanced at the ornate shelf clock atop the mantel over the fireplace, noted how much time had elapsed . . . and smiled his grudging respect. *So the American woman thinks to keep the British duke waiting.*

Every tick of the clock past the one-hour deadline he'd given her further raised Sam's ire. Not so much because she'd defied him, but because she'd given him too much time to think—and mostly about her. Sam narrowed his eyes, recalling how he'd first found her. Her slender back had been turned to him and he had not yet seen her face. Even so, a shock of numbing force had traveled through him, leaving him speechless. And then, when he'd spoken to her and she'd turned around, his breath had damned near left him.

He'd known in that instant that this woman would be his undoing. Or perhaps she would save him.

That thought had Sam tensing. *Save me from what?* he demanded to know of tormentors unseen. *I'm not lost. I know exactly where I am.* Yes, he knew—in his brother's house and bearing his brother's title and carrying his brother's responsibilities. Sam clenched his jaw. What a turn his life had taken. First, and because of Sarah, he'd lost everything in America that he'd been working so hard to achieve. Then he'd had to abandon America and Sarah altogether because of his brother's death. In essence, he'd been forced to walk away from life as he had chosen to live it to come back here to a life he'd never wanted.

Grimacing, Sam closed the mental door on that path. He'd already traveled it until it was worn with worrisome ruts.

There was nothing he could do about what had happened in America, so this brooding was getting him nowhere. Impatient now, he marked the present time yet again and frowned. *Has the damned clock stopped?* The hands didn't appear to have moved since the last time he'd looked at them.

Well, of course they hadn't, he chastised himself. He'd only just glanced its way a few seconds ago. And in the woman's defense, Sam now argued with himself, little more than the allotted hour had passed. Still, patience and excuses be damned. His muscles bunched as if urging him to jump up, storm out of the study, charge up the magnificent sweep of stairs to the third floor, drag his uninvited guest out of her room and back down here to his study—

*And then what?* he asked of himself.

Why, exact some answers from her, of course. Sam tried to convince himself that the only reason he didn't act accordingly and accost his guest was because such behavior would hardly be worthy of a duke. A scoffing chuckle put the lie to his caring how it would seem. He didn't give a damn. But such a scene would upset his staff. And this irony amused Sam. His own servants were more expectant of proper behavior on his part than he was. So, that being true, and the proprieties being what they were, he would sit here and wait.

Sam narrowed his eyes . . . he didn't wait well. And a certain American woman was about to find that out if she didn't put in an appearance soon. He didn't know whether to applaud the very striking Miss Calhoun—if that was really her name, and he still had his doubts—for her pluck or to berate her for being so headstrong. A grin toyed with the edges of his lips. *Probably applaud.*

Sighing, forcing himself to relax, Sam looked about, finally settling his gaze on his desktop, or more exactly on the cluttered stacks of papers under his nose. He knew that he should be using this time to go over the accounts and contracts that needed his attention. Earlier he'd abandoned these same onerous obligations for the simple delights of a rainy day out in the horse barn. Well, he hadn't gotten far, had he? Here he was right back where he'd started and here his obligations were, dutifully awaiting him.

"Let them wait." His jaw tightening, Sam arrowed a glance up at the room's vaulted ceiling. He wished he could see through it to the floor above and then to the ceiling above that, all the way to the third floor and down the long west hall and into the woman's room to see exactly what it was that she was doing that was taking her so long and was so important that she thought she could keep a titled duke, no matter his opinion on the proprieties, awaiting her presence after specifically having been told—

A knock on the closed door cut off Sam's burgeoning tirade and had him staring its way. His gaze focused narrowly on the door. *At last. The American.*

*Well, my lady, turnabout is fair play.* Glowering now, his temper simmering, Sam took a slow sip of his smooth whisky, savoring it for a long and purposeful moment. He then eyed the near-empty glass appreciatively, wondering if he wanted a refill. Perhaps. Thus he passed a few pleasurable moments. Only when he decided that he'd kept his guest waiting long enough did he call out a gruff invitation.

"Enter."

The door opened. In stepped the woman. She closed the door behind her and stood across the way, her hands folded primly in front of her. She struck a penitent pose, yet she boldly met his gaze, her chin raised a notch, her green eyes defiant.

Sam ignored his suddenly thrumming heart, blaming impatience and anger for its quick pacing. She'd taken off her traveling coat, he noticed, and had arranged her hair. A very striking woman. Yet, even from across the room, he could see that she looked tired. Try as she might to disguise it, she still gave herself away. Her shoulders weren't as squared as they could be. Her chin didn't tilt up to the degree she'd managed only an hour ago upstairs. She looked ready to drop. And she said nothing. That in itself was very telling.

Sam held her gaze, content for the moment not to break the silence between them that threatened to burst into desire and have him striding across the room to her and—*stop it.* His grip on the whisky glass tightened with his self-remonstrance. Never looking away from her, Sam inhaled deeply, held the air in his lungs as long as he could, and then exhaled softly. *Have the decency, man, to be a good host and not lust after your mysterious guest, uninvited though she may turn out to be.*

That brought him around. Shouldn't he at least offer her a chair? Ask her to sit? A simple courtesy, really. Offering a chair didn't have to mean that he cared one way or the other about her. Because he didn't.

But his conscience would not allow him to lie to himself. It told him differently: he cared that this woman looked drained of stamina. But why he should, and so quickly, was the part that he didn't understand. It was also the part that made him very uneasy. He bristled defensively and broke the silence by behaving like an ass. "Do you know who I am?"

She started and her eyes widened. "I believe so. You're the Duke of Somerset."

"Exactly. Do you know what that means?"

Frowning, she shook her head. "I'm afraid I don't take your meaning."

Rudely not arising from his chair, not even putting his feet on the floor, Sam sought to educate this American. "Etiquette, Miss . . . *Calhoun,* if that is your real name."

She stiffened, her expression hardening. "I assure you that it is."

"So you continue to say. But that is a discussion for another time. Namely, when my mother returns to either confirm or deny your story."

"It's not a story. It's the truth."

"Of course it is. Which brings us back to my point. The *proper* behavior and form of greeting to be used when one comes into the presence of a duke."

"I see." She tilted her head at a challenging angle. When she did, a curling lock of copper-red hair freed itself of its pins and fell softly to her shoulder. Sam could not take his eyes off it. Then she spoke, bringing his attention back to her perfectly oval face with its pink and creamy skin. "Perhaps you'd care to instruct me in those areas where I'm lacking?"

"Indeed?" Sam allowed an arch and frankly sensual expression to claim his features as he blatantly raked his gaze over her shapely person. When he heard her intake of breath, he met her eyes. They blazed with anger. Sam sent her a triumphant grin as he raised his whisky to her in a salute. "It would be my pleasure to instruct you in whatever you wish."

She started to say something—no doubt, some tart comeback that would roundly put him in his place—but apparently she thought better of it and closed her mouth, firming her lips together.

Sam bit back a chuckle at her response. No doubt, his intended etiquette lesson, given what he knew of independent-thinking Americans, would not sit well with her. Especially since he meant to exaggerate the customs greatly.

"Very well, then. Lesson one," he began, managing to sound quite pompous. "The proper forms of address are, as you may know, 'Your Grace' or 'Duke.' Now, when you enter into the presence of a duke, Miss *Calhoun*, you are to curtsy and keep your eyes downcast. You may say 'Your Grace' as a greeting, but other than that you await the duke's pleasure. Meaning, you speak only when spoken to. And you certainly do not question him or speak sharply to him."

"I will endeavor to remember that . . . Your Grace."

Enjoying himself too much, Sam admonished, "And never interrupt a duke. Now, lesson two: you stand unless asked or told to sit down. In short, you remain subservient at all times. Is that clear?"

From under lowered yet far from subservient brows, Miss Sarah Margaret Calhoun met his gaze. Her vividly green eyes flashed fire that should have left Sam charred. Instead, he felt triumphant, much as if he'd won a battle. No doubt, with her answer, she would begin the war. An exciting war, one he admitted he was intentionally goading—not simply for sport, but because he felt compelled to do so, for many reasons. Among them was her odd presentation here with that highly improbable story and name. Add to that the instant antagonism that had arisen between them. And the attraction. Yes, the attraction . . . the desire . . . the mutual wariness. In some ways, he and this woman were like circling dogs sizing each other up.

Her continued silence finally goaded Sam into speaking. "I'm waiting, Miss Calhoun."

As if that were her signal, she hunched her shoulders and lowered her gaze. Her hands remained clasped together in front of her. "I apologize, Your Grace, for keeping you waiting. I also apologize for my ignorance of your customs and do heartily regret my embarrassing faux pas. Would Your Grace please allow me to correct my mistake by removing myself from your presence and then executing a proper entrance?"

Sam frowned. How disappointing. This was not what he'd expected or wanted. But now he was caught. "Certainly. Leave the room, then knock, and await my reply as you did before. We'll proceed from there."

"Very well, Your Grace." Still not meeting his gaze, she curtsied awkwardly and all but sidled meekly over to the closed door. Fumbling with the knob, she finally got it open and fled the room, closing the door behind her.

Alone now with only the ticking of the clock and his surprise, Sam shook his head, chuckled, and waited for her to knock . . .

And waited for her to knock. Only silence greeted his ears. Slowly, his grin faded. He shifted his weight about in his chair and finally put his drink down atop his desk. Still no knock. "What the bloody hell?" he muttered.

In one agile movement, he had his booted feet on the floor and was standing, staring at the door across the way. Still no knock sounded. And still he waited. He glanced at the clock and then eyed his bookcases, as if they could provide a clue. His jaw slowly tightened and his eyes narrowed. She was toying with him. She wouldn't dare. There had to be another explanation.

Instantly into his mind popped images of him and his abominable behavior. And her meek response. Why, he'd scared her, the poor little bird. Even now, she was perhaps gathering her courage, perhaps even rehearsing what to say and how to curtsy properly. He pictured her out there, nervous and scared, trying to remember the protocol. The vision she made in his mind unexpectedly affected Sam's heart and had him urging her on. *Come on, you can do it. Don't be frightened. Don't disappoint me.*

And so, feeling magnanimous, he waited longer, wanting to give her more of a chance to take this brave step and face him again. But all too soon, given the continued lack of a knock upon the door, he became agitated. Why didn't she knock?

Sam skirted his desk and stood in the middle of the room, planting his hands at his waist and staring at the damned door. Maybe he needed to say something. Maybe she was waiting for him to tell her to knock. Of course. That was it. Feeling slightly ridiculous, he called out, "You may knock now."

But she didn't.

"What the bloody hell . . . ?" Sam stalked over to the door and jerked it open. "I said you may knock—"

He cut off his own words. The hallway was empty.

# Chapter Five

Much like a woman's shawl does her shoulders, the elaborate gardens of Stonebridge graced the manor's grounds. With seemingly not a care in the world, Yancey ambled along the gravel walkway. The enchanting path meandered its way through the pleasing geometric grid that surrounded whimsical statues, neatly trimmed shrubs, and colorful flowerbeds. Stopping in front of a particularly interesting bed of roses, she leaned over to smell a freshly blooming blood-red specimen dotted with iridescent raindrops. She inhaled deeply. So sweet, its perfumed scent. A smile claimed her lips. It was nice out here in the garden, though a bit damp and cool and windy and dark.

She cast a sidelong glance toward the manor house to see if the duke were making a storming advance on her yet. He wasn't, not that she could see. But she expected he would soon enough. With a secret smile claiming her lips, Yancey again devoted her attention to the flowers, coming to the complimentary conclusion that the English certainly had a way with gardens. In this one's middle was a lovely three-tiered fountain surrounded by bedding plants and park benches. At the garden's end began a maze comprised of tall greening hedges that looked inviting. A perfect place for a lovers' tryst.

Yancey's arm was suddenly grabbed, eliciting a gasp from her as she was whipped around. Though startled by the suddenness of the attack—he hadn't been there only a moment ago—she wasn't surprised to realize that her heart was pounding with fright and that she would find herself staring up into the wickedly angry gray eyes of the Duke of Somerset.

"Don't tell me you weren't expecting me, Miss Calhoun."

"Well, of course I was. You just startled me with the suddenness of your attack. How did you sneak up on me without my seeing or hearing you?"

"First of all, I do not *sneak*. And second, I came around a side way across the lawn."

Yancey had nothing to say to that. She'd pulled a neat trick on him inside, but now it didn't seem so funny. A functioning part of her mind committed to memory how extremely impressive the duke was—in size and in temper. With him this close, with only mere inches of rose-scented air separating him from her on the garden's path, Yancey knew a moment of belated fright.

"Cat got your tongue, Miss Calhoun?"

"No."

"Good. May I assume, then, that while standing outside my study"—his voice was a low warning purr, like that of a crouching jungle cat—"you were suddenly seized by an overwhelming desire to have a stroll through the gardens without giving anyone any notice of your intentions?"

Yancey swallowed, her earlier courage and sense of victory having now abandoned her. "Yes."

"I see." The duke firmed his lips together, then inhaled and exhaled, looking around and making a show of surveying their surroundings. Then, suddenly, his gaze swooped down on her. "And do you find the half-planted flower beds to your liking, especially on such a lovely gray and wet afternoon as this one is?"

He couldn't have sounded more pleasant or more deadly. Yancey tipped her tongue out to moisten her suddenly dry lips. "Yes."

He nodded as if finding her answers pleasing. "Excellent.

And did you think there would be no consequences for making me feel the fool?"

Who did this man think he was? And what was she doing allowing him to handle her like this? "I don't recall wondering or worrying what you might think, Your Grace. Probably if I had, I wouldn't have done what I did. But then again, I might not have walked away if you hadn't first behaved like such a—"

She clamped her lips together, short of calling him a name. There was valor, and then there was discretion.

The duke cocked his head as if trying to hear her better. "I'm sorry? Like such a what, Miss Calhoun?"

He didn't think she'd dare say it. Yancey tried not to. She really tried. But failed. "Pompous ass. I'm sorry for the name, but you'll have to forgive me. I haven't been around many dukes. For all I know, every last one of you might behave this way."

Her words had transformed him into every inch the insulted blueblood. The duke glared at her with narrowed eyes. "Given your very precarious position here, do you actually think it wise to call me names and to insult my peers?"

His grip on her arm tightened painfully, but Yancey refused to flinch or to struggle against his hold—or to be further intimidated by his hard-muscled size. Still, the heated anger that radiated off him in waves threatened to melt her where she stood. Calling upon her reserve of daring, Yancey found her voice. "I would remind *Your Grace* that you began the game. I merely played out my turn."

His face a mask of anger, he inhaled stiffly, the action flaring his nostrils and raising his eyebrows. "Then allow me to end our little game with yet another reminder. Your position here is tenuous, at best. And you remain here only at my discretion and with my permission. Therefore, continued flippancy on your part will only get you and your trunks summarily thrown off all Somerset holdings—"

"Fine. Have my trunks repacked and please send for a—"

"Do *not* interrupt me." He pulled her to him and lowered his head until his nose almost tipped against hers. "Somerset's boundaries are considerable. So I would advise you to look about you at this wild country and how much you are at my mercy before you next speak or behave rashly." He used his free hand to make a sweep of their environment. "The mountains behind you. The hills around you. The farms, the forest, the very road you traveled over to get here. Everything you can see, Miss Calhoun, no matter in which direction you look . . . is *mine*."

Outrage at his high-handedness again won out over her fear of him and had Yancey jerking hard to free her arm. The tall duke released her suddenly, causing her to stumble backward before regaining her balance. With her hands fisted at her sides, Yancey all but launched herself at him. "Oh, you misspeak, sir, because not *everything* hereabout is yours. Make no mistake—I do not belong to you or to anybody. And you would do well to remember *that* . . . Your Grace."

Standing defiantly in the middle of the rain-puddled garden pathway, Yancey craned her neck up in order to meet the duke's thunderous gaze. The sheer blackness of his hair and the steel-gray of his eyes matched the rolling storm clouds overhead and gave him the appearance of being a force of nature in his own right.

"Your own woman? Perhaps in America. But not here. Not when you are in *my* charge. Remember that. And tell me—who exactly *are* you? And what *are* you doing here?" He pointed a finger at her. "And I warn you, I will not listen to or even consider the story you told me earlier."

"Well, then, that being so, Your Grace, you leave me nothing to say. Because I've already told you the truth." Well, as much of it as she intended to divulge at this time, she added to herself.

The angry duke crossed his arms over his chest and shifted his weight to one muscled leg. For long moments, he remained silent, frowning, staring down at her. He seemed to be struggling for control. Or insight. Yancey had no way of knowing. All she could do was wait.

Slowly his expression changed, finally smoothing out and becoming more contemplative than angry. "What *am* I going to do with you, Miss Calhoun?"

The smile lines that crinkled the corners of his eyes and

his almost affectionate tone of voice disarmed Yancey. She sent the duke a sidelong glance rife with suspicion. "Am I to assume you have something definite in mind and you're asking me to guess what it might be?"

His chuckle surprised her more than had his grabbing her arm, which still ached from when he'd gripped her so tightly. "No, Miss Calhoun. Hardly. I'm admitting that I have no idea how to proceed from here. Unless it's to have you drawn and quartered. Which I'm not inclined to do. At least not yet."

"I'm grateful for that, as you can imagine." Yancey didn't trust this calm of his. Still, she shrugged her shoulders. "But given that's how you feel, it would appear we're at a stalemate."

"Yes, it would. As long as you're not willing to tell me more about who you are and what you're doing here. And as long as I'm not willing to torture you to get the information out of you. And as long as my mother is not here to ask . . . well, we're stuck with each other as we are now, wouldn't you say?"

"I suppose so." She continued to look for hidden meaning or veiled threats in his words, but could find none.

The duke pivoted his shoulders to look back toward the manor, then again sought Yancey's wondering gaze. He hooked his thumbs in his waistband and favored her with a polite expression. "Would you care to join me for tea?"

Dumbfounded, her mouth agape, Yancey stared up at the extremely handsome and powerful man standing before her. "Tea? You're asking me to come inside and have *tea* with you? I don't understand."

"Surely you've had tea before. Even in America—"

"I've had plenty of tea before, thank you. I'm talking about us." She pointed from him to herself, adding for good measure, "You and me."

Frowning, he shook his head. "I wasn't aware there is an 'us.' "

"There is, and we were only just at each other's throats. And now I'm invited in for tea."

The duke grinned broadly. The transformation was

astounding. He was truly handsome and arousing . . . devastatingly so. Yancey had to stiffen her knees against the effect on her pulse of his sudden good humor. "Well, it is teatime. And as I'm certain it's already prepared, I would hate to waste it. But beyond that, you'll find ours is a most polite society, Miss Calhoun. Even in a time of actual wars, we have stopped the day's fighting out of regard for teatime. So I see no reason why our own private little war here can't be put aside long enough for the civilities to be observed, do you?"

What could she say? "No, I don't suppose I do."

"Excellent. A truce, then? Meaning we'll talk no more of important or upsetting matters until you are better rested. Say . . . on the morrow?"

Yancey searched for a trap in his words but could find none. And he was right—she was awfully tired. Her thoughts and reactions were threatening to become sluggish. That would be dangerous, given her purpose for being here. "All right. Truce."

"A wise decision." He offered her his arm, as politely as you please. "Shall we, then?"

To her own utmost surprise, Yancey took it, feeling his well-developed muscles flex and bunch under her hand. But almost immediately she regretted her decision to walk with him because his nearness actually soothed her. He felt so solid, so warm and dependable. Frightening Yancey was her sudden urge to lean on this man's strength, to lay her cheek against his sleeve and cry. No one had ever affected her this way. No one. If she had any sense, she admonished herself, she'd let go now and walk under her own power.

But she didn't. Instead, and as if she'd done this every day of her life, she allowed him to guide her steps back toward the safety and security of the mansion. From inside, warm and welcoming lights dispelled the afternoon's gloom. But instead of uplifting her, the sight dismayed Yancey terribly. She wanted nothing to do with such a domestic scene. She felt weakened somehow, without power, under the weight of such an inviting setting. The welcoming lights of a home, any home, always put her in mind of her mother, a sad woman who had accepted the safety and security of a home, and had paid for her mistake with her very life.

Dispelling the painful images of her beloved mother's face, and under cover of her eyelashes, Yancey sent a sidelong glance up to her companionably quiet escort's face. His unguarded expression revealed strength and intelligence in the high forehead and proud cheekbones. But a touch of sadness, which was revealed at the edges of his mouth, surprised Yancey, as did the hint of kindness that shone from his eyes. The man was an enigma. One moment raging, the next offering her his arm and inviting her inside for tea. She found him very intriguing.

And for that reason alone, Yancey's heart threatened to flip over with excitement. Nothing could be worse. She couldn't allow that. Excitement was danger. She knew that. Why else would she be a Pinkerton undercover operative if not for the danger and the excitement and the freedom? But this, what this man did to her fluttering heart, was not the same thing. Not the kind of excitement she needed.

Indeed, Yancey reminded herself, her own mother had urged on her an unconventional life. She'd begged her only child, her daughter, not to succumb to the traditional or to the domestic, not to live an ordinary life, one of wifely servitude and fear as she had. She'd also warned Yancey to beware the ways of love and of tying her heart and her body to one man's will.

For these reasons and more, Yancey knew she had to get away from the duke. And soon. Even if it meant not solving the mystery of his mother's misdirected letters to her or the murder of the Sarah Margaret Calhoun who had met her untimely death back in Chicago. Then Yancey heard herself and felt ashamed. That she would even consider such a cowardly move as abandoning an assignment, which to her would mean a compromising of her ethics, told her all too plainly just how dangerous this man striding so confidently beside her was to her professional state of mind.

Then she thought about the long and intimate evening that stretched ahead of them. Hours upon hours of each other's company. Teatime. Then later, supper. Conversation. Always

. . . conversation. How prolonged and painful it would be, given that they'd agreed not to discuss anything of import. All that left for discussion were the inane and the mundane. Certainly, Yancey's many undercover assignments in which she'd played the part of the coquette or the simpering miss had made her a master of those arts. But it was too late to masquerade with this man in such a way.

Earlier upstairs, he had already glimpsed who she really was . . . a strong and capable woman of secrets. No doubt, under the guise of polite conversation, and over the course of the evening, he might endeavor to pry those secrets out of her. She would have to watch every word, weigh every action, and right now, she was simply too bone-weary to be up to the task.

Therefore, the very notion of such a tension-filled evening caused Yancey's strength to flag. She leaned more heavily on the quiet duke's arm. After tea, she decided, she would beg off for the evening and remain in her room, away from him. All she wanted was a bath and that delicious bed. And a good night's sleep. No doubt, she'd feel differently in the morning. Stronger. More capable. More immune to this tall and powerful man at her side. No doubt, tomorrow she'd be better able to stand on her own two feet without help from anyone.

In the deep, dark hours of night, at a time just before daybreak, Sam thrashed about in bed, caught in the throes of a too familiar nightmare. In it, a woman in a white nightgown, her dark hair wild and tumbling, her face contorted with madness, screamed at him. He was struggling with her. He tried to hold on to her wrists, tried to stop her from lashing out with the long-bladed knife she held in her grip. She meant to kill him. She was strong, almost too strong for him to hold off. She jerked this way and that in his grasp, calling him vile names, accusing him of trying to kill her, of not loving her. Sam fought desperately to maintain his hold on her, but she twisted about until she was out of his grasp. Sam stumbled back. She lunged at him yet again with a slash of the knife—

With a cry of his own, Sam wrenched himself out of his dream. Awake now, his heart pounding with fear, he lay there, breathing rapidly and gripping the sheet under him. As he'd learned to do in the past when this particular bloodcurdling nightmare visited him, he worked hard to assure himself of the benign normalcy of his surroundings. *Dark bedroom. Alone. My bed. Bad dream. Safe now.* Hearing himself, he grimaced, hating that he felt like a frightened little boy who needed his mother's reassurance. He was a grown man, for God's sake.

Angry with himself, and ashamed, Sam fought his heavy, restraining covers, pushing them away as if they'd insulted him. Once he was free of them, he jackknifed to a sitting position. His knees bent, he braced his elbows atop them and clutched at his aching head. "How bloody long am I going to keep reliving that scene?" he asked the otherwise empty room.

Blinking, trying to clear away the last dregs of sleep that still fogged his brain, Sam stared fixedly into the faint reddish-yellow light cast by the glowing embers in the massive fireplace. He frowned. The damned room seemed to want to spin. No doubt, an evening spent alone with a whisky bottle accounted for that charming effect. Taking deep breaths and sitting quietly, hoping to calm his racing pulse and appease his raging headache, Sam concentrated on listening to the sounds of night. There were none to be heard. Only silence greeted him. Entombing silence. What had he expected?

Suddenly the silence surrounding him seemed hushed, expectant, as if holding its breath and awaiting the next sound. Sam tensed. What would he hear—a loud bump in the night? Something heavy falling to the ground? A scream? No, that couldn't be it. Not a scream. That had been in his nightmare. *And it's a damned good thing, too,* was Sam's now self-deprecating conclusion because he wouldn't be of much help to anyone. Not weak-kneed and hungover as he was right now. *That damned dream. It's always the same.*

"Leave it be, Sam," he cautioned himself just above a whisper. "There's not enough whisky in the world to wash away that guilt. What's done is done." He knew that, knew that it was over, that those times were past. But that knowledge didn't change anything. Especially not the way he felt about what he'd had to do, what circumstances had forced him to do. If only Sarah hadn't—*No. Stop right there.* Exhaling forcefully, as if that would relieve him of his guilt, Sam concentrated on the present—the very quiet present.

Had he missed something? Was something amiss outside his nightmare and inside his home? He truly did not think so, but still his mind insisted on a roll call of those in his household. It lit first on the most vulnerable member. Nana. Her bedchamber was several doors away. If she had cried out, if she were in any distress, her nurse would see to her. Unless, of course, her nurse had been the one to cry out against an attack on her person. Sam could only tsk-tsk at that. Who exactly in his household would be attacking the very stout and capable Mrs. Convers? Not Nana, who was dotty but not dangerous. Or even Scotty, who was neither dotty nor dangerous. Just big.

A chuckle escaped Sam, going a long way toward lightening his dispirited mood. What an odd assortment of people he had in his charge. Unorthodox, at best. But they were well-meaning and he cared more than he'd believed he would about them all, especially Nana. Given all that, Sam could only wonder what was wrong with him right now that he suddenly had the females under his care in distress and crying out against imaginary attacks. And what event had dredged up his old nightmare that had finally awakened him?

Then he remembered. Not an "event" at all, but a person. Her. The American. The woman with the same name as his wife. Sam glanced the way of the dressing room door that connected his bedroom to hers. He'd left it open on purpose so he could hear her, should she stir or sneak about. Could it be that she was up and stirring? Had she maybe bumped into something and cried out? Surprising Sam was how much he wanted that to be true. He wanted an encounter with her.

But telling himself he was merely suspicious of her, he cocked his head and listened.

He didn't have to wait long. A keening moan of terror, one that ripped upward along each of his vertebrae, became a scream that issued from the bedroom adjoining his. For an instant, Sam was frozen with shock. His spine seemed to stiffen and he could only stare at the open door across the way. Then his mind began to work, telling him that either she was having a bad dream, or—"Dear God, someone is trying to kill my houseguest."

Sam hopped quickly out of bed—and nearly went to the floor. The damned room was spinning again. Blinking and cursing his wooziness, he clutched at a bedpost and forced himself to take deep breaths. Blessedly, and in only seconds, the room righted itself. Thankful for that, though lacking a weapon and clad only in his small clothes, Sam sprinted . . . in a somewhat weak-kneed and meandering way . . . across the carpeted bedroom. Finally, he achieved the open doorway of the dressing room. Plunging in, he felt his way along the wall and navigated the darkness that enveloped the small familiar room that joined the lady's bedroom to his.

Once at the opposite end of the room, Sam halted at the barrier that was the closed door when he ran into it, nose-first. Cursing, he felt his nose with one hand and searched for the damned doorknob with his other. He found it and gave it a wrenching, twisting turn to open it as he told himself he'd have no one killing his quarrelsome guest before he'd first had a chance to do so himself. It was only fair, given all this upheaval she was causing just by being here.

Thus determined, Sam pushed open the door and slipped into the room, blinking rapidly to adjust his sight to the dawn-gray light that greeted him through a gap in the closed draperies. Tensed, ready for anything, he made a quick visual sweep of the room. No flurry of secretive or desperate activity met his inspection. All was still and quiet.

But at that moment, another cry arose, causing Sam to jump and direct his attention to the canopied bed across the way. The sound was a bleat of fright so heart-wrenching that it could have been wrung from a wounded baby animal.

Though Sam's heart lurched, he exhaled a sigh of relief. No one was trying to kill Miss Calhoun. At least, not in the waking world. She was having a bad dream.

Instinctively, Sam started for the bed—but suddenly stopped, wondering at himself. This dream, or nightmare, and especially this woman, were none of his affair, his conscience told him. What did he think he was going to do? Gently awaken her? Hold and comfort her? Sam couldn't actually see himself doing either of those things, but already he'd again set himself in motion across the room—in the direction of the bed.

Once there, but before he could reach out to touch her, the sight of her stopped him cold at the bed's foot. A silvery shaft of light spilling in through the windows across the way had illuminated for Sam his sleeping guest.

She'd kicked her blankets off. Covered only by her long white nightgown, she lay on her side, balled up and shaking, her hands fisted. Moaning, tossing her head from side to side, she twisted her expression into a mask of terror. As if he were locked in the dream with her, Sam's pulse picked up and he fisted his hands at his sides. He wanted to reach out to her. He also wanted to turn away, to leave. But oddly his muscles wouldn't allow him to do either thing. Locked, rigid, they held him in place as the two desires warred within him.

Compassion won the upper hand. Sam slipped onto the bed with her. Leaning against the many pillows at his back, he gathered the small, fine-boned woman into his arms. She resisted at first, crying out, fighting him. But Sam knew how to deal with this behavior. He persisted, gently tugging her across his lap, holding her close and making soothing, shushing sounds. Sitting in profile to him, her head was tucked up under his chin. On his lap, her slender body trembled like that of a frightened bird. Sam softly called her name, thinking to wake her, but the nightmare had too deep a hold on her.

That left him only one thing to do. He would comfort her. With an arm wrapped around her back, and her cheek resting against his bare chest, he stroked her long, unbound hair from her temple to her shoulder. Soft waves of silky curls felt luxurious under his hand. Sam marveled at how delicate and fragile she felt against him, like a twig that could be easily snapped in two. As he held her, he concentrated on soothing her and stroking her hair, her arm. He even heard himself shushing her, telling her everything was fine and she was safe. He kept expecting her to wake up at any moment, but she didn't. She remained asleep and gradually quieted.

As she relaxed, so did Sam. But then, with a sigh, she encircled his waist with one arm and smoothed her other hand up his bare chest. Sam's heart damn near stopped, even as his body responded with a surge of desire. Only too well did he realize that theirs was an intimate pose, one easily misunderstood—especially by her, should she rouse and come around. It didn't take much to recall what a spitfire she was when awake. It did, however, take Sam another moment to realize that he was smiling while thinking of her earlier tirades against him.

She'd certainly given him no quarter since she'd arrived. He could respect that. How brash she was, to just show up and install herself in his home and use the name that she did and yet offer no explanations. And what about him? Here he was in the middle of the night holding her in his arms while sitting atop her bed. Had he lost his mind? Perhaps. But she excited him so, made him feel alive. She gave him an argument. He liked that, and the fact that she apparently was not the least bit impressed by him or his titles.

So very intriguing. And what man wouldn't be intrigued by this green-eyed woman who looked him right in the eye and stood her ground? Well, plenty of men in his acquaintance wouldn't appreciate her cheek. But he did. He'd spent too many years in America not to be affected by the independent spirit that pervaded that country. He admired it, in fact, just as he admired her putting him in his place late yesterday afternoon. A grin of self-deprecating humor quirked Sam's mouth as he pictured himself and how he must have looked standing there alone in his study and wondering why she didn't knock on the door so he could give her an etiquette lesson.

What an ass he'd been, one who deserved exactly what

she'd done in retaliation. Then he heard himself. So now he was defending her. A bit troubled by this admiring reaction to her, Sam glanced down at the warm bundle on his lap . . . and shook his head. Had he really only known her for one short afternoon and no more? It didn't seem possible. Yet it was true. Already he was wondering what he'd done with his time before she'd arrived here.

Almost too late, alarm bells sounded in his head. He could not be having these thoughts about this woman. As he'd already told himself, she was danger personified. He knew nothing about her. More importantly, she knew nothing about him. And that was how it needed to stay. Truly unsettled now by how quickly she seemed to have enchanted him, Sam renewed his efforts to extricate himself from her without waking her up.

So, how to escape undetected? That was his dilemma. One thing he knew: he wasn't going anywhere unless he sat up straighter. Along those lines, Sam contracted his stomach muscles, thinking to sit forward and get his hand under her legs, so he could lay her on the other side of the bed and then slip off it himself. But when he moved forward, she fussed in low murmurs and gripped him tighter. Grimacing lest he wake her, Sam relaxed, again leaning back against the pile of pillows at his back. He shook his head, finding the situation faintly amusing. But only faintly.

*Well, this is a fine kettle of fish.* Unable to clearly see her face, he could nevertheless smell the fresh, sweet scent of her hair from its washing last evening before she'd retired. He could also feel her warm and pleasant weight atop his lap . . . against his chest and against his lap—a part of himself that remained intrigued and very awake. That was about the last thing he needed right now. Sam's agitation and heated blood had him stretching his legs and rotating his ankles. The more he moved, though, the more she clung to him, whimpering and shifting about, essentially grinding her bottom against his now very happy lap.

Sam instantly but too late sat still. Thanks to her innocent movements and his lascivious thoughts, he was now hard enough to cut diamonds. Every nerve ending in his body thrummed and he was finding it increasingly difficult to breathe normally, much less keep his hands to himself. He thought about that and corrected himself. He wasn't keeping his hands to himself. They were already on her. He had an arm around her back and his hand resting against her hip. His other hand, his left hand, he'd smoothed up under her hair to cup her cheek and neck. So, essentially, he was embracing her.

The only thing separating him from the feel of her bare skin under his touch was the thin fabric of her nightgown. All he had to do to kiss her was raise her chin. God knew he wanted to and had ever since he'd first seen her in this very room only a matter of hours ago. Sam's mind wandered now, presenting him with images of himself claiming her lips, of his tongue inside the warm moistness of her mouth, of his hand on her breast, his thumb caressing her nipple—

*Bloody hell. This simply will not do. Think about something else, man.* Taking his own advice, he searched through his many business ventures and concerns for something of sufficient weight to distract his mind from the reality of the sweet-smelling woman atop his thighs. The cattle he'd had shipped from America to strengthen his stock? He shook his head. No coherent thought would form regarding livestock. The fine horses, then? No. The fact that Parliament was sitting without a Treyhorne in attendance? Hardly. His mother's imminent return from his aunt Jane's? No. His brother Geoffrey's sudden illness and death?

Sam shook his head as if to physically dislodge that remembrance. If he dwelled on that, he'd be the one with the nightmares. Or a different one, at least.

Sam gave up. The thought simply did not exist that could render him unaware of the petite, redheaded, green-eyed woman in his arms. She was too potent a presence. Too warm a weight. Sam exhaled and leaned his head back against the bed's headboard. He closed his eyes. What was he supposed to do, then? Stay like this until the morning? No. He'd already ruled that out.

Well, damn his uncharacteristically kind instinct in coming in here in the first place. Look where a bout of compassion had landed him. Yes, just look where. In the bed of a very desirable woman whose mystery and flashing green eyes excited him beyond belief. But a woman who had no inkling that he was presently in her bed. A woman who would not be amused in the least to find him here. He needed to leave, he knew that, and go back to his own bed. Now. Before he fell asleep. Before the room's silvery moonlit grayness and absolute quietness seduced him into dropping off. Before the wonderfully comfortable mattress underneath him lured him into its depths.

And before the enticing sleeping woman in his arms had him simply shrugging them both down atop the bed and pulling the covers up around them. Sam blinked and yawned, feeling his muscles relax, feeling the lethargy of sleep slip over him. He started to nod off. He felt his hand drop from Miss Calhoun's neck to her thigh, where his palm lightly rested against her skin. His other hand fell away from her hip and onto the sheets.

Several peaceful moments slipped by . . . then Sam started, coming to and shaking his head, trying to clear his mind. He took a deep cleansing breath, blinking rapidly and admonishing himself. *Just get up, man. Simply lay her down and leave. You're not a schoolboy. This isn't the first woman's bed you've been in. You've made getaways before. You can do it this time, too.*

Right. He needed to leave. What he had to face, though, was that he didn't want to leave. He wanted to stay. He wanted to continue to hold her. He liked the way she felt in his arms. He liked the way her hair smelled, the softness of her skin. Sam heard himself and called himself four kinds of a fool. Curse it all, he was making this worse by even entertaining thoughts such as those. But there it was: he liked being here with her. It was as simple as that. Simple or not, he didn't have her permission to be here. Worse, he had no right to be here, no matter how pure his motives had been at first. Beyond every other consideration—and they all paled when held up to this one—he was a married man. He had taken vows, sworn an oath of fidelity.

While he hadn't yet broken them, his behavior here tonight proved him to be no kind of gentleman. He might not be polite society's idea of a gentleman, but he did have his own convictions regarding honor and his own standards of conduct, none of which he was currently upholding. An ironic grin claimed his lips. The only thing he was upholding was a delicious armful of sleeping female—who would, no doubt, scratch his eyes out if she awoke to find him in her bed.

That image did it. Where shame or good sense held no sway, the possibility of being blinded for life prevailed. Renewing his grip on her, as well as his resolve to get himself free and remain unscathed, Sam tensed his muscles and sat forward, scooping his feminine burden up into his arms. Done with efforts at gentleness and doubts, he rocked forward, trying to get his balance so he could twist and lay her down. But he came too far forward and lost his balance, falling heavily onto the mattress—atop her and squashing her under him.

A moment of stunned silence followed. Then, a muffled feminine squawk from somewhere under him, between him and the sheets, told him his worst nightmare was now awake.

# Chapter Six

In one split second, deep sleep became a painful and frightening awakening. The only thing Yancey's shocked mind would register was that she was in a bed and something had fallen atop her, something that lay across her back and was crushing the life out of her. When the weight had hit her, her breath had left her lungs in a muffled whoosh that under other circumstances would have been a shriek. Where was she? She couldn't remember. What was happening? She had no idea. All she knew was that something warm-blooded and heavily muscled—and deadly—held her pinned down.

That was when, in the next second upon being forced awake, her situation became crystal clear to her. She'd been attacked in her sleep. Terrified, yet determined to die with dignity, she stiffened, preparing to fight back. One thought reigned uppermost in her mind. *Get to your gun under your pillow.* Yes. If only she could. But, frighteningly, she realized that the weight atop her was so heavy that she couldn't even draw enough air into her lungs to scream, much less to mount any kind of an effective attack. She was lying on her stomach and couldn't even turn her head. Nor could she get so much as a hand out from under whoever was atop her.

*So this is how it will end,* a very calm part of her mind remarked. No. She wouldn't accept that. Not without a fight.

With a surge of determination lancing through her, Yancey struggled in earnest, wriggling about and straining ever upward. That was when she heard the voice—an irritated and pompous one that stopped her cold with disbelief.

"Would you bloody well hold still a moment, Miss Calhoun? We're tangled together here, and I'm trying to get you free."

The duke! Anger and outrage combined with fear and flooded through Yancey. When the weight gave some, finally lifting off her neck, she turned her head to the side so she could grit out her words through the tangle of her hair that covered her face. "Get *off* me, you big overbred ass."

The mattress under her shifted with the man's efforts to extricate himself from her. "I assure you that is *exactly* what I am trying to do . . . you underbred little guttersnipe."

Yancey sucked in an insulted breath, or tried to. All she got was a pained attempt. "How *dare* you?" she bleated into the sheets.

"How dare I? I'll tell you how I dare. This is *my* house."

Suddenly the weight was removed completely from her back. Extreme relief coursed through her as, gasping for each breath, she remained flat on her stomach, her arms out to her sides. Every blink of her eyes revealed tiny stars dancing across her vision. They gradually receded as she shoved her hair away from her face and raised her head. Moonlight—or perhaps the beginnings of sunlight—peeking through the closed drapes across the way revealed that she now mysteriously was lying sideways to the bed and at its foot. She could make nothing of that as she concentrated on sucking in huge drafts of sweet and wonderful air.

When her breathing became more normal, she pushed herself up and sat cross-legged atop her bed, a hand to her chest as she stared at the duke.

He'd hopped off the bed and was now lighting a threesome of fat candles that sat atop a bedside table. A golden light suddenly suffused the room, pushing the gloom back to the corners. Yancey watched in disbelief, thinking how common and ordinary a task he'd just performed under these most extraordinary of circumstances. What did he think he was about? Then she realized that she was now capable of speech and made her demands known. "What in God's name were you doing in my bed? And if you expect a 'Your Grace' to follow that, then you have a long wait, sir."

"I expect nothing, I assure you," the duke said, now standing beside the small round table, his body suffused in the candles' glow as their combined light danced over his skin.

*His skin?* Blinking her surprise, but then instantly captivated by him, Yancey raised her chin and looked at him through different eyes. She slowly slid her gaze up and down the duke's length.

A sensual awareness flooded through her, finally pooling low in her belly and leaving her limbs feeling heavy. The appreciative female part of her brain registered that the duke was a magnificent specimen, just as she had supposed he would be. Perfectly proportioned. Broad across the shoulders and through the chest. Narrow at the hip. Hard-muscled. Breathtaking. And almost completely unclothed. Yancey softly blew out her breath—then realized with a suddenness born of embarrassment that she was ogling her tormentor and thinking very unladylike thoughts of him. And he knew it.

"Are you done?" His voice was low, husky . . . faintly taunting.

"For now," Yancey replied boldly, raising her chin. In order to meet his arrogant gaze, though, she had to tear her own away from the sprinkling of crisp curling hair that graced his broad chest. The candles' insufficient light masked his gray eyes, but she could see that he had arched an eyebrow in a suggestive way that she deserved but didn't particularly like.

She refused to look down at herself to see what, if anything, she might be exposing to his gaze. "I expect that at any moment now you will tell me what has happened here?"

"Certainly." He crossed his arms over his chest. His bunched muscles spoke of power and health. "You cried out."

"Of course I did. I awakened to find you atop me and crushing the life out of me with your bulk. Anyone would cry out."

"No. I meant before."

"Before what?"

"Before I came in here to see about you. You cried out."

"I never."

"You did. And more than once."

This was unsettling news. But uppermost in her mind was her growing sense of immodesty in her pose. She subtly pulled at her gown, tugging it down over her legs and holding the gown's fabric wadded up in her lap. "Say I did cry out in my sleep. I doubt that I called out for you."

"Not for me. Not for anybody, actually. Just cried out. A moan of terror. You were apparently having a nightmare."

Sitting there, considering him as much as his words, Yancey decided that she believed him. Certainly the frightening images that had been burned into her memory by repeated nightmares over the years could have assailed her once again. The dreams were always the same: the day her father came home when she was thirteen. Five years of hell had followed that, ended by an afternoon of violence that only she had walked away from. Or run, was more like it.

Yancey felt her throat tighten and her face heat up with remembered emotion. "I see. A nightmare," she finally commented. "And you thought the best way to wake me from it was to jump atop me and try to smother me?"

His expression hardened as he lowered his chin. With his face partially in shadow, he looked positively sinister. "Had I had been *trying* to smother you, Miss Calhoun, there would be no need for this conversation because you would already be dead."

Yancey's breath caught in her throat. She reminded herself of her gun under her pillow and her own proximity to it. "I'll strive to remember that," she replied. "And given that's the case, please accept my apologies. I never meant to malign your abilities or your motives."

He ducked his chin regally. "Apology accepted. Now, if you will excuse me, I would like to finish my night's sleep."

Again, and just like out in the garden last afternoon, his change in manner was so sudden that Yancey could only watch in disbelieving silence as the duke—acting as if they were fully clothed and stood in broad daylight, as if he'd only just met her on the street and they'd visited amiably—stepped away from the table and skirted the end of her bed.

Yancey crabbed around none too ladylike atop the mattress in order to keep him in her sight. The fear that he would again leap atop her and crush her no longer held sway in her mind, despite her warning to herself only moments ago. Instead, it was the breathtaking sight he made in only his smallclothes. They did nothing to hide his masculine endowments. Yancey's gaze remained helplessly riveted to his body.

When the darkly sensual duke reached the open door of the dressing room that joined her bedroom to his, he stopped and turned to her. She'd thought he meant to say something, yet he didn't. Instead, with a hand holding on to the doorjamb, he merely stared her way. Yancey's heart beat slowly and dully. *What now?* she could only wonder, still under the spell of his overt sexuality that had her breathing in and out through her flared nostrils.

Then . . . he did speak, his voice a husky purr. "Good night, Miss Calhoun. Or should I say good morning?" He touched his fingertips to his brow in a mock salute to her. "I hope the remainder of your night, or day, is less eventful."

"Yours as well . . . Your Grace. You'll forgive me if I don't leave my bed and curtsy this one time, won't you?"

His chuckle was decadent. "Oh, I think under the present circumstances, we can forgo the formalities. But only if you'll forgive me for how much I enjoyed holding you while you slept."

She'd overslept. And it was no wonder, given her extreme tiredness of the day before and then the unusual but titillating events of the early morning hours. Refusing to dwell on his comment about how wonderful he had found it to hold her in his arms, and following a late breakfast alone in the very formal dining room, Yancey had set about some detecting duties. She didn't know exactly what she was searching for in each orderly room she invaded. But, to her, it was enough that she was diligently on the job. Something, no doubt, of a suspicious nature would present itself to her trained eye.

But it wasn't to be because no matter where she'd roamed, or into whatever room she'd slipped, she'd been politely confronted by some servant or another wanting to do her every bidding. It hadn't taken her long to get full of that and to retreat in irritated self-defense to her own elegant suite of rooms upstairs.

Standing now in front of one of the tall windows in her bedroom, her arms crossed and her features set in lines of vexation, she stared at the landscape spread out before her. Hulking mountain peaks formed a jagged backdrop to the green hills and the thatch-roofed cottages closer by. Cattle and horses dotted the land. And an occasional farm wagon trundled by, headed in the direction of the village in the distance. Though the setting was beautiful, much like a fine pastoral painting, Yancey just couldn't appreciate it today. Not when she needed instead to be working on a plan to solve the case for which she'd been sent here.

And that case involved the duke. Despite her best efforts not to indulge in fantasies of the man, her mind insisted on reliving the feel of his wonderfully lithe body and sensual presence in her bed only a matter of hours ago. Immediately Yancey responded, tensing with a yearning she found hard to control. She caught her breath and exhaled it slowly in an effort to cool her blood. Hoping to distract herself from what could only be ruinous yearnings, she lowered her gaze from the middle distance of the English countryside to focus on the formal gardens right below her window. Any distraction would do at this point.

Below her, the gardeners were revealed to be about their duties. The flower plots were overrun with an army of men who, like so many ants, were busy with potting and pruning and planting. And there was that scrappy little dog, Mr. Marples. Yancey grinned at his canine antics. Tearing about, he seemed to be purposely getting in the workmen's way, only to be shooed irritably. Undaunted, grinning, his tongue lolling out the side of his mouth, he hurried to the next man and helped with the digging, throwing dirt and chaos everywhere, only to be shooed again.

Yancey then spied the dog's three shadows . . . the cats Alice, Mary, and Jane. Taking the sun, the felines were elegant white splotches draped lazily over the various ornamental benches set around the fountain. Comparing her plight to theirs, Yancey called herself the very image of the damsel in distress from ancient times, withering away and locked inside her ivied tower.

And that was when it occurred to her: there was indeed an ivied tower here, one simply begging for exploration, if for no other reason than to see the view from its top. Just then, something pinged against the glass, at a spot only a few inches from Yancey's nose. Startled, she blinked and pulled back. *What in the world . . . ?* It happened again. Another sharp, startling ping. Much as if a small stone—

Someone was throwing rocks at the window. She leaned toward the glass pane and peered outside. And there he stood . . . the duke. A thrill of excitement chased through Yancey's veins. The barest of smiles slipped onto her lips. Then she caught herself. *No.* She stiffened her knees and warned herself to adopt an attitude of diffidence toward this man. To do otherwise, to respond warmly or wantonly, could be the death of her, she reminded herself.

But her cautions to herself died a sudden death, and it was the duke's fault. There he stood, dressed in much the same type of clothes he'd worn yesterday. Black boots, corded breeches, and a white shirt. He had his hands planted at his waist and he was staring up at her. Apparently realizing that he had gained her attention, he grinned and waved at her, signaling for her to come down and join him.

Join him, indeed. She couldn't stop the seductive smile that claimed her lips, even as a fresh wave of desire-filled tension washed over her, raising the fine hairs on her arms and at the nape of her neck. She nodded her reply to the man below, signaling that she would join him. She raised a hand, sending him a tentative little wave in return to his more boisterous gesture.

Without thinking, Yancey flattened a palm against the

cool pane of glass and held it there . . . as if awaiting his touch in return. Below her, standing with his feet apart, much like a ship's captain on the main deck, his upturned gaze seemed to bore into hers. Awareness, not dulled by distance or panes of glass, flowed between them. Yancey couldn't look away. Worse, she didn't want to look away. In fact, if she could stay just like this for the remainder of her days—

She heard herself and gasped, jerking her hand away from the window. "Dear Lord, what am I doing?"

"Beg your pardon, Your Grace?"

Yancey gasped and spun around, her hands fisted around her skirt.

Across the room stood a slender, dark-haired girl in a maid's livery, who proffered a quick curtsy and an apology. "I'm so sorry, Your Grace. I didn't mean to startle you."

Stung, embarrassed, wondering how much the girl had seen, Yancey all but barked out, "How long have you been standing there, Robin?"

Her eyes wide, the maid took a step back. "Not long, Your Grace. I've only just now come into the room."

"I see. Well . . . then, good." Yancey eyed the young girl with whom she'd already lost one struggle this morning. Robin had insisted that she'd been promoted to lady's maid to assist Yancey. And as this was a major elevation in the girl's status in the household, she wasn't about to relinquish it. And so, over Yancey's protestations, Robin had assisted with "my lady's toilette." And now, here she was again. Though she owed the girl no explanation, Yancey heard herself giving one. "Over there, by the window, I was just, uh, *thinking* and didn't hear you come in. And there's no need to call me 'Your Grace.' "

The girl curtsied again. "Yes, Your Grace." And continued to stand there at attention, her brown eyes wide and expectant.

A confused silence crowded the space between them until Yancey caught on that the girl possibly awaited her permission to speak. *Damned stupid custom,* was Yancey's unvoiced opinion. Still, "Did you want something?"

"Oh no, Your Grace. Not me." With her hands knotted

together in front of her, the girl waited, yet looked ready to hare off at the slightest provocation.

Yancey wasn't quite sure how to proceed. After another bit of awkward silence, she ventured, "Then . . . perhaps I can do something for you?"

"Oh no, Your Grace. Not at all."

Really stymied now, Yancey brushed at a stray lock of hair at her temple and stared at the girl. "Then I find, Robin," she began, "that I have no idea how to continue this conversation. Unless you came in here to ask me something specific or to—"

"I have a message for you, Your Grace." she blurted. "From His Grace."

"Really?" Striving to appear unaffected, even though a now familiar thrill shot through her, Yancey crossed her arms, feigning nonchalance. "I'd love to hear it."

Taking a deep breath, Robin pulled herself up to her full height and proudly, loudly, announced, "His Grace the Duke requests that, if you are not otherwise engaged, you attend him in the gardens, Your Grace."

No doubt, Robin had rehearsed that title-heavy speech all the way up the stairs. Yancey suppressed a grin. "Oh, I see. Well, yes, I knew that, Robin. He just now threw a rock at the window."

The girl's eyes widened, no doubt out of surprise at the unfathomable antics of her betters. "Yes, Your Grace."

"What I meant was I was standing at the window, looking out, when suddenly a stone hit the glass and I looked down and there the duke was, signaling to me. And then here you were and . . ." Yancey's voice trailed off, leaving her feeling silly for having divulged all that to her lady's maid. "If that's all, Robin?"

The girl gave a start. "Yes, Your Grace." She curtsied and began to turn away, but then turned back to Yancey. "Begging Your Grace's pardon?"

Already in motion, her feet being moved forward by an impatient desire for fresh air and sunshine—and nothing more, she stridently told herself—Yancey stopped short and met her maid's gaze. "Yes?"

"I was wondering, Your Grace, about the rest of your trunks."

"The rest of my trunks?" Yancey frowned her confusion. She'd brought all her clothes with her, not knowing how long she'd be here or what she might need. And only this morning Robin had told Yancey that she'd unpacked them last evening while Yancey had been at tea with the duke. Even knowing there weren't any others, Yancey asked, "What about them?"

"The ones with your gowns. I didn't find any, and I thought that exceeding strange, yourself being a duchess and all. Forgive me for asking, but will they be arriving from America soon?"

Now, how to answer that without giving herself away? Yancey decided on brevity . . . and a lie. "Yes."

Robin's expression cleared and she smiled widely. "Oh, Your Grace, I just knew they would be right along. I just knew it."

The girl's happy response gave Yancey pause. Was there perhaps discussion belowstairs about the impoverished state of the, uh, duchess's wardrobe? And had Robin been defending her mistress? Yancey's conscience reminded her that the maid's trust in her would soon be dashed when no trunks appeared. Feeling guilty, Yancey added, "Hopefully, my trunks won't be lost in the shipping. That happens more than one cares to think about."

Robin was now agog with affirmations. "I've been told as much, Your Grace. We can only hope and trust to God that it won't be so."

Yancey came very close to chuckling out loud. "I hardly think it's as dire as all that. We are talking about clothing here, and not a person's life, Robin."

Instantly contrite and red-faced, the girl dropped another curtsy. "I beg Your Grace's pardon. I didn't mean to overstep my bounds."

"But you didn't." Yancey's fleeting reflection was that she and Robin were both novices at this mistress-and-lady's-maid relationship. In truth, and well Yancey knew this, she had more in common with the maid than she did with any duchess. "And I'm certain it will turn out well," she added—only to be interrupted by another well-aimed stone pinging against the window behind them.

The duke was obviously becoming impatient. Yancey met her maid's startled gaze and smiled a tight little smile as she again set herself in motion to cross the room. "Perhaps I'd best go before the duke unleashes a barrage of stones that brings the house down around our ears."

"Yes, Your Grace. The duke is not a man to be denied long."

Yancey's pace didn't slow but inside she was aflutter with nerves. Her traitorous body had given Robin's innocent answer a different spin and left Yancey unsettled. Meaning that was exactly what she feared—that she would not be able to deny the duke anything . . . or for long.

# Chapter Seven

She'd come down to him like a lamb to the slaughter. And now, Sam reflected, to lead her down the garden path, as it were, and penetrate her façade. Anything to get to the woman underneath.

"You have quite the unorthodox method for gaining someone's attention, Your Grace."

"Many of my methods are unorthodox, Miss Calhoun. But I assume you mean specifically my tossing pebbles at your bedroom window?" Sam smiled lazily at his very striking companion as they wound their way through the garden's maze. Composed of high green hedges that blocked the soft breeze, it made the sunlight feel almost too warm upon Sam's shoulders, just as the woman at his side made him feel too warm all over.

"Yes. Startling, to say the least."

"I hope I didn't frighten you?" He couldn't have been more solicitous of her tender feelings. Or more apologetic in his attitude.

"It takes more than a few tossed pebbles to frighten me, Your Grace."

"I can well imagine that it does." They'd reached an intersection in the maze. "And which way would you suggest we turn, Miss Calhoun?"

She glanced up at him, giving Sam a perfect picture of a delicate feminine jaw and slender neck. Feathery reddish-orange curls laced her hairline at her temple. And he found himself drawn to her lips, which were pink and full. "You wish me to choose? But you've been leading us so unerringly."

"Out of sheer habit. I've navigated this maze since I was a child."

"I see. So my choosing our direction now is to be a test of my skill?"

"Skill. Chance. Luck. Whatever you wish to call it. We can only go left or right. So you have even odds for being right or wrong."

Her arch expression told him plainly enough that despite his disclaimer, she knew full well that he was toying with her, testing her, but not on any level that had to do with the maze. With a knowing smile curving the corners of her sensual mouth, she ducked her chin in acknowledgment of the thrown gauntlet. "Ah. Even odds. The words seem to cancel each other, don't they? Like so much in life, Your Grace, and just like in this maze we currently find ourselves."

"Really? An interesting observation. Tell me how you think this maze has anything to do with life."

"Well, it's obvious, isn't it? Look here." She swung a pointing finger from left to right at the intersection in front of them that faced a wall of hedges. "Just like life. Each of our actions and decisions brings us only as far as the next crossroads. Then we're shown only bits and pieces of what lies to our left and to our right. But still we must choose at each juncture, even without fully knowing what is around the next corner."

Sam found himself completely engaged in this mental exercise. "I see where you're going. But a maze differs from life in that it remains a fixed shape."

"Meaning it doesn't reconfigure itself with our decisions?"

"Exactly. The maze here doesn't change for us. Should you take the wrong path, the only consequence is you will waste a bit of time because, once you've discovered your error, should your decision prove to be one, you remain free to simply turn around and try another path."

She pointed at him, her green eyes bright with enjoyment. "Ah. But life is again similar. With each decision we make, we cannot know if it is right or wrong until we act upon it. And one wrong turn in life can change its outcome, too. It may seem unfair, but we are actually only guessing our way through at any particular point because we can only see our present choices, and not those of the future."

"But our present decisions directly affect the future, which in turn doesn't begin to take shape until we make a decision one way or the other in the present."

"So far as we know."

"True." He slanted a meaningful look her way. "Still, I worry more about being forced to choose when I suspect that not all of my options have been made known to me."

She sent him a sidelong glance from under her eyelashes. "You mean by others who don't wish you to succeed?"

"Exactly. What do I do then, Miss Calhoun, when I suspect there might be hidden information that could affect my decision, yet I'm not made privy to it?"

She shrugged, shaking her head as if she were innocent of any such actions as he'd just described. "Well, Your Grace, either you must wring more information out of the offending party, or make your decision to the best of your ability based on what you do know."

Feeling himself duly forewarned that she'd be a formidable adversary, Sam softly clapped his hands together. "Bravo, Miss Calhoun. A fine bit of logic and philosophy."

She sketched a formal curtsy. "I share the triumph with you, Your Grace." Then she stepped out into the intersection and looked both ways.

Now captivated by her figure as much as he was by her mind, Sam crossed his arms and watched her work on this problem. Sparring verbally with her left him wanting nothing more than to take her in his arms and kiss her soundly. He found himself wondering what she would do if he did . . .

She turned around abruptly, facing him and smiling,

pointing to her right. "This way, Your—" Her expression sobered, her eyes rounded.

So he'd been caught with his thoughts on his face. Sam arched his eyebrows, doing nothing to hide the intensity of the desire he felt for her. "To my left, then?"

"Yes," she said a little breathlessly. "Am I correct, Your Grace?"

He nodded. "You are." He started toward her. "Tell me how you knew. Or did you guess?"

Though she still appeared distracted by his approaching nearness, she stood her ground and shook her head in the negative. "Not a guess. It was simple, really. The gravel is more displaced in this direction. The path is more worn. Anyone who knew his way through here wouldn't consistently take wrong turns. So I merely followed your footsteps, as it were, Your Grace."

Sam had to chuckle. "Undone by my own habits. Outsmarted by a fox, I'd say, Miss Calhoun."

Her expression blanked and she pulled back, looking startled. Sam sobered in reaction to her response. "Are you quite all right, Miss Calhoun? Did I say something untoward?"

She recovered quickly—curiously so—and smiled brightly, talking a bit too rapidly. "Oh no, it was nothing, Your Grace. Nothing at all." She gestured toward the correct way out. "Shall we? I find it a bit too warm and close in here just now."

Sam considered her a long, silent moment, then indicated she should precede him. "Please, then. After you, Miss Calhoun."

She turned and walked off, giving him time only to wonder about her puzzling reaction to something he'd said and to notice the enticing sway of her hips, when she spun around, forcing him to stop in his tracks or risk running into her.

"I find it rather curious, Your Grace," she said, "that your servants still believe me to be your . . . well, your American wife, the duchess. You obviously know I am not. So why do you allow the charade to continue?"

Her bluntness took Sam by surprise. He crossed his arms

and shifted his weight to his other foot, two delaying actions which gave him time to formulate an appropriate answer. From the number of options coursing through his mind, he finally decided on the one certain to spark outrage in her heart. "Because it pleases me to do so, Miss Calhoun."

She pulled back in surprise. "It *pleases* you? I believe I have a right to know in what ways it does, since I'm a party to this deception."

"Merely a party? I believe you to be the instigator, Miss Calhoun."

Her cheeks pinkened, and she had trouble meeting his gaze. "I have tried to right that wrong, but your servants won't believe me."

He fought to keep a grin off his face. "I'm sorry to hear that. But as regards me, I need no other reason than that it pleases me. Since I am a duke, I am free to behave according to my every whim or mood. And no one will gainsay me or think to correct me. That is, not if he—or she—wishes to remain in my good graces, which I am sure you do . . . given your, uh, position here in my household."

Sam watched the effect of his words on her. Her green eyes radiated momentary confusion, even a bit of fear. She seemed to shrink back. He didn't like that he'd frightened her, but it couldn't be helped. After all, he had no idea who she really was or what her purpose was in being here. Until he did, he had a duty to protect what was his, and he saw no reason to make life simple for her, no matter how much she affected him. He'd given her good advice—and she'd be wise to heed it.

When she still made no reply, Sam indicated the path ahead of them. "Shall we—now that we know the correct way of things here?"

Without a word, she turned away from him and faced the path ahead. Behind her, quirking a grin of victory as he watched her straighten her shoulders and march onward, Sam pronounced himself content enough for the moment to walk behind her to the accompaniment of buzzing bees, happy songbirds, and the crunch of gravel under their feet.

She was being very quiet. He'd always heard that someone with something to hide was best served by remaining silent. Then, hadn't he better draw her out? "Tell me, Miss Calhoun, what do you think of the gardens of Stonebridge?"

Not slowing the least or even casting a glance over her shoulder, she said, "Very impressive. I especially like the roses. Although I don't think I've ever seen anything quite like this before. So much variety. So intricate and surprising. A fountain here. A tiny grotto around that corner. And there a pond. Something unexpected around every corner."

Her last words put him in mind of their dealings together so far. Something unexpected around every corner—and behind every word. "That there is. Much like life again, wouldn't you say?"

Her steps faltered, but she bravely carried on, still refraining from giving him her direct attention. "I'm not sure. How do you mean?"

"Well, I daresay you never expected to find yourself here. And I mean in England."

"But of course I did. I wasn't drugged and tied up and thrust on board a ship bound for your fair country. I came here on purpose. A ticketed customer. It was all very aboveboard."

He chuckled. "Very clever. What I meant, of course, were the circumstances that caused you to be on that ship."

Just as he said that, they exited the maze and found themselves face to face with a knot of workmen who immediately abandoned their tasks to clear a path. As they did, they pulled off their caps and bowed in a show of respect. Several "Your Graces" followed Sam and his enigmatic and lovely companion around another corner on the outside of the maze.

As they moved past the deferential men, Miss Calhoun finally looked up at him. Sam's breath unexpectedly caught. Did the sunlight have to add such a glow to her peaches-and-cream complexion? And then glint so brightly off her curling hair in such brilliant hues of gold and orange and red? Only yesterday he'd wondered what her unbound hair would look like in sunlight. And now he knew. Today she'd caught her hair back with combs and left it to hang down her back in a long, lush wave. Sam itched to stroke her hair, to feel it slip through his fingers and perhaps cascade across his bare chest.

And her costume, a dark blue simple skirt and a white blouse that showed off her arresting figure to its best advantage. Where did it end? Did she never stop in her mounting attractions? Oh, how well his body remembered how it felt to hold her when only her nightgown was between them.

"I said, do you never get tired of all that?"

Blinking out of his reverie, and cautioning himself to keep his wits about him, Sam realized he had no idea what she meant. "I beg your pardon? Tired of what?"

"All that bowing and the 'Your Grace' this and 'Your Grace' that. Is it ever tiresome?"

"Most certainly. Especially since returning here after many years spent in America. I found I'd become quite comfortable with being simply Mr. Samuel Treyhorne."

She nodded. "That sounds very American. I like it."

"Then you must call me Sam."

She shook her head no. "Oh, I don't think I could. Not here."

Relenting a bit, if only for the moment, Sam teased, "Not here in the garden? Then how about in the drawing room?"

"Now you're teasing me."

He shrugged. "Blame it on the welcome sunlight and the enchanting company."

"And now you're flattering me."

"Are you going to pass judgment on every action and word of mine?"

"I'm sorry. It's my nature to always be weighing things."

"I see. They could certainly use you in a counting house, then. But tell me, what in your life cultivated such talents?"

Now it was her turn to shrug. "Nothing in particular. More of a natural inquisitiveness, I suppose."

"Ah, I see. A Calhoun family trait, then?"

Her expression sharpened. "Yes. Is that where you've been leading me? To a discussion of family names?"

He nodded. "Yes. And to this most inviting bench here." It sat just off the gravel pathway. Tall elms surrounded it on three sides. "The shade from the trees will cool us." He held a hand out for her to precede him. "Care to join me, Miss . . . Calhoun?"

Again she turned those magnificent green eyes of hers up to him, this time to openly assess his expression, as if his features would reveal his intent. Sam met and held her gaze. Without warning, his body tightened, telling him plainly enough just how much he wanted her. He struggled to appear nonchalant, but he had to discreetly fist his hands to do it.

"Of course," she finally said, breaking the spell and showing him she wasn't afraid of him.

"After you, then. Careful, though, mind your skirt. The grass is still wet from yesterday's soaking and then the dew this morning. It could be slippery going for you."

Again she sent him an arch expression. Clearly, she didn't trust him any more than he did her. "Yes," she drawled, "I'll keep that in mind."

Sam watched her holding up her skirt as she made her way safely across the grass and over to the bench. He had to exhale and shake his head. Besides being a most pleasing picture of femininity, she also appeared so impossibly small and vulnerable. What was he to do with her?

Sam finally followed her, behaving much as if she were leading him to his own execution. He must remain on guard with her, he chastised himself, only to instantly defend himself with the notion that he always meant to be, but her effect on him was too great. In fact, even now, though not knowing the first thing about her, except that she purported to have the same name as his wife, he wanted nothing more than to grab her up and toss her to the ground right here and have his way with her. He wouldn't be male if he didn't.

But stopping him, aside from a sense of decency and mature restraint, was his suspicion that such a thing was her game. Only yesterday he'd thought that she'd found out about Sarah and meant to capitalize on her knowledge. Perhaps she meant to seduce and then blackmail him.

That set off the proper alarms in him. And put him in the correct frame of mind for dealing with the mystery that was this woman who'd simply shown up on his doorstep yesterday in a driving rain and with a preposterous story. Sam narrowed his eyes as he stared at her slender back. Then she turned around, facing him, a questioning look on her face. "Surely you don't mean for us to sit here, Your Grace? The bench seat is as dewed as the grass."

He looked at the bench in question. "Ah. So it is. Allow me."

As she stepped aside, Sam pulled out his handkerchief from a pocket and very self-consciously yet gallantly dried the wooden seat as best he could. When done, he signaled for her to be seated. Affecting a benign smile, he watched her smooth her skirt under her and sit down. She then looked up at him and held her skirt out of his way so he could be seated next to her. Tossing his wet and dripping handkerchief to the grass, Sam joined her.

Once they were both settled, their shoulders touching . . . or, rather, her shoulder pressed against his arm, given that her stature was so much shorter than his . . . she took up the conversation, and in a surprising vein. "I feel compelled to tell you yet again that Sarah Calhoun is my real name. I am who I say I am, Your Grace."

He'd expected her to avoid that subject, yet here she'd brought it up again. So either she was innocent of the things he suspected her of, or she was very good at her game. "I'm certain that you are, Miss Calhoun. I never meant to imply otherwise."

Of course, she saw right through his answer, but she smiled, saying nothing as she looked all around them at the cultivated land and drew in a deep breath. "It's very appealing out here. I like it very much. Is every May this pleasant in England?"

"It varies from yesterday's weather to today's. And it can change rather quickly, too. It doesn't do to be caught too far away from a safe haven."

She directed her gaze to him. "Is that a warning?"

Sam crossed his arms over his chest and looked away from her. "Yes. But only a friendly one."

"Then I must thank you, Your Grace. And yet you've led

us away from the manor and now even the garden. I'd say we're quite out in the open."

"No. I'd say we're quite on our own. Away from everything. And everyone."

"Are you trying to frighten me again?"

He looked over and down at her, so tiny and ramrod straight sitting there next to him on the bench. His heart unexpectedly turned over in a way that had him feeling protective of her, when there was no reason why he should be. "If I were trying to frighten you, would you say I'm succeeding?"

"No." She lowered her gaze to her lap and made a show of arranging the folds of her skirt. "Failing abysmally is more like it."

Caught off guard, Sam laughed out loud, garnering for himself her surprised attention. She didn't laugh with him, but he saw lights dancing in her eyes and her lips quirked at the corners. Feeling a bit more at ease with her, Sam nonchalantly put his arm around the back of the bench and her shoulders. She didn't protest. And again, he had expected that she would. With her under his touch, he became aware that she did not wear a corset. Such an unusual woman, to flaunt custom so. Yet he could respect that, being someone who also bucked tradition every chance that presented itself. "You are a delight, Miss Calhoun, and I really wish you weren't."

She pulled back as if to see him better. Her movement sent her intoxicatingly perfumed scent his way. She raised her delicately arched eyebrows quizzically. "Really? Why is that?"

"Because I don't know the first thing about you or what your intentions are here at Stonebridge."

She pursed her lips and pointed a finger at him. "That reminds me. I have yet to see the stone bridge. Where is it?"

Sam raised his eyebrows in surprise. "You want to see a stone bridge?"

"Not *a* stone bridge. *The* stone bridge, the one I assume gave rise to the estate's name. Surely there is one?"

"Yes, there is." He frowned, wondering what this need

was of hers to see a simple stone bridge. "But you want to see it *now*?"

"Well, no, not if it's a bother." Then, in a mercurial change of mood or tactics, she stood abruptly, giving him no chance to reply before she began smoothing her skirt. "I apologize for taking up so much of your time, Your Grace. I've only just realized that's what I'm doing. And I'm certain you must be a busy man with much more important things to do than—"

"Not so busy as you'd think." He stood also, remaining purposely close to her so he would tower over her. "In fact, my first order of business, since your arrival, Miss Calhoun, has become to discover exactly who you are and what it is you're doing here. All else is secondary."

Instantly a picture of injured innocence—or so it seemed to Sam—she held her eyes artlessly wide as she gestured her apparent confusion. "But there is no mystery, Your Grace," she swore. "I told you yesterday, and truthfully, that your mother wrote to me in America—"

"Where in America?" He'd surprised her with his question. Her expression lost some of its innocence as her gaze darted here and there. Clearly, she was fishing around with the truth. "Just answer the question, Miss Calhoun. It's bound to come out as soon as my mother returns home, which could be as soon as today or tomorrow."

She firmed her lips. "I have no reason to keep anything from you. And, as your mother will confirm, Chicago is the answer to your question."

A thrill of fright and guilt shot through Sam, making him wish he'd never asked her. "Chicago. I see."

She cocked her head at a questioning angle. "What do you see?"

"That you're no innocent, Miss Calhoun. You show up here with the same name as my wife and from the same city as she is. No mere coincidence, that."

The very enigmatic Miss Calhoun frowned. "I agree. But where exactly *is* your wife, Your Grace? Is she with your mother? Will I meet her today or tomorrow when they return home? Or is that possible?"

Extreme anger seized Sam in its grip, stiffening his stance. "I warn you to leave off right there. How dare you question me like this?"

She raised her chin, and her green eyes sparked with a strong emotion. "Because you're the duke, you mean?"

"I do not. I mean because you're rude. This has nothing to do with rank or title, but simple courtesy and respect for me and my privacy."

She cocked her head as if in disbelief. "Oh, really? That same courtesy and respect that had you sneaking into my bed early this morning, uninvited—and unwanted, I might add—*Your Grace*?"

Sam couldn't even remember grabbing for her, but in the next instant, his heart pounding painfully, he had seized his guest by her arms and pulled her hard against him. "Tell me who the hell you are—and I mean right now." He saw the fear in her eyes and heard how his voice shook with rage. But he couldn't seem to stop himself. By God, he'd done nothing more to his wife than he'd been forced to do. And he was through paying for it. "Talk to me. Tell me how you found this place, how you know about my wife."

"I know *nothing* of your wife." He'd all but shaken the words out of her, and her voice was a cry of pain.

But Sam was beyond being moved by it. "You *lie*. What do you hope to gain by coming here to prey on my troubles? Is it money you want?"

She shook her head vehemently, causing her hair to swing viciously about her shoulders. Finally it came out of its combs and fell into her face, which was red with her exertions as she tried to wriggle out of his grasp. "No. Let me go. I want no money. I came here because I was asked to do so. I swear it. Please. You're hurting me."

And that was when Sam came to his senses. As shocked as if he'd just come upon the scene and saw himself shaking a helpless woman, he released her. "Dear God, I'm sorry, Miss Calhoun. I have no idea what came over me."

But Miss Calhoun, no doubt scared for her life, was having none of his apologies. Stumbling backward, feeling for the bench behind her, yet not taking her eyes off him, she held her mouth in a grimace of fear as she did her level best to sidle around the park bench to get away from him. She shoved her hair back and pointed a shaking finger at him. "You stay away from me, you bastard, or I'll claw your eyes out."

Sam took a conciliatory step toward her. "And I wouldn't blame you a bit if you did claw my eyes out or worse, Miss Calhoun. I am so very sorry. Please believe me."

"Get back," she growled, her hand held palm out to him. "I warn you—I will defend myself if I must."

Although he had serious doubts that she could do any damage to him, Sam knew this wasn't the time to remind her of his superior strength or size. She was overwrought—with damned good reason—and he, no matter how much he might want to make amends right now, would be best served to just let her go. So, backing up and stepping out of her way, effectively clearing a path for her to get safely back to the house, Sam told her, "I won't stop you. You're free to go."

Much like some cornered little animal, she warily watched him as she edged along the back of the bench, holding on to it as if it would afford her some protection from him. Not once did she look away from him. For Sam this was a waking nightmare. He saw Sarah, his wife, all over again in this woman's pose and in her fearful expression. Sam then realized that Miss Calhoun had no more of the bench to put between her and him, so he retreated farther. "I said I wouldn't stop you, and I won't. And again, I'm so very sorry. I can't *tell* you how sorry I am."

But she was already tearing off. Sam held a hand out to her, but she never saw it. Holding her skirt up, she ran, her long red hair whipping wildly to and fro in her desperate flight away from him.

*"Damn!"* Sick with disgust for his own behavior, Sam could only helplessly watch her go. He couldn't look away from her and didn't, not until she was lost to him when she made a mad dashing turn at the far outside corner of the maze and passed out of his line of sight.

"Rotten bastard," Sam muttered to himself. With the tightness of regret in his chest, he continued to curse himself as he stepped over to the bench and sat down heavily upon it. Defeat had him leaning forward over his legs to prop his elbows atop his knees. Then he held his face in his hands and sat there a very long time, slowly shaking his head from side to side.

Badly shaken, and wanting only to be away from the volatile duke, Yancey had entered the round stone tower through a blessedly unlocked wooden door at its base. Propelled by demons she couldn't name, she had run up the seeming hundreds of spiraling, twisting steps that led to the top. Stumbling, half-blinded by her hair that insisted on matting long, loose strands of it to her perspiring face, she'd lost her footing more than once and tripped over her skirt, banging her shins or skinning her palms. But on and on she'd run as if on some instinctive level she'd known she'd be safe if only she could achieve the top of the tower.

And finally she was here. Sweating from her exertion and weak-kneed, she braced her hands against the cool dank walls of the tower itself. Bent forward, gasping for air, she kept her gaze on the closed door that greeted her at the very top of the ever-narrowing steps. Yancey reached out and pushed on the door . . . it swung easily inward. Surprised yet grateful for that, she forced her trembling legs to lift her feet just one more time so she could take the last stair and step over the threshold.

When she did, she found herself in a small room, one that was crudely furnished. Beyond that she noticed nothing as she sagged to the floor with the blessedly cool wall at her back. Bending her knees, she drew her legs up until she could anchor her shoes' heels against the worn stone floor under her. She rested her arms atop her knees. Closing her eyes, she leaned her head back, concentrating only on getting air into her lungs and nothing more.

As her breathing slowly began to return to a normal rate, she opened her eyes, wiped at her cheeks, and was surprised to find them wet with tears. She stared at her hands. She'd been crying? Certainly, she was justified, but it was humiliating to think the duke had reduced her to tears and made her run away just by raising his voice and shaking her a bit. In her many cases for Mr. Pinkerton, she'd been dealt much more than that. And yes, sometimes running away had been the only smart thing to do. In her mind's eye she again saw herself running out of the whorehouse in Chicago with Clara shooting at her.

So it wasn't that which had her so upset. Could it be her lingering tiredness from the long journey here? After all, she didn't yet have her detective's feet under her, to put it one way. Or could it be the strangeness of the place, of Somerset and its inhabitants? Or the constant state of vigilance forced upon her by not being able to trust anyone here? Certainly, any or all of those would unhinge anyone. Or could it be the duke himself?

Yancey didn't have to think overly long about that. It was true, and how she hated knowing that it was. Yes, he'd shocked and frightened her just now. And her first instinct had been to put a safe distance between him and her. He needed time to calm down, and she needed time to rethink how they'd come to such an impasse so quickly. But of more concern to her was her own heart. What if what was plaguing her now was something she simply did not want to acknowledge but must if she expected to keep herself safe?

*All right, then, go on,* she urged herself. *Admit it.* What if the duke—a man who appealed to her on so many levels, a man who had already drawn more sensual and even angry passionate responses from her in less than a day's acquaintanceship than any other man ever had—turned out to be the mastermind whom she was seeking? Could she bear it?

She shook her head no. Well, like it or not, if he was guilty, she told herself, then she'd just neatly made of herself a cornered mouse in this tower. All the enraged duke would have to do now was climb the steps and toss her out the narrow window above her. *Lovely.* Not trusting herself to be able to stand, and with no strength left to defend herself, even should a knife-wielding villain burst in, Yancey sat where she was and belatedly surveyed her surroundings, looking for anything she could use to defend herself, providing she had the strength left to pick it up.

Across from her, a narrow hewn-wood bed—its head abutting the stones of the thick wall across the way and its length jutting out into the room—boasted a sagging and torn mattress through which straw poked out and trailed to the floor. The work of rats, she told herself, though blessedly none appeared to be around at the moment. The only other furniture proved to be a roughly cut chair that was pulled up to a small table that listed to one side. To Yancey, the furnishings had the appearance of dollhouse furniture made by a giant—or for a giant.

Instantly to mind came the hugely broad Scotty, the butler. The man spoke to her as if she were a dog. Sit. Stay. Yancey shook her head. No. This wasn't his room. He'd never fit through the doorway, much less atop that bed. Besides, the room did not have the air about it of daily use. The narrow window wasn't covered to keep out the weather. And the bed wasn't mended, nor did it have any linens. Nor was there any clothing or other personal items to be seen. Could it be, then, that it was simply someone's retreat, just as it was now hers?

She didn't know. Nor did she care, she told herself. All that did matter to her at the moment was that she was the one up here now at the top of the round tower. She was the one alone—and still ashamed for having allowed a mere man to scare her so. Never mind that he was more than twice her size. And never mind that she slept in his house and ate his food and was under his control. Never mind any of that. Because, as he'd so innocently or otherwise reminded her, she was the Fox. And a seasoned Pinkerton operative. As well as a mature woman, to boot.

Then why was she sitting here on the floor of a stone-tower room and using a bit of her petticoat to wipe her eyes? Because sometimes even the strongest of women fall. Because even the most mature and independent are susceptible to the occasional emotional undoing. But she'd never thought it would happen to her. Not until the Duke of Somerset came into her life. Yancey feared she'd met her match in this man. Feared it, yet refused to accept it.

"Oh, leave me be," she tiredly told her scolding conscience. "Just please leave me be."

As if there were an actual person in the room with her from whom she wished to hide, Yancey slumped in on herself, turning away from the door and resting her cheek against the wall's blessed coolness. A sudden sense of utter aloneness in the world settled over her like an onerous weight. This was sorrow . . . and suddenly she was crying again. She cried for her mother. She cried for what her father had done and what she, Yancey, had then done to him. She feared she'd never be free of those awful images. And yes—this was so difficult for her to admit—she had run from her yearning for the duke, a wanting that persisted despite everything she had at stake here.

Yancey covered her hot cheeks with her hands. "Dear God, I am so undone. And I am so confused. Why? *Why* does *this* place and *this* man unsettle me so?"

"Don't fear, child," a warm and sympathetic voice suddenly said behind her. "You don't know it yet, but you belong here."

# Chapter Eight

Sam experienced the very devil of a time setting his world to rights following Miss Calhoun's fleeing from his presence out in the garden. Then, and making matters worse, by the time he'd recovered enough to retrieve his handkerchief and her hair combs and make his way to the manor with the intent of apologizing yet again to his distraught guest, every servant seemed to know of his despicable behavior toward her. How they transmitted this information among themselves with a speed to be envied by the fleetest of Thoroughbreds, Sam believed he would never know for certain. But somehow they did—most logically, he believed, from gardener to page to maid and so on throughout the house—but however it was accomplished, the lord of the manor was now paying in spades for his outburst.

Inside the manor house, as he passed through it and encountered various members of his household staff, their sepulchral quietness vied for the upper hand with their judgmental solemnity. Under less trying circumstances, Sam would not have stood for it. But this time, and in this instance, having deemed it more than called for, he stoically ran the gauntlet of his servants' disapproval. Time and again, he was told that the lady was not in the manor proper. She had not passed this way.

Sam wasn't satisfied with that. Perhaps she'd instructed the servants not to tell him where she was. In that case, if she had, he would not ask them to break their word to her. Yes, it rankled a bit to think his servants would feel more loyalty to her than they did to him. But given his behavior with the lady, he couldn't fault them, he supposed. And that being so, he did the only thing he could. He made his own search of the house, top to bottom. It proved fruitless. But Sam couldn't say he was totally unhappy with his results. At least his staff had told him the truth—the lady was not in residence.

Then where the devil was she? He was forced to conclude that Miss Calhoun was, in actuality, nowhere. Which was a ridiculous notion because everyone must be somewhere. It was a law of nature or of some such related science, wasn't it? Frowning, and worried that he'd driven her to do something foolish like leave on foot, Sam sought out the only person he had yet to question. Scotty. He found the hulking giant in the butler's pantry.

Seated on an impossibly small stool next to a tiny table which he dwarfed, the big man was engaged in, lo and behold, cleaning a gun. Surprise laced with a jet of apprehension had Sam raising his eyebrows. "Dear God, Scotty," was his greeting to the enigmatic butler. "Has it come to this, man? You need a gun?"

Scotty's response was to glance up at his employer from under his heavy brow ridge and then silently resume his quiet task. "No. Your gun."

Well, that explained nothing. Sam exhaled. "I see."

Following that, Sam wondered how exactly to proceed from this point with his butler of very few words and, worse, very unpredictable responses. If he didn't frame a question with precise and simple wording, Sam reminded himself, then he would get the answer he deserved. Watching his butler, who'd been an orphaned babe taken in all these many years ago by Her Grace Nana with no forthcoming explanation to anyone as to where she'd got him or under what circumstances, Sam suspected that the man understood more and felt more than he let on. Sam also believed that Scotty didn't lack so much in intelligence as he did in language, for whatever reason.

Finally Sam believed he had it—the most politic framing of his simple question. "Scotty, have you seen Miss, er, the duchess?"

Still singularly occupied with his task, the big man didn't look up, but he did answer. "Yes."

Excitement raced through Sam. If one didn't mind pulling hen's teeth, then one could get results with his butler. "*When* did you see her, Scotty?"

"Yesterday."

Sam's breath left him in a disappointed huff. "Yesterday. Not today, then? Not at all?"

Scotty kept polishing the gun's barrel. "No."

Impatience and irritation had Sam quirking his lips. "Are you certain?"

Now the butler raised his head, looking Sam in the eye. "Yes."

"Then no one has seen her. Yet she can't have disappeared into thin air."

"No." The butler put the gun and the cloth down on the table and stood up . . . always an impressive sight. "Her Grace Nana knows." He then pointed a thick finger in a vague direction, somewhat northwest of where they stood now. "The tower."

Sam slumped with relieved revelation. "Of course. The tower. She went to the tower." She was safe. Sam stepped forward and clapped Scotty on a huge and solid arm. The butler's stance and expression did not change. But that didn't stop Sam from being grateful. "Thank you. The tower. I would never have thought of looking there."

Then he sobered, just then realizing the import of what Scotty had said. "Did you say that Nana is with the, uh, duchess in the tower?"

"Yes."

"Alone?"

"Yes."

"Well, then, where the devil is Mrs. Convers? How did Nana get away from her nurse?"

"She hides."

"And Mrs. Convers?"

"She looks."

"Of course. But doesn't find her."

"No."

This was an insane conversation and well Sam knew it. "Do we know where Mrs. Convers is, then? What has Nana done with her?"

"Carriage house."

Sam rolled his eyes. "Not again. Locked in, I suppose?"

"Yes."

Sam eyed his butler and wondered how to proceed. There were rules regarding these things, rules known only to Nana, who wasn't to be trifled with. Sam was quite convinced that she could turn them all into toads if she so chose. "I see. May I at least assume that we will be letting her out soon . . . Mrs. Convers, I mean?"

"Yes."

Well, that was a relief. Mrs. Convers was the third nurse this year, and here it was only May. Sam shook his head as he took another tack and did his wondering out loud. "So Nana is up in the tower. There must be a hundred or more steps. How in the world does the old dear get up all of them?"

"One at a time," Scotty supplied seriously.

Sam's question had of course been rhetorical, but that point would be lost on the hulking butler. Still, a bemused chuckle escaped Sam. "Yes. I suppose then that I will have to take a page from her book and do the same thing."

"What book?"

*Dear God.* Sam momentarily closed his eyes and rubbed at his forehead. "I mean I will have to climb the tower steps in the same manner. One at a time."

"I'll come, too."

Sam shook his head in the negative. "No, there's no need."

"I'll come, too."

Sam eyed the big determined man, looking him up and down. "Of course you will. Never any question about that."

* * *

Her tears dried, and feeling somewhat calmer now, Yancey perched sideways atop the torn straw bedding in the tower's room. Her Grace Nana mimicked her pose and sat at the bed's other end, facing her. The perfectly white cats, Mary, Alice, and Jane, had accompanied her up here and had arranged themselves around the room. One sat in the window's wide sill. Another perched on the chair. And the third sat atop the table. Like silent sentinels, they watched the two women.

Bemused as much as befuddled by their appearance here, Yancey allowed the tiny older woman to hold her hand and stroke her palm. A harmless activity, yet it seemed very much to please the ancient lady, who looked up at her now and said, "You're a magical person, my dear. But you don't know it."

This white-haired peer of the realm kept saying such mysterious things as that, just as she'd done a bit ago when she'd made her presence known to Yancey. But taken aback nonetheless—not knowing if she was in the presence of the insane or the insightful, but suspecting both—Yancey tried to extricate her hand. The ancient woman's grip proved to be surprisingly strong and unyielding. More curious than alarmed, Yancey relaxed, refusing to struggle with her.

Eyeing their joined hands, Yancey said, "I wish you wouldn't say things like that, about me being magical and belonging here. Because I really don't know what you mean by them."

"I know you don't. But you will come to know."

Yancey raised her head until she met Her Grace Nana's gaze. A beatific smile lit the sweet little woman's wrinkled face. "In time, Sarah Margaret, you will know."

Yancey froze. That name. That hated name. It was all she heard. She knew the elderly woman believed she was talking to the duke's wife and had no idea who she really was, but that didn't forestall her emotions. Defiance born of years of hurt and betrayal reared its jutting head in Yancey's heart.

"I don't wish to be called by that name. It is detestable to me."

"I know—"

"No. You don't know."

She'd spoken more sharply than she'd intended but Her Grace Nana appeared unperturbed. "Oh, but I do. You won't always hate it. It won't always be so for you."

Yancey tried now in earnest to pull her hand out of the older woman's grip. This time, Her Grace Nana allowed it. With her hand free, Yancey smoothed her hair behind her ears, nothing more than a nervous gesture. "How can you know? How? And yes it will always be hateful to me. Always."

Yancey's benign tormentor smiled her sympathy and patted Yancey's arm. "Poor wounded lamb. Nothing lasts for always, my dear. Nothing. And I am right. You will see, and you will come to know."

As if that were the most innocuous of comments needing no further elucidation, Her Grace Nana pulled herself to her feet, shuffled over to the table, and stroked the purring cats, talking in silly love tones to them.

Yancey could only stare at the woman's age-hunched back and remind herself that Her Grace Nana's talk was so much prattle. And if she seemed to know things that she really couldn't know, then it was probably because she was referring to some knowledge she had of the real duchess, someone Yancey knew nothing about. So of course, Yancey reminded herself, it was only natural that she should feel as if she were in the dark. But frighteningly, she reflected, with her gaze still trained on Her Grace Nana's shawl-covered back, the lines between herself and the other Sarah Margaret were beginning to blur, even in her own mind.

*But why wouldn't they?* she argued right back. She'd taken on the other woman's identity and life, hadn't she? Yes. Her only hope now was that she wouldn't also suffer the woman's fate—and even that was assuming that the murdered Sarah Margaret Calhoun back in Chicago was in fact the actual duchess these people believed Yancey to be.

Unbidden, the duke's handsome yet menacing face

popped into Yancey's mind, immediately racing her pulse with awareness of him as a man as well as fear of him as an adversary. She frowned, putting a hand to her temple. She mustn't allow her woman's heart to respond to him. She must instead think rationally about this man. He knew she wasn't his wife. Yet he hadn't told anyone differently. And without his corroboration, her protestations otherwise to the servants this morning had fallen on deaf ears.

Yancey's question remained: why wouldn't he tell them she spoke the truth when she said she was not the duchess—a woman they'd obviously never met? The unsettling answer was that it served some purpose of his to allow her charade to continue. Could that purpose be to get away with murder? After all, how could anyone say his wife was dead if she was right here in attendance? A possible truth, then, was that Yancey's own masquerade had played innocently, yet perfectly, right into the duke's scheming hands.

A very daunting notion. She still did not want to believe him capable of murder. She still wanted to think him innocent. Because she was so attracted to him? *Yes.* A self-loathing filled Yancey. She'd always prided herself that being female was her greatest asset in her profession. And now here it was in danger of being her greatest weakness. Always before, she'd never had a problem keeping her heart out of her work. But here and with this man, she was finding it increasingly difficult to do so, even after only one day. How difficult would it be next week, then? Or the week after that?

Exhaling, Yancey rubbed a hand over her face. This was awful. The whole thing. A convoluted mess. Then an ironic smile claimed her lips. Of course if it weren't, she'd have no need to be here. And if there'd been an easy or even a discernible answer to the mystery of the duchess, she would have had no need to go to such lengths—physically and geographically—to solve this case of simple mistaken identity that had led her into this intrigue.

Frustration ate at her. If only she could come right out and ask the duke what the truth was. She'd certainly intended to do exactly that, but that had been before she'd met him.

And now that she had, now that she'd felt his irresistible masculine tug on her female heart and body, she wasn't so sure she really wanted to know the truth. And that alone could get her killed.

Yancey suddenly felt physically ill. She clutched at her stomach, concentrating on breathing and forcing her incriminating thoughts back to where they belonged, back to some dark place at the back of her mind where they could no longer accuse her or cloud her judgment. And thus she sat quietly, repeating to herself that she had a job to do. She'd come all this way to do it, and do it she would. She would allow nothing and no one to interfere with that, least of all the duke or even her present companion.

Yancey sat there until she believed her own conclusions, until her mood lifted and she felt more her practical-minded self. Shifting her weight atop the clean straw mattress, she told herself that it now seemed silly that she had allowed this ridiculous conversation with this ancient little woman to upset her. Yancey concentrated now on Her Grace Nana. What she finally saw was the truth—a dear but dotty woman whose white hair wisped about her head like a halo, whose skirts trailed the ground, who played hide-and-seek, and who talked to cats.

And so it was with a chuckle that Yancey called the woman's attention away from the cats and back to herself. "All right, then, Your Grace Nana, *how* will I know? Tell me that much."

Coming back over to the bed and again perching a hip atop it, much as if she sat sidesaddle on a horse, Her Grace Nana smiled a knowing smile as she took Yancey's hands in hers. Yancey's heart softened at the feel of the warm small-boned, age-gnarled little hands that held hers. The older woman's disconcertingly lucid light blue eyes met Yancey's. "I cannot tell you . . . except to say that you will know. You will be left with nothing more than knowledge. And nothing less."

Yancey frowned. *Now, what the devil does that mean?* Her sympathetic gaze roved over the other woman's impossibly sweet face. She was to be pitied and indulged, but not believed. As if to prove all this to herself, Yancey took another, more practical, tack in her questioning. "I see. Now, dear, tell me how you knew I was up here, or if you even did, I suppose I should add. I mean, you could have been coming up here anyway and simply found me here."

"No. I came up here to see about you. Alice told me." She released Yancey's hands and pointed to the white cat still seated regally on the foot-wide stone windowsill. Unbelievably, the sleek cat ducked its head in seeming acknowledgment. "She saw you come running in here. From behind the garden. Over by the benches under the elms. With Sam. And then she came and got me at the carriage house."

Disbelief coursed through Yancey. She hadn't seen any of the cats there. Or Nana. Yet that was exactly where she had been with the duke. How could Nana know that? Surely one of the gardeners had told her. But something else nagged at her. "Did you say the carriage house? What were you doing in the carriage house? Did the dowager perhaps arrive?"

That would be awful. Yancey just didn't feel up to another confrontation today.

"No, no. I was locking Mrs. Convers inside."

She said that as if it explained everything. Yancey stared at the wizened old woman. "I'm sorry, but who exactly is Mrs. Convers?"

Her Grace Nana waved a hand in dismissal. "Sam calls her my nurse and companion. I call her my warden." She leaned in conspiratorially toward Yancey, all but whispering now. "Mrs. Edgars is next, you know."

Yancey frowned, seeing in her mind the tall, angular, unsmiling, unwelcoming woman who had shown her to her suite of rooms yesterday. "Do you mean the housekeeper?"

"Do you mean the housekeeper?"

Startled to have her words repeated, Yancey sat back, roving her gaze in an assessing manner over the much older woman's face. To Yancey's dismay, Her Grace Nana's eyes seemed suddenly cloudy, not so focused, and her expression slack. Yancey slumped. The poor old dear was gone, at least in mind and spirit, if not body. Now what had caused that?

"A little bird told me I might find you two up here."

The unexpected sound of the masculine voice from behind her jerked Yancey around and had her leaping off the bed in one movement. Her back to the wall, she faced the duke, her heart pounding, her hands fisted.

"Samuel, dear," Her Grace Nana greeted him, her voice full of affection. "I seem to have misplaced my nurse."

Yancey looked from the man to his nana and back to him when he replied, his voice patient and warm. "I've heard. But I think we've found her in the carriage house."

"Ah," the old lady remarked, sounding as if a great mystery had just been solved. "So that's where she's got to."

"Amazing, isn't it?" The duke had directed his comment to Yancey.

But she was in no mood for idle chatter. "What are you doing up here?"

Standing just across the threshold, with his arms crossed over his chest, he lolled with a shoulder leaned against a wall comprised of cold, massive stone blocks. "I used to come up here all the time when I was a boy. Sometimes with my brother on a rainy day. We'd be here for hours fighting many imaginary battles and countless invading armies. But now, when I want to be alone, when I want to see something eternal, something bigger than myself—I mean the mountains—I come up here. But I believe, in this instance, what *you're* doing up here should be my question to you."

He hadn't advanced on her, but she still felt a need to step back. As it was, she had to tip her tongue out to moisten suddenly dry lips. She roved her gaze over him. Was he actually bigger? Taller? Even more muscular and imposing than he'd been out of doors? Or was it the room's confining dimensions that made him seem so? That had to be it. Just as she'd done yesterday when he'd surprised her in her bedroom, Yancey wondered how long he had been standing there and how much he had heard. In her mind she damned the well-oiled door to this room for not squeaking a warning to her. She also damned the cats as well for having done nothing to give away their master's presence.

"Any one of the cats here got your tongue?" He idly pointed to the three felines in attendance.

He always asked her that. Perhaps if she weren't so tongue-tied around him . . . Yancey raised her chin. "Very amusing, Your Grace."

"Ah, then they don't. Excellent." Holding her attention with his piercing slate-gray eyes, he held a hand out, as if he wanted her to take it.

Never. Yancey took another step back, only to butt into the table behind her, which elicited a startling yowl out of the offended cat sitting there. Yancey whipped around, her hands held to her chest. The white cat crouched down and hissed at her. Yancey jerked back.

"Jane, stop that. You're being a bad girl."

This reproof had Yancey pivoting to Her Grace Nana, who'd just chastised the cat. The older woman caught Yancey's eye. "It's not you, dear. It's Scotty. She doesn't like him."

"But Scotty's not . . ." Yancey thought her voice sounded weak and so far away . . . as if she were at the other end of a tunnel. All of a sudden these people seemed oddly strange to her, as if they were malevolent and were closing in on her. She didn't know whom to trust or what was real or imagined. She put a hand to her temple, wondering what was wrong with her, why the room was slowly spinning. Did no one else feel it?

She put a hand out, seeking a solid presence to cling to, but finding none. "Scotty's not up here," she got out, hearing the slur in her words.

"But you're mistaken, Miss Calhoun. Scotty is right here."

This came from the duke. As if made of lead, as if unable suddenly to control the movement of her head, Yancey did her utmost to lift her gaze until she could see the duke. And there was Scotty standing beside him.

"No," Yancey whispered. He hadn't been there but a moment ago. She could not make heads or tails of this. Had the butler materialized out of thin air? In a puff of smoke? Had they all gone mad—or had she?

"Help me," she begged, her knees feeling weak, a hand outstretched to the duke.

With an oath and a frowning look of sudden concern, he started toward her. But that was when the floor rose up to meet her . . . and the world went black.

"Shhh. She's coming around. Be quiet now. Don't scare her." Sam punctuated his admonitions with a fierce frown all around the canopied bed, in the center of which lay Miss Calhoun, who was returning to consciousness following her swoon in the tower.

Standing in the circle around her bed were Scotty the silent butler, Robin the tearful lady's maid, Mrs. Edgars the glaring housekeeper, Mrs. Convers the recently rescued and irate nurse, Nana the oblivious, her three cats—Mary, Alice, and Jane—and Mr. Marples the dog. The cats were on the bed. The short-legged dog yapped frantically, wanting also to be atop the bed. One of the cats hissed at him. Stiff-legged with outrage, the terrier growled right back.

"Quiet that dog, or I'll clear this room," Sam all but growled to Miss Calhoun's lady's maid.

Wide-eyed with fright, yet dropping a curtsy, the girl wordlessly plucked the frantic wire-haired terrier off the carpet and held his squirmy body in her arms. Petting it, she shushed it and stared at Sam.

He nodded his thanks to her, which seemed to frighten her more, and then turned to the florid-faced Mrs. Convers, his nana's nurse. "Dampen a cold cloth for her head." Scotty's turn was next. "Open those windows. The breeze will do her good."

Nana nodded, repeating, "The breeze *will* do her good."

As Scotty lumbered past, bent on doing Sam's bidding, the stout nurse curtsied to Sam, said, "Yes, Your Grace," and hurried over to the washbasin and dry sink tucked away in a corner of the room. In a moment she was back with the dripping cloth and made as if to place it on Miss Calhoun's forehead. Before she could, Mrs. Edgars plucked it from her, saying, "Give me that. You're dripping it everywhere. I will tend the duchess."

But Sam surprised his housekeeper—and himself—by taking the rag from her. "In fact, I believe I will tend her."

His housekeeper looked as if she could slap him. "I must protest, Your Grace. I hardly think you—"

"You hardly think at all if you think to gainsay me, Mrs. Edgars." Sam leaned in toward her, daring her to say another word. Wisely, she did not, instead firming her severe lips into a straight line. Satisfied, Sam righted himself and said, "Leave us. All of you."

En masse, they all turned and, following Scotty, filed out. Mrs. Convers gripped Nana's arm, so the cats fell in, single file, behind them. Still holding the dog, the lady's maid was next. Mrs. Edgars was at the rear and herding them all as if she were a shepherd and they her flock. Once she stepped over the threshold into the suite's sitting room, she arrowed an angry look Sam's way. But she did close the door behind her. Sam didn't know what to think about her impertinence. Perhaps he'd had too lax a hand with his household staff of late. Perhaps he needed to pay more attention.

But alone at last with Miss Calhoun, Sam dismissed his housekeeper from his mind and placed the washcloth on his supposed wife's forehead. But Miss Calhoun, in a semiconscious state, frowned and swiped at it, dislodging it. Sam spoke low and soothingly to her and put it back in place. Slowly she writhed, moving her arms and legs and tossing her head from side to side. The cloth again dislodged and a tiny moan escaped her. Sam plucked the wet rag up and tossed it to the nightstand. Obviously she wasn't going to hold still for its cooling benefits.

He perched a hip on the side of the bed and watched her. He knew that should she awaken and find him thus, his positioning would appear at best unseemly to her. But for the life of him, he couldn't step away from her. Nor could he help but notice at such close quarters how disconcertingly young she appeared with such pink cheeks and the childlike pout of her full lips, her slender neck, and unblemished skin. She was beautiful. Delicate. Like a flower. Or perhaps a nymph from the sea. More affected than he cared to admit, Sam had all he could do not to caress her cheek or stroke her hair.

He focused on her long red hair, trying to name for himself its color. Auburn? Burnished gold? Copper? None of them, yet all of them, seemed to fit. It depended on whether or not she was in the sun. And even now the thick tresses had fallen like silken waves about her.

Just then she moaned again and writhed with an unintentional sensuality that nevertheless stunted Sam's breathing. Instant carnal images burst into his mind's eye, as much appalling him as exciting him. The things he saw the two of them doing together hardly seemed appropriate under these circumstances with her in an impaired state. But there they were, even despite her being fully dressed and only semiconscious, for God's sake. Not for the first time in his life was Sam chagrined by the willful turns his masculine brain would take when shown a beautiful woman. Very unsettling, much as if a rutting beast lived within him.

He'd grown used to that aspect of his nature, but did prefer instead the idea of the civilized gentleman able to control his baser instincts. Yet . . . here the images were, and Sam's moment of shame was bowled over by his desire for her. Causing him increasing physical agitation, his mind insisted on showing him pictures that boiled his blood, images that depicted her as God made her, naked, beautiful, proud, writhing atop a bed—his bed—and moaning, under him, and calling out his name—

She opened her eyes, revealing them to be a deep forest-green. Sam felt his heart rate pick up. Still, he managed what he hoped was a neutral enough smile.

She didn't return it but blinked rapidly, as if still in a daze. Then, suddenly, her gaze landed on him and held. She frowned, much as if she couldn't quite place him. Sam said nothing, giving her a few moments more to clear her mind. He knew the moment conscious awareness came to her because her eyes opened wide and she froze, croaking out a single, accusatory word. "You."

# Chapter Nine

"Yes. Me." The duke's gray eyes, the rich color of slate, roved lingeringly over her as she lay there on the bed. Yancey had all she could do not to squirm under such scrutiny. "Do you remember what happened, Miss Calhoun?"

Her first response was to nod and murmur, "Yes. I think so." Certainly, consciousness had come back to her in a rush. So had memory. And she believed she had the morning's events pieced together. They weren't flattering to either one of them, so Yancey shied away from bringing them up. However, she did call herself relieved to realize that though they were alone in her bedroom, they were both fully dressed. That left only one thing to nag her now. "How did I get here?"

"I carried you, of course."

A shock of awareness, tempered with embarrassment, had Yancey blurting, "Oh, I hope I wasn't too heavy."

He chuckled at her expense. "Spoken like a true female. Allow me to reassure you that your weight is trifling, Miss Calhoun. I wasn't even winded when I laid you down here."

Upset with herself for being so typically female, something she liked to think she wasn't, Yancey lowered her gaze. "Well, still, I'm glad to hear that."

Only belatedly did she realize that in order not to look

into his eyes, she'd settled on the man's powerful biceps and his broad chest. All she could think was he'd held her close and tight against his body for the entire distance from the tower to this room. Try as she might, she had no memory of the experience, but of course, she concluded, she wouldn't. She'd been unconscious. Her next intruding thought told her that this was twice in as many days that she'd been held in his arms without her consent and without being conscious of it.

Before she could decide how she felt about that, the duke shifted his weight off the bed and caught her attention, pulling her back to the moment.

He stood and leaned over her, fisting his hands atop the bedding and to either side of her. Startled at this bit of familiarity on his part, and though still a bit fuzzy-thinking and so very thirsty, Yancey instinctively tensed. She felt small, an insignificant presence, a person of no defenses, and she didn't like it. Her heart pounded. What could he mean to do?

As if answering her unasked question, the duke said, "I would ask you to forgive me, but I find I'm not the least bit sorry for what I'm about to do." With that, he lowered his head to hers and kissed her possessively on her lips.

The shock of initial contact rocked through her, intense and riveting, awakening her senses. His lips against hers were warm, full, firm . . . and questing. His clean scent, so very male and musky, his body still retaining the elemental scents of the outdoors, heated her blood with desire. Yet, shocked by the suddenness of his ardor and his actions, Yancey felt pressed into the bed and gripped fistfuls of the bedding under her. Almost immediately, though, and before the kiss could deepen, the duke pulled away from her.

Yancey opened her eyes, distressed to realize that she had at some point closed them. Didn't that lend at least the appearance of her acquiescence to what he'd just done? Well, he mustn't think such a thing, and she must tell him so. But she didn't know what to say. Her next—and rebellious—thought was, *Why should I have to say anything?* She wasn't the one at fault. She hadn't taken liberties. He had. And she should look to him for an explanation of his actions.

But as he'd so plainly stated but a moment ago, he wasn't about to ask for forgiveness. And she knew he wasn't in the habit of explaining himself. As it was, he stood there beside the bed, watching her. With her mouth slightly open and her lips still wet from his kiss, Yancey wanted to be angry with him. But the unsettling truth was she wasn't. Instead, staring up at him, she could only pronounce herself glad to be already in a prone position. Surely, if she'd been on her feet, her knees would have given way and she would have fallen to the carpet, so powerful was the effect of his lips against hers.

Gone, certainly, were any lingering dregs of her faint. But adding to the confusing mishmash of emotions and responses he seemed to engender in her was the realization that she had liked his kiss. She welcomed his advances. How distressing, given her circumstances in being here. If only he would say something, Yancey silently begged him, anything to end this agony of staring and knowing.

Instantly, he complied. "As you appear to be unharmed by your swoon, I will leave you now."

Stung, humiliated, and dismissed, apparently, Yancey pushed up against the bedding and supported her weight with her elbows. "What? You'll leave me now? That's it? That's all you have to say for what just happened?"

He cocked his head at a considering angle. Then his expression cleared. "Oh, of course. I owe you an apology, don't I?"

Feeling vindicated and thinking that this was more like it, Yancey nodded. "Yes. You do."

"Very well." He crossed his arms over his muscled chest, an expanse only barely covered by his open-throated white shirt. "I apologize again for my behavior out in the garden."

Yancey shook her head as if to clear it of cobwebs. She stared wondering at him, thinking, *Arrogant male.* "The garden? Hang the garden, man. What about what just happened here?"

He shrugged his shoulders. "But I told you I wasn't sorry for what I meant to do. Tell me . . . are you?"

*Yes* was on the tip of her tongue, but the blasted word

would not be spoken. Then it was too late to answer. Her silence had given her away, she knew. And so did he.

"Well, then, if that's all . . . ?" He trailed his words off and proved himself a man of his word by turning on his heel and stalking toward the open door of her bedroom.

Though in a state of disbelief, Yancey watched his retreating figure, instinctively noting the broadness of his shoulders, the narrowness of his hips, and the swagger in his walk. The combined effect of the man's parts momentarily stunted her breathing. And because it did, she finally became angry with him. His swagger told her he felt triumphant. She couldn't allow him that sense of victory over her, especially not after her appalling display of female weakness both up in the tower and then right here with his kiss. She must regain the upper hand. At this point, pride was all she had.

Yancey struggled up to a sitting position. She'd expected to feel residual dizziness or weakness, but there was none. Glad for that, she refused, however, to credit his kiss—as if he were the prince and she the sleeping beauty—with fully awakening her. Instead, she insisted, it was her iron constitution and years of training that accounted for her alert, wide-eyed status. Swinging her hair out of her face, she braced her palms behind her and atop the bedding.

"Hey, Duke," she called out, being purposely insolent.

He stopped as if he'd hit a solid yet invisible impediment. Grinning, feeling the pendulum had finally swung back in her favor, Yancey nevertheless blanked her smirk of triumph as . . . ever so slowly . . . the insulted peer pivoted to face her. His expression as much as said she should be put to death at the next sunrise. A knee bent, his hands planted at his waist, he drawled, "Yes, Miss Calhoun?"

"What do you think you're doing, kissing me like that? You have no right."

He merely raised an eyebrow at that. "You'd be hard-pressed to find anyone in this household to support that statement, Miss Calhoun. And, amusingly, you have none to blame but yourself. After all, you are the one who introduced yourself as the duchess. Deny it all you want, but we both know that's exactly what you did."

Guilt brought an instant heat to Yancey's cheeks. "I admit nothing. Still, you and I know differently. I am not your wife, and you will take no further liberties with me, sir."

Irritatingly, he chuckled, making the sound at once erotic and threatening. "I still claim that I have every right. I am the Duke of Somerset. And Stonebridge is my ancestral seat. I told you that when you first arrived. And I also told you, Miss Calhoun, that everything here, everything on this land and in this house . . . is mine."

Yancey's breath caught in her throat. The way he had said *mine* in such a slow, growling purr had made her feel the word as a vibration down low in her belly. Though sensually unhinged by his voice as much as by his commanding stance, she narrowed her eyes. "I'm afraid I must correct you, Your Grace. I also told you yesterday that there was one exception. And I am it. That remains true, sir. I belong to no man."

A challenging light claimed his eyes and lifted his eyebrows. Looking perfectly dangerous, he sketched a formal bow for her and then straightened, meeting her gaze. "Perhaps not now, Miss Calhoun. But only for now, I assure you."

With those words hanging in the air between them, he pivoted on his heel. Though shocked . . . and titillated . . . Yancey again helplessly raked her gaze over his body. Her mind registered his power and his virility, but she refused to give in to his charisma. And so, unchallenged, he exited the room and disappeared from her view as he entered the sitting room.

Still atop the bed, Yancey sat as one in a trance and stared at the empty doorway where only a moment ago the duke had stood. Though she seemed to feel every bone and muscle and cell in her body, she couldn't move her limbs. His spell, despite her best intentions otherwise, still held her in its thrall.

"I think I'm in trouble," she murmured.

* * *

Sam stood in his study on the first floor, his back to the room, his arms crossed over his chest as he stared out the window at the meadows where his prize stock of horses grazed contentedly in the English sunlight. The scene, though tranquil and inviting, made barely an impression on his consciousness. Instead, his thoughts were turned inward on the woman upstairs. He wondered exactly how long it would take Miss Calhoun to seek him out in order to continue their spat. A check of the mantel clock told him he'd left her over an hour ago. Much the same as it had been yesterday when she'd kept him waiting. But given what he now knew of her impetuosity and her spirit, she was overdue.

With a start he realized that he was eagerly anticipating their next confrontation, much as if this were some sort of merry game between them. It was nothing of the sort. So why was he behaving as if he couldn't wait to see her again? Certainly, she was an entertaining distraction and she excited him physically. A man would have to be dead not to respond to her. But he was over the top with his reaction to her. Here he was as excited as a schoolboy at the prospect of a holiday.

A frown of concern ate at Sam's expression. He couldn't allow himself to be taken in by her. He tried to tell himself he was merely biding his time with her, playing cat and mouse. He'd thought that if he didn't respond to her, she would eventually expose her game. But the truth was she excited him in ways he hadn't ever been excited before. Not to this extent. And he remained intrigued by her, no matter the many possible explanations that lay behind her presence here. Whatever they were, none of them would be favorable, he suspected.

Certainly, he had in mind all the right questions and suspicions regarding her. His eyes were open on that score. She was up to no good. He knew that. But he didn't give a damn right now. He was too intrigued by her. Too, she didn't appear to be any real physical threat to him or to those under his protection. So . . . let the game continue.

Sam chuckled. How very jaded of him. He meant to string her along in her own game. He hadn't known he was capable of such a thing. All it took, apparently, was the right woman.

It was enough for him now that she relieved for him the boredom of isolation at Stonebridge. And he hadn't lied when he'd told her that he allowed her to be known as his duchess simply because it pleased him. It did. Very much. He'd asked himself what life would be like to have a woman like her as his duchess. And he'd liked the answer: it would be infinitely exciting.

But Sam had a more logical reason for allowing her charade to continue. Simply put, by not calling her on her lie, he'd locked her into the role she'd thrust upon herself. Now if she didn't wish to continue as his duchess, she'd have to tell him and his household the truth. Then she would be exposed, and by her own hand. Sam nodded. He liked it. Besides, by not challenging her, by not simply tossing her out as he'd threatened yesterday, he had gained the upper hand. She was now completely isolated here with him and her own story. Completely at his mercy and where he could watch every move of hers.

What he had better do too was watch his own moves more carefully. In his mind's eye he could see her shocked expression when he'd kissed her. The contact had been exquisite and his body had damned near exploded with desire for her. He'd had all he could do not to leap atop that bed and take her. Sam closed his eyes and rubbed hard at the pounding space between his eyebrows. The woman excited him to passion and to violence, to tenderness and to sarcasm. She was very dangerous and very desirable.

Even standing there alone, he thought he could feel her lips, soft and yielding. The scent of her skin, delicate and feminine. And the sultry fire he'd felt against his mouth, the fire that had threatened to consume him—the same fire that had him pulling away from her before he fell into her feminine trap.

Yet here he was wishing to tumble right back into it. This simply would not do. Sam stepped back from the window and paced angrily around the room, skirting such things as the sharp corners of his desk and avoiding the protruding bookcases. Why this woman? It was the most incredible thing, the way she of all women affected him. Certainly he'd known more beautiful women—more tractable women, to be sure. But for some reason, his body ached for her and his thoughts always returned to her.

Could it be possible that they'd only met yesterday afternoon? No. Surely he'd known her forever. Why, he could already feel her in his very marrow. And he wasn't the least bit happy about that. How had she done it? How had she so quickly tangled his emotions up with hers? Was she better at this game than he'd given her credit for being? Was he already lost and he just didn't know it?

That was entirely possible. Probable, even. Then, hang it all, from this moment on, and until he knew better, he would treat her as the enemy. But with a change in tactics. Where pomposity and confrontation hadn't drawn Miss Calhoun out, cordiality and courtliness might. Sam liked it. This could work. It was a good plan. Feeling better now for having one, he set off in a long-legged stride across his study. In his mind's eye he saw himself charging up the stairs and drawing Miss Calhoun out of her room and hauling her downstairs and—

He stopped again, his hand on the doorknob as he faced the blank façade of the solid door, not six inches from his nose. *And doing what?* He had no idea, but he would think of something. With that, he opened the door, only to have his chest beat upon by a feminine fist.

"Oh, I'm so sorry—"

"Miss Calhoun!" Excitement, as much as surprise, had Sam's heart pounding. The mere sight of her slender body with her feminine curves and the overall effect of her widened green eyes and long red hair on his sensibilities was staggering—and unsettling for being so. *Manners, man. Remember your manners with her. Be courtly, yet distant. Preserve yourself.*

"Oh, I do apologize, Your Grace. I meant only to knock upon the door and not your person."

"No need to apologize. I was just on my way to get you."

"You were? Really? Why?" Smiling, she leaned in toward him. Bright, expectant lights danced in her eyes.

Sam's first impulse was to grab her and ravish her right

there. Though a certain other part of him stiffened, as well, he tensed his body against the base urge and took a deep breath. Thus steeled, he managed to reply in a calm manner. "Please. You first, Miss Calhoun. What did you want with me?"

Tugging her hair behind her ears, she suddenly looked everywhere but at him. "Actually, permission to have a saddled horse or a carriage placed at my disposal so I might go into the village."

"The village?" An outing. A place away from here. It was perfect. She was playing right into his hands. A sudden calm and calculation came over Sam. This was a game he could handily win. Get her alone with him in the carriage and question her. But obliquely, of course. "How intriguing, Miss Calhoun. You wish to go into the village. Hoping to find its idiot, are you?"

It was a fabulous opening he'd given her, one he could see she struggled not to respond to. She was actually grimacing and sputtering. Oh, those words wanted out in the worst way. Feigning a sincere smile, Sam raised his eyebrows and waited, knowing she wanted to blurt out that she'd already found the village idiot, and he was it.

"No, hardly, Your Grace," she finally gritted out. "Instead, I simply find myself in need of a . . . of a—"

"Of a what?" he prodded, watching her struggle. Suddenly he didn't think his plan of courtliness and good manners was what was called for, after all. Perhaps a military campaign or a fencing duel with well-placed parries and thrusts that forced her to respond in kind or be skewered.

"Of a dressmaker," she finally blurted.

"A dressmaker?" Sam barely bit back a guffaw. "That's the best you can do?"

She sobered, apparently insulted. "I don't take your meaning, Your Grace."

"Oh, I think you do."

"And I'm telling you I don't, Your Grace."

"Truthfully?" He crossed his arms and leaned a shoulder against the doorjamb. "Have it your way, then. I apologize if I've offended you. But tell me, have you received an invitation I'm not aware of, one that necessitates new gowns?"

"I've only just arrived, Your Grace. Who would issue such an invitation to me?"

"I have no idea, as I know not the first thing about you. For all I know, you are boon companions with everyone hereabouts."

"And if I were, you too would already know me, am I correct?"

She had him there, but he wasn't about to admit it. "Proceed then, Miss Calhoun."

"Thank you. Robin—my lady's maid, you may recall—has informed me that I must dress for dinner. She's very concerned that my, uh, trunks with my . . . gowns haven't arrived yet and that I will therefore make a poor showing. So I thought perhaps the local dressmaker might have some ready-mades I could purchase for the occasion."

"How very sympathetic of you. One wouldn't want one's maid's sensibilities to be offended, would one? However, I find it curious that you have more trunks coming. I mean no offense, Miss Calhoun, but for just how long did my mother invite you to stay?"

Her face colored. With embarrassment or guilt? "She didn't actually put an end date on it, Your Grace. But you are free to do so. As you've pointed out to me, everything hereabouts is yours, so I assume even time spent here is under your control?"

"Yes, it is." Sam's body thrummed with excitement. Such a quick and refreshing intellect she possessed. She certainly kept a man on his toes . . . and more. Exhaling for calm, reminding himself yet again that she was no innocent, Sam managed a schooled response. "However, I will defer to my mother's invitation to you and to whatever her wishes may be for how long your visit should last."

"Very sporting of you, Your Grace. And as it should be."

They were like circling dogs, looking for an opening. Sam felt she'd handed him one, and he didn't intend to leave it unchallenged. "Would you like me to accompany you into town, Miss Calhoun?"

Her eyes rounded with surprise. "Oh no, Your Grace, I'm

sure you're much too busy to attend to something so silly. I would never dream of presuming on your time."

So she didn't want him to go. Well, then, go he would. "Nothing silly about it, Miss Calhoun. I find the fitting and making of women's dresses to be an endlessly fascinating spectacle."

She eyed him as if he were a dirty, pawing old man. "I don't doubt that you would." Then she smiled. "Well, then, Your Grace, if you insist on going, far be it from me to deny you your bit of entertainment."

She then caught him completely off guard by executing a full and formal curtsy—the first one he'd wrung out of her. And hadn't it come at an interesting moment? Sam nodded his head in regal acknowledgment of this show of respect and courtesy on her part, though he expected she meant it in a disparaging sense.

Indeed, her expression as she looked up at him from under her eyelashes could only be termed daring. "I would be honored if you would accompany me."

"Good. Then it's settled. We'll go after luncheon, which should be ready just about now. And as luck would have it here in the country, we don't dress formally for the noonday meal." Sam pulled away from the doorjamb and held his crooked arm out to her. "May I escort you into the dining room, Miss Calhoun?"

She smiled brightly, accepting his offered arm. "By all means, Your Grace."

# Chapter Ten

Luncheon consisted of cold meats and an assortment of breads and fresh greens, which were followed by an offering of cheeses. In the formal dining room and seated at the other end of the long table from the duke, Yancey remained quiet as she ate her fill. A need to be fortified for her upcoming jaunt into town with him accompanying her lay behind her behavior. She couldn't believe this twist. Shopping for gowns had only been her excuse and certainly not her intention when she'd come downstairs and knocked on his study door. As it stood now, though, she would actually have to engage in the tiring activity. *Damn.* How the devil would she pay for a wardrobe of gowns? Mr. Pinkerton would not be amused should she be forced to put them on her expense account.

All she'd wanted from the duke, when she'd knocked on his study's closed door, was his cooperation in ordering a vehicle, or at least a saddled horse, to be placed at her disposal. Only he could give such an order. Then, once she had her conveyance, she'd meant to slip away to the village and post a letter—a formal report she'd written this morning and so couldn't possibly send from the manor because it was addressed to the famous Mr. Pinkerton.

Even now, the letter to her employer was tucked into her

skirt pocket. Though not heavy in its own right, it held the emotional weight of a good-sized stone weighing her down. She had created it and now had the responsibility of it. A very incriminating thing it would indeed be too should it be discovered by anyone here. She'd have a lot of explaining to do. Still, despite that risk, she was glad she had composed it. The very act of writing it had put her firmly back on track with her mission here. She'd of course left out her embarrassing faint and then the kiss. A very complicating kiss from a very complicated man.

Stealing a glance at the duke as he spoke patiently to Her Grace Nana, also in attendance at table with them, Yancey exhaled her distress. The handsome, arresting man was a craving she could not satisfy. Around him, she had no sense of objectivity, much less decorum. She wanted only to run her hands over his body, tear her hands through his hair, and pull him to her.

Such heated thoughts, accompanied by sensual visions, had Yancey inadvertently tightening her hand around the warm, buttered bun she'd all but forgotten she held. Melted butter ran between her fingers. Shocked and dismayed, but undetected, she surreptitiously plopped the mess onto her plate and wiped her hands clean on the linen napkin in her lap.

*Imbecile,* she admonished herself. *Around him, you behave more the harlot than the seasoned detective. You could be swimming in murderers and you wouldn't even know it. Pay attention to your job and not your . . . heart.*

Easily said, but it wasn't her heart that was throbbing at the moment. Yancey fidgeted in her chair, trying her best to subjugate her desire to her will. She worked to convince herself that she was suffering only a momentary weakness and she had only herself to blame. But the truth was she was angry with him. Did he really intend to pretend that he hadn't kissed her? As a duke, had he thought nothing of taking whatever lay under his roof—or atop one of his beds? Well, she couldn't say he hadn't warned her. Still, should he try it again, now that she wasn't recovering from a swoon, he'd have a big surprise coming. She knew a thing or two about disabling a man, whether he be amorous or murderous.

Thus fortified, Yancey took her last swallow of a white wine they'd been served. As she did, she again eyed her handsome and enigmatic host at the other end of the long table. He was pointedly ignoring her. Evil man. Yancey's grip tightened on her wine glass. Fearing it would go the way of the bun, she carefully set it down and lowered her gaze until she stared at her plate. She needed to remember that she was a woman of twenty-six years with six years of undercover detective experience behind her. Why, she even had a notch on her gun. Not that she was proud of the life she had taken, and not that it was the first one . . . but there it was, nonetheless.

And regarding this duke her body so yearned for? She needed to remember that, despite her not wanting it to be so, he could prove yet to be the enemy here. She must focus on that and nothing else. Along those lines, how, with the duke in attendance, was she going to post her letter? And again, how would she pay for those gowns? Well, she'd just pray the dressmaker had no ready-mades. Suddenly it occurred to Yancey that she didn't have to buy a thing. A lady could simply not like what was shown her. There. Solved. She felt better for that. But other problems remained.

Namely, she hadn't counted on—and she didn't think the duke had, either—the general excitement the announcement of a trip into town had caused. Her Grace Nana had insisted on forgoing her nap and going along into town. Absolutely insisted. And won. That meant, as it turned out as lunch proceeded, that Mrs. Convers, Nana's nurse, would also have to go.

Then Mr. Marples, perhaps sensing the excitement in the air, had chased around and yapped until, in the interest of sanity, the terrier had won a place in the carriage, as well. And that meant someone would have to go along to watch the dog. As it turned out, Scotty was awarded that office as he was the only two-legged creature the dog would obey. Yancey amused herself envisioning the sight that huge man would make with a tiny dog on a lead held by him.

But petitions to go along to town hadn't stopped there.

Over fruit and cheese, Mrs. Edgars, the dour housekeeper, had presented a very lengthy list of needed household goods that the duke had read and grown testy over, finally telling her it would be simpler if she came along and purchased them herself. And then that sober lady had asked His Grace for Robin's addition to the party since she was now a lady's maid and needed to observe how to choose personal items for "my lady."

That was when everyone had looked at Yancey, and she'd been reminded that *she* was "my lady."

By this time, too, near the end of luncheon, the duke had been obliged to call for two vehicles to be readied. Which meant that both drivers and various pages would now also be in attendance. This had put the duke in a decidedly foul humor. He'd all but yelled that only in this most singular of households would a duke be taking his entire household on a jaunt into town. He certainly hoped they all realized that were this London, it would not be occurring, and as it was, this was a one-time event that would *not* be repeated in future.

Through all this, Yancey had kept her head down, her thoughts to herself, and pronounced herself glad she was isolated at the other end of the table . . . and apparently beneath the man's notice.

"What? No cats?" the duke had roared when, about thirty minutes after luncheon ended, they'd all assembled in the grand foyer. The women had been pulling on gloves and hats and chatting amiably with each other up until that point, when they all froze, Yancey among them.

At that roared question, Nana had raised the lid on the basket she carried to reveal one of the cats. And so their parade . . . or "damned traveling circus complete with animals" as the duke had called their troupe . . . was completed.

And now, here they all were on the road to the nearest village and, no doubt, Yancey feared, high adventure on this warm and lovely spring afternoon. Around them birds sang happily and bees buzzed softly. A light breeze seemed to accompany them of its own accord, and the air smelled sweet with hay and the scent of wild flowers. Spirits were high.

And Yancey sat smashed against the duke in the crowded barouche that led the way to the village. Across from her and facing them sat Her Grace Nana and her silent nurse. Suddenly, to Yancey, this was an amusing turn of events, and she bit back a smile that surely would require explaining. She'd had the sudden thought that she could buy all the gowns she wanted. After all, she was—to everyone's thinking—Her Grace, the Duchess of Somerset. So, then, could the man sitting next to her deny her anything? Would he dare? She was about to find out. And turnabout was fair play.

"You're awfully quiet, my dear."

*My dear?* Pulled back to the moment by the duke's endearment, as much as by his comment to her, Yancey glared at the man behind whose shoulder she was all but stuffed in the thankfully open barouche. Her first instinct was to put him in his place, but then she caught his very pointed stare at her.

Yancey cocked her head in question. He angled his chin in the direction of their carriage companions. Realization dawned. He was playing his part as her husband. And she was the one who had foisted this masquerade on them both. So she must play her part . . . until he relieved her of it. "Am I that quiet, Your Gra—Mr. Trey—uh, Sam?" What the devil should she call him in public and in front of a servant? "Does my silence concern you?"

His amused expression surprised her. "Had I good sense it would."

What a wonderful opening. Yancey smiled sweetly up at him, fluttering her eyelashes. "Well, then, thankfully, you have none to upset you."

He chuckled and shook his head. "A well-aimed barb. Touché, madam."

Pleased with herself, barely hiding her smirk of victory, Yancey looked away from the duke and caught the gaze of the nurse seated across from her. The woman's florid complexion capped her round-eyed stare of evident confusion.

No doubt, she found this exchange most interesting and would, in all probability, carry tales back to the manor about the duchess who didn't seem to know what to call her husband. And how the two of them spent the ride into the village insulting each other.

But as for Her Grace Nana, that sweet little woman was cheerfully oblivious and occupied with holding on to her cat. Whichever one it was—Mary, Alice, or Jane—she held it up, allowing it to take in the rolling hills of the countryside. At every turn, respectful bows and curtsies were sent their way by people walking on the roadside or traveling past in wagons.

"Well, then, *Sarah,*" Sam, the duke, said into the quiet. He stretched his arm out to put it familiarly around her shoulders, knowing there wasn't a thing she could do about it. "Perhaps I should instead fear your wit and quick tongue. I feel certain you could use both to weaken the kingdom. Or lighten my purse."

Yancey sent him a look she hoped would fry him on the spot, but disappointingly didn't. "You assign me great powers. Or capability for great treachery, I don't know which."

"Both, actually." He ducked his chin and stared into her eyes, his own gaze bearing the bright gray sheen of pewter. "But am I off the mark in my assessment?"

Damning her own heart for pitter-pattering over the tantalizing feel of his thigh intimately brushing her leg and of his arm around her shoulders, Yancey smiled and lifted her chin, managing to look away from him. "It remains to be seen, doesn't it"—she paused for effect—"my dear *husband*?"

The duke's reply was a husky laugh, a knowing sound a lover would make in the privacy of his bed after lovemaking. Yancey felt a delicious shiver slip over her skin, one that awakened her anew to the dangers this man posed to her sensibilities. Just how far away was this village? she fussed irritably. How much longer must she suffer being so openly and intimately corralled by a man who had her pulse fluttering at just the sound of his voice?

Just then, as if her plaintive thought had conjured it up,

the village appeared around a bend in the road that passed between two hills dotted with cattle and horses.

"And here we are, my sweet," the duke announced with a sweep of his hand in the direction of the clustered stores and houses ahead. "Lakeheath-on-Somerset. I hope you find it to your liking. After all, it is mine. Or, rather, ours."

She ignored his last mine-and-ours statement, focusing instead on his saying he hoped she found the village to her liking. Interesting. Yancey looked up at the duke, whose attention was on the fast-approaching town. She noted his determined jaw, his square chin, and his clean-shaven skin. Undeniably handsome.

But her mind was racing with other realizations. His wife had never been here. Otherwise, he wouldn't have expressed a hope that she liked the village. Yancey supposed she shouldn't be surprised, given that no one in his household had known any different yesterday when she'd told them she was the duchess. Still, she found it exceedingly odd that he had not brought his wife, to all appearances, back with him to England.

Suddenly he looked down at her—and caught her staring. An amused grin lit his features. "Yes?"

"It's lovely, Your Gra—Sam. The town, I mean." Yancey stopped her sputtering and took a deep breath for calm. Then she subtly leaned toward him, all but whispering in an effort not to be overheard. "What the devil should I call you? Sam? Samuel? Your Grace? After all, we are in public, and I don't know the correct form."

His grin, which showed white and even teeth, had Yancey catching her breath. Would the day ever come when her body didn't jump to show its appreciation for him? "Oh, I'm certain other dukes would prefer the formal. But blame my years in America for relaxing the rules in my own household—this unorthodox outing being a prime example—and for giving me a liking for informality. In other words, you may call me Sam." He paused, as if thinking about that. "However, for the sake of propriety, I suppose you should refer to me as His Grace to the town's people."

Glad that was cleared up, she nodded and turned her attention once more to the looming village. And found it was indeed lovely. Neat. Clean. Flower boxes and flower beds abounded. As their carriage approached the town square, in its center Yancey saw a water well encircled by bench seats. These were occupied by a well-dressed assortment of the young and the old. Over here were women laden with shopping baskets and small children. Over there, gentlemen strolled along the narrow streets, entering and exiting shops of every variety, including a pub and an apothecary. All around them, older children ran to and fro, usually followed by a barking dog or two. Young mothers with babies stood in knots, chatting and comparing infants and, no doubt, husbands.

All in all, Yancey noted, commerce seemed to be thriving and the people appeared prosperous. Surprising her was how proud that made her feel. As if she'd had anything to do with it. Then she realized that her pride was in the duke. Sam. Her . . . husband. She hadn't thought much of the British system of hereditary land ownership and titles, but here was evidence of it working at its best. All of this prosperity was possible because of Sam's and his predecessors' efforts, she concluded.

Then she heard herself. *Sam's?* Yancey marveled at how easily his name was coming to her mind already. How natural it seemed. Sam. Samuel. Samuel Isaac Treyhorne. Her husband. The Duke of Somerset. No. Not her husband or anything else. Merely a person involved in her active and ongoing investigation into a crime.

Just then the Duke of Somerset leaned in close to her ear to whisper something. When he did, Yancey felt the soft little hairs on the back of her neck stiffen in response. "Just do as I do," he offered helpfully.

"What do you mean?"

"Look around you."

Yancey did and saw that evidently word of their approach had preceded them. And now, much like a soft wind that carried their titles aloft and whisked and whirled them through the narrow hard-packed dirt streets of the town, whispers of conversation came to her ears. "The duke." "It's the duke." "His Grace and his lady." "The duchess! At last, the duchess." "What does she look like?" "How does she seem?" "Is the duke well? Is his lady?" "Look—it's Her Grace Nana, the grand old lady." "Oh, this is a glorious day."

As the two carriages passed, one in front of the other—Scotty, Mr. Marples, Mrs. Edgars, and Robin being in the second barouche—conversations ceased and everyone rose to their feet. Looking agog with excitement and wonder, the women curtsied and pulled children to them, getting them out of the way of the vehicles. While the older children stared boldly, the toddlers shyly peeked out from behind their mothers' skirts. The men doffed their hats and bowed. Amazingly, to a last person, they showed their respect and deference.

Yancey had expected that her American blood would hate what she called bowing and scraping. In fact, she had feared she'd see resentment and ill will on some of the people's faces. But she found none. Didn't that say something about the Treyhornes, that they would be held in such esteem? It must. Indeed, the villagers behaved as if the carriages were stocked with conquering heroes.

To her utmost surprise and chagrin, Yancey liked the attention. She basked in it, wanting to wave and greet these people as if she'd known them all her life. How to explain this response of hers? Even in Chicago, she hadn't behaved this way. Instead, she was aloof, a loner, preferring not to be noticed. But here in Lakeheath-on-Somerset, a lovely town actually built on the shores of a large blue lake surrounded by carpets of blooming heath, she felt at home. What was this feeling? Where was it coming from?

"Just ignore them for the most part," the duke said out the side of his mouth.

"I will not," Yancey protested in a harsh whisper. "How rude."

The duke's exhale had the quality of a long-suffering sigh. "They will expect you to. But if you must, a discreet wave or regal nod of your head"—he demonstrated both in the direction of the delighted citizens he'd thereby singled out—"will suffice. It's not necessary to hug everyone and kiss the babies."

"I had no intention of—"

"No doubt. But let me assure you the barest form of notice from you will be bragged about for weeks and can cause hard feelings or accusations of favoritism. I promise you there will be aggrieved feelings and, before long, you will have petitioners on the doorstep wanting your notice and favor, too."

So he wasn't simply being pompous. The duke knew his people and he knew his business, which, it occurred to Yancey, was being a nobleman. "I see," she said, contrite, yet with a growing sense of the heavy responsibility that was placed upon the shoulders of the realm's peers. "Thank you for that lesson, Your Grace."

He chuckled. "My, my, I am honored. A thank-you from you. How much did that cost me?"

Just then, the carriage drew to a stop. Yancey glanced to her right. The dressmaker's shop. She smiled her widest smile for the duke. "Not nearly as much as my gowns will . . . my husband."

He caught her meaning and his wonderful gray eyes widened. "You wouldn't dare."

"Oh, but I would . . . Sam, darling."

That evening, with a double shot of a fine whisky as his only company, Sam sat alone in the lavishly furnished and carpeted drawing room. Achingly formal, the long, wallpapered room wasn't his favorite one in the manor. But he did favor its high ceilings and the double sets of French doors, closed now against the night's chill. His mother had expertly decorated it with names like Wedgwood and Chippendale. Porcelain vases stuffed with fresh flowers and ornamental bric-a-brac of exquisite quality owned every tabletop. Surrounding him too were a swirl of tall potted plants. Scattered about the room were three separate arrangements of brocaded suites meant to allow for intimate conversation.

Dressed no less formally than the room, Sam awaited Miss Calhoun and his dinner. *Miss Calhoun.* A grin tugged at his lips. He shook his head and chuckled. She'd certainly won the day—and ten new gowns, all at his expense. The woman was a force of nature. He hadn't fully realized that until he'd seen her with the people of Lakeheath-on-Somerset. They'd immediately adored her. No matter which shop she'd frequented—and she had frequented them all—she'd woven a spell of cheer over the entire town. How happy the people had been to see him at last with his lady.

Sam frowned. What would they say when they found out she was nothing more than an impostor? No doubt, his tenants would storm the manor with pitchforks and torches held aloft. Surprisingly, the fact that she was so obviously American hadn't seemed to bother the townspeople in the least. They'd thought her charming and had told him so. And there he'd been, forced into the background and allowed only to stand around grinning stupidly in her wake and toting all of her purchases.

The proper husband. The picture of connubial bliss. Sam's smile faded into a frown. Connubial bliss. Had that been what he'd experienced today? He'd never known it with his real wife. And yet he had with Miss Calhoun. Infectious happiness. Peace. Warmth. Conviviality. With a sinking feeling in his stomach, Sam realized that he couldn't allow this warm feeling of contentment to own him. He already suspected that his delightful little impostor was charming him for some nefarious purpose. And he wasn't proving to be too difficult a mark, was he?

Just as he'd done earlier that afternoon, Sam reminded himself that he knew what he had to do. Have it out with her, or attempt to. He sipped at his liquor, feeling its warmth curl around in his stomach as he stared into the fireplace where a fire roared. He would ask her direct questions and expect direct answers. If she refused to answer him, or if he wasn't satisfied with her answers, then she would be leaving tomorrow morning—and hang his mother's alleged invitation.

In truth, and he was only now willing to admit it, he feared less any treachery in which Miss Calhoun might be involved than he did the fact that increasingly he didn't care what it was. He wanted her here, plain and simple. And that could put her in physical danger. It hadn't hit him until they'd been on their way back to the manor this afternoon, but he'd suddenly realized that allowing her to pose as his duchess—which he did hoping to divine what her reason might be for such a pretense and to see how far she would take it—could conceivably put her in harm's way, if any of his suspicions regarding Geoffrey's death proved to be true. Meaning, if he was the next target, then she could also be.

Sam drained his measure of whisky. Eyeing the fireplace, he fought his urge to hurl the glass against the cold marble fronting it. *Damn.* He must call her bluff and send her away. For her own good.

Would he never know peace? Or happiness? The words were a familiar lament to him. What had he done that he didn't deserve it? First, a little over a year ago, things with his wife Sarah had come to a head. And right on the very heels of what he'd gone through with her, Geoffrey's sudden, suspicious death had occurred. And that had forced Sam to return here to shoulder the responsibilities of being a duke. He'd much preferred the freedom of being a fortune-seeking second son.

And now? Just when he'd come to grips with it all, and just as he was making peace with this new life, this new Sarah had arrived. A riveting and desirable woman of mystery. He thought of her now, recalling how she'd felt in his arms last night . . . warm, sweet, feminine. How she'd raged at him today like a tiger. And how her mouth had tasted this morning when he'd stolen that kiss . . . hot, inviting, questing.

A grin of purely male lust claimed Sam's mouth. What would it be like, he wondered, to possess such a woman fully? Would she be like a summer storm that comes out of nowhere and threatens the day's calm? A sudden squall that could swamp a ship at sea? A woman who could make him forget he was supposed to be a gentleman bound by rigid dictates of polite behavior? One who could, with but a sign from her, and in a rage of lust, sweep her off her feet and carry her up the stairs to his bed, only to—

The heavy double doors into the room opened behind him. Sam jumped to his feet, not an easy thing to do given his state of arousal. Self-consciously, he cleared his throat and tugged on his vest with his free hand. He straightened his formal swallow-tailed coat. *Like a preening peacock,* he irritably accused himself. Still, excitement filled his veins and rooted him to the spot. He gripped the glass in his hand so tightly that he expected it to shatter into shards.

In walked the huge and lumbering, very sober Scotty. He caught Sam's eye and said, "The duchess."

The very words weakened Sam's knees. For one ironic second he didn't know exactly who to picture. In quick succession, he saw his mother's face . . . then his wife's . . . then Miss Calhoun's. He blinked, realizing that Scotty could only mean Miss Calhoun. "Very well. Show her in, Scotty."

The butler stepped back, making way, and in swept Miss Calhoun. Just inside the room, she stopped suddenly and stared at him as if she'd never seen him before in her life. Sam's breath caught in his throat. The distance between them in the long room seemed to disappear as if in a rush of attracted bodies. He felt as if she were only inches from him, and that he had merely to reach out to touch her. Yet she remained so very far away and out of his grasp.

Sam raked his gaze up and down her. In a word, she was stunning. Gone was his desire to question her, to be abrupt, or to confront her. He wanted only to hold her and make her his own . . . in every lofty and carnal way possible. Hang the consequences, moral or financial.

She said nothing. Was she giving him time to note details about her? Perhaps so. And so, greedily, Sam did. Her hair was artfully arranged atop her head in a mass of curls and ribbons. Several trailing auburn tresses fell across her bare alabaster-white shoulders. She wore no jewelry. She needed none. Sam sought her eyes and beheld there sparkling emeralds in their green depths. Her gown left her shoulders and a good amount of her breasts bared. Nipped in at the waist, the full crinoline-supported skirt floated around her like gossamer wings. He could see only the tips of her silver shoes.

He raked his gaze back up her length until he again looked

into her eyes. Looking very anxious, she tipped her tongue out to moisten her pink lips. The gesture was not lost on Sam. Innocent. Provocative. It all but staggered him. As he held her gaze, he felt his body tighten with need. Sheer, physical need. But it was more, so much more. Deeper even than his need for food and water and air. He knew he was lost. He wanted to cry out with the truth that he wanted this woman above all others. And that he meant to have her at all costs. All costs. Even certain death.

Staring at her, Sam fought an urge to shout out his rancor to her. Why, in God's name, had she come here? But he didn't really want to know why because he feared he couldn't bear the answer.

# Chapter Eleven

Still standing across the room from him, Miss Calhoun remained innocent of Sam's torture. Without moving or saying a word—indeed, he didn't believe himself capable of either—he struggled for a control that still eluded him. He swallowed, felt the lump in his throat, but couldn't make himself smile or greet her in any way. This was insane. Had he been turned to stone? Had he become a statue doomed to stare longingly and futilely at her for all of eternity?

Then a movement by the doors caught Sam's eye. He saw Scotty showing uncustomary sensitivity by quietly closing the doors behind her and leaving Sam alone with his enigmatic guest. Moving somewhat mechanically, much like clockwork, Sam returned his gaze to Miss Calhoun.

For her part, as if suddenly prodded from behind to break their stalemate, she dropped into a deep curtsy, which exposed to Sam's hungry eyes an enticing expanse of her ripe bosom. She arose and spoke her greeting softly. "Good evening, Your Grace."

Sam did her the honor of bowing to her, even as he marveled that he could, given how stiff he felt . . . and he didn't mean only in his legs. "Good evening. You are absolutely stunning in that gown, Miss Calhoun."

"I have you to thank for it." Her smile was uncertain, her voice shaky.

"Nonsense." Dare he hope—never mind that he didn't have the right to hope—that she was as affected by the sight of him in black formal wear as he was by her in this stunning emerald evening gown shot through with silver threads? "It was my pleasure to obtain it, and the others, for you since I have the honor of seeing you in them."

Her smile slipped away from her, only to be lost in a wide-eyed look of uncertainty. "You're very kind. But all ten of them, Your Grace? I don't see how you could call it an honor. I tricked you into paying for them, and we both know it." She looked very guilty and contrite . . . and totally endearing. "I forced their purchase on you."

Somehow, her being uncertain—or at least appearing to be so—restored Sam's equilibrium. He pointed at her and made a mock accusation. "You're absolutely right. You did trick me into making these purchases. I shall bill you for their cost. Or better yet, I say we should take them back."

Instantly stricken, she lowered her gaze to her skirt and smoothed her hand over the fabric. Her childlike gesture said she was in love with her new dress and would sooner die. She looked up, disappointment edging her rounded eyes. "If you like, we can take back the ones we brought home. They're not all unboxed as yet, Your Grace."

Sam called himself the worst kind of cad. His teasing her had gone awry. "No. You keep the gowns and all the essentials that came with them. Call them my gift to you, Miss Calhoun."

Again she curtsied. "You're very generous, Your Grace."

"Sam. Please call me Sam. Blame the influence of my years in America. All these titles put distance between people and make conversation so stilted. I find I yearn for familiarity from at least one person."

"Then I'm to be that person, I take it?"

"Yes. You're American. Who better than you to understand?"

"Point taken. But only if you'll call me Yancey."

Sam frowned. "I beg your pardon?"

Her chin came up a proud notch. Sam wanted to kiss it . . . and her neck . . . her shoulder . . . her breast. He wanted to take her into his mouth and—"It's the name I go by," she said, breaking into his lurid thoughts of her naked and atop him, moaning with ecstasy. "I don't like to go by Sarah."

A jet of belated suspicion, never far from the forefront of his thoughts where she was concerned, shot through Sam. "But isn't that your name?"

"Yes. But not one I favor."

"I see. Then . . . Yancey it is. I shall think of it as a private endearment for when only the two of us are in a room." He gestured to the settee beside him and said, "Please. We'll wait here until called for dinner. It shouldn't be long. And then you can tell me how you came by that most singular name."

She set herself in motion, coming toward him. "It was my grandmother's name before she married," she remarked, her voice full of challenge. "I've just always preferred it. I never felt much like a Sarah."

"Indeed, you don't look much like one, either." Smiling at her as she approached the intimately arranged brocaded suite of two chairs and a settee separated by wood-carved tables, Sam stepped up to offer her his hand for assistance in being seated. Only then did he realize that what he held out to her was his empty whisky glass. He met her gaze and saw her amused grin. Even though it was at his cost he realized that he was delighted with her response. "Perhaps I could offer you your own drink, Miss Calhoun?"

"Yancey, remember. And yes. I'll have what you're drinking."

"Are you certain? I'm drinking whisky."

She pursed her lips in a stubborn pout. "Then that's what I'm having."

A chuckle escaped him.

"You find that amusing?" She sat down rather delicately, further winning Sam's admiration, given the expanse of crinolines and yards of fabric with which she had to contend.

"Yes. I am amused to at last find a whisky-drinking woman, that is. I must say that you continue to surprise me

. . . Yancey. And you should be flattered because very little amuses me."

"Then you share that trait with Scotty."

A burst of laughter escaped Sam, but then he feigned horror. "Has he been dragging you along? He tends to think that's the best method of moving around those people left in his charge."

She nodded. "*Dragging* is a good word for it."

Sam grimaced. "Well, it's better than being hurled down the stairs like a lance. We've only just broken him of that behavior."

"Only just?" She arched her delicate eyebrows. "Then I'm glad I didn't arrive one day sooner. And I shudder to think how you broke him."

"Perhaps *broke* isn't the correct word. Still, it wasn't pretty." Then he bowed to her. "If you'll excuse me, I'll serve our drinks."

"That would be lovely."

Sam stepped over to the striking gold-inlayed liquor cabinet and small bar that ruled a corner of the room and set about measuring out the liquor. This put him behind his guest, who sat demurely with her back to him and looked around the room. Sam realized two things: his hands had stilled in his task, and he was staring longingly at the sweet nape of her neck. Feathery tendrils of curling hair graced her upswept hairline. He wanted very much to grip her by her bare shoulders, bend over her, and place hot kisses against her warm, soft skin.

What would she do if he did? Certainly he'd seen the invitation in her expression earlier today when he'd kissed her. Dare he try it again? Then, he heard himself sounding like a schoolboy angling for his first kiss. Disgusted, a bit embarrassed even, Sam turned his hand and his mind to the purely physical task of pouring out the fine whisky he stocked. With a host's smile on his face, he then rejoined his guest. As they awaited their call to dinner, he remained the perfect host by regaling her with his impressions of that afternoon's events and the people she'd met in town.

He made her laugh with his rendering of Mrs. LaFlore,

the excited shop mistress who had reaped the benefit of Yancey's shopping spree. *A nip tucked in at the waist and a bit more let out in the bust,* Mrs. LaFlore had sung out as she'd fluttered joyously around the ill-at-ease "duchess." She'd informed them that their timing was impeccable as she was just back from London with a new stock of fashionable samples to tempt the well-to-do ladies of the village. But she would be most delighted to sell them all to Her Grace the Duchess.

"No doubt she would have, too," Sam now remarked to his "duchess."

"She almost did," Yancey said, grinning.

Sam shrugged as if his generosity were of no consequence. "It was my pleasure. And a well-deserved punishment for my abominable behavior this morning . . . Yancey." He'd disliked the name at first, but somehow it seemed more fitting. It was unconventional . . . just like her. And wasn't his wife's name, either. "Again, I apologize for my barbaric behavior out in the garden."

Her expression sobered and she looked down.

Sam rushed on, wanting to restore the cheery feeling they'd achieved. "At any rate, ten gowns and all the appropriate underpinnings seemed like a nice round number. I feel certain Mrs. LaFlore will set all her seamstresses to work, now that they have your measurements, and will have the remainder of the gowns delivered by tomorrow."

Yancey favored him with a teasing smile. "And what about your nana's new traveling costume? Do you suppose it will arrive tomorrow, as well? She was so very excited by your purchasing it for her."

"Yes, she was. Though God alone knows when or to where she'll be wearing it. Perhaps in London at some point, I suppose. Still—and forgive my language—there will be hell to pay if it doesn't come tomorrow. She doesn't wait well. That grand and impossibly ancient lady *will* have her way."

"I have noticed that. But she couldn't be a sweeter, more endearing little woman. May I admit to some curiosity about her and ask how she's related to you?"

"Certainly. She's my great-grandmother on my father's side. Her actual name is quite intimidating. Margaret Mary-Alice Jane Thomas–St. Adair. And then Treyhorne, of course."

"Good Lord. But wait—Mary, Alice, and Jane? Those are her cats' names."

"Yes. She doesn't seem to be aware, though, that those names are also hers. At any rate, I hadn't anticipated her insisting on new dresses for herself, her nurse, then Robin, and even the redoubtable Mrs. Edgars."

To Sam's delight, this beautiful woman who wished to be called Yancey laughed . . . a sweet, soft sound that in his younger days would have had Sam on a knee in front of her and asking her to marry him. But given who he was now, and who she may or may not be, he simply sipped at his drink and awaited her.

"I remain certain," she said, "that it was not a usual event for someone in your position, Sam. Still, it was very good of you to stand back and allow their impassioned frenzy."

Sam basked unashamedly in her praise. "Yes. Wasn't it good of me?"

He then relived with her their lively party's departure from the shop, dress boxes in hand, and their triumphant march over to the men's tailor and haberdashery shop. There Sam had been informed by his nana that a new hat and suit of clothes was needed by Scotty as he was still a growing boy. The giant had stared dully at him to show his rampant appreciation.

Their spree had taken the entire afternoon. In between times and shops, Sam now told Yancey, he had spoken with several of the men regarding spring harvests and livestock prices. He'd even shared a pint with some of the local dignitaries at the pub while she and the rest of the women had been sorting through the various market stalls and making further purchases—all on his bill, of course.

At this point in their cheery discourse, and—as Sam remarked to himself—just as they were becoming comfortable with one another, Scotty opened the room's doors and announced dinner. As he'd done at luncheon, Sam offered Yancey his arm . . . and escorted his lady into the dining room.

In the deep, dark recesses of the night, Yancey was startled awake from her fitful slumber by the drawn-out creaking of a door being furtively opened—into her bedroom. Lying still, tense with apprehension, she slowly raised her head from her pillow and cocked her head at a listening angle. While her mind worked feverishly with the possibilities, she trained her gaze in the direction of the noise.

The room was as dark as if she'd loosened the tiebacks on the canopy's hangings and had immersed herself in their draping cocoon of warmth. But she hadn't, and even the dratted fireplace had gone cold. Not even repeated blinking could accustom her vision to the thick blackness of her bedroom. Indeed, it seemed to press right up against her eyes.

Since she couldn't see, she would have to rely on her other senses. And they told her that the sound had come from the dressing room door, the one that connected her room to Sam's. She knew that creaking sound. The door only made it when it was being pushed open, but not closed. So whoever this was, he was just now entering the room.

A frown of consternation found its way to Yancey's face. Did Sam mean to accost her every night in her sleep? Would she be rudely awakened, only to find herself flat on her stomach with him atop her and their limbs tangled? A sensual image of them thus entwined flitted through Yancey's mind, leaving her to shake her head at its insane workings, given the situation that now faced her.

*But what if it's not Sam?* Someone could have slipped through his room without awakening him. Or maybe had done him harm—her heart sank—and was intent on doing the same to her. But who, in heaven's name and in this household, would that be? Nana hadn't the strength or the evil intent. Scotty hadn't the intellect to be sneaking. Mrs. Convers, the nurse, was terrified of her shadow, as well as of Nana. And Mrs. Edgars, the imperious housekeeper, she

. . . Well, Yancey admitted, that woman was a definite possibility. More than once Yancey had caught her glaring at her for some unknown reason.

The creaking sounded again. Yancey's heart pounded against her ribs. Not with fright now, but with determination. She narrowed her eyes. Won't he—or she—be surprised to find that the intended victim, namely her, had a gun in her hand? Ever so slowly, Yancey smoothed her hand up under her pillow until she gripped the cold steel of her weapon. She fixed it in her grip and then turned over onto her back, counting on the rustling sounds her bedding made to pass for those she'd make in a natural sleep.

Ready now, her hair brushed out of her face, she waited. But not for long. Suddenly a huge form took shape right next to her bed. She had time only to gasp before a big rough hand was clamped over her mouth and warm breath bathed her face. Though terrified, and with a muffled cry escaping her, Yancey nevertheless managed to jerk her gun up and stick it against the first solid part of her assailant she could. She cocked her weapon. The sound was unmistakable and deafeningly loud. So was the man's startled curse.

"Son of a *bitch*!" Instantly his hand was lifted from her mouth and the dark shape retreated from the bedside. "You've got a gun! Don't shoot, Yancey. It's me—Sam."

Her heart pounding now with as much relief as anger, Yancey shot up as if she were spring-loaded. With her free hand she shoved her covers back. "What are you doing, Sam? Have you taken leave of your senses?"

"Put that gun down."

"I will not. I may yet want to use it. Don't think that just because you're you that I won't shoot you. Because I will."

"You will not. And keep your voice down."

"Why should I? Most ladies would be hysterical and screaming their heads off about now."

"And yet you remain calm and in possession of a gun."

"I'm nowhere near calm. Or feeling much like a lady right now." Several ticks of the clock went by. Sam said nothing. Yancey frowned, listening for any sound of his movement. "Sam?"

"I'm right here. Bear with me a moment."

She cocked her head in the direction of his voice. "What are you doing? You had best not be removing your clothes—"

"You flatter yourself. I'm fumbling my way over to the bed table to light a candle. Can I do that without getting shot?"

"Remains to be seen, doesn't it?"

"Will you *please* keep your voice down?" His whisper was urgent.

Yancey's matched his. "Will you tell me why? Have we been overrun by a marauding horde of heathens?"

"Hardly. But my mother has returned."

"Oh." Yancey's stomach flopped sickly. With the dowager duchess in residence, the moment of truth for Yancey's story had arrived. Her next thought had her frowning. "She risked the roads in the middle of the night?"

"She did, but it's not now the middle of the night." Yancey heard sounds that told her he was readying to light the candles by her bed. "It's after six A.M. already."

That was surprising. She'd had seven hours of sleep, yet she didn't feel the least bit rested. Thankfully, though, her mind seemed to be functioning. "Your mother rode all night in order to get here this early? That smacks of urgency, Sam."

"Very astute. Only she didn't return alone," he added cryptically.

That drew a sigh out of her. "Sam, I am no good first thing in the very early morning without coffee. So if you expect me to surmise who accompanied your mother, you're in for a long list of very bad guesses."

"I don't expect you to guess. Only, hold on a moment." Sudden light flared into the room, causing Yancey to blink. "There." Sam had put the match to the candles.

Feeling suddenly silly for holding a gun on him, she placed it next to her on the sheet. Now that she could make out his presence, she saw he was dressed decently enough in pants and a shirt. But his face, with his jaw shaded with stubble, appeared haggard in the candlelight that lit his profile. She inhaled deeply, feeling not only his sensual tug on her heart but a surprising urge to comfort him. "Sam, what's wrong? You can tell me. I'll help you."

Yancey surprised herself with the realization that she truly did want to help him. And she wanted him to trust her.

Sam closed his eyes and rubbed a hand over his forehead, then met her gaze. His gray eyes looked so haunted. "I'm not certain you can."

"I can do more than you realize, Sam. You can trust me."

He didn't say anything. He didn't have to. Clearly he doubted her—and with good reason, she knew.

"You *can* trust me, Sam, I swear it." She wanted to take his hand and hold it to her cheek. He'd been such a perfect gentleman at dinner and had taken great pains to entertain her. Despite his unorthodox way of awakening her, and the fright he'd given her, Yancey felt warmly toward him. Knowing that the time was fast approaching when she would have to tell him who she was, meaning a Pinkerton, she added quietly, "I'm not your enemy."

She could only hope he wasn't hers.

Sam exhaled a sigh. "I'm glad to hear you say that. Because I need you, and I have to ask you to do something."

Perhaps it was because they were in her bedroom, such an intimate cocoon of a setting. Perhaps it was because she was in the bed and he was standing so close to it and telling her he needed her. Perhaps it was because his shirt wasn't quite tucked in and was open at the throat, where she could see dark, crisply curling hair peeking out. Whatever the reason, she felt a softening in her belly and heard herself yielding to him. "Anything, Sam. Whatever you want."

He startled her by coming to the bed in a rush and taking her hand in his as he abruptly sat down. "I have to ask you to be my wife."

Yancey jerked, pulling her hand back. "Are you insane?" She stared in wide-eyed shock at the duke. "My pretense was nothing more than that—"

"I am fully aware of that. And I have had my reasons for allowing the charade to continue. But now, today, I truly need you to masquerade as my wife. It's very important, Yancey. Life or death."

She arched her eyebrows, her detective's instincts coming to the fore. "Life or death? Good heavens, Sam, who did your mother bring with her? The very devil himself?"

Sam let go of her hand. He sat with a hip perched atop the bed and his muscled leg dangling over the side. He rubbed a hand over his jaw, a frown shading his grim expression. "You're not very far off the mark. It's my cousin. Roderick Harcourt."

Well, that didn't sound so bad. Yet, given Sam's behavior, if the man wasn't the devil, he'd at least sold his soul to the beast. Yancey cocked her head, intent on digging for information. "I assume that this cousin is your aunt's son, since that's where your mother was?"

Sam nodded. "Yes. Aunt Jane is my mother's sister. Roderick is a first cousin. And much more. He is the Duke of Glenmore. And a very dangerous man steeped in court intrigues. He knows much more than he should about most people and isn't afraid to use the knowledge to his own gain."

Yancey leaned forward, gripping Sam's arm. A part of her mind noted that his skin felt warm and smooth, and his flesh hard, much as if he worked the fields. "What does he know about you that he could use against you?"

"I don't know. Maybe nothing."

"Maybe nothing? Then it could be something?"

"Possibly. It's hard to say."

Yancey considered him and his evasive answers. "Sam," she said carefully, "why are you so concerned about your cousin's being here?"

"Because of what I suspect *him* of."

"And what is that, Sam? You need to tell me."

Sam exhaled sharply. "I suspect him of somehow, if not directly, contributing to my brother's death."

A cold sickness invaded Yancey's limbs. "Your brother? Then your mother doesn't know of your suspicion, I take it? Otherwise, she wouldn't bring him here. If she's like most mothers, she would tear his heart out if she suspected such a thing."

"You're right in saying she knows nothing of my suspicion. To her, he's simply her nephew, her sister's son. And I intend to leave it at that unless I can and do prove otherwise. There's no sense in causing a needless rift between her and her sister, whom she loves dearly."

"Very good of you, Sam. But why do you suspect your cousin? And of what? I don't understand."

"I don't expect you to, not all at once." He shifted his weight as if signaling a change in subject. "I've taken the liberty of sending down to the kitchen to have our breakfast—mine and yours—brought up to my private sitting room. I came here to ask you to join me."

This was a startling—and an amusing—turn to Yancey. "Really? Sneaking around in the darkness and clamping your hand over a person's mouth? You have an odd way of inviting a lady to your room. I wonder that your entire breed didn't die out for such tactics."

At last, she'd wrung a grin from him, one that quickened her pulse. "I assure you I'm much more accomplished under less strained circumstances."

Smiling, Yancey raised her chin. "I shall take your word for it. And I shall be honored to join you for breakfast. I assume our topic of conversation will be your cousin and why you want him to believe that I am your wife?"

"Very astute of you. Will thirty minutes be enough time for you to dress and then join me? Do you need Robin's services?"

Yancey shook her head no. "I can manage without Robin, although the very idea that I can seems to break her heart. However, I'm used to taking care of myself."

Sam picked up her gun and brandished it pointedly between them. "I can see that."

"Yes. But where are your mother and cousin now? What are they doing?"

"They've both gone to bed. As you surmised, they've been on the road all night and are exhausted. I don't look for them to be recovered and up and about until late this afternoon at the earliest. Which is good because it will give you and me time to get acquainted."

"I thought we already were."

He still held her gun, smoothing his hand over it, hefting it for balance. "Nice weapon." Then he captured her gaze. "I don't think we are acquainted at all . . . Yancey."

Not if it meant her very life could Yancey maintain her eye contact with him. Instead, she picked at a thread in the bedcoverings and thought of all he needed to know about her. And all he didn't need to know.

Sam silently held her gun out to her. Meeting his gaze, seeing the questioning expression on his face, she took it from him. He surprised her by running his fingers over her cheek and jaw. His touch was feather soft. Then he exhaled, shook his head, and stood up.

Yancey struggled for something to say to break the spell. "Sam, you never told me why your cousin accompanied your mother here. A mere social call, perhaps? Or did she invite him?"

A smile that held a world of tenderness and intrigue claimed his features. "No mere social call. Roderick and I despise each other, but in this instance, I believe he's playing the solicitous nephew. To answer your question, he accompanied Mother because she's absolutely distraught. She was in no condition to tell me why she is, so Roderick did."

Sam looked away from her and swallowed. Even in the dim candlelight Yancey could see his throat work. Fear for him had her speaking his name softly. "Sam? What did he say?"

He gave her his attention, saying, "In short, Roderick—who looks like hell, I must add—said that on my mother's last day at his and his mother's home, she received a letter from America."

"Is that usual, her getting mail at her sister's home?"

"No. That's very odd."

Yancey could barely breathe. "Who was it from?"

Sam rubbed tiredly at his forehead. "He didn't say." Then he frowned. "And gave me no chance to ask. At any rate, Roderick said Mother received a letter that put her into a swoon and then had her insisting on making for home straightaway." Sam's expression became baleful, naked and exposed. "Apparently she's been told that my wife is dead."

Shocked, Yancey blurted, "He just said it out like that? My God, Sam, that is cruel. I am so sorry. You poor man."

Even as she spoke, she thought guiltily of what she knew about that poor woman back in Chicago who had been murdered. Had she been Sam's wife? Yancey stared up into Sam's haggard, hurting face. If all of this was true and that woman turned out to be his wife, Yancey knew she could swear with a clear conscience that Sam hadn't known until this moment that his wife was dead. It was there in his face. He was innocent. She expressed her condolences again. "Sam, I am so, so sorry you had to learn it this way."

He brushed away her words with an agitated wave of his hand. "Dress and join me in my room, Yancey. We have much to do."

He gave her no chance to respond or to further sympathize with him as he turned and walked away. After no more than a few steps, the room's darkness swallowed him up.

Yancey slumped atop her bed, her mind whirling with her thoughts. Uppermost was her growing suspicion regarding the Duke of Glenmore. With the arrival of this man, could it now be that the villain was in residence? With each passing second, she became increasingly certain of it. So certain that she would stake her reputation on it. And her life, if need be.

Her life. Would it come to that? Could it? She nodded. Yes. She suspected that should she agree to continue in her masquerade as Sam's wife, it could come to that. Her very life. Or possibly Sam's.

# Chapter Twelve

In a little less than thirty minutes, Yancey had quickly bathed and dressed in a belted rust-colored skirt and cream blouse. She had her hair pulled back and tied at her nape with a bit of ribbon. As she passed through the adjoining dressing rooms, she couldn't help but smile at how messy Sam's side was. If she wanted to be kind, she would say the details of life were of no concern to him. But he, no doubt, would say that that was what he had servants for.

Her conclusion carried her into his bedroom, where she stopped suddenly at the threshold and, filled with a sense of awe, looked around her. Here at last was the man's room revealed in all its masculine glory and not framed in partial detail by an open doorway, her only means before now of satisfying her curiosity. *So this is Sam's lair. Here is how he lives in private. And these are things with which he surrounds himself.*

Even while breathing in the unique masculine scent that permeated the very air, Yancey told her clanging conscience that she was simply being a good Pinkerton. Noticing the details, as it were. Like the heavy draperies done in a rich maroon. They were flung open, allowing in the day's dawning sunlight. And such masculine furniture the light revealed: the writing desk with papers spread messily across it, and the massive, rumpled bed with the coverings thrown back. To one side hunkered a huge armoire that revealed, through open doors, his considerable wardrobe. And a tall chest of drawers attested to Sam's harried state of mind. The drawers were pulled out and items such as underthings and shirts spilled out of them.

A fond yet ironic grin claimed her mouth. *Does the man not have a valet to pick up after him?* She thought about that and realized she'd heard no mention of one. Then who assisted him? Scotty? She shook her head no. She couldn't picture that slow-moving giant attending to the small fussy details that filled a valet's time. She concluded that Sam, then, must see after himself. Interesting—and unexpected. Yancey took another moment to notice Sam's more personal items lying about. If she was to masquerade as Sam's wife in earnest, then she should know some intimate details of his habits, shouldn't she? Things like how he flung his hairbrush aside. How he allowed his shaving mug to foam over. And there he'd tossed a wet towel over the dry sink's mirror. And here were last night's formal clothes draped over a chair.

Yancey knew one thing: if she were really his wife, this state of affairs would be rectified. The man would have a valet, mind you. Feeling slightly superior for her neat ways, Yancey crossed Sam's carpeted bedroom, intent now on joining the duke in his sitting room. Through the open doorway she smelled the wonderfully tantalizing aromas of bacon and coffee. But her next thought had her wondering if Sam was messy like this every day. Or if today was different because of the news he'd just learned about his wife.

*His wife. That poor woman.* Yancey wondered if any proof of her death had been given Sam. His Grace, the duke. *My duke,* she amended, since his cousin also carried the same title. A private smile tugged at Yancey's lips. She inexplicably found that she liked his lofty titles and formal forms of address. Absurdly, they now held a note of familiarity and of intimacy for her. An intimacy she was not entitled to with this man, her conscience railed.

Raising her chin stubbornly against those admonitions, Yancey reached the threshold of the sitting room, where she paused, a hand on the doorjamb as she looked around. Where was Sam? There was the breakfast cart, but the room, Spartan in decoration, yet somehow appropriate to the man it served, appeared to be unoccupied. She stepped farther into the room and looked around. Then she saw him. Her breath caught in her throat. So tall and commanding a presence he was. He stood across the way, staring out a long narrow window set in an alcove.

With his back to her, he was sipping at something, presumably a cup of coffee . . . although under these trying circumstances, Yancey avowed, whisky would have been forgiven. She noted that he was dressed like he'd been when he'd stolen into her room earlier to wake her up, only now he appeared neater. Certainly she'd seen the evidence as she'd passed through his bedroom that he'd cleaned up for the coming day.

Such a picture of masculine power and beauty he was. Yancey had to bite back a sigh of appreciation, not wanting to alert him just yet to her presence. First she wanted to drink her fill of the man . . . his black hair, so thick and wavy. His neck, a strong column. Such broad shoulders, narrowing to a slender waist and muscular buttocks. His long legs were encased in riding pants and Hessians.

Having traveled down his length, she flicked her gaze back up him and made a face of feminine despair. Why did her heart do a light, tripping dance with her pulse every time she saw him? Why did her blood sing and her belly softly throb? And what would she do with all those emotions when she had to leave? Not wanting to hear the answers to those questions, Yancey cleared her throat discreetly. "Sam?"

He turned around, his gaze warm, riveting . . . inviting. "Yancey," he said, a look of delight and relief edging his eyes. "Come in. Please. I'm sorry. I didn't hear you enter."

Mindful of his mourning state, she returned his smile and made excuses for him. "You were deep in thought, and I didn't wish to intrude on that."

He arched his dark eyebrows, his expression somewhere between amused and suspicious. "Then you've been standing there observing me?"

The fierce heat of embarrassed guilt bloomed on Yancey's cheeks. "Oh no, not long. Only a moment. Less than a moment." She willed herself to be done with chattering, but failed. "Actually, I just arrived."

"I see." He started toward her, striding confidently and gesturing to the breakfast repast spread for them. "Will you join me?"

"It would be my pleasure."

"Excellent." Standing at the table now, he placed his coffee cup in its saucer. "Please allow me to pull your chair out for you."

"Thank you." A bit puzzled by his formality, Yancey suddenly realized that a certain amount of rigidity might be the only thing that was holding him together. She made a mental note to watch him for signs of fragility or shattering. They seemed odd, those two words applied to this hale and hardy specimen of manhood. But no one was immune, and he had received quite a shock this morning.

Yancey smiled up politely at the duke as he seated her. She prepared to express her thanks, but the words never left her mouth. His nearness, as he hovered solicitously over her, enveloped her in the bay rum and the shaving cream and soap scents that were so much a part of him. When he picked up her napkin off the plate and placed it across her lap, Yancey fought wanting to close her eyes and inhale again out of sheer ecstasy. Only the fear that she would fall into a swoon and tumble right out of her chair kept her from indulging.

If he was aware of his effect on her, he didn't show it as he skirted the round white-cloth-covered table to take his seat opposite her. Employing a more offhand manner with himself, he plucked up his own napkin and draped it across his lap. Then he smiled at her, showing her his brilliantly white and even teeth. "See anything to your liking?"

*You.* Yancey blinked, wide-eyed . . . but then realized she'd only thought the word and hadn't spoken it aloud. Staring helplessly into his amazing gray eyes, she couldn't get her mouth to work correctly. Suddenly her jaw and teeth and tongue were not familiar with the other's workings.

"The food, Yancey. Is anything to your liking?"

Blessedly, she recovered the use of her faculties. "Oh. The food. Yes. Of course." In a tizzy of swirling sensations, she looked down at the breakfast offerings before her. Bacon, scrambled eggs, sausages, potatoes, toast, scones, coffee, cream, sliced fruit, and an assortment of pastries. Her stomach growled rudely. Yancey clutched at it, her eyes wide as she met the amusement dancing in his gray eyes. "Well, allow me to second that, Your Grace. I am obviously hungry."

He chuckled, leaving Yancey to realize that she liked making him laugh. "Shall we serve ourselves?" he suggested. "We can talk as we eat."

Yancey nodded. "Certainly."

The next several minutes passed in relative quiet, broken only by the sound of silver striking china as they filled their plates and began eating. After a relatively companionable interlude, Sam broke into the silence between them. "Tell me, do you have any distinguishing marks in any intimate areas of your person that I as your husband would know about?"

Unfortunately, his shocking question came at the same moment Yancey swallowed her bite of toast. It didn't go down correctly. She choked and coughed and couldn't speak, not even with the help of a generous gulp of water. Finally, she got it down—and stared wide-eyed at Sam through her tears.

The very picture of innocence while holding his knife and fork, he rested his wrists against the table's edge. "I'm so sorry. Did I embarrass you?"

Her voice rasping and watery, Yancey replied, "You came closer to killing me, Sam Treyhorne."

"Again, I apologize. I was simply trying to think ahead to any situation in which we might find ourselves where such knowledge would be essential."

Yancey leaned across the table toward him. "An example being . . . ?"

He shrugged. "My cousin could ask."

Yancey abruptly sat back. "Your cousin? Good Lord, Sam, the obvious impertinence on his part aside, should he dare to ask something so personal, you are assuming that I have agreed to this latest pretense of being your wife, are you not?"

"I am. And since you put it that way, you have yet to tell me why you came here using her name."

Yancey arched her eyebrows. "And you have yet to tell me why you allowed me to continue masquerading as the duchess."

"But I did. I told you quite plainly I did so because it pleased me."

"Ah. I do recall you saying that. And the other? Why you now wish me to portray your wife in earnest?"

His expression was every bit as arch as hers. "Because, for one thing, everyone here and in the village already believes you to be my wife. Therefore, it will be simpler to have you continue in that role for now than it would be to tell them all otherwise. We've not the time. And for another, I wish to throw Roderick off the scent. I want to see how he'll respond to seeing you obviously alive and well. And to see what he'll do next, like go home if there's nothing to be gained by staying."

"Good enough. But your poor mother? What will she think? Are we to lie to her, also?"

"It can't be helped at the moment."

"I don't like it, Sam."

"I don't ask you to like it. I ask you simply to play along just while Roderick is here. When he's gone, we'll tell everyone the truth. Of course, you'll have to tell them your portion of it as I don't yet know it."

Well, he certainly had her there. And she intended to ignore that he did. "So we're having a bit of sport with Roderick?"

"I'd hardly call it sport."

"Then what, Sam? You really must give me something to go on."

Sam sighed as if irritated by all her questions. "Yancey, Roderick is a very dangerous man politically. I'll have him knowing nothing of my private affairs that he could make public and ruin me and therefore my mother."

"While I can respect that, it is no kind of answer." Now

Yancey was irritated. "If I'm to be a part of this scheme, then I must insist on a straightforward answer. What exactly could he find out? What do you not want him to know?"

His expression stony, Sam glared into her eyes. "I can't tell you. I won't. Except to say I don't believe there is any physical danger to you, or I wouldn't be asking you to cooperate. Beyond that, I implore you to trust me and to help me, Yancey. I don't ask lightly. And I don't ask you to do anything that you haven't already been doing."

She didn't know quite what to say to that. Yet she suspected that with the arrival of Roderick Harcourt and Sam's response to him, she was now very close to the truth of the mystery that had sent her here in the first place. So she nodded, giving in for now. "All right, Sam. I'll do as you ask. But only because I wish to see how you explain *me* to your mother in the face of her having apparent proof that I—I'm sorry—that your *wife* is . . . please forgive me . . . dead."

Sam shook his head. "I've seen no proof. And my wife is alive and well."

"You mean me?"

Sam hesitated for a moment longer than an innocent person might. "Yes."

Yancey's mouth dried. "Sam, do you think that your wife *is* actually still alive?"

He sat back. "What an odd question. Of course I do."

"Then where is she?" Yancey's agitation—and barely admitted jealousy—had her leaning forward. "Why isn't she here?"

"She can't be. Now, please, Yancey, we don't have a lot of time to put our masquerade together. Roderick or my mother could awaken much sooner than I think they will. So please answer my question."

She blinked. "I'm sorry. I've forgotten what it was."

"Have you any distinguishing marks hidden about your person?" he repeated, clearly impatient with her.

Yancey put a hand to her cheek and stared at the man. "Again, Sam, I find it hard to believe that this cousin of yours would have occasion or the nerve to ask you such a personal thing about your wife."

Sam glanced at her, put down his fork, and picked up his coffee cup. He surprised her by shooting her a teasing grin. "You're right, of course. I just thought it was worth a try."

More titillated than offended, Yancey cried out. "Why, you scoundrel!"

Sam chuckled. "I never said otherwise."

"Well, what about you, sir? Any scars or moles I should know about?"

She refused to dwell on the fact that his real wife would already know. His very much alive wife. A sinking feeling in Yancey's stomach revealed more than she wanted to know about her own emotions where this man was concerned.

Sam eyed her over the rim of his cup as he took a swallow. He set the cup down and then his knife. "As a matter of fact, on my right thigh is a scar from a childhood run-in with an angry sow whose piglet I had the misfortune to be holding and making squeal."

"Dear God, you could have been killed."

"Exactly what my father said—right before he tanned my britches with a switch."

"I don't wonder. What in the world possessed you to do such a thing?"

"Say, you're very good at this. That is exactly what my mother said when she came to dry my tears. You see, my brother and I did it on a dare. The bet was who would stand there the longest, holding an unhappy piglet while the sow charged."

Yancey could only shake her head in disbelief. "Did you at least win?"

"Of course. And like I said, I have the scar to prove it."

"Of course. Silly of me to doubt you. How old were you?"

"All of eight. Geoff was ten. Both of us old enough to know better. But ever since then, the only time I care to see a pig is in the cured form." As if for emphasis, he picked up and chomped down on a piece of bacon, then waved the remaining portion at her. "Now it's your turn."

"All right, Your Grace." Yancey weighed what she should say and then decided it was high time to come clean. Besides, the shock of her story would serve him right for asking. "I have a fresh scar on my right upper arm that I got in a whorehouse fight when one of the ladies of ill repute shot at me as I was running away after I killed a man in her room."

Her honest confession had the desired effect. Sam choked on the bacon. Really choked. His face was red, his eyes teared up, and he was wheezing. Alarmed, Yancey jumped up, sending her napkin to the floor as she raced around to Sam's side of the table. She jerked his arm up over his head, shaking it as she pounded repeatedly on his back, which was what her mother used to do to her. He waved her off with his free hand and gasped in a huge breath. Yancey let go of his arm and stepped back. Coughing, he reached for his water and took a big gulp. And everything went down fine.

Relieved, a hand over her heart, and proud of herself for her successful intervention, Yancey swaggered back to her chair, sat down, and then leaned over to retrieve her napkin. She straightened up to see the duke, still teary-eyed, glaring at her. Placing the napkin across her skirt, she rounded her eyes to a look of innocence. "I'm sorry. Did I embarrass you?"

"What the hell"—his voice was rather raspy—"kind of story was that?"

"The God's honest truth."

He coughed hoarsely, still sounding wheezy. "You're telling me you're a whore?"

Yancey stiffened with offense. "I most certainly am not."

"Then what were you doing in a . . . a whorehouse?"

She took a deep breath. "I was working undercover." She saw him arch his eyebrows and realized that her wording was unfortunate. "Not under the covers in the way you're thinking. Not like the ladies of the house."

With his elbows on the table, and his color approaching his normal ruddy tan, the duke folded his hands together and stared unhappily at her. "I'm afraid the subtlety is lost on me, Yancey."

"Oh, all right. I'm a Pinkerton agent." There. She'd said it. She crossed her arms under her bosom and waited.

"And I, dear lady, am the King of Prussia."

"So pleased to meet you, Your Highness. At any rate, the

whore was the lady friend, shall we say, of a train robber. And I was in disguise as an elderly Christian woman come there to save her soul . . . and to question her about her man."

"You're starting to scare me."

"I scare many people. But it explains the gun—why I would carry one, and how I know how to use it—doesn't it?"

His changing expression, a begrudging, fatalistic one that involved lowered eyebrows and a decided frown, said he agreed that it did. "You're actually a Pinkerton agent?"

"I am actually a Pinkerton agent."

He shook his head. "So you say. However, I remain unconvinced."

"And pompous in your attitude."

He nodded. "A shortcoming of the breed, I'm afraid. But say you are a Pinkerton—"

"I say nothing. I am. And a darned good one, too . . . when I have more to do than pose as a duchess and make forays into villages to buy gowns I have no need of."

"Expensive gowns, I'll add. Now, I'm willing to concede the point for the moment that you're a Pinkerton because I know the man employs women. Still—forgive me, I cannot get past the very idea—what the devil are you doing here?"

"I told you. Your mother begged me to come."

He smacked his palm on the tabletop, causing the dishes and Yancey to jump. "I'll not listen to that. You're trying to get me to believe that my mother involved the famous American detective agency in an investigation of . . . what exactly?"

"Of nothing. We focus mainly on protecting the concerns of the various railroads."

Sam narrowed his eyes. "Did my mother have a sudden concern for the state of the railroads in England, then?"

"Dear God." Sighing, Yancey rubbed at her forehead. "She did not hire me, Sam. But I *am* a Pinkerton, and I *did* come here to help."

"Why? Why are you here at Stonebridge?"

Yancey thought of the ongoing review of her past cases that Mr. Pinkerton had initiated and of how she could be found negligent. "I have many reasons, some of them personal and to do with my employment back in Chicago. But to answer your question, I *am* here at your mother's bidding, mistaken though she was in her choice of correspondents."

"And what does all that mean, pray tell?"

"She wrote to the wrong woman. Me."

"Ah. The famous letters."

"Yes, the famous letters. I have no idea how she got my address. But she did, and she wrote to me several times. At any rate, my having the same name as your wife, and pretending to be her, got me inside your house. And then, very early this morning, *you* asked me to help you."

Sam's doubting expression remained unchanged.

Yancey leaned forward over the table, pushing her plate out of the way. "Less than an hour ago you asked for my help—*before* you knew I was a trained detective. And now that you do know, you hesitate? Sam, I can handle myself. But how the devil you expect me to help you unless you trust me and give me something to go on, I just can't say. And yes, only a few minutes ago I said you could keep your secrets, but now that you know who I am, I've quite changed my mind."

She sat back, making her point by stabbing a finger on the tabletop. "To be honest, it's a bit muddled from where I'm sitting, Sam. And I mean what exactly is going on here. So I'd be damned foolhardy to proceed from here—from this very table—without being better informed." She paused, staring levelly at him. "So what's it going to be? Do you want my help or not?"

He sat back, a stunned expression on his face. "Good God, you *are* a Pinkerton."

Pleased, Yancey gave a nonchalant shrug. "I told you so."

He looked at her differently, as if seeing her with new eyes. His delighted and curious gaze roved over her face, much as if he'd sighted a celebrated person of myth. "I understand you Pinkertons have code names."

"We do. And no, I'm not telling you mine. Now, I meant what I said. I won't help without first knowing everything that you know. Start with your brother."

Sam's expression fell. "Very well." He paused, exhaled, and then launched into his story. "Geoffrey was first-born and the heir. He was a good man, basically, and very well suited to the title. Or so I thought. As it turns out, he had gambling debts I didn't know about until recently. And I only found them out when the markers were turned in by the men he owed. The total sum is staggering, but one he could have well afforded to pay. They would have had no need to kill him over it. But add to that his penchant for other men's wives, and you begin to see a broader picture."

"Indeed. And I understand he died almost a year ago?"

"Yes." He looked taken aback. "How did you know that?"

"Scotland Yard."

"Scotland Yard? What the devil? Why would they be involved? I've told no one that I think his death is suspicious."

"They're not involved, but they have heard rumors. And more than one of them called your brother's death suspicious. At any rate, I went there first on some Pinkerton business unrelated to this. And men like to talk to a pretty face." Yancey grinned and batted her eyelashes at him. His eyes widened and he sat back. Yancey proceeded. "How did he die, your brother?"

"In his sleep, actually. I wasn't here then. I was still in America. But he passed away at our London residence. And Mother said the doctors believed he had succumbed from natural causes."

"But you have no faith in their assessment?"

"No. He was only thirty-three at the time. Two years older than me. Mother said he appeared troubled in his last days. She also said he was pale and dropping weight."

Yancey raised her eyebrows. "Gambling debts weighing heavily?"

"Perhaps. Though it sounds like an illness of some sort."

"Could have been. So why do you suspect your cousin of foul play?"

"Do you know, I really can't say. But I have from the very moment I received Mother's letter informing me of his death. The instant I read that her sister and Roderick were visiting them when Geoff took ill and died, I have had my suspicions."

"Did you do anything about your suspicions? Confront your cousin? Hire an investigator?"

"When I first came home and found out about Geoff's debts, I had a scene with Roderick where he denied being involved beyond the gambling. Still, I had my solicitor have someone discreetly look into the circumstances surrounding my brother's death, but nothing came out of it. No proof, at least. I admit I let it go, or at least kept it in the family, wanting to spare my mother and her sister."

"I see. So there was nothing as obvious as—forgive me, I don't mean to be insensitive—gunshot wounds or a knife?"

Sam shook his head no. "Nothing like that."

Yancey worried her lower lip with her teeth. "Hmm. Who discovered that Geoffrey was dead?"

"Actually, Mrs. Edgars, the housekeeper."

Yancey winced. "Lovely woman. But what was she doing in his rooms?"

"Checking the maids' work, evidently. Only they hadn't been in yet because he hadn't awakened. So, poor Mother. Until I could get here, there she was with only her sister, Jane, the dowager Duchess of Glenmore. And that bastard Roderick."

"You really don't like him."

"I never have. But it goes deeper than simply not liking him. He's cruel. Like a badger. Even as a child he was sly and underhanded. Always cheated at games. And tattled on Geoff and me. He even tormented poor Scotty."

"My. A most unlikable man."

"Exactly. And as I said earlier, he's very much involved in court intrigues and the seamier social swirl of London. And the bastard had involved Geoffrey in his dealings, too. Corrupted him, he did."

"Certainly Roderick sounds jaded and unscrupulous, but, Sam, what would he stand to gain from your brother's death? What does . . . I'm sorry, *did* your brother have that Roderick might want? The answer to that is your clue."

Sam eyed her. "I don't suppose I can say. Roderick has

his own title and lands and wealth. But he's always been jealous of my brother and me. He says everything came so easily for us and so hard for him. When we were young, his own mother would throw our accomplishments in his face." Sam stopped talking and frowned. "Poor bastard. I can almost feel sorry for him when putting it like that."

"He does seem pitiable."

"Well, if he was, he certainly outgrew it. Or grew into it, perhaps. He went on to become a nasty, vile man."

"Well, jealousy is certainly enough of a motive for some people to kill. No wonder you don't wish him to know your private affairs. Is Roderick married?"

Sam made a scoffing sound. "No. No self-respecting mother would consider him for her daughter. And that's despite his being a duke. He's simply not welcome in the finer homes. It's that cruel streak of his, coupled with his well-known gambling and indiscretions of the bedroom. That sort of thing has cachet in some circles, but not in genteel drawing rooms or salons."

"No doubt. How old a man is he? I ask because from what you say it sounds as if he were a playmate."

Sam quirked his mouth. "Not by choice but by blood. But to answer your question, he's thirty-five."

"Interesting. For some reason, I supposed him to be older. As if one must have many years behind one to be so accomplished at treachery. However, my many cases have proven otherwise."

"You sound very much the world-weary and seasoned detective. How many years do you have behind you?"

"Twenty-six."

"A mere child. And never married?"

"No. Well, yes—to you, actually, and for the several months before we ever met."

He looked askance at her. "I fear I'm going to hate myself for asking, but will you clarify that for me, please?"

"Certainly. Your mother thought I was your wife and wrote telling me that you were in trouble and needed my help."

Sam's expression soured. "Why would she think I needed my wife's help?"

"She didn't say in her letters. Perhaps with one son gone, she simply wanted her remaining son's wife to be here with him and her."

Sam's expression hardened. "That wasn't possible."

And here was another, very interesting piece of the puzzle. "Again, may I ask why?"

Sam looked away from her before answering. "All right. Because we were . . . estranged, at best."

"I see. Estranged." Yancey was embarrassed for him and what had to be a painful admission. She watched Sam another moment before trying for his attention. "Sam?" He swung his gaze to her. "Is that, the estrangement, why no one here, with the exception of you, of course, knows that I'm *not* your wife?"

"Yes. Like you, Sarah is American. We met and married in America and lived there. And separated there."

Yancey nodded. "And your mother knew of this estrangement?"

"Of course. Now you tell me why my mother would think *you* are my wife."

"For two reasons. I have the same name, and I live in Chicago."

Sam shook his head wonderingly, roving his gaze over her face. "An amazing coincidence."

"I thought so, too. Now, from this point on I'm only guessing, but I have a theory based on many years of experience in matters such as this one."

"Guessing about what?"

"Your mother. My guess is, for whatever reasons she has, she hired an investigator to find your wife. Not a very good detective, evidently, since he concluded I was your wife and reported my address to her. Obviously, she had him send his reports to her sister's and not here since she didn't want you to know of her activities. We know that much since Roderick told you she received a letter there."

"Go on." Sam considered her with deepening gray eyes.

Yancey's next thought had her mouth opening in surprise.

"But wait, I've just thought of something else. The address she gave me to answer her—and how I knew to come here—was this one. Why would she do that if she didn't want you to know what she was doing?"

Sam raised his eyebrows. "She probably hadn't thought it through that far."

"This is very frustrating. Why don't we just wake her up and ask her?"

Sam's expression was one of mock horror. "No. You don't know my mother, Yancey, but she is . . . dramatic. Easily overwrought. You'd have better luck right now getting answers from Mr. Marples the dog than you would her. I love her dearly, but I would rather be dragged behind horses than confront her with anything when she's got herself into such a state as she was this morning. It could go on for days. It's best to allow her to rest for now."

"Oh. I see. Well, perhaps you could look at her letters to me and see if you can discern any meaning in them that may have been lost on me."

"I would love to do just that, Yancey," he drawled meaningfully, "except you said you don't have them."

Caught. Yancey picked at a crumb on the table. "Oh. That." Then she smiled brilliantly at him. "Well, *that* I lied about. I do have them."

He remained unamused. "You lied. How, then, am I supposed to believe you now when you say you are a Pinkerton come here to rescue us all?"

"Because I *do* have the letters from your mother. They *are* addressed to me in Chicago. And if you need further proof of my employment, I have a letter I wrote yesterday to Mr. Pinkerton, one I tried unsuccessfully to mail since *someone* wouldn't allow me to go into town unaccompanied. Now, why would I do that if I didn't work for him?" Sam said nothing. Yancey exhaled her irritation. "I repeat . . . *would* you like to see the letters, Sam?"

"Yes. I believe I would." He tossed his napkin onto the remains of his breakfast and stood up, signaling for her to precede him. "After you."

"As you wish." Yancey stood and, swishing her skirt out

of her way with a practiced gesture, escorted the duke toward her rooms. As they passed through his bedroom again and into the dressing room, she commented, "I can certainly complain convincingly to your cousin—strictly from a wife's point of view, of course—that you are a messy person."

Behind her, he grunted what was no doubt a comment of her opinion. "That's what servants are for. If I wished to clean up after myself, they would have no employment."

Still walking, Yancey threw her response to him over her shoulder. "I knew you'd say that about the servants. Tell me, did you have servants when you were in America?"

"No. I did for myself."

"Not very well, though, I take it?"

# Chapter Thirteen

Sam could not believe her. Here he was trailing after her through her . . . yes, very neat . . . side of the shared dressing room and into her bedroom. And she was insulting him. "I'll have you know that I did very well in America without servants. I had no problems," he finally responded to her question.

She whirled around. "No problems? Let me count them out for you. You tell me your brother died under suspicious circumstances." She ticked his life off on her fingers. "You left your estranged wife in America. Your mother writes frantic letters to her—or me—begging me—her—to come here and help, but she doesn't say why. Then, when I get here, you don't disavow anyone of the notion that I am *not* in truth your American wife. And now you *want* me to masquerade as your wife to fool your family. I still don't know why. *And* you have Roderick whom you obviously suspect of some foul deed or the capability to commit one. And you say you have no problems?"

About halfway through her tirade, Sam's growing impatience had tightened his jaw. He worked it now, feeling a muscle there jump. "What I said was I didn't have any problems with *neatness* while in America. But allow me to ask some questions of you."

Petite, fiery, she gestured widely, her green eyes guileless, her dark auburn hair framing her lovely face. "Ask away. I have nothing to hide."

"We'll see about that." Sam steeled himself against his intense attraction to her because he had only a matter of hours to get everything in place before they faced Roderick, as well as his unsuspecting mother, that poor, dear woman, who would awaken to find that her daughter-in-law, whom she believed dead, had been miraculously resurrected and plopped down in England.

Just as Sam opened his mouth to ask his questions, he heard behind him, back in his rooms, a rustling around and dishes clattering. The staff clearing away the breakfast? Damned quick and efficient—and inconvenient—of them. "Bloody hell. I'll not suffer interruptions."

"Where are you going?" Yancey called out to his back.

"Nowhere." He strode over to the door to the dressing room, encountered the surprised Mrs. Edgars across the way as she entered his bedroom. "Mrs. Edgars, what *are* you doing in here?"

She curtsied. "I thought I heard something, Your Grace."

"Indeed? Like what?"

She folded her hands together in front of her. "I'm sure it was nothing."

Sam suffered the unsettling feeling that she'd perhaps been listening outside the door in the hallway. He certainly hoped not, given his and Yancey's revealing conversation. But then he dismissed his disquiet. Mrs. Edgars was merely doing her job, and today he was suspicious of everyone, it seemed. "Well, carry on, then. Have this breakfast cleared away."

"Yes, Your Grace."

Sam nodded to her, and then closed the door forcefully, making a point that he'd best not be bothered in his *wife's* chambers. He marched over to Yancey, grabbed her arm and, ignoring her widened eyes and outraged sputtering protests, hurried her to her sitting room on the other side of her bedroom, where he also closed that door behind them. Still with her in tow, he took them to the windows where he finally released her and threw open the heavy drapes to light the dim interior of the room.

Standing in profile to the long window, he turned to his guest, whom he needed most desperately to play the part of his very-much-alive wife. "And now, Miss Pinkerton Agent, you're going to answer my questions." He crossed his arms over his chest and, bending a knee, shifted his weight to one leg.

Facing him, barely one-third his size, she mimicked his pose, right down to crossing her arms. "Ready when you are, sir."

"Fine. Earlier you said that my mother had written you letters, meaning more than one was sent to you. My question is, why did you allow her to go on thinking she was corresponding with my wife?"

"There was no correspondence in the strictest sense of the word. Meaning I didn't answer her letters."

"Not even to tell her she had the wrong woman?"

"No. My work keeps me out in the field for weeks on end. So my mail is held by my landlady until I can retrieve it. By the time I got around to reading it all, your mother had written me four letters, starting last November."

This surprised him. "Why, I'd been here as long as four months before she sent the first one—"

"Four months?" Frowning, Yancey began counting on her fingers.

"What are you doing? Did I say something significant?"

"I don't know. Maybe. So you left Chicago last July?"

"Yes. Almost a year ago. Why?"

She smiled up at him. "I'm so glad you told me that."

"Glad? Why? What in the world did my mother say in her letters?"

"You may read them, if you like. But they all say the same thing, really. That she was very concerned about you and wanted your Sarah to come to England. She wrote that you desperately needed her help. But she didn't say why you did."

Agitation seized Sam. He ran a hand over his jaw and planted his other hand at his waist. He looked away from

Yancey and stared out the window. Then he heard himself speaking his thoughts aloud. "This is all so very strange. I must ask her first thing when she awakens."

"I'm sure she meant well, Sam. From the tone of her letters, I believe her heart was in the right place."

Sam turned to look at Yancey and was struck by her petite size and by the absolute fragility of her. Coupling that with her exquisite beauty and coloring, he could only compare her to the porcelain dolls little girls played with. "What am I doing drawing you into this intrigue, Yancey? You're a stranger. An innocent in all this. I can't involve you further and shouldn't have in the first place."

Yancey knitted her brow into a show of surprise. "I'm afraid it's not your decision. I involved myself by coming here to Stonebridge."

Sam hated that answer. "And I can end your charade right now by sending you away."

She struck a defiant pose, her hands planted at her narrow waist. "Are you speaking now as the imperious duke who owns everything and who can order me off the place? Because if you are, I'd best remind you that while you say you don't need your wife's help, you do say you need mine to help you fool everyone into thinking I'm her. And I still don't know why. Not really."

"It's not a simple thing to talk about, Yancey. In fact, it's very painful."

She dropped her pose and looked uncertain. "Oh. I'm sorry."

"No need to be. Instead, tell me why you came here, knowing my mother had the wrong person."

"Because about the time the first of your mother's letters arrived, my cases—all of them undercover—began to go sour. Then someone exposed my identity. Remember the whorehouse?"

His very droll reply was, "I shall never forget it."

"No doubt. In that incident, my identity was exposed to the lady of the night, who would surely talk, thus making me vulnerable. And that can be certain death in my line of work since I unavoidably make so many enemies among the criminal element. Mr. Pinkerton thought I should journey here to see if there was a connection."

Despite himself, Sam found himself intrigued. "Well, it does make a certain amount of lopsided sense, I suppose, given that your name is the same as my wife's. Do you think, now that you're here, that the events *are* connected?"

She shrugged. "Too soon to tell. But given your concerns with Roderick and your suspicions regarding your brother's death, and the fact that the people involved—I include your mother, however innocent her involvement may be—seem to be coming right here to us all at once, I have to admit that I am intrigued." She laughed. "I've never had a case like this one where I've not even had to leave the house to investigate it or to solve it, where the suspects arrive on the doorstep, as it were."

"Indeed." Sam ran a thumb over his bottom lip and stared at Yancey's beautiful face. "Tell me, why *did* you present yourself as the duchess when you arrived here? Why not the truth?"

She exhaled. "When I was on your doorstep, it became apparent to me that the truth was not as expedient as a quick lie."

"How so? I don't follow you."

"I know. Allow me to explain. Think about you and me and our intellects, Sam, and how difficult all this is to sort out between us. Also think about how much explaining we're having to do to each other." She paused as if to allow time for those points to sink in with him. "And now remember that *Scotty* answers your door."

Sam frowned. "What does he—?"

"A kind soul, Sam, but not a towering intellect. Now add to that a driving rain when I arrived."

"I remember. So, a complicated story, Scotty, and a driving rain. With you so far."

"Good. He didn't want to let me inside."

Understanding finally dawned. "Ah. Of course. So you said the only thing that would cut through his thickness. You said you were the duchess."

"Exactly. Sam, where *did* you get him?"

"I didn't. Nana did. It was right after my father died. She simply appeared one day with this big, big boy of about eight years of age and said his name was Scotty and that she was keeping him. That's all anyone knows."

"You never questioned her further? Or Scotty, either?"

Sam raised his eyebrows. "You're free to try your expert hand at it with either one of them."

"No. I think I shall refrain. However, I did expect *you* to put the lie to my duchess story. Which you didn't."

He had to look away from her. Cursing himself for being so tongue-tied around one tiny woman, Sam focused instead on the scene outside the window . . . the sun rising over the green hills, the spring day beginning, the countryside stirring. "I had every intention of doing so, believe me."

He sought her gaze. He wanted to see her face, see her reaction. "But then . . . I saw you. Right here, in fact, in front of this very window. You had your back to me. And I was intrigued. A part of me wondered what it would be like to have a woman like you as my duchess. And another part of me wanted to see what your game was, how long you would carry on the charade."

With her face uplifted to his and her lips apart, she was utterly entrancing. Sam wanted nothing more than to kiss her soundly. He was lying. He wanted nothing more than to *begin with* kissing her soundly. She then surprised him by stepping in closer to him and putting her hand on his arm. Her touch was warm, riveting. Sam clamped his jaw shut and braced his knees. Much more of this intimacy and he'd be carrying her off to bed.

"Sam, you knew, didn't you, even before you saw me on the day I arrived, that your actual wife couldn't possibly be here? Am I right?"

The warmth of the moment fled. Sam stared down at her. An old hardness that not even Yancey's nearness could dissipate infiltrated his bloodstream and left him cold. "Yes, you are right. I knew better. But I don't like talking about this."

"I know. You've said." She removed her hand from his arm and stepped back. "And yet I'm afraid you have to, if you want my cooperation."

"You have no idea what you're asking of me, Yancey."

She held his gaze with the strength of her own. "You're asking a lot of me, too, Sam. I can tell this is hard for you. But it has to be this way. I admit that until now I've been the one to involve myself. But if I'm going to agree to help you from here on out, then I have to know everything."

Sam roved his gaze over her high forehead, across her delicate cheekbones, and down her jaw. She had the pinkest skin and lips and the greenest eyes. Quite arresting. But more importantly, and he'd only just realized this, she looked kind. In fact, her entire demeanor was that of a caring woman. Why hadn't he noticed this before? *Blame lust,* he accused himself. "All right, Yancey," he began slowly. "Despite what my mother was told and what I told you this morning, my wife is *not* dead."

"You sound awfully certain of that."

There was a tone to her voice that Sam couldn't identify. Suspicion. Or challenge, maybe. He didn't like it. "That's because I know all too well that she is alive." Yancey raised her eyebrows, increasing Sam's irritation. "All right, then, I suppose I'm *assuming* she is alive. At least, she was when I left America." Yancey said nothing, merely nodded. Sam braced himself to speak aloud—and for the first time—of his personal cross to bear. "What I'm about to tell you not even my family knows. But I believe Sarah to be alive and well in Chicago. I say 'well' but that's not completely accurate."

"Then what is, Sam?"

"I mean she's physically well. At least she was at last report. But she's in an asylum, Yancey . . . for the mentally infirm."

Yancey's surprised exhalation of breath came out on one word. "Oh."

"Yes. Oh." Sam steeled himself for her further response.

"So that's why you weren't distraught over news of her death," she said, frowning in concentration. "You believed she wasn't dead." Then she nodded. "Yes. I daresay your behavior makes sense now."

Her comment on his behavior aside, Sam couldn't have been more surprised by her very practical and unemotional response. For years he'd lived with the oppressive shame and guilt of his wife's growing mental instabilities and with having to commit her. He'd feared being looked upon as coldhearted or conniving for having her put away. And perhaps he still would have to face that from other people. But apparently not from this woman. A grateful warmth for her spread through Sam.

Then, some new thought apparently struck her and had her turning widened green eyes up to him. "Oh, Sam, oh no. You poor man. Your wife."

"Yancey, what's wrong?"

Looking supremely sad, as if the life had been drained out of her, she closed her eyes and slowly shook her head.

Sam gripped her arms. "Yancey? What is it? Tell me."

She opened her eyes. They brimmed with sympathy. "Sit down, Sam."

"I will not." He let go of her and stepped back. "Not until you tell me what you mean."

"Oh, Sam, I'm so sorry to be the one to tell you." She covered her face with her hands and then lowered them, showing him her sad eyes. "The report your mother received may not be wrong. In fact, I'm very much afraid it's not."

Sam couldn't move, couldn't speak. He stared at her, feeling suddenly hollow and cold throughout. "What do you know? Tell me."

Her expression intensified. "Sam, you really need to sit down. I've got some bad news for you. News you've already heard once today, but which I must verify, I'm afraid."

Yancey sat with Sam on the grassy crest of a rounded hill situated between the ancient stone manor and the Cumbrian Mountains that provided its brooding backdrop. Barely a breeze blew and the air smelled sweet with the riotous blooming of colorful wildflowers. Only the occasional bumbling bee that buzzed curiously by and a songbird, happy with its existence, dared disturb their conversation. Not that there was any at the moment. Instead, she and Sam were sitting quietly. Yancey waited upon whatever Sam might want to say.

She exhaled sadly. There was nothing worse than being the bearer of bad news. She'd told Sam about the other Sarah and why she believed that woman might have been his real wife. He'd become quite agitated and almost unmanageable. Yancey had quickly suggested that they come outside, that they walk some and put a bit of distance between themselves and the oppressive though sleeping presence of his family. Her hope was that the soothing countryside and the cool yet rapidly warming day would settle Sam's troubled heart, even if only for the space of an hour or two.

Suddenly he pointed off into the distance. "Look there, Yancey."

"Where?" A thread of alarm unraveled along her nerves, making her wish she'd brought her gun along. She strained to see what had caught his eye. He directed her attention down the hill and off to his right. Since she was seated to his left, she got up on her knees, steadied herself with a hand on his solidly muscled shoulder, and peered around him. "What am I looking for, Sam?"

As if it were the most natural thing in the world for him to do, he put his arm around her waist to steady her. "See that cottage down there? The one next to the mill? With the many pens behind it?"

"I think so. Yes." Yancey could barely think with his hand on her. His touch seared through her clothing, leaving her a bit breathless. Then she caught sight of what he meant, and realized it looked a perfectly innocent cottage. "What about it?"

"That's where Geoffrey and I played our game of dare with the sow."

How odd that he would think of that in such dire circumstances. Yancey glanced down at Sam's profile and saw his faraway look and soft smile. Perhaps it wasn't so odd, she decided. Maybe right now he needed the memories of a more innocent time. Yancey played along, even laughing. "And look—there are still pigs down there."

His chuckle accompanied her sitting back down as he

gripped her elbow to steady her. Yancey arranged her skirt around her legs. "I have to thank you, Sam. Because now, if suddenly asked by Roderick where the pig farm is, I'll know."

He smiled, showing even, white teeth. "Then perhaps you should also know that the stone bridge for which the manor is named is located over there." He swung his arm to her left. Yancey's gaze followed his lead. "You can't see it from here," he informed her. "But that's where it is. Those trees meandering along that trickling stream over there hide it. It's not very impressive. Small, even. But now you know."

"Now I know," Yancey repeated, more interested in watching Sam's face. It alarmed her that she cared so deeply about his state of mind and his every mood. Her mother's warning to her about never marrying, about not giving up her independence, once so loud in her ears, now seemed to be fading further and further away, the longer she spent time in this man's presence. So did Mr. Pinkerton's admonition to his agents not to entangle their emotions in their work.

"It's not as it seems, Yancey. I didn't just abandon my wife," Sam said suddenly, riveting her attention to his face. "I had no means, beyond heavy and continual sedation, for getting her back with me to England. She was in one of her violent moods at that time. In fact, she'd already tried to kill me twice before I finally admitted defeat three years ago and called in a doctor."

"Dear God, Sam. She tried to kill you?"

His frowning expression intensified. "Yes. Once she set a fire in our bedroom—with me in the bed."

*They shared a bedroom*, was all Yancey could think. A more logical part of her mind reminded her that she was not his wife, no matter the pretense, and well she would do to remember that salient fact. Yancey blinked back to the moment and heard Sam still talking.

". . . put it out quickly without realizing at the time that she'd set it deliberately. But there was no mistaking her second attempt. She came at me with a knife. I never knew what would upset her or what I'd done, if anything." He pulled at a blade of grass and heaved a sigh. "And I still don't. Worse, early on, I never knew, when I left the house, what state I'd find her in when I came home."

A sudden insight had Yancey asking, "Was her . . . behavior why you didn't have servants in America?"

He nodded. "Yes. We had a small staff at first. But as her madness progressed, how could I leave some poor, unsuspecting maid alone with her? I did try hiring companions, but they never stayed. Too afraid. I don't blame them. There at the last, I had no choice except to care for her myself."

"I see. Her family couldn't help you?"

"She had none. She was alone in the world. An heiress from New York. That's where I met her. The impoverished second son—that's me—takes a well-to-do wife. And she was ten years older than me." Sam looked into Yancey's eyes. "Not exactly a love match, is it? Or 'was' it, I suppose I should say."

Yancey lowered her gaze to her lap and picked at a fingernail. "I'm so sorry, Sam." She looked up. "But what about your mother? Couldn't she have helped?"

His expression hardened. "No."

Yancey lowered her gaze. "Of course. You never told her about Sarah's madness. Otherwise she wouldn't have written to her daughter-in-law."

"Exactly." The look he sent her was hard, proud. He didn't say anything for a moment more, but then his expression clouded. "I sounded resentful just then, didn't I? I mean about losing everything because of Sarah's sickness and especially when it was her money to begin with."

Swept with sudden sympathy, Yancey shook her head. "Sam, only if you were a saint could you not have at least some hard feelings."

"Well, I'm certainly not a saint. I've barely been accused of being a gentleman."

"I think you are. A gentleman, I mean. And while you may not be a saint, I do think you behaved nobly with regard to her."

He shook his head. "You can't say that. You weren't there. It was an awful struggle. And I wasn't always kind . . . as you yourself have seen."

Yancey smiled her sympathy. "None of us is always on our best behavior, Sam."

"Now *you're* being kind and forgiving me too easily."

He was right. She was more than ready to forgive him anything. Feeling as transparent as a pane of glass where he was concerned, she carefully avoided meeting his eyes. "I just don't see how you or anyone else could have been unfailingly kind in that situation. You had to have been exhausted at times. And very frustrated." In truth, Yancey felt so sad for the young husband he had been, probably full of ideas and ideals, all of which he'd been forced to abandon—as had his wife. *That's right*, she reminded herself. *His wife*. She now looked up at him and found him watching her. "Tell me about your Sarah."

He looked away from her. "My Sarah. Funny. I never thought of her in that way." He exhaled. "But you asked me about her." He was quiet a moment, then began by repeating her name—and Yancey's real one. "Sarah. Her madness came on slowly. In between episodes, she was loving and kind. She tried hard and didn't ever seem to remember her . . . worst moments."

"And you didn't tell her, either, did you?"

"No. What good would that serve? At any rate, and even on her best days, she hated the ranching country where we lived. You see, I was experimenting with cattle stock, how to improve it. And I got involved in horse breeding. Mostly Thoroughbreds."

"That explains the beautiful animals I've seen here."

He smiled as if genuinely pleased. "You noticed. All I had to bring back with me were my ideas and experience and use them here."

"Well, at least that's something, Sam."

"Yes." His expression became far away. "You'll get around to thinking of it at some point, Yancey, so let me just say now that I did not have my wife killed. I can't say the thought didn't ever cross my mind. I am only human. But when I got to that point with her, of actually considering it, I allowed her to be committed."

"I believe you, Sam," she said quietly, knowing in her

heart that were he capable of violence, all he would have had to do was . . . kill his wife and bury her. Yancey knew firsthand that it was very easy, out on the prairie, to explain away a missing person. Snakebite. Sickness. A bad fall. Happened all the time. Just shoot them and bury them. That was all it took. And no one would ever know. She saw herself digging the two graves . . . her parents' graves. Eight years ago.

"Good," Sam said suddenly, pulling Yancey back to the moment and holding her gaze with his gray eyes the color of slate. "I'm glad you believe me. More than anyone else in my life, I very much need you to."

Moved, her throat working, Yancey fought to keep an understanding smile on her lips. "I have to tell you something else, Sam. Before I left Chicago to come here, I told as much as I knew of all this to Mr. Pinkerton. I showed him the letters from your mother. And he knew about the man in the whorehouse I shot. And he also knew about the other Sarah Calhoun being killed. Now, the description of her murderer matched that of the man I shot. So Mr. Pinkerton began an investigation that very day, Sam."

"What are you saying, Yancey?"

"I'm saying that I believe the agents he put on the case will probably have already found the trail to the asylum where Sarah was—or maybe still is. The only way we'll know for sure if your wife is actually dead or alive is to see if she is or isn't there. If she isn't, they'll find out soon enough what happened to her. They're good. They'll find out where she went, too, and why she was released, things like that."

He nodded, his throat working. Sam looked down at the ground and then up, but still facing away from Yancey. "She wouldn't be released. She—There was no hope that she'd ever . . . get better."

Yancey wanted to cry, it was so sad. "Maybe she escaped."

He shrugged. "Unlikely, but possible. She could have." He was quiet a moment. In an increasingly emotional state herself, Yancey studied his troubled profile. Then, with vehemence, he all but cried out, "God forgive me, Yancey, I hope she is dead. I don't like to think of her suffering, and I would never do anything to harm her. But being alive, for her, was more suffering than a person should have to bear. When she wasn't violent, she was withdrawn and confused. There was no joy, no understanding for her."

Yancey could only stare at him, wondering how she should proceed with him—a man who had sacrificed his life for a woman who probably had no idea he had, for a woman who had tried twice to kill him in her demented rages. It was time for Sam's hurting to stop. It was time for him to live again. Yancey reached out to him, putting a hand on his arm. "Sam?" He settled his hurting gaze on her. "Don't do this to yourself. You've suffered long enough."

His face colored with high emotion, and his expression hardened. He nodded and again looked away from her. After a moment, he said, quietly, hoarsely, "Perhaps. Go on with what you were saying."

Yancey thought quickly. What had she been saying? Then she had it. She lowered her hand to her lap and said, "We were talking about the investigation in Chicago. I don't believe it's inconceivable, Sam, to think that the agents may already have the answers for us. You see, with my life in danger, Mr. Pinkerton made this case a priority and had agents assigned to it right away. Now, that was over a month ago when I left Chicago. So if they found something weeks ago, and accounting for the length of time it would take to get a letter here to me, one could arrive at any moment from them."

Sam swung his gaze her way. Yancey was relieved to see that he looked more himself now, more caught up in living. "That makes sense. Would they know you were here, though? Or would they think you were in London at my residence there? After all, this is the height of the season and they could reasonably assume you'd be there if I was."

"Mr. Pinkerton will send his findings to Scotland Yard. They know where I am and would send it along. Remember, I was in London before I came here."

Sam nodded. "I remember. But what was I supposed to

think, Yancey, before today, before you told me who you are, if a letter had arrived for you from Scotland Yard?"

"I'd been worried about that," she confessed, grinning guiltily. "I suppose I would have had to tell you at that point."

"Obviously." He looked at her as if she were some sort of new mechanical marvel that had caught his eye. Then he frowned. "However, I'm not so sure the doctors at the asylum *will* tell your agents anything. I pay handsomely for Sarah's privacy."

"They'll go undercover if they have to, Sam. Don't underestimate them. But did you say you 'pay'? You still do?"

He blinked, surprised. "My God, yes. Why didn't I think of that before?" He tapped his forehead. "I'm not thinking straight. But Yancey, I received a statement for their services from the asylum not too long ago. And from what you're telling me, she's been dead for six months."

"Well, maybe not, Sam. Either I'm wrong and she's alive, or the people running the asylum aren't as honest as they should be."

Sam scrubbed his hands down his face. "Dear God. I turned Sarah over to hyenas."

"You don't know that, Sam. Even if the doctors are dishonest, you did nothing wrong. Your heart was in the right place."

"No. I just wanted rid of her, Yancey. And they were the only ones who would take her."

Yancey felt so desperate, so in over her head. "But *your* heart was still in the right place, Sam. You wanted help *with* her and *for* her. It's not your fault if the doctors turned out to be crooked."

His expression was rough, ragged. "I don't know. I just hope we haven't underestimated the power of my money to buy those doctors' silence regarding the truth. Otherwise"—his gaze roved slowly, tenderly over her face—"I may never have a chance to truly . . . live, Yancey."

Her heart leaped. She had the distinct impression he had been about to say "love."

# Chapter Fourteen

Sitting there on that hillside in the warm sunshine, Yancey basked in the warmth of the look Sam was giving her. She didn't see how she could keep her heart detached from her mind's workings in this case. Then she had an idea. "Sam," she began, "I think you ought to officially retain the Pinkertons to act on your behalf in this matter."

"No."

Yancey blinked. "You don't even want to hear my reasons why?"

"No."

"But you said you want to know the truth."

"And I do. But you don't fool me for a minute, Yancey Calhoun. You mean I should retain you, don't you? You're the only Pinkerton around. You're asking me to *officially* put you in harm's way."

Yancey puckered up sourly, as if she'd just bitten into an unripe persimmon. "I'm already in harm's way, Sam. I'm here and pretending to be your wife, aren't I?"

"Oh, I see. You would prefer being professionally retained by me, then. Is that because I don't have such a good record with wives?"

Yancey gasped. "You stop that right now. I won't listen to it." She pulled herself up to her knees. "One more word like that and I'll leave you sitting here on this hill by yourself to rot, is that clear? And that's not even all I'll do. I swear to you I will"—she cast about for something severely threatening—"go tell your mother on you, Sam Treyhorne. Don't think I won't."

His face was red, his eyes were the darkest gray she'd ever seen them, and he was already pointing at her, no doubt intending to roundly tell her off. But then he blinked and started laughing. "You'll what? You'll tell my *mother* on me?"

Embarrassed, laughing at herself, Yancey plopped back down beside him. "Oh, be quiet. You were being so awful to yourself, and it was the only thing I could think of."

"Yancey Calhoun, you are an absolute delight. And you will be the death of me yet."

"Actually, I was hoping to preserve your life, Sam. Not end it."

"Come here." He surprised her by pulling her to him and soundly kissing her, this time with no hesitation and no holding back.

Delighted to the tips of her toes, her heart singing, Yancey recognized this for the opportunity it was and threw her arms around his neck, giving him every ounce of passion she felt for him. Immediately, Sam's arms went around her and he held her tightly to him. His kiss said he was every bit as hungry for her as she was for him. Indeed, his hands roved over her back, kneading her muscles. His breathing erratic, he fisted her skirt in his hands, pulling at the material, pushing it up her legs, then his hands were on her thighs, caressing her bottom through her underclothes.

Yancey gasped, moaned into his mouth, then planted tiny, biting kisses along his lips as she pushed herself against him. The next thing she knew, Sam toppled over backward, taking her with him. He was lying on his back with her atop him. Startled, her hair flying everywhere, her arms still around his neck, and her breasts crushed against his chest, she looked down at him. He was grinning up at her. Though her passion was aroused and she could barely breathe, Yancey pulled back to stare wide-eyed at him. "What just happened, Sam?"

"You got yourself hired, that's what. Is this how you interview every prospective client? No wonder you Pinkerton women are so successful."

Into the dead silence that followed this, Yancey heard a horse neigh. A bird chirp. A dog bark. Men calling out to each other some distance away. She and Sam had behaved like wantons and outside, under God's blue sky. "Oh, dear heavens, Sam."

"What's wrong?"

She pulled her arms loose and disengaged from him, sliding off him sideways, gracelessly, struggling to sit up. She tried to right her clothes and her hair. "We are out here in the open. Anybody could see us." She smacked at him just lying there and grinning at her. "I'm serious," she cried. "What were we doing?"

Sam jackknifed to a sitting position and then arranged himself with a knee bent, an arm resting atop it. His expression was droll, his eyebrows arched. "You aren't seriously going to tell me you don't know?"

Yancey stared at him in exasperation. How was it possible for the man to be so supremely handsome even now, when here she was, her clothes twisted around, her hair a fright— "Of course I know. Don't be ridiculous. But we're out here in the open, Sam. We could be seen."

"Please don't expect me to be upset about that. If we were, then we would certainly make a very good case for actually being married, wouldn't we?"

"Oh, you're impossible." Then she stopped, suddenly recalling what he'd said several moments ago. "I'm hired? Really?"

He shrugged, a grin tugging again at the corners of his mouth. "I can deny you nothing. Jewels, furs, employment, whatever you want."

He was teasing her. She knew that. Yet she couldn't help but feel ashamed somehow, as if she had used her feminine wiles to bring him around. She lowered her gaze to her lap. Trying not to feel how kiss-swollen her lips were, she smoothed the folds in her skirt, just for something to do.

"What's wrong, Yancey? Didn't I do as you wanted?"

She met Sam's questioning gaze. "Yes. I just hope it wasn't for the wrong reason. I'll do a good job, Sam. I swear I will—"

"Shh." He'd put his fingers over her lips. "I know you will."

Then he sat back and watched her, making Yancey feel awkward, ill at ease. His gaze on her body made her feel undressed and made her wish she were. Feeling on the brink of forgetting herself and her mission here, she fell back on professional behavior. "Maybe we should talk about the case. Tell me more about Sarah. Before we, uh, sidetracked ourselves, you were saying she was worsening."

He looked askance at her abrupt shift of tone and subject—Yancey felt her face heat up—but then he blessedly complied. "All right. At the time, I had no idea what I was dealing with. Then her bad moments came more frequently. Obviously I knew she was disturbed, but I never suspected the depths of her outright insanity."

Yancey suspected he was glossing over the awful episodes and the fear he'd felt. She didn't blame him a bit, though. Certainly, living through it once was more than enough.

"The doctors convinced me that her condition would only worsen over time. They strongly recommended that I commit her for my own safety and hers. I didn't want to, Yancey. You have to believe me. But I did it. Right then. I put her away."

Yancey put a sympathetic hand on his arm. "It sounds to me as if you had no choice."

He looked away from her, showing her his stern profile and set jaw. A muscle jumped as if he were clamping down on his back teeth. So different from the laughing man who'd just kissed her. "Choice? I was just so *damned* relieved to hear that she was beyond my help. I wanted only to be rid of the burden of caring for her. And now my decision may have killed her."

Yancey tightened her grip on Sam's arm. He looked at her hand as if he'd had no idea she was touching him. "You did the only thing you could, Sam. You didn't cause her death. Perhaps I shouldn't have said anything about this other Sarah Calhoun in Chicago."

Sam glared at her. "Don't do that. You think it's her, don't you? You wouldn't be here otherwise."

Yancey released his arm and exhaled. "Yes, I do believe this other woman was your wife." And she'd been carrying a child. Sam's child? He didn't seem to know. Yancey looked into Sam's pained eyes and made a decision on the spot. Not until she knew without a single doubt that it was indeed his wife who'd been murdered would she divulge that dreadful news to him—and maybe not even then. She would have to weigh his right to know, she told herself, against what the news of that final tragedy would do to him. The truth or the greater kindness? That was what she needed to consider.

"She begged me not to leave her." His voice sounded hollow, strained.

Yancey's heart constricted. She wanted so badly to hold him and comfort him. "I can't even imagine. It must have been awful for you, Sam. And for her."

His expression cleared as he focused on her. "Yes. It would have been better had she had no awareness of her surroundings. But she did. I visited when I could. But it turned out to be less and less often. I had to pursue a living so I could pay for her care. But more often than not when I did go, I couldn't even see her because she'd be having a spell. After a while, I didn't go at all anymore."

"That's understandable."

"Is it?" He was acting as judge, jury, and hangman to himself. "Not too long after I sent her away, I had to mortgage the ranch and sell off the cattle. Then finally the land. All to pay for her care." He was quiet for a few moments, but then again took up his narrative. "At precisely the point when I was having to consider exactly how I could support myself and Sarah, I received word that Geoffrey was dead. Ironic, isn't it?"

"Ironic? How do you mean?"

"I mean, I came back to England because of my brother's death, which endowed me with great wealth and a title and all this land. Except for the title, it has turned out be everything I could want. But I wanted them in America. Only that certainly wasn't to be. Still, my brother's death also afforded me the means to pay for my wife's care. Ironic, as I said."

"More ironic than you know. It's a good thing you were in America when he died, Sam," Yancey said wryly. "Otherwise—and for all those reasons you just gave—you'd be my prime suspect in your brother's death, not Roderick."

"My God. I suppose that's true, isn't it? And now I'm not a suspect in Sarah's death because I was in England when she was killed."

Yancey nodded. "There's nothing like the width of an entire ocean to act as your alibi. But you know, Sam," she began, "the Sarah Calhoun in Chicago, by all accounts, lived quietly and worked as a maid in a boardinghouse. I just don't see how that poor woman and the violent woman you're describing to me could be one and the same."

"I can. When she wasn't in a state, she was just bewildered and timid. But she could take care of herself. In fact, she liked keeping house. So being a maid, in some simple way, might have been something she understood. Too, it was my understanding that at the asylum the doctors believed that performing simple chores, doing for themselves, was good for the patients."

"I see. Then it makes more sense. But what do you think she was doing out of the asylum?"

"I have no explanation for that. She wouldn't have been released without my being informed. Even if she'd escaped somehow, the doctors would have told me." Sam frowned. "Assuming they are honest."

Yancey slumped. "Oh, Sam, do you know how much I hate all of this? All I can do is assume. I know nothing. Usually on a job I enjoy this part, the search for motives, trying to find out how all the pieces fit together. But in this instance I hate it. I hate it because for the first time I know the people involved and I care. It makes everything different. Harder. I don't want to tell you my theories. This is your wife we're talking about. Well, *maybe* your wife. There. I've done it again. Do you see what I mean? I can hardly throw my suppositions out and look for the logic in them without seeming the worst kind of callous woman."

Sam gripped her wrist. "I don't see it that way at all. You're not upsetting me. I want to know. I hired you, remember? And even though it may not seem like it at the moment, I have come to terms with what I had to do regarding my wife. It's something I must live with. But I *want* you to talk to me. I *need* for you to tell me everything. Besides, I think if we talk long enough we'll find out how Roderick fits into all this."

Yancey chuckled as she covered Sam's hand that held her wrist and squeezed it affectionately. "You're very certain that Roderick is our villain, aren't you?"

He pulled his hand back and frowned hugely. "I don't like the man. I've been looking for a reason for years to poke him in the nose. Or worse."

"I know you have. And I don't blame you. But that brings up something else. Earlier you said that one of the reasons you need me to masquerade as your wife was so your cousin wouldn't know your affairs. By that I assume you mean Sarah's . . . madness?" He nodded. "I thought so. What are your other reasons?"

Sam's face colored, surprising Yancey. "If you weren't introduced as my wife, who exactly could I say you were, Yancey? You're an unmarried, unchaperoned woman in my home. And your bedroom suite is next to mine."

Assailed by a sudden shyness, Yancey looked down. "I see the problem. That would not do."

"No, it wouldn't. So, it's easier for now—at least while Roderick is here—to say you are my wife."

"But you have to tell your mother the truth, Sam."

"No. You don't know her. She can't keep a secret."

"She kept her letter-writing a secret from you."

His puckered expression said he didn't like being reminded that he'd been duped. "Perhaps I should have said she's not a good actress, that she can't be trusted not to misstep and give the game away accidentally. No, I would feel safer if, while Roderick is here, she doesn't know."

"As you wish. But in that case, and given what you've

told me of her"—Yancey grinned—"make certain I'm *not* here when you do tell her the truth."

Suddenly sober, Sam winced as if something had hurt him. Very quietly, he said, "I can't imagine you not being here, Yancey."

Taken by surprise, but afraid her heart was in her eyes, Yancey lowered her gaze to her lap. "Still, your poor mother," she murmured, choosing to ignore his last remark. "She thinks her daughter-in-law is dead."

"Not for long," he said, cupping her chin and raising her head until she met his warming gaze. "Not with you, the green-eyed evidence to the contrary, staring her in the face."

Yancey smiled and Sam returned it, taking his hand away. Then, as if seeking a position on the ground conducive to being practical, he shifted about and ran a hand over his jaw. "We need to worry more about Roderick, actually."

"I agree. You said he looked like *hell,* I believe was your word. What do you make of that?"

Sam shrugged. "Well, he had been on the road for two days with my overwrought mother. I can almost sympathize with him, yet I feel he deserves that and more. What concerned me more was his mannerisms and the things he was saying, how he was saying them. They seemed *off* somehow. Artificial. Smug. As if he knew something that we didn't. I know I sound vague, but that's the best I can do."

"Not as vague as you think. You might make a good detective yourself, Sam. The other agents and I, once we get a few facts together, turn them all over to see how they feel. We go more by instinct or blind feeling at the beginning of a case than I almost care to admit."

That seemed to please Sam. "Do you mean it? Do you think I'd have a future as a Pinkerton?"

Yancey chuckled. "Dear God, no. I don't think Mr. Pinkerton is currently hiring titled nobility."

"Oh. A shame. I think I'd like it."

"You'd hate it."

"I don't think I would."

"You would. And you'd have to take Her Grace Nana and her nurse and Scotty along. And Mr. Marples and the cats."

"I would not."

"Shall we go inside and put it to them? They'd want to go. And I cannot imagine a bigger nightmare, Sam. Think about yesterday and a simple jog into the village. We had nearly a dozen people, two carriages, and an assortment of animals."

Sam's grin was bright and teasing. Yancey wished for a big spoon with which to lap it up. "I see what you mean," he conceded graciously.

Then he surprised her by jumping to his feet and towering over her still seated there on the grass. "Enough of this sitting around," he declared, holding his hand out to her. "Come on. We're going back inside and set our plan into motion."

"We have a plan?" As if it were the most natural thing in the world for her to place her hand and her fate in this man's keeping, Yancey accepted his assistance and allowed him to tug her to her feet. The feel of her hand in his, of his much larger fingers intertwined with hers, of his palm, his skin, against hers, sent tiny shocks up Yancey's arm. But that didn't mean she hadn't enough presence of mind to question him. "What plan, Sam? I didn't know we had a specific one."

"We don't." Still holding on to her, he set off energetically down the hill at such a clip that she struggled to keep her feet. "But you'll think of something," he informed her over his shoulder. "It's what I'm paying you for—beginning right now, Miss Pinkerton Agent."

Hours later, they were in the vast formal drawing room, she and Sam, and they were plotting in earnest. They'd pulled their chairs close to each other's, and their heads were all but together in a conspiratorial pose. Upstairs, Sam's mother and cousin still slept, and he had left orders not to awaken them. Luncheon with Nana had come and long since gone. That sweet lady napped upstairs now, as well. And the afternoon sun, slanting warming rays in through the open French doors, verified by the shadows it cast that the four o'clock time displayed on the mantel clock was correct.

Much had already been accomplished on this fateful day. As soon as they'd come in from sitting on the hill, Yancey had given Sam his mother's letters, the ones sent to her by mistake, to read for himself. And he, in turn, had drafted his letter officially retaining the Pinkerton Agency to act on his behalf in their ongoing investigation in America. Once written, it had been tucked in with Yancey's updated one from yesterday, and that provocative packet had been sent with a footman to be posted in the village.

Then the two of them had bathed . . . separately . . . and dressed in their best afternoon attire. Yancey's heart had beat happily and with relief when Robin had excitedly told her that the costumes purchased yesterday at Mrs. LaFlore's shop had arrived while she and Sam had been outside earlier. Yancey came close to kissing Robin's forehead when she'd made her announcement. Thank God for that ill-conceived trip into the village yesterday or, as Yancey knew, she would never have been able, without the proper clothes, to convince Sam's family that she was a duchess.

It was along those lines now that Sam was rapidly instructing her. Yancey worked hard to understand and retain all of the practical information she would need to know in order to pass herself off as a long-married duchess. Sam had first reminded her that his mother thought that he and his wife were estranged. So Yancey's story would be that his mother's letters had convinced her to give Sam another chance. Instead of answering them, and after much thought, she had simply shown up and surprised him and they'd had a private reunion. It was simple and romantic and his mother would love it.

"However, Yancey—"

"Sarah, Sam. Not Yancey."

"Damn. Exactly. Sarah. All right, we've been married for five years, and we had money, for all they know. Given that, you would know how to handle servants—"

"Tell that to Scotty."

Sam's expression became very droll. "First, don't tell Scotty he is a servant. You could get bitten. Never mind the servants. They mind you better already than they do me.

Let's discuss the dinner service. Being American will not be a valid excuse for poor table manners."

"I have bad table manners?"

"No. But it can get complicated. If you get confused, just watch my lead to see which piece of silverware to use."

"How hard can it be, Sam? All we're going to do is eat."

He rolled his eyes. "In a formal setting, Yancey—much more formal than last night—there will be as many as fifteen different knives, forks, and spoons, each one with a distinct use. You wouldn't want Scotty to smack your hand for using the wrong one, would you?"

"Dear God," was Yancey's despairing remark. "Maybe I should take all my meals in my room."

"And have them think you're indisposed, or perhaps with child?"

Yancey's eyes widened. "No. That won't do." Flitting through her mind were thoughts of the other Sarah and her baby. "But why *didn't* we have children, Sam?"

Did he not want children? Yancey had to wonder. This was interesting—and his answer would be very telling.

Sam sat back in his chair, looking every inch the aristocratic gentleman as he lounged there, an elbow resting on the chair's arm and his chin and jaw supported by his thumb and forefinger. "I beg your pardon?"

"We've been married for years, Sam. Why are there no children?"

He cocked his head at a considering angle and ran his gaze over her person, finally capturing her eyes with his. The warmth she saw there clearly said he'd found her to his liking. Yancey fought her body's tightening response to his intense notice. She barely stopped herself from crossing her arms over her chest in a gesture of modesty to hide the evidence of her nipples hardening into tiny buds. How distressing. Why had she brought up children? Or lack thereof?

"Do you want children, Yancey?"

His low, seductive bedroom growl did nothing to calm her nerves. In fact, his tone of voice alone had her babbling. "It's a little late for that. Unless you intend to produce several in the next few hours."

He grinned evilly. "We could certainly try."

Outraged . . . and titillated . . . Yancey tsked. "We most certainly can *not*."

"Too bad."

"And that is not what I meant. I marvel at you, sir."

"On what score? You're the one who reminded me that I am among the living and should behave accordingly."

"Do not toss my words in my face for your own advantage. Here our very lives hang in the balance—"

"Perhaps not."

"Oh? What's changed?"

"My thinking. Roderick is only one man. And he and I are not children any longer. If he is responsible in any way, then he has more to answer for than we do. So, if it's a fight my cousin wants, it's a fight he'll get."

"I don't like the sound of that, Sam. Remember, you hired me to—"

"To uncover facts, Yancey. Not fight my battles."

"Be that as it may, I—"

"No. Hear me out. I am no longer the young and penniless second son. I am now the Duke of Somerset. And that may well be because of Roderick's machinations. I refer to Geoffrey's death, of course. I owe Roderick, Yancey. And I find myself in a mood to pay him back in full—and then some."

"Again, Sam, I don't like the sound of this."

"Really? How do I sound? Hard? Bitter?"

"You have every right to be both. And I don't blame you. But what you are is vengeful. Which means you're not thinking clearly and you'll make mistakes. We cannot afford mistakes, Sam. There have been two deaths already."

Sam shot forward in his chair, his expression hard and bitter, just as he'd described himself. "And there will be another one before this is over, I assure you."

Yancey exhaled slowly, knowing Sam was in no mood to be mollified. She'd have to choose her words carefully. "Have you ever killed a man before, Sam? I have. Two, actually. And what it does to your soul is unspeakable. No matter how much the man might deserve to die, what it does to you is much worse." She stared soberly at Sam. "Much worse."

Sam gestured, spreading his hands wide. "I'm sorry for you, Yancey. But what would you have me do? Clap Roderick heartily on the back and say all's forgiven?"

"Hardly. But I think you're purposely not hearing me, Sam. You're toying with me, and I don't like it."

A complete transformation came over him. Grinning at her and arching an eyebrow, he smiled. "Would that I were toying with you, dearest. It would be much more pleasurable an activity than instructing you in which spoon to use."

Yancey felt her face heat up. Yes, she knew what he was doing. He was trying to distract her from lecturing him on seeking vengeance. But, God help them both, she was going to allow him to do so. "We were not talking about spoons. We were talking about children."

"Yes. We were. We would have beautiful children together, Yancey." The dancing lights in his eyes raced her pulse.

They shouldn't be doing this. She knew that. But this banter, this sensual web they were weaving, felt so good and so delicious that a shiver of anticipation slipped over her skin and had her smiling just as archly as her duke. "We'll never know, though, will we? You forget, Your Grace, this marriage is our masquerade . . . and nothing more."

Sam's gray eyes warmed with awareness as he languidly sat forward, every inch the aroused panther ready to pounce. "Would you like for it to be more?"

Yancey's breath caught. Was he speaking from his heart? Or merely trying to seduce her? If so, he was doing a wonderful job of it. But much more of this and she would faint. She had to put a stop to it. Had to get them back on an even keel. "You ask me a question I have no way of answering. And then you don't answer a question I need answering. I refer, of course, to children."

Her duke slumped back in his chair. "Oh. Them. I say we have four. Two girls. Two boys. That has a nice ring to it."

"Indeed. Four in five years. Quite a feat, given our estrangement."

"Very true. We'll not mention children to her. Can I at least give her hope and tell her we're trying?"

"You are outrageous, sir."

"And you are beautiful, Yan—Sarah. About your name. You don't like to be called 'Sarah,' if I remember correctly. Would you prefer I bastardize 'Margaret' and call you 'Maggie'?"

Yancey raised her chin. "You do, and I'll call you Sammy."

He narrowed his eyes. "Vile creature. You wouldn't?"

"I would."

A thunderous knock upon the door had Yancey shooting out of her chair, her heart pounding, her pulse racing. She wadded handfuls of her skirt in her hands and stared wide-eyed at Sam. "They're here. It's them. What are we going to do? There's so much you haven't told me. I'm not ready."

Sam was on his feet, too. He gripped her arms and stared down into her face. "No, it isn't them. They'd simply sweep in. That's Scotty, most likely, since the door almost splintered. Come on, now, where's the charge-ahead woman who lectured me at breakfast? The one who so calmly questioned me outside on that hill and came up with probability after probability and then likely solutions? Where is she?"

"You're right," Yancey said, hating that her voice sounded so breathy with nerves. "They would expect me to be nervous, wouldn't they? But they're not going to come in looking for faults, are they?"

"Of course not," he lied, and she knew it and loved him for it. "No doubt, upon seeing you alive and well, they'll be the ones we'll have to revive. Then, once she adjusts, my mother will be thrilled. She will also have a lot to answer for with those letters of hers. And Roderick? Ah yes, my cousin. He will be shocked and then falsely charming and mannerly. Watch yourself with him. He fancies himself a ladies' man. He and my brother apparently cut quite a swath together through London."

Feeling better for these benign characterizations, Yancey squared her shoulders. "Well, his best efforts will all be for naught with me, I assure you."

"Spoken like a true and faithful wife." Sam surprised her by tugging her to him and kissing her forehead lightly. His lips against her skin were firm and warm . . . and so welcome. When he released her, Yancey's steps faltered. She hadn't realized that she'd been leaning in toward him.

"I'd best see what Scotty wants before he becomes impatient and comes through the door. It wouldn't be the first time."

Yancey had no reply. She watched Sam's retreating figure, thinking he looked so strong now, and not the least bit diminished by his more formal attire. If anything, he seemed more powerful, more sure of himself. It was as if they'd reversed roles from this morning. Now she felt uncertain and faltering. And Sam was steady as a rock. Not that she should be surprised. He wasn't the impostor here. She was. He couldn't slip up with a lie. She could. He couldn't give the game away and get them both killed. She could.

Yancey hated these misgivings. She'd never experienced them to this degree on previous cases. Always before, she'd felt excited and on edge, looking forward to the challenge, but not here at Stonebridge. And not with Sam. She placed the blame for her present uncertainty squarely on the broad shoulders of the man across the room from her. She cared about him. And it was making her . . . scared.

Sam opened the door and spoke in low tones to Scotty. She assumed it was Scotty because Sam had said it was, but all she could see was Sam's profile and his hand on the partially opened door. Then he shook his head no. Yancey's palms felt moist. What were they talking about? Why was Sam whispering? What had happened now?

"Sam?" she called out. "Is something wrong? Something I should know about?"

He nodded at Scotty, said something else to him, then stepped back into the room and closed the door. "Yes and no," he said, coming toward her, frowning in consternation.

"Well? What is it? What's happened?"

"It's one of my horses. A prize mare. She's pulled up lame all of a sudden and refuses to allow her foal to suckle.

Daniel, my stableman, came to the back door, asking for me to come investigate and render a decision. I'm afraid I must go."

Yancey clutched at his coat. "What? Now? Are you mad? You cannot leave me here to face them alone."

Smiling, chuckling, Sam rubbed his hands up and down her arms. "You won't have to face them alone. Mrs. Edgars says they're not even awake yet. You'll be fine."

"I'm not worried about being fine. I've played undercover parts before. It's just that this time, the news—or the reality of me, Sam—and given what's at stake, well, it needs your presence." Yancey was still wadding his dark blue frock coat under which he wore a snow-white shirt and dark waistcoat and matching trousers.

"I agree. And the sooner I go see about the mare, the sooner I can be back." Gently he extricated her from his person and caressed her jaw lightly with his fingers. Yancey's breath caught and held, and her heart raced. "Dear Sarah." Then he frowned, looking troubled. "Strange. I find it oddly disconcerting to call you by *her* name."

"It's also my name, Sam. One I hate but there it is." She hesitated and then plunged on. "I know I have no right to ask you, but can you not just think of me when you say it?"

He smiled, looking both tender and wounded as he roved his gaze over her face. "That's the problem. You are all I think about, Yancey."

Desire poured through her in honeyed waves. She grabbed Sam's waistcoat and pulled him to her, tilting her face up to his. "Kiss me, Sam. I really need for you to kiss me. As if I were your wife. I want to know how a wife feels when the man she loves kisses her."

Sam needed no further prodding. An arm instantly around her waist, he held her tight and cupped her chin in his other hand. His gray eyes warmed to pewter as he stared down at her. Then he lowered his head until his lips met hers . . . and claimed her mouth.

Instantly seared and weak-kneed, yet wonderfully alive and sweetly lethargic, Yancey clung to Sam, hungrily deepening their kiss. She stretched up to meet his questing lips, wanting to have all of him, wanting not to miss any part of him. Barely able to breathe, so wonderful and fulfilling was his kiss, much like coming home and being welcomed with open arms, Yancey embraced the pooling tension low in her belly and felt Sam's answering hardness, despite the hindrance of clothing, pushing against her. In her heart Yancey knew that this was what she wanted, this man, his body, his strength, his weaknesses, his compassion, his love.

She couldn't have said which one of them broke their kiss. All she knew was it ended, and they were both gasping for air and clinging to each other. Breathing as raggedly as she was, Sam stared down into her eyes. He appeared dazed or overwhelmed. Yet Yancey reveled in the knowledge that her lips were dewy with Sam's kiss, her mouth heated by his ardor, and her body warmed by his passion for her.

"Oh, Sam, my God." She could barely get the words out. "I don't think I've ever felt anything like that. I mean that strongly. I feel so overwhelmed."

"I, as well." Sam shook his head as he peered into her eyes. His own eyes widening, he told her, "When this is over, Yancey, when all is said and done, I—"

She put her fingers over his mouth to stop his words. "No, Sam, don't say another word. Please." She rested her forehead against his chest, and he held her to him.

"What's wrong, Yancey? What did I say? I meant nothing wrong."

She could only shake her head no. Yancey could feel his heart beating thunderously with health and vigor and passion. So very much alive, this man was. She knew on some elemental level that he could very well be the man for her. But again she heard her mother's words, warning her not to give up her freedom, perhaps her very life, to any man.

In a flash of awful memory, the images from the past, from that fateful day, poured over Yancey. She saw her mother's body lying pooled in blood. She saw her father, five years after returning home, standing over his wife, his fists red and slick with her blood. Then Yancey saw him spying her and his realization that she'd seen his crime. He came after her. Then she saw the rest . . . and finally she saw herself, a terrified eighteen-year-old, running . . . running . . . running away. Never to look back. Never to go back.

And she heard as well Mr. Pinkerton telling her she must never, never become involved with anyone from any of her cases. It was grounds for instant dismissal because it compromised everyone . . . her, the client, the other agents, the entire agency. She was already under review; and here she was, in the arms of the man who had only that morning retained her services as a Pinkerton, the profession Yancey had gravitated to so she could keep men and love at arm's length.

"Yancey? Talk to me. What's wrong?"

Snapped out of her nightmare, Yancey pulled back from Sam, releasing him. She looked away from the confusion in his eyes. Staring instead at a small round table situated between the two chairs where only a few moments ago she and Sam had been sitting, their heads together in what had seemed an exciting masquerade, one in which they were a happily married couple, Yancey inhaled slowly for calm and exhaled rapidly for courage.

"Go, Sam," she told him, defeated by her own past. "Go see to your mare. I'll wait here for you."

"Look at me." She did. Sam's expression was hard with determination. "I'm not going anywhere until you tell me what's wrong. I know it wasn't the kiss. You wanted me to kiss you. You asked me to."

"I know, Sam. It wasn't the kiss, and yet it was. Just . . . please don't say anything else. Not now. Please." She hated the ragged emotion in her voice. Hated the frown of concern on his face. Why did she have to care so much? Why? She'd been here only three days. Three intense days. But never before, with any man, had she involved her heart. But now, with this man, it was already too late. And it was awful.

From the corner of her eye, she could see that Sam held a hand out to her and that he'd taken a step toward her. She turned on him, much like a wounded animal striking back. "Stop, Sam. Right there, I beg you." He did. Yancey's voice was no more than a jagged sob of desperation. "I was wrong to kiss you. *We* were wrong. Both of us. We can't—"

"No." Angry now, his coloring heightened, his eyes blazing, Sam pointed an accusing finger at her. "We weren't wrong, Yancey. And we weren't carried away simply by the moment. We both know better. And I won't let it go at this. I won't. You can't kiss me like that and not expect me to know your true feelings."

"You know nothing."

"I *know*. I felt it in your kiss, and in the way you clung to me. It was there, how you feel." Sam softened his stance, now holding an imploring hand out to her. "Yancey, you're not alone in this. Don't tell me we can't do this, that we can't feel this. We *can*. We do. It's too late to step back from each other, Yancey. Too late."

She feared he was right. But all she could do was stand there in her aloneness and stare at him and deny what her heart wanted and what her mind railed against. As if in physical pain, Yancey wrapped her arms tightly around her waist. "You're wrong, Sam. We're wrong. But it's not too late to make it right." She had to say these hateful things. If she didn't, she'd lose herself in him. Yancey hardened her heart and turned away from him. "Go see about your mare. We have a job to do."

# Chapter Fifteen

Walking away from her, leaving the drawing room, sweeping past the staircase, and directing his steps down the long hallway and out the back door, forcing himself away from her and across the lawn, then down the meadow, and keeping himself on course and aware of his surroundings was the hardest thing Sam had ever done. Before this, he'd thought that walking away from Sarah, leaving her in the asylum, hearing her screams begging him not to go, to please take her away with him, had been the single hardest steps he'd ever had to take.

But now Sam knew better. That had been nothing compared to what he was doing now. Was this, he wondered, how life paid him back for his act of desperation and what he had hoped was a kindness to Sarah? Was this his penance for doing nothing more than seeking help for her? Must it be that he had now to walk away from the one woman he believed he could truly love in his whole life? Here he stood on the precipice of joy and happiness . . . and a long, hard fall it was, indeed.

Sam's jaw ached because of how tightly he had his teeth clenched. His forehead creased with his pain. His temples throbbed with the hurt. If he appeared stern and worried, he knew it could be passed off to many causes, but none of them would be close to the truth . . . that he'd walked away from his wife's love for him and now, in turn, he had been put off by the one woman he could love.

Life didn't abound with purpose, Sam was coming to believe. It abounded instead with irony. He pictured idle gods with a huge chessboard and, without thought or compassion, moving the human players about at will, choosing their next move solely on the basis of how hurtful and confusing and devastating the outcome would be to the pawns they held in their ethereal hands. It had to be thus. There was no other explanation, none that would satisfy him in his current black mood.

Sam's brooding thoughts carried him into the gray and welcome shade of the horse barn's interior and out of the day's bright and cheery sunshine. This earthy yet murkier atmosphere instantly suited his mood. As he walked farther into the huge barn's interior, with a practiced eye and out of habit, he noted the orderliness of the structure, the neatness of the hanging tack, and the air of industrious labor. A sudden pride in ownership raised Sam's spirits a bit. He breathed in the clean smell of the hay and the familiar scent of horse. Here was something he understood. This was a place in which he felt comfortable, more at home even than he did in the manor . . . than he did in all of England.

Up ahead, outside a stall, Sam saw waiting for him . . . for his direction and for his decision—God, he didn't want to think, didn't want to be responsible for the fragile life of any other living creature—the stablehands and Daniel, the man whose life revolved around the care and feeding of Sam's prized horses. Immediately upon spying Sam's approach, even though he was still yards away, the men and boys all bowed, echoing a chorus of "Your Grace," showing respect and deference, both of which shamed Sam.

He had nothing about him of a state of grace. He was not among the forgiven, and this, his life, was hell. Still walking toward them, Sam raised a hand in silent greeting, thinking to spare his employees his mood. They'd not caused it and should not bear the brunt of it.

*Very noble,* a more sardonic part of his mind smirked,

seeming to laugh also at the maudlin bent of Sam's ranting conclusions about his life. It urged him to cheer up, saying that Yancey lived, she was under his roof yet, would be for the foreseeable future, and was posing as his wife. And therefore, with such reasons to hope coupled with their imposed intimacy—no matter the fabricated nature of it—he'd have every opportunity to break down her defenses and win the day. And the woman.

Sam's protest was instant. He'd prefer not to have to break down defenses. He'd like to think she would welcome him. But the truth was, she hadn't. All they'd done was share kisses, he reminded himself. Yes, kisses they both had clearly wanted. But then she'd pulled away, upset and wanting nothing more to do with him. Surely, the fault didn't lie in the way he kissed. He had too much experience, coupled with no complaints, to believe that. Still, Sam's heart refused to give up. *You felt her ardor,* it told him, *and it was the truth . . . and nothing is lost. Everything is possible. Everything.*

No. No, it wasn't. Not if she didn't want his ardor. Only this morning he'd been excited at the prospect of her posing as his loving wife. But now, as events stood, he believed the ruse would only be the next poke of the devil's pitchfork in his backside as the nasty little demon pricked away at Sam's disgustingly optimistic conscience.

Now upon the knot of concerned horsemen awaiting him, Sam stopped in front of them. Deferentially they stepped back and away, much like a receding tide, to make room for him among them.

Shrugging out of his frock coat, Sam hung it on an available hook and began rolling up his sleeves. Another irony. He'd greet his mother and cousin while smelling of horse and manure. Entirely appropriate in Roderick's case was Sam's conclusion. Prepared now to go to work, he looked from the men to the open stall and the agitated, head-tossing, neighing mare that occupied it. "She wouldn't let you inside, would she?"

"No, sir," Daniel answered for them. "You're the only one can do anything with her, Your Grace."

Sam chuckled. So the only female, it seemed, who would

gentle under his touch today turned out to be a mare. "All right, then, let's see what we can do."

*What the devil is taking Sam so long? How long does it take to look at a horse?* Fuming, her mind racing as fast as her feet, Yancey paced the length of the drawing room, wringing her hands and drilling herself on every detail regarding Sam that she could think of. Second son. Thirty-two. Gray eyes. Spent adult years in America. Loves horses and cattle. Scar on his thigh; put there by the angry sow. His brother's name was Geoffrey, who died—or was killed—almost a year ago. Duke of Somerset. Stonebridge. Ancient tower.

She stopped, staring blankly ahead of her, vaguely aware of a huge oil painting of some ancient battle scene that hung on the far wall. *Dear God, is that all I know about the man?* She shook her head. *Surely not.* She knew his kiss and the way his hands felt on her body. Though the memory of it stirred her blood and had her sighing somewhat lasciviously, even to her own mind, she could hardly hear herself bringing that up.

She tested such a sentence out loud, holding her hand out as if offering it to an imaginary dowager duchess. She curtsied. "Hello, lovely to meet you, Your Grace." Yancey frowned. "Mother Treyhorne?" She shook her head no. "Mrs. Treyhorne? Rosamond? Oh, bother. I'll ask her what I should call her." That settled, Yancey smiled brightly and said, "So pleased to meet you. Your son is a wonderful kisser."

Instantly, while the words still hung in the air, Yancey made a face, shaking her head in an emphatic no. "I'd sooner die than say that to her."

She set off on another circuit of the room, which she was beginning to know intimately, given her many turns around the pieces of furniture and the equal number of times she'd stopped to pick up and examine what were no doubt priceless pieces of sculpture and porcelain. Yancey feared she'd have a groove worn in the thick Aubusson carpet before she was rescued by Sam's presence.

Thinking of him had Yancey wincing with shame and guilt. *Poor Sam.* Why had she said such upsetting things to the man before he'd left? Wasn't this charade going to be hard enough without her having made it more complicated? Couldn't she have left well enough alone? Why had she thought she needed to make something simple, a wonderful kiss, so hard? Now everyone would know, by how stiff and awkward she and Sam would be around each other, that they had argued. So distressing.

Again Yancey eyed the closed doors to the room when she passed them, alternately cursing and blessing them for not opening. The difference lay in who might walk through them when they did open. Sam she would welcome. Just about anyone else she wouldn't. Well, maybe Her Grace Nana. She hadn't seen that grand old lady since lunch. Was she still resting, the frail little dear? Yancey eyed the doors again, wondering if everyone, sensing fireworks, was avoiding her. A lovely thought. Just when she needed familiar company around her, even if it was based on a three-day-old acquaintanceship, she had imprisoning solitude.

Of course she could leave this room and go seek Nana out. Only to turn a corner on the way and run into Sam's mother or his cousin, no doubt. So it would be better to wait here, where Sam knew she was, than it was to wander the manor over and risk a chance meeting that could end badly. Besides, Yancey assured whatever portion of her mind she was speaking to, she could hardly see herself skulking along the walls until she got to her suite of rooms upstairs. In all likelihood she'd be spotted by Scotty, who would promptly throw her down the stairs and order her back into this room.

For all she knew, came Yancey's next thought, Scotty was outside the double doors at this moment, just standing there . . . a scowl on his face, his massive arms crossed, and guarding the door, keeping all comers out until Sam returned. Yancey smiled. *How sweet.* Then curiosity of the intense variety that killed cats and detectives seized her. Was the giant out there? Had Sam left an order that she was not to be disturbed until he returned? An exhalation of relief over such a possibility left her sighing. Yet, she had to know. First looking around the room, as if there were some lurking presence here with her whose detection she must avoid, Yancey all but tiptoed over to the doors.

As quietly as she could, she turned the knob and edged one of the doors open . . . only enough to afford her a peek into the hallway. Well, that answered her question. If she could see the hallway—and she could—then Scotty was not present. Just then, her diabolical mind treated her to a scene from three days ago—the day she had arrived and had stood in the grand foyer and Her Grace Nana had done this very same thing, only from the front parlor. That brought Yancey back to sanity.

"Well, then." She straightened up and closed the door, self-consciously clearing her throat and fussing with her gown's scoop neckline. *My goodness, they're low this year.* It seemed a scandal to show so much bosom this early in the afternoon.

So she was better off right here, alone. Apparently. Yancey smoothed her hands down her skirt. At least she looked presentable. The only accessory she lacked was her gun. Yet her day dress of thick textured silk, pale green in color, had no pockets for concealment of a weapon. It was just as well, she decided, because as nervous as she was—much as if she were in reality meeting her true in-laws—she just might lose her nerve and shoot them. And that wouldn't do, she was certain of it.

Yancey's circuit this time, now with the room's doors behind her and to her right, had her stopping at the thrown-wide French doors that afforded her the benefits of the spring air and the happy sounds of chirping birds and the sight of working gardeners. She frowned, standing there with her back to the room and her hands folded demurely together in front of her as she watched the busy men. Always planting, digging, pruning, shaping. They worked incessantly, it seemed. Like so many ants. At whose direction? she wondered, not really caring but pondering these things in a concerted effort not to think about the day's drama yet to unfold.

What she needed to do, Yancey told herself, still looking out over the wonderful flagstone-paved, half-moon-shaped terrace, was pull herself together and behave as a Pinkerton and remember that this was a job she was doing. And nothing else. She made a face, hating that idea because she couldn't even imagine packing up and leaving Sam or this place in a matter of weeks, maybe days. Could it be that she belonged here with him? Pained by that realization, and telling herself no, Yancey closed her eyes and exhaled. *See this for what it is, Yancey. A case you're working on, and nothing more. When it's done, you'll go home and start your next case. That is your life, the one you've carved out for yourself.*

Feeling as bereft as if she'd suffered a terrible loss, Yancey opened her eyes and was greeted by the sight of the huge glazed flowerpots that sat atop the concrete railing at even intervals. So very cheerful, they offered up riotous colors of purple, red, yellow, and blue. The low stone benches, she decided, almost required one to cross to one of them and sit and relax and let one's troubles float away on the spring breeze. If only she could. Then it occurred to her . . . why couldn't she? The thought becoming action, she smiled and, gathering up her skirt, took a step toward the great outdoors.

"A lovely sight, isn't it?"

Gasping in surprise, Yancey all but jumped out of her dress and her skin. She whirled around, a hand over her heart and hearing her detective's conscience railing at her that here she'd had all this time to worry about the doors opening, and when the time had finally come, she hadn't even been aware.

"You startled me," she told the tall man . . . the impeccably dressed, very handsome, square-jawed, dark-haired, sensually wicked, tall man . . . who stood framed in the open doorway of the parlor and boldly raked his gaze over her.

Stunting Yancey's breathing was the man's eerily similar appearance to Sam. But it was in a sinister way, as if he were Sam's opposite, someone in whom the more frightening urges of men went unbridled. She watched silently as her visitor bowed elegantly to her.

"My apologies," he drawled. "I should be flogged for upsetting such a wonderful creature as yourself."

Yancey refused to be flattered or to give any quarter. This man was the enemy. Despite her pounding heart and moist palms, she managed to speak in a normal tone of voice. "Fortunately, it's not required . . . the flogging, I mean."

"You're American." The man's voice was a purr of surprise—or dawning suspicion.

The vibration of his words brushed over Yancey's skin, irritating the fine hairs on her arms. A thrill of the sort that warned one of danger shot like a lance through her nerve endings. Her heart wanted to pound right out of her chest. Where the devil was Sam? "Yes, I am an American. You're very astute."

"Astute? No. Your provincial accent gives you away, my dear. But, ah, America . . . a wonderful country, our former colonies."

Insulting cad. He'd raised Yancey's patriotic dander. "Yes, it is wonderful. In fact, you ought to see the improvements we've made to the place in the last hundred years or so."

He laughed, a rich, throaty sound that accompanied his steps into the room. He closed the doors behind him. "And witty, too. Very intriguing."

Yancey very subtly narrowed her eyes. *You have no idea, mister.* But when she swallowed, she was surprised to realize how dry her mouth was. Quickly she assured herself that this thrumming tension inside her was not fright. Instead, it was anticipation of the chase. She was the Fox, and she'd be damned if she'd allow this man to be the hound that ran her to ground. Her next calming breath helped prepare her to meet this devil.

The man stopped in front of her, all but clicking his heels together as he again bowed, this time over her hand, which she remembered to offer him. "Roderick Hamilton Harcourt, the Duke of Glenmore, at your service."

Using her free hand to hold her voluminous skirt out of her way, Yancey dropped into a formal curtsy, thinking this ought to be a very telling moment. "So pleased to meet such a close cousin of my husband's, Your Grace. I am Sarah Margaret Calhoun."

She'd used her "maiden" name on purpose and got the response she wanted. The Duke of Glenmore squeezed her hand overly hard and immediately straightened up, releasing her and sending her a hard stare. Yancey had drawn first blood. Because she had, she felt calmer, more in control of the situation, and better able to act her part. She began by affecting a light, trilling titter of laughter. "Oh, so silly of me. I of course meant Treyhorne. Sarah Margaret Treyhorne, the Duchess of—"

"Somerset, I know. You cannot be my cousin Sam's wife."

She ducked her chin regally. "Oh, but I can and I am . . . unless you know something I don't, Your Grace?"

"Forgive me, but I was told you are . . . *dead*."

Yancey put a hand over her heart. "My goodness, the way you say *dead* gives me the shivers. But here I am, very obviously alive. Of course, Sam told me this morning that you and my dear mother-in-law had arrived with the news of my unfortunate demise. I find myself most distressed."

Roderick's bold eyes narrowed even as he affected concern and executed a bow. "I apologize if my obviously erroneous news of your demise caused you any distress."

Yancey returned his comment in kind. "And I apologize to you, sir, if my being alive has caused *you* any distress."

She surprised him with that. His hawk's gaze met and held Yancey's. She refused to blink first and distracted her mind by detailing the man's features. Most notably, his eyes weren't gray like Sam's. They were blue. A very hard, chipped-flint blue. But they went well with his mouth, which had a cruel set to it.

"Far from distressed," he said a little too late, a little too insincerely. "In fact, I am truly delighted to find my cousin's wife so obviously alive and well."

Yancey allowed herself a smile. "Such a sweet man you are, Your Grace."

"Please. Under the circumstances, you and I being family, even if only through marriage, please do me the honor of calling me Roderick."

"Why, I'd be delighted. But you must call me Sarah, in return."

"Then . . . Sarah, it is."

"Oh, forgive me my lack of manners, Your—I mean Roderick," Yancey fussed, playing the distracted hostess. She indicated an intimate arrangement of chairs that fronted the cold fireplace. "Would you like to be seated? I can ring for tea"—wouldn't they be surprised in the kitchen? Yancey suffered a second's fear: what had Sam told the servants? But wait, they already believed her to be the duchess; they'd cooperate without question, wouldn't they?—"or we can step outside to enjoy this lovely day."

"What's your pleasure . . . Sarah? I defer to you. This is, after all, *your* home." His voice was tight, as if it had cost him dearly to spit the words out and admit her ownership. Yancey found that interesting.

"Why don't we sit in here?" She indicated the chairs, received his nod of acceptance, and preceded him over to them. Eschewing the settee, not wanting to give the man a chance to sit so close to her, Yancey sat in one of the chairs and arranged her skirt about her, much as if she took callers every day in this room.

For his part, the Duke of Glenmore chose the settee, sitting and crossing his legs much as if *he* owned the place. Yancey eyed him, wondering at the vehemence behind his earlier comment about Stonebridge being her home now. She would have to ask Sam some questions. Such as, did Roderick's land share a boundary with Sam's? Was he looking to expand his holdings? How big was his property? Was it profitable? Did this man have the money to support his duchy? Much of the peerage didn't nowadays and sought rich American wives who were hungry for titles—

"It's a pity that we couldn't have met you before now, Sarah. Yet I find you a lovely creature, and don't blame Sam at all for keeping you to himself in America all these years."

Though he pretended not to, Yancey reasoned, Roderick had to know—through Sam's mother's many visits to her sister, this man's mother—of Sam's alleged estrangement from his wife. What a snake. She smiled. "You're too kind, Roderick."

"I've often been told that is a fault of mine."

"No doubt." Yancey remembered to smile, to appear attentive to her guest, even though she would have given her right arm to be able to tie him to the danged furniture and hold a gun to his head until he told the truth, the villain. "Although I must say I'm glad I'm here now. Otherwise, these reports of my death might persist." She leaned over, toward the hateful man. "I find myself wondering who would tell you such an awful lie, Roderick. And why they would."

She waited politely, pointedly, for her guest to reply. But inside, she was fretting. *Where the hell is Sam? He needs to hear all this. If he doesn't hurry up and get back here, there's going to be another death later on. And it will be his.*

Roderick's answering smile Yancey judged to be very much like that, no doubt, offered by the serpent in the Garden of Eden. "Well, this is most awkward, my dear, sweet cousin."

"Isn't it, though?" Yancey agreed conversationally, clasping her hands together in her lap. She paused for a count of three, then added, "And your source for that most distressing news you brought with you . . . Roderick?"

"Forgive me, Sarah," Roderick began, appearing puzzled, "but I wonder why Sam didn't tell me straightaway early this morning that you lived. His dear mother was so distressed—and still is, I remain certain—to learn that Sam's wife was, uh, no longer with us."

So . . . no sources revealed. Roderick was proving to be quite the slippery little eel. Yancey adopted an expression of sweet innocence and tried again. "Sam's poor, poor mother. I myself am very distressed that someone—and you *must* tell me who—is spreading these tales that are upsetting everyone."

If he wasn't going to answer her questions, she wasn't about to answer his. And so she waited. Roderick said nothing, only tilted his head this way and that as he considered her, much as he would a ripe fruit ready for the plucking. Yancey's smile stayed in place as if she'd plastered it there. "Yes?" she asked, encouraging him. "Who did you say wrote to . . . Mother Rosamond"—dear God, she hoped that was a correct form of address for Sam's mother—"and upset her so? What a villain this person is, I must say."

Roderick's tight smile only tipped up the corners of his thin slash of a mouth. "Very much the villain, I assure you, dear lady. One can only hope he will be dealt with accordingly for having passed along such incorrect information."

Yancey did not doubt in the least that whoever the bumbling informant was, he would be dealt with severely—as soon as Roderick got away from here.

Just then he became the very picture of cousinly solicitousness and charm, leaning forward in a show of attentiveness. "And now, my dear, you must tell me how it was that you and Sam met."

Yancey's smile fled from her face. She had no idea how Sam had met Sarah. None. She recovered quickly, becoming the trilling, cheerful hostess. "Oh my, that's a story for Sam to tell you." Through gritted teeth, she added, "If only he were here, that dear, dear man." She eyed the closed doors of the suddenly suffocating drawing room. "I wonder *what* can be keeping that husband of mine. He should really, really be here."

As if in response to her inquiry—or prayer—the doors to the drawing room opened. Yancey had to grip her chair's arms to keep from jumping up and shouting hallelujah.

# Chapter Sixteen

But it wasn't Yancey's "husband" who rattled in behind the tea service. No, it was Scotty. Yancey wanted to die. Where the living hell was Sam? How many horses did he have, and were they all ailing?

As the Duke of Glenmore had jumped up—out of guilt? Wariness? A need to watch his back because he was up to no good?—and now faced the doors, Yancey fanned her face with her hands and exhaled hard enough to puff her cheeks out. This grateful feeling she had for Scotty right now had to be how settlers felt when, surrounded by marauding Indians, they saw the cavalry coming on the run. Of course, in Scotty's case, there was no running.

"Why, Scotty," she chirped, knowing full well she hadn't rung for refreshments, "how nice of you to bring tea."

"I brought the tea," Scotty repeated, continuing his rattling way across the room, and not sparing the furniture's legs—or the villainous duke's. Had the man not sidled out of the lumbering giant's way at the last moment, he would have been run over. Scotty waited until he had settled the silver service at Yancey's side, next to her chair, between her and Roderick, to offer more conversation. "The horse is sick," Scotty told her. "The duke is delayed."

"Yes, I can see that," Yancey said pleasantly, every facial

muscle involved in smiling now sore and tired. She did wonder, though, exactly how long Scotty had known this tidbit of information. Hours, it had to be. Veritable hours. Yancey patted at her hair and sent Scotty a sidelong glance. "Did the duke happen to say, Scotty, exactly how long he would be delayed?"

"No." He pointed a sausage-like finger at the steaming pot of tea. "Pour this," he said, "in here." He now, of course, pointed to a fine bone china teacup in its equally delicate saucer.

Dismayed, Yancey forced a chuckle and felt her face heat up. "Thank you. I know how to serve tea, Scotty. You may go now."

But he didn't. He just stood there . . . between her and the Duke of Glenmore. Scotty's dull gaze seemed somehow to skewer the man in place.

Yancey glanced the way of the now reseated duke and saw him dividing his suspicious attention between her and her monster-sized butler. "No doubt," Yancey said, directing her "fair warning" comment to Sam's cousin, "you have a long acquaintance with Scotty and know how . . . protective he can be of those he serves."

"Yes," the duke said smoothly. "A most singular creature."

Creature? Not man? Instantly angry, all Yancey could think about was Sam's telling her earlier how Roderick used to torment Scotty when he'd been a helpless boy. Well, the duke certainly didn't seem inclined to do so now. No doubt, Scotty's size had something to do with that. But size or no, should anyone of any rank think to torment anyone under her charge, Yancey silently fumed, they'd have to go through her first.

Tipping her face up to the butler, trying to convey that she was fine here alone with the duke, though she felt anything but fine, Yancey smiled and said, emphatically this time, "Thank you, Scotty. You've been most kind, but you *really* may go now."

The hugely intimidating man, who was proudly wearing his new suit of clothes, complete with his new hat—a strange twist for indoors—straightened up to his considerable awe-inspiring size. Cutting his clear-colored gaze from her to Roderick and back to her, he said, "I cleaned your gun. It's back under your pillow."

No doubt, he thought himself the soul of subtlety. But Yancey nearly shrieked. She certainly had Roderick's undivided attention now. Surely, he was wondering why the lady of the house felt compelled to sleep with a gun under her pillow. "Oh my. Uh, thank you, Scotty." Yancey looked up at the butler, pleading with her eyes for him to leave.

"Her Grace Nana filched a crumpet off the tray."

He wasn't going to leave. Defeated, Yancey could only stare up at the man. They were speaking two different languages, she and Scotty. She cleared her throat. "Really? Why didn't she simply join us if she's up and about?" Yancey was actually beginning to feel sorry for the Duke of Glenmore. They must all appear insane to him.

"She's hiding."

Genuine distress seized Yancey and had her turning to the duke. "Excuse me a moment, Roderick. Please forgive this bit of domestic drama." The man nodded, looking as if a cannon had gone off right next to his head. Yancey turned in her chair to better see the butler. "Where, Scotty? Where is Nana hiding? Tell me."

"Under her bed. She's eating the crumpet."

"And you're supposed to be looking for her, aren't you?" He nodded. "Then I expect you to do so. Scotty, she is approaching three hundred years old, if she's a day. So if you're going to engage her in a game of hide-and-seek, there will be none of this allowing her to hide and your not looking for her. Now, what do you have to say to that?"

Scotty lowered his impressive brow stubbornly and poked his thick bottom lip out. "Mr. Marples made potty in the dining room."

Yancey stared at the big, big man. "Dear God." She then squeezed her eyes shut and pinched the bridge of her nose with her thumb and forefinger. In that pose, she told her guest, "You'll be glad to know, Roderick, that Mr. Marples is a very bad little dog."

When she opened her eyes, Scotty was lumbering off in his hulking way and Roderick the villainous duke was staring at her as if she'd just shed a skin. "You really *are* Sarah Margaret, aren't you? You *are* the American duchess."

Yancey cocked her head at a questioning angle. "Why, yes I am. But what an odd thing for you to say. I told you straightaway who I was. Did you doubt me?"

"No," he said, tugging thoughtfully at his clean-shaven chin, his eyes narrowed in consideration of her. "No, I didn't."

Yancey watched him, knowing that as of this moment, with the Duke of Glenmore now convinced of her identity, her life was in danger. She would have to be very careful from now on. After all, her suspicion was that he'd killed, or had caused to be killed, one Duchess of Somerset, for whatever reason, and so he wouldn't hesitate to kill another one. The most dangerous creature on earth, she knew, was a man who had already killed once. Maybe twice. She thought of Sam's brother, Geoffrey.

Still playing hostess, though, and still smiling, she poured Sam's cousin a cup of tea and offered him a biscuit. As he made his selection, she looked up and happened to catch Scotty's eye. Behind the Duke of Glenmore, out of the man's sight, but directly in Yancey's line of vision, the butler stood at the open doors, facing her, and was making ready to close them as he exited.

He'd obviously been waiting for her to notice him. Yancey glanced her guest's way and saw he was occupied with staring longingly, perhaps possessively, out the open French doors off to his right. With him thus occupied, she set down the plate of biscuits and met Scotty's waiting gaze, her eyebrows arched in question.

He did the most remarkable thing, something she would never have believed if she weren't seeing it herself. His face split apart . . . into a grin. Then he winked, which made Yancey blink with surprise. Why in the world had he done that? But almost immediately, she knew. The butler's performance had been just that. A performance to show Roderick that Yancey knew the ins and outs of the household. A performance to convince a skeptical and dangerous man that she was who she said she was. Scotty was her co-conspirator.

A sense of wonder filled Yancey as the butler pulled the doors closed and left her alone with Roderick. At least now she had the serving of the tea to occupy her hands and the fussing with the dishes to supply her with reasons for pauses to gather her thoughts. Maybe Sam had told Scotty, on his way out to the horse barn, to come to the aid of the duchess because she was new here. That could be, but she had no idea what to think about that gun business. How did Scotty know where she kept her gun? Sam's doing, again? Possibly. She would have to ask him. And, for the tenth time, where *was* he—off inspecting the queen's stables in London?

Just then, the closed double doors to the room opened again. So quick was this on the heels of Scotty's departure that Yancey thought it must be the giant again. With her guest, the villainous duke, she turned expectantly, waiting to see who would join them now. Yancey's silent prayer, of course, was that it would be Sam. But no. To her horror, in swept an elegantly dressed, silver-haired middle-aged woman who could only be the dowager Duchess of Somerset, Sam's mother and the writer of the desperate letters to her daughter-in-law in America.

Unescorted—meaning, again, Sam wasn't with her—she stopped suddenly, stared wide-eyed at Yancey, who'd slowly risen to her feet, along with Roderick, and said, "Who are you?"

All but frozen inside, and refusing to look Roderick's way, Yancey replied smoothly, "I'm Sarah, your daughter-in-law. You wrote to me in Chicago, and here I am."

The attractive woman with the sweet face took a moment to absorb that. Then her expression softened, became wondering. "Then . . . you're not dead? You're Sarah?" Her face lit up. "It is you? You're really Sarah? And you're really here?"

Yancey credited the woman's inane questions to her shock. "Yes, it is I. And yes, obviously, here I am. And I am very much alive."

The dowager shook her head, still not believing. "I don't

understand. Roderick told me—And then Sam said you had—Oh, dear." She put the back of her hand to her forehead as if feeling for fever. "Forgive me, I fear I'm going to . . ."

And then she did. She fainted dead away.

Sweaty, frustrated, and smelling of the horse barn, but with events there satisfactorily resolved—a stubborn stone had been removed from a prize mare's hoof and then, free of pain, she had finally accepted her hungry foal to nurse—Sam now carried his jacket tossed over a shoulder. Grim of expression, he rolled his sleeves down. With the afternoon sun beating down on his head, and his mounting worries beating down on his mood, he trudged up the steep hill that led from the meadow up to the formal garden and then to the manor house.

He couldn't really say that he was anxious to go back inside. Not while he and Yancey were at odds. And not with Roderick here. And especially not with his own mother in residence. He loved her deeply, heart and soul, and she was a good woman. But she could ask more unanswerable questions than Roderick could because she had more of a right to do so.

Sam still debated with himself whether or not he should tell his mother the truth about Yancey. For one thing—

"Sam! Oh, thank God, here you are!"

Sam jerked his head up and saw Yancey standing atop the hill he was just starting up. She was waving and urging him to come to her. Obviously, something had happened. A jet of fear weakened Sam's limbs, but then galvanized him into action. His mind suffered from dire images of what could have transpired in his absence. Gunplay? A life-and-death struggle? A stabbing, a poisoning, a choking? His mind spared him nothing. He knew he'd never forgive himself for not being there.

Swinging his coat off his shoulder and tossing it to the ground, he charged headlong up the hill to meet Yancey, who was stumbling down to meet him. They met halfway up, and she fell into Sam's arms, putting them in grave danger of nearly crashing and rolling back down to the meadow in a twist of arms and legs. But Sam held fast, digging his heels into the earth as, his muscles tensed, his heart pounding, he pushed Yancey's hair out of her face. "Yancey, what is it? What's happened?"

Breathless and gasping, she was capable only of shaking her head and clinging to him as if all the demons of hell had been chasing her. *What the bloody hell has happened?* He may not know what, but he felt certain he knew who lay behind it. His eyes narrowed with steely resolve, Sam wrenched his gaze up to the top of the hill over which Yancey had just come. He fully expected to see at least one of the devil's minions, with Roderick's face plastered on it, pop into view. Should that happen, Sam fully intended to knock the bastard right back down the other side of the hill, if for no other reason than that he owed him from their childhood. But he didn't appear, and Sam thought it was just as well because he was fully occupied with the distraught Yancey.

"Yancey, tell me what's happened. Did Roderick harm you or Mother in any way?" Sam took hold of her arms and tugged her resisting body away from him until he could see her face.

She'd run all this way—the manor still remained a good distance away—and her face was reddened to prove it. Her hair was coming undone, she was gasping in great drafts of air, and shaking her head. "No, he didn't. And I'm fine. But it's your mother, Sam." It was all she could get out.

Sam's heart sank. "My mother? Yancey, what about my mother?"

She ignored his question and, suddenly looking surprisingly calm and in control, asked him, "Did anyone follow me?"

Though a bit confused over this abrupt change in her demeanor, Sam looked up the hill again, saw no one topping the rise, and focused again on her. "No. Not that I can see. Why?"

"Good." She pulled away from him, calmly fussing with

her hair as she looked up at him. "Your mother fainted, Sam."

"My mother?" Shock stiffened his legs. "You met my mother? She's been downstairs already?"

"Oh yes, Sam, she has."

Sam stared at Yancey, his mind churning with the implications of that simple statement. But it was Yancey's glaring green eyes that told him he was in trouble with her, plain and simple. "I should have been there."

A tight smile tinged her usually generous lips. "Yes. You should have."

"I'm so sorry. But my mother . . . she fainted? That's why you came running out here?"

Yancey arched her eyebrows. "Were you hoping for something worse?"

"Hardly. But why did you come haring out here and scare me? Why didn't you just send a boy to get me? Scotty would gladly have tossed a little beggar out the back door for you. There was no need for this, forgive me, hysterical display."

"But that's exactly what it was, Sam. A display only." Very calmly, she straightened her pretty pale-green dress around her.

And Sam watched her appreciatively. Yes, there was tremendous upheaval occurring all around them, but he was a man, after all. And he wasn't dead. When she raised her hands to brush back her loosened hair, Sam's gaze followed them. He saw that she was watching him watch her and apparently found this worthy of pursing her lips.

"Are you paying attention to me, Sam?"

"I thought that was rather obvious." Her answering scowl forced him to confess. "I'm sorry. What *did* you ask me?"

"I didn't ask you anything. I was telling you about your mother's faint. And was about to tell you of my delightful tea with Roderick."

Sam came to attention. "Dear God, Yancey. Tea with Roderick? This won't do at all. I had no idea he and Mother were even stirring. Mrs. Edgars told me they were still abed, or I never would have left."

"She was wrong."

"Indeed. Forgive my language, Yancey, but *damn.* I am so sorry."

His speech appeared to mollify her. "Apology accepted. You couldn't know what was occurring. At any rate, I took matters in hand and proceeded on course."

Sam smiled. "No doubt, very capably." He watched her duck her chin in acceptance of his compliment. What an exciting woman she was. Very stirring. Standing there with her so close, he felt the pull of her magnetism, the heat of her femininity. Sam cleared his throat, struggling to stay on the subject. "Did you ever tell me *why* my mother fainted?"

Yancey startled him by smacking his arm—hard—and planting her hands at her waist. "Is it not obvious? Could it have had something to do with how surprised she was, Sam, at the idea that she could have tea with a *dead woman*?"

Sam's stomach clenched. "Blast it all! You had to tell her who you were, didn't you? Damn." Sam put a hand to his forehead and rubbed tiredly. "Forgive me again, Yancey. You've had much to deal with alone, I know. I can only thank God for your help and your quick thinking. How was Roderick through all this?"

"Surprised. Not pleased. Suspicious. But he never let on, not openly. Perhaps someone with a less trained eye than mine would not have even noticed that he was anything less than kind and relieved. While he avoided answering any of my questions, he did prove most helpful when your mother fainted."

There was no reproach in her voice, but her wording made Sam wince. He should have been there. Damn that Mrs. Edgars! "Helpful? Roderick? I find that hard to believe. In the past, my cousin has proven himself fit only for fertilizer of the rankest sort."

"And yet your dear cousin scooped your mother up and carried her to her bedroom upstairs . . ." Yancey paused. Sam felt certain he would not like what she had to say next. She proved him right. "*Where*, you'll be glad to know," she continued, "your insane little nana was hiding under the bed."

"Dear God. We inhabit a madhouse."

"I've thought so since I arrived. However, to continue. I

found out that your nana was under your mother's bed when she grabbed my ankle as a prank and nearly sent me to the floor in a swoon—"

"Yancey, I'm so sorry—"

"Don't interrupt. Her Grace Nana's nurse finally flushed her out. Apparently, she'd been under her own bed for hours—your nana, not Mrs. Convers—only coming out long enough to make her way downstairs in a well-timed foray to steal a crumpet off the tea cart . . . just before Scotty, who was suddenly struck chatty, wheeled it in to Roderick and me and told us that Mr. Marples had made wee-wee on the floor in the dining room, Sam."

Sam found himself wincing again, this time because of his insane family's antics and because of Yancey's continuing aggravation with him for not being there to help. He wasn't the least bit fooled by her chirping voice and smiling face. She was angry.

"Then," she was saying brightly, "your mother woke up to a fluttering of maids and myself and Roderick all clustered around her, et cetera, et cetera, Nana, my ankle, you already know that part. Following all this, then, that dear, dear lady—your mother—had many questions, Sam. Many very specific questions. All of them directed at me, who I will remind you again was operating without your presence and therefore in the dark."

"The mare had a bad hoof and wouldn't nurse her foal," Sam blurted guiltily and unhelpfully.

"I'm so sorry to hear that."

"It's better now."

"Well, thank God." Yancey spared him a tight grin and held forth with her tale of woes. "At any rate, your mother *is* very happy to see me, Sam. Though she did wonder—in front of Roderick, mind you—why my hair and my eyes aren't brown. And why I'm several inches shorter than *you* told her I was in your *many* letters to her over the years while you lived in America. What a good son you are to have kept up such a chatty correspondence."

"I can explain."

"I'm sure you can. But I'm the Pinkerton here. I should

have thought to ask you. Mr. Pinkerton would not be happy. He'd call that slipshod."

"Don't be so hard on yourself."

"Oh, I'm not," she remarked cheerfully. "There's plenty of blame to go around."

Sam felt suddenly stubborn. "I've accepted my part in this."

"Have you, now? Well, there's more, Sam. Much more. Your mother—a sweet, sweet woman, by the way—asked me, and I remind you again that all of this was in front of Roderick, about my paintings. She wondered had I brought any examples with me." Yancey paused . . . long enough for Sam to realize he was sweating. "I can't paint, Sam," she added fatalistically. "Not even a wall, much less a portrait, mind you. And then there's the piano." She stared pointedly at him.

Sam knew all too well where this was going. After all, he was the author of all the glowing, detailed letters outlining his wife's many accomplishments—all of them out-and-out lies—for his mother. He'd done so to spare her the truth of Sarah's insanity and his burden. But now his kind deed was coming back to haunt him. Still he heard himself, quite stupidly, echo Yancey . . . "The piano?"

"Yes. The piano. She'd like for me to play it for her this evening. And sing. Apparently you've told her that I do that very well."

Sam felt pained, aggrieved, and so very much in trouble. "I don't suppose you can play the piano, can you?"

Yancey shook her head. "Not a lick. And I sing even worse. Are you beginning to see my dilemma, Sam?"

"I left out a few details."

"Yes, you did."

Sam absently, guiltily, scratched at his head. "And so you feigned this hysteria in order to get to me first, didn't you?"

Yancey smiled brightly in much the same way one would at a particularly dense child who has finally, at long last and after much instruction, given a correct answer in the schoolroom. "You're very good at this. My first thought was you deserved to walk right into that hornet's nest."

"And your second thought, the one that had you running out here, was?"

"Was that such a course of action is not what you're paying me for." She was serious now.

Sam nodded, stared down at his boots, at the bits of manure and hay he could see were stuck to the soles of them, and then glanced up at Yancey. "This isn't the first time I've stepped in it with you today, is it?"

Also staring at his boots, her arms now crossed under her magnificent bosom, she shook her head no. A guilty sigh escaped Sam and brought her attention back to his face. For something to do, he ran a hand through his hair. "You'd like to shoot me about now, wouldn't you?"

"I would. And if I did, it would be with my newly cleaned gun." Suddenly warmer than the day could account for, Sam didn't say a word . . . not one word. "Sam, how would Scotty know about my gun being under my pillow?"

"I have no idea. He doesn't snoop. Perhaps Nana found it and told him."

She nodded, and Sam stared into her brightly sparkling green eyes and thought how beautiful she was. He knew better than to tell her that right now, though. And, fully realizing the depth and the breadth of the trouble he was in with Yancey, Sam looked longingly over his shoulder, yearning for the relative quiet and masculine environs of the horse barn. That he understood. He also understood, now returning his gaze to her face, that she was apparently at the end of her tirade and was awaiting comment from him, all while giving him the cold shoulder and staring pointedly off into the distance.

Watching her, Sam was unexpectedly struck anew at how petite she was and how exquisitely fragile, like a piece of fine porcelain. He could only stare at her. No doubt, she fancied herself invincible. Certainly she had a wonderful wit and intellect, both of which stood her in good stead, along with her years of experience with the Pinkertons. But if he had his way, Sam knew he would suit her up in the heaviest armor he could find and then stand guard over her day and night. Anything to keep her safe and from rushing headlong into danger.

Momentarily overcome with the depth of his feelings for her, and equally mystified that he'd come to care so quickly, he stared at his dirty boots and tried to accept several truths. He didn't have the right—or her permission—to protect her, to keep her safe and happy, or to love her, much less to have her in his life beyond the foreseeable future. Neither had she expressed any desire to remain with him. Indeed, her life was in America and her heart lay in her work. And he and his problems were merely her present case for her employer.

"Sam? What's wrong?"

He met her gaze and saw that she frowned. Concern for him shone in her eyes—concern of the woman for the man, and not the detective for the employer. Obviously he'd revealed, through his expression, something of his state of mind.

Unexpectedly, anger welled up inside Sam. He wanted her and hated that he did. Wanting a woman like her could only lead to more hurt. She was like the wind and would not be tamed. Sam wanted to turn away from her and tell her to leave. He hated how his damned heart flopped around in his chest whenever she was near, and how she filled his every waking thought. He opened his mouth to speak but thought better of it. He firmed his lips together and shook his head.

"Sam? You can tell me."

He sent her a sidelong glance, considering her and considering the foolhardiness of what he was about to say. Then he decided to hell with it, might as well say it. "All right, Yancey, I'll tell you," he said at long last. "You're going to leave one day soon, aren't you?"

She blinked, appearing surprised by his question. "You know I am. When I'm done here."

"Exactly. I and my problems are just another case for you." When she didn't rush to gainsay him, to tell him that he was different, that she felt more for him than that, disappointment and resignation fought to be first to close Sam's throat. He swallowed the hurtful lump lodged there and continued. "So you'll go back to America and take up your life where it left off, correct?"

Her expression could only be called wary. She raised her chin as if to signal she was prepared to defend herself. "What choice do I have?"

What choice, indeed? He could offer her several, but believed she wouldn't be receptive to any of them. He recalled all too well everything she'd said earlier following that heated and hungry kiss they'd shared.

"I would go with you, if I could," Sam said quietly, obliquely, offering her an opportunity to say she too wished he could go and that maybe together they could find a way.

"But you can't."

Sam's heart felt pinched at her rejection. He had only pride left to him. "I agree. My life and my responsibilities are here. You've seen them. They are formidable. There is no more America for me."

She cocked her chin at a questioning, considering angle. "This is a mighty strange conversation we're having, Sam."

"Yes, it is. But these words need to be spoken."

Yancey met that observation with a frown. "Why do they?"

"Because I'd never forgive myself for letting you go without at least having said a portion of what I feel. Yancey, I want you to know that I—"

"Don't, Sam. Please." She squeezed her eyes shut and held up a cautioning hand. "What you're about to say cannot make either one of us happy."

"Happy?" His angry word had her opening her eyes. "I'm not certain I know how that feels, Yancey. Do you? Have you ever experienced 'happy'?"

She looked at him as if she hated him for putting her through this, for making her think about such things. "Just say what you have to say, Sam."

"All right. Before you go, before I'll never see you again, Yancey, I'd like to make love to you."

She drew back in shock, her eyes widened and her mouth agape.

He held out a hand to forestall her stalking away, should

she be thinking to do so. "Forgive me for being so forward. I don't believe there is another woman in the whole of England I could or would say such a thing to, Yancey. But you're not other women, and I don't have the luxury of time to woo you."

She narrowed her eyes. "Why, you pompous, overbearing ass." Now she shook an accusing finger at him. "Make no mistake, sir, while I am no untried miss, neither am I a fast woman. Do you think I'll jump into your bed simply because *you* desire it . . . *Your Grace*?"

Sam leaned in toward her. "No, I do not. But I think you will because *you* desire it, too. Tell me I'm wrong. Tell me, after that kiss in the drawing room, that I'm wrong, Yancey."

She said nothing, but her throat worked, as did a muscle in her jaw. Her eyes blazed with high emotion . . . and with the truth. He'd hit a nerve, and she hated him for that. Still, Sam had all he could do not to grab her to him passionately and have her right here on this hill. But instead he steeled himself, body and soul, and made the most impassioned speech of his life.

"Yancey, I meant no disrespect to you. I spoke my desires badly. What I mean is you are the only woman in all of England I would risk saying such a thing to. And that's because you are also the only woman in all of England or even the world about whom I care a fig. I want you. I desire you. And yes, I feel so much more for you than I have a right to feel. What I don't have are months upon months to gently seek your affections. And if I can't have you for always, then I want you while you're here. I know you can't give me more than that, but I'll take that, Yancey. If it's only days or weeks, I'll take that. I want that. And if you do, too, then I shall be, for the first time in my life, the happiest of men."

Clearly, he'd surprised her with his declaration. She couldn't seem to meet his sincere gaze. She lowered her own and toed her satin slipper through the dirt. "I don't know what to say."

The cold sweep of dread shot through Sam. "You don't have to say anything, Yancey."

She looked up at him. Sam's heart seemed to catch in his throat. He thought he detected the shine of tears in her eyes. Then she smiled at him. "I've never had any of those pretty things said to me before in my life, Sam Treyhorne."

Though she didn't say how she felt about having now heard them, she was smiling. Sam dared a grin of his own and also dared to hope, though his heart still thumped dully and felt too heavy for his chest. "Do I at least get high marks for a pretty speech, then?"

Looking suddenly shy, and with her dark auburn hair seeming to absorb and reflect the day's waning sunlight, she nodded. "You do."

Had she said yes or not? Sam felt he stood not on a hill but at the crumbling edge of a cliff that overlooked a deep and dark ravine. Not really knowing how to wring an answer out of her, he planted his hands at his waist and nodded over nothing. "Good. Good. That's good to know. High marks."

She chuckled at his expense. "Glad to hear you're so pleased."

He had to know. Yes or no. He sent her the most direct and sincere expression he could muster. "It's all I'll ever ask of you, Yancey. I swear it."

"I believe you, Sam," she said quietly, looking down and then away. "But you won't try to keep me here . . . afterward, will you? Because I can't stay, and I can't be who you want me to be."

"I know." His heart leaped with joy and thudded with resignation, all at the same time. What had he expected, he asked himself—for her to say she loved him and would stay forever? Ridiculous. But wanting now to be gentle with her, Sam asked, "Is it too much, Yancey, what I've asked of you?"

She shook her head no and met his eyes. "No. It's not too much. As long as we both know it's not forever."

Sam nodded and then stood quietly with her, wanting her, not knowing how to reach out to her, or even how to touch her at this moment. He just stood there on the side of a hill in the English countryside while the sun slipped stealthily down the unsuspecting sky. Sam thought about making love to Yancey. He could see it in his mind . . . their bodies intertwined, the feel of her under him, the way her satiny soft skin felt, the sounds she might make.

He'd said he would let her go. But he didn't see how that would be possible, not after he came to know her in such an intimate way. He simply couldn't get his mind to wrap around the idea of a life spent with her existing only in his memories of her. That was no life at all.

After a bit, Yancey turned to him. "We still have to do something about Roderick and your mother, Sam."

How very practical of her. Here he was on fire for her, and here she was concerned about her job. Of course, that was only as it should be, given that her occupation placed her squarely in danger. "Yes, *we* do."

Yancey smiled at him. "Go get your coat, Sam. Then we'll go inside and face the music together."

Just to lighten the mood and their burden, Sam teased, "Face the music? I thought you said you can't play the piano."

She chuckled. "Shut up, Sam."

# Chapter Seventeen

That evening, seated on the tiny cushioned stool that fronted the mirrored vanity in her stunningly feminine bedroom, Yancey was, for the most part, absorbed in her own thoughts of the coming evening she would spend with Sam. Such a delicious topic he was. So distracted, she was catching only snippets of Robin's complaints as she handed the girl hairpins when needed.

"I tell you, Your Grace, they've no right to treat me so. Even Mrs. Edgars, who's been ever so kind to me since I became your lady's maid, said so. She told them I'm on a level with them now, I am, and they was to show me respect and courtesy."

"Good for her," Yancey commented distractedly. From what she had heard so far, Robin—who stood behind Yancey and brushed, combed, and curled her hair—was alternately fussing about the dowager's maids' shabby treatment of her and about Yancey's too thick and troublesome hair. In the girl's snit of a mood, she tugged Yancey's head this way and that, leaving her to fear that she'd be bald before Robin was done.

Apparently, Yancey sighed, no one in the household had experienced a successful day. Still, a bright spot existed in the later evening for Yancey . . . and for the duke, if he only knew it. She smiled the secret smile of the seductress. Certainly her duke had an inkling of what was to come, being the one who had initiated their pending liaison. What the man didn't know, however, was that she meant to make His Grace woo her.

He'd said there wasn't time. But he was mistaken. There was. They had the entire evening before them. She intended to make him put it to good use, but without telling him, of course. Where was the fun of informing him? He was an intelligent man. Let him figure it out.

". . . and them with all their traveling they've done with Her Grace the dowager," Robin was saying. "I expect I'll be doing the same with you one day."

"I expect so," Yancey idly mumbled, thinking now on the events from earlier this evening when she and Sam had come in from the hill.

She'd been spared from having to prove she could neither sing nor play the piano or even begin to discuss painting because Sam's mother had already retired to her room for the evening and had sent word through one of her maids that she was not up to being sociable this evening. She cited her gruesome trip home in a jouncing carriage, followed so closely by the shocking revelations of the day, which had taken their toll on her strength. Therefore, she would stay in her bedroom and take her evening meal there.

When Robin raised her voice with a fresh complaint, Yancey blinked back to the moment. ". . . telling me, they were, all them snippy maids of Her Grace the dowager, that I was only a newly elevated lady's maid. Like that makes a difference. And them thinking they can teach *me* the way of things. I told them I haven't had any complaints from my lady." Robin sought Yancey's reflected gaze in the mirror.

"No. I have none. You're doing a wonderful job."

Clearly delighted, Robin executed a quick curtsy. "Thank you, Your Grace. That's exactly what I told them myself." Then she tsk-tsked and pulled on a hank of Yancey's hair. "Will you look at this? It won't do a thing I want it to do. Got a will of its own. Wants to be about its own business, I expect."

Robin's last comment recalled to Yancey how Roderick had also surprised her and Sam. He had saved them all an uneasy evening by announcing he'd sent word to a family in the area that he was at Stonebridge and he'd been invited to pay a call that evening. Sam had immediately offered to make available to him a carriage and driver, but Roderick had insisted a saddled horse would be just fine for his purposes. He fancied a bit of exercise and fresh air after the enclosed carriage ride here, he'd said. Besides, his friends lived close by and he would have a jolly evening with them and not return until late, maybe not even until tomorrow midday.

*What the devil is that man up to?* Yancey had wondered, somewhat alarmed not to have him where she could see him. She'd been instantly suspicious, of course, as had Sam, so she'd sought Scotty out and he had verified Roderick's story of a message sent and an answer received. Still, she doubted that Cousin Roderick's activities of this evening were as innocent as they were nefarious. The man was up to something.

Well, whatever it was, short of following him, she couldn't know until he returned and said or did something to give himself away. Patience was the strongest virtue a Pinkerton operative could cultivate. How well she knew that. Besides, she was glad the man was gone because that left her alone with Sam, her current prey.

"What do you think, Your Grace?"

Yancey gave a start, having no idea to what Robin referred. "What do I think about what?"

"Why, your hair, of course."

"Oh. My hair." She appraised it critically in the mirror, turning her head this way and that. As always, Robin had piled it high atop her head and had cascading curls falling over Yancey's shoulder. "It's nice. I like it."

"Well, I don't," Robin grumped, pulling pins out and fluffing the curling mass of long auburn hair all about, ruining the whole effect. "I want to try something else, if Your Grace wouldn't mind."

With her hair now completely wild and disheveled, with it looking much as if she'd been caught in a ferocious windstorm, there wasn't much Yancey could say but, "No, I don't mind."

With Robin happily pulling, tugging, and twisting her hair again, Yancey was free to retreat back into her increasingly sensual thoughts that caused a tightening and a low, pulsing throb deep in her belly. She couldn't stop the smile that claimed her lips. She would have Sam all to herself this evening . . . and this night. He wanted to make love to her.

Yancey recalled for herself that wonderful speech he'd made standing there on that hill. So tall and handsome and sincere. He'd certainly won her over with his words. *Making love to Sam* . . . the very idea and the images it conjured up gave Yancey a case of the delicious shivers.

"Are you cold, Your Grace? You just shivered."

"Oh. No, Robin, I'm fine." Embarrassed, and feeling the heat of it bloom on her cheeks, Yancey said the first thing that came into her mind. "By the way, this mauve gown is a perfect choice for tonight. Thank you."

Robin preened under Yancey's compliment. "Oh, Your Grace, you look so lovely in it. The color is perfect. It's a simple design, really. Very much the thing. And easy to get into and out of."

Robin's innocent comment acted on Yancey's sensual frame of mind. Smiling into the mirror, she pictured Sam undoing her dress's fastenings later. "Good," she told Robin. "That's perfect."

Yancey's next thought was that so many aspects of her own behavior since she'd been here at Stonebridge were unlike her. Here she'd readily turned over to a maid the intimate details of her toilette. She'd never been pampered before and had been certain she would hate it. But she didn't. Just as she didn't hate the idea of Stonebridge and of masquerading as Sam's wife. And she'd thought she would.

She didn't know whether to attribute the changes in her to the unique facets of this case, not the least of which was her setting herself up as the specific target for a murderer. She wondered what Sam would say if he knew that she had never done anything like this before, not on any of her cases. Always before, she'd simply adopted a disguise—like the elderly Christian lady one she'd used with Clara—and played a part to gain information from thieves' wives, girlfriends, or mothers. Then she'd take that information back to Mr. Pinkerton and the male agents, so they could use it in tracking down the thief. But never before had Yancey actually been the lamb tied to the stake to attract the hungry predator.

*But,* came the startling thought, *what if I'm not the lamb? What if Sam is?* It made sense—sickening sense. Sam was the last in his line. His mother was no threat to anyone. She wasn't likely to produce any further heirs. But Sam certainly could. And his wife, if the murdered woman proved to be her, had been with child, the heir. Tense with this new revelation, and fearing for Sam's safety, Yancey told herself the first question she would ask him was: in the event of his death, who inherited Stonebridge? Yancey felt certain she already knew. Roderick Hamilton Harcourt, the Duke of Glenmore. "Diabolical bastard."

"Excuse me, Your Grace?"

Yancey popped back to the moment and saw Robin's smiling, questioning visage reflected in the mirror in front of her. Obviously she had muttered her curse aloud. "Nothing, nothing. Forgive me. Are we almost done, Robin?"

"Yes, Your Grace. Sorry to be taking so long. It's your hair. It won't . . ."

Yancey tuned the girl out, leaving her to fuss about Your Grace's hair as Yancey returned to her mounting concerns for Sam. It was a very good thing, she decided, that she was playing the role of his wife. That way, she and her gun could be with him day and night. Day and night . . . the phrase echoed in her mind. Here she was pretending to be a married woman, something she never intended to be in reality. Certainly in the past, she'd adopted the role of a respectable married woman, but there had never been a husband. She had merely alluded to one.

But Sam was different. He was no illusion. He was very real. So she could lay these changes in her at Sam's door, couldn't she? His bedroom door, to be specific. That had her smiling. His bedroom door. She was going to allow him to make love to her. And that had nothing to do with the job.

Then she heard herself . . . *allow him to make love to me. What an odd way of putting it.* As if she were simply going to lie there and let him have his way with her. How . . . submissive of her. How wifely. Certainly, she'd never behaved that way before with a man, and she certainly didn't intend to with Sam, a man she very much desired and a man this entire household believed already to be her husband. Oddly, that belief on their part lent her and Sam's coming liaison the cachet of legitimacy. She had a husband. "My husband."

"Pardon me, Your Grace? Did you say something?"

Dear God, she must have murmured that aloud, too. Yancey gave a quick, embarrassed shake of her head. "No, no, I didn't. Well, I did. But just . . . carry on, Robin."

"Yes, Your Grace."

Yancey returned quickly to her thoughts of Sam, going so far as to stand him next to her in her mind's eye so she could see him as her husband. Not so much as he was in this masquerade, but how he might be in actuality in her life—a life she would have to live here in England if they were truly married. As Robin continued her fussing over Yancey's hair, she considered a life spent here with Sam. Lost in the image, a shimmering mirage of something that could never be, Yancey forgot herself and shook her head.

"Oh, steady, Your Grace," Robin cried. "I've got a handful of hairpins here. I'd hate to scratch your head with one as I put it in place."

"Sorry, Robin." Yancey immediately straightened up, knowing the girl was still a bit pouty because of her shabby treatment by the dowager's maids. As Robin gave her critical attention to different styles, still brushing and combing and piling Yancey's hair this way and that, Yancey suddenly felt much like a bride preparing for her wedding night, except she was getting dressed instead of undressed. Still, the sensual specter of a honeymoon night loomed.

A parody of a loving couple, that's what they were and nothing more. She needed to remember that. A spate of unexpected guilt assailed Yancey. She felt as if she had betrayed her mother's memory by even thinking of being married. Yancey realized that not all men were like her father. But she did believe that all marriages were the same in some very basic aspects. They were restrictive for the female. They signified a loss of the woman's independence. A subjugation of her will for his. No, Yancey couldn't see herself ceding those freedoms to any man. Not even to Sam, as much as she wanted him.

And she did want him. She was more than eager to be in his bed. Or to have him in hers. Since she'd first laid eyes on him, this evening's outcome had seemed inevitable. She'd been drawn to him, to his dark, handsome looks, to his air of potent sexuality, and to the aura of barely leashed sensual urges that emanated from him. How could she not be drawn to him? After all, she was a healthy woman of normal appetites.

Yancey stopped right there, marveling at her own attitude. How had it come about, given her mother's marriage and the awful way her life had ended at the hands of Yancey's father, that she, the daughter, would enjoy the pleasure of men's company, much less those of the bedroom? She smiled a secret smile. Ah, but she knew how.

It came from working with the men who respected her. Her attitude also came from respecting herself, from making her own way in this world, from being independent, and from being the one to say yes or no. She and her sister agents were a breed apart from other women and prided themselves on that. *A breed apart.* Yancey frowned. Always before she'd gained much satisfaction from being different. From being tough-minded and independent. But now that she'd met Sam, now that she'd experienced Stonebridge and its strange and wonderful inhabitants, all she felt was lonely at the thought of the single room in the boardinghouse that awaited her in Chicago. Suddenly, for the first time, she felt as if her profession put her in danger of having love pass her by.

*Oh, that would be awful.* Yancey stared at the troubled young woman with the creased brow who stared back at her from the mirror. *Awful? Since when?* But the question wasn't when. The question was who. Since who? And her answer was . . . since Sam. He scared her. What if he proved to be an appetite she could not satisfy? She feared she would want more and more of him. And that she wouldn't be able to let him go when the time came. Or worse, that she would lose herself in him. She hadn't yet, but the potential to do so certainly loomed large. This sort of fear was a first for her. A frightening first.

Yancey stared wide-eyed at her reflection. *Dear God, I'm falling in love.*

Would that be so awful? her softly feminine side asked. What is there to go home to? it wanted to know. Think about it. A room in a women's boardinghouse. And the next case for Mr. Pinkerton. No friends. No loved ones. No one she could be close to, or wanted to be close to. Certainly she felt gratitude and loyalty to Mr. Pinkerton, and a certain amount of daughterly affection. But beyond that, and beyond the job, she had nothing.

Until now, until Stonebridge—until Sam—she'd believed her life had begun in Chicago at the agency and would continue to be there. But not so much anymore. Now she wanted to be here . . . with Sam. And that meant the end of her as she'd been for the past six years.

"There you go, Your Grace," Robin announced triumphantly, pulling Yancey yet again out of her troubling thoughts. "All done. And you look lovely, if I must say so myself."

Smiling at her maid's reflection in the mirror, and feeling her scalp tingling all over from the prolonged brushing her hair had just undergone, Yancey considered her new hairstyle. She'd be darned if she could tell any difference between this arrangement and the one Robin had pulled down a few minutes ago. But she'd also be darned if she'd voice that. "Lovely, Robin. Absolutely lovely. Much better. You've outdone yourself."

The girl beamed, looking abashed as she shrugged her shoulders and proceeded to rid the brush and comb of a considerable amount of Yancey's hair. "You're very kind, Your Grace. And a great lady you are. We're all most thrilled to have you here at last with us. Well, most of us are. Her Grace the dowager's maids aren't. They like lording it too much over the rest of us that they work for the lady of the manor."

Finally, here was some ammunition Yancey could give Robin in her struggle for pecking order. "The lady of the manor? No, they don't, Robin. Not with me here, as you said. I am now the lady of the house." She tried not to feel guilty over the pretend nature of that designation—or its short duration. "And you are my lady's maid," she continued, feeling worse with every word for having started down this road. "I would think that gives you rank over them."

The girl's brown eyes, as well as her entire face, lit up with dawning realization and only made Yancey feel worse. "Why, Your Grace, you are absolutely right. Just let those old cows—I mean, those women—say something to me now."

In light of the girl's enthusiasm, all Yancey could think about was how humiliated Robin would be when the truth came out and she lost her exalted position. Her life among the other maids would forevermore be one of sneering looks and snide remarks. The devil of it was there was nothing Yancey could see that she could do to forestall that future. Except to stay here and become Sam's wife for real.

Just then, with Yancey in shock from her own conclusion, Robin reached around her to untie the light cape she'd placed over Yancey's shoulders while dressing her hair. Pulling it off her with a happy flourish, the newly confident lady's maid brushed away any stray hairs that might have escaped her prior notice and then stepped back, saying, "And there you are, Your Grace. Ready for your evening."

As she stood up, smoothing her silk gown with Robin's help, Yancey wished she could agree with her. Suddenly, she felt anything but ready for what was to come. Maybe she should tell Sam that this wasn't such a good idea, what they had planned for tonight. Then . . . her woman's mind treated her to a vision of herself in Sam's arms, made her taste his kiss, feel the weight of his body atop hers in a big bed, both of them undressed, the night dark and close—

"Shall I wait up for you, Your Grace?"

Her senses humming, her body filled with yearning, Yancey turned to her maid, her decision made. Whether she was right or wrong, only time would tell. She smiled, thinking of Sam and how he'd looked standing there on that hill and struggling to tell her how he felt. "No, Robin," she said softly, "I don't think that will be necessary."

The meal was almost concluded. Sam couldn't have been more pleased with it. His cook, a large, sweet-faced woman named Mrs. Sutton, who wielded absolute power in the kitchen, had outdone herself tonight. He had asked her earlier to prepare something special. And she apparently had scoured the larder, the pantries, the icehouse, the countryside, and the lakes to please him. Every manner of fish and fowl and game and green vegetables and sauces and breads and puddings and cakes had been produced and presented with a flourish, each course being accompanied by its own wine.

Adding to the air of pomp and celebration were his impeccably liveried and wonderfully mannered servants. They silently performed their various tasks under the scowling and watchful eye of Scotty, who continued to wear his new hat indoors. No one had the heart or the courage to tell him to take it off.

Seated on Sam's right, and looking stunning in a mauve gown designed to drive him insane, given its squared neckline and fitted waist, a dress meant to give more than a hint of the woman beneath, Yancey leaned over to whisper to him. "All this food. It's marvelous. And so wonderfully seasoned. I think your cook may be trying to seduce you, Your Grace."

Sam leaned in toward her. "And she just might succeed, too."

"Oh, dear." Yancey startled Sam by coming abruptly to her feet and placing her napkin beside her plate. No less than three of his liveried men rushed to hold her chair and stand ready to assist her otherwise. But she had eyes only for Sam. "I had no idea you had romantic designs on your cook," she chirped endearingly, putting a hand to her chest, over her heart, and adopting a maudlin poet's stance. "Though crushed, I shall step aside and allow true love to—"

"Oh, for the love of—Sit down, goose." Chuckling at her, Sam clutched her wrist, so poignantly tiny that his fingers more than met and lapped over each other. He couldn't help but think of the fragile bones of a bird, so easily broken if not held tenderly in one's hands.

But no sooner had Sam spoken than the three men jumped to help her: one at her elbow, one holding the chair, ready to push it in, and the third already holding her napkin, intending obviously to arrange it on her lap once she was seated. Sam continued to stare in wonder at this display on their part. They'd certainly never been so overly zealous when considering his needs. And here he was the one who paid their wages. Sam was more amused than jealous. Was everyone enamored of the woman? Not that he could fault them their taste. She was delectable.

Yancey sat down with a dramatic silken plop. Her gown's skirt billowed around her like a cloud before finally settling gracefully over her lap. Sam was reminded of a swan coming to rest on a lake. But far from swanlike at this point, Yancey's wide green eyes, high color, and slightly tipsy air amused Sam and warmed his blood. Her expression was the wide-eyed one usually found painted on a doll's face. She appeared shocked that she'd landed so hard. Instantly the servants went to work, performing their tasks and then fading back into the woodwork until they were needed again.

Sam gave them no more notice as he found himself absolutely enchanted with his American duchess. He leaned over toward her and, pretending to wipe at his mouth, hid behind his linen napkin and whispered, "Far from my cook trying to seduce me, my sweet, I fear more that this extravagance of food is a ploy on Mrs. Sutton's part. I am rapidly coming to believe that she and the rest of them here have joined forces and intend to stuff me so full that I shall be rendered incapable of seducing *you*."

Yancey sat back abruptly. "The hell you say, sir."

She cut her gaze around the room, sighting suspiciously

on the variously stationed men who stood stiffly about, much like sentinels. Then she leaned in toward Sam. Her nose very nearly touched his. "You won't allow that to happen, will you, Your Grace?"

"I assure you I'd sack the lot of them first," Sam growled, lightly hitting his fist on the tabletop for emphasis.

Then seized by a sudden impulse to be alone with her and away from these smothering individuals, Sam again took hold of her wrist and scooted his chair back. Before he could even stand up straight, again the servants snapped to and assisted, all quite needlessly to Sam's mind.

"Come with me," he implored Yancey. "I think we need to take the air."

She came to her feet, ceding her chair and her napkin to the hovering men. "Take it where, Your Grace?"

"Why, outside, of course." Sam was now dragging her the length of the impressively long table and toward the room's closed doors. Two other men opened these and bowed as they approached. At his side, Yancey hurried along, her gown rustling appealingly as she did so. "Don't we always keep the air outside, Your Grace?"

"Not all of it, my dear," Sam said amiably over his shoulder. "We keep some inside, or we wouldn't be capable of having this conversation."

"True. Then it's absolutely ingenious of you."

"Thank you." He stalked through the doorway and took them down the long hallway, aiming for the drawing room and, more specifically, the wide terrace that graced the grounds outside it. "I thought of it all by myself, you know."

"I'm not the least bit surprised, Your Grace. You're the smartest man I've ever known. Imagine, keeping air inside."

Quite inane, their conversation, and exactly as Sam intended. The truth was he suffered from no small amount of nervousness and unease, which grew out of his intentions toward this woman before the night was up. He could stand it no more. It had seemed there at the end of the meal that his employees had been multiplying like rabbits. Where earlier there had been only one, in the next moment there were three—and they were all over her. Dammit, he wanted the woman to himself and his hands the only ones touching her.

"Slow down, Sam. Where are you taking me?"

The sound of Yancey's voice surprised him into doing just that. He pulled her to his side and put an arm around her bare shoulders. Her closeness, and the warm, sweet feminine scent of her, sent Sam's blood rushing southward. This wouldn't do . . . not in the drawing room.

He tried to dissuade his willful body by teasing lightly with her. "I do apologize. I'd quite forgotten you were here."

She stopped cold, forcing Sam to do the same. They stood just outside the drawing room doors. Such an enticing vision of bright colors she was, Sam noted. Much like a hummingbird, it suddenly struck him, with her green eyes and deeply red hair, like emeralds and rubies. Perhaps she didn't need jewels. She'd put them to shame, no doubt. Still there was one particular piece he thought she should have.

"You're doing it again." The sound of her voice brought Sam around. He blinked, saw that Yancey had lowered her eyebrows in a clear sign of vexation. "That forgettable, am I, Sam? Even while you had a grip on my wrist? And now while you're standing here in front of me and staring?"

She was completely insulted. Sam chuckled, trying to ignore how his body, the damned thing, was tightening in response to her nearness. And why wouldn't it? He'd tantalized himself all afternoon, as he'd worked the estate's accounts and then bathed and dressed, with carnal images of him and her locked in loving embrace after loving embrace. "Hardly forgettable," he told her now. "I was merely lost for a moment in thought."

"Oh, were you? You will only get out of this quagmire you're rapidly sinking down into, my friend, if you can say those thoughts were of me. Which you can't because you've already said you forgot about me."

"Well, I can't possibly prevail, then, can I? However, I can say truthfully that you were included obliquely."

"I beg your pardon?"

Sam looked down the hallway, back toward the dining room. "Shh. Don't say anything yet."

Yancey tensed, straightening her posture. "What is it?"

Sam held a cautioning hand up until he was certain no one had followed them. "I think we're alone now. Come with me out to the terrace where we can talk."

Suddenly she was as sober as a judge. "It's about time. Playing the mindless little coquette was really beginning to wear on me."

# Chapter Eighteen

Sam blinked in surprise, staring down into the piquantly doll-like face that hid a will of steel. "That was an act? All that teasing and flirting? The tipsiness, too?"

She made a tsking sound. "Of course. What did you think—that a bit of wine would put me under the table?"

Feeling the fool, Sam stared at her, wondering if he would ever know the real Yancey Calhoun, the woman beneath the undercover Pinkerton operative that she was. "Why were you pretending?"

She pursed her lips as if exasperated with him. "I wish for our behavior to be reported as loving and flirtatious, just as a newly reunited couple's would be."

"Reported by whom and to whom, exactly, Yancey?"

"Well, that's exactly what we don't know, isn't it? And, as we have no answers yet, and so don't know who might be involved, we must guard our actions and our words when in the same room with anyone else."

He frowned. "Then, you think my servants—"

"Possibly. How better to keep oneself informed of the goings-on in your household than through your servants? A well-placed bribe goes a long way toward deflecting loyalty, Sam."

Sam swung his gaze toward the dining room and took a

step in that direction. "By Jove, I'll get to the bottom of this right now—"

"No." Her hand on his arm stopped his forward progress. "You can *not* do that, Sam. We cannot afford to say or do anything right now that gives the appearance of our suspecting that anything at all is afoul."

Disbelief fueled Sam's anger and sense of betrayal. "Then we're damned sitting ducks until our villain decides to act? Is that it? We behave as if nothing is the matter?"

"Exactly. We can only remain alert and be patient, Sam."

"The hell you say." He tugged against her resisting hold on him.

But she held him tighter, even planting her other hand against his chest. "Listen to me. What exactly do you propose we do, Sam? Who exactly should we confront? You'd get only denials, and you have no proof of anything. All you would end up doing is having to fire your entire staff—all of whom may be innocent—and thereby alerting our villain that he needs to be more circumspect. And that is the last thing we want, Sam. We want him to think we're unaware, so he'll be careless and will make a mistake. And not us."

"Damn your years of experience at this, Yancey. And how dare you make complete sense when I feel like acting the jackass?" He was angry and he meant it. But still, he chuckled at his own expense . . . right along with her.

"Sorry to ruin your fun," she quipped, letting go of his sleeve and conscientiously smoothing the fabric.

"No you're not. And I hate it that you're right. I much prefer acting to waiting. But there's no help for it, is there?" He paused a moment, trying to make himself believe it. "Damn." He exhaled, finally feeling more in control of himself, and smiled down at her. "You're very good at this, you know. I have tremendous respect for your abilities."

Though looking suddenly shy, she did grin at him. "Let's see if I can keep us all alive before we hand out congratulations, shall we?"

"A good plan. I'll help you." With that, he stepped around her to open the double doors of the drawing room. "After you, my dear." She raised her eyebrows, and Sam added, "For the servants. In case they're listening."

"And of course, if they are, then they will have heard you say that, too."

"Damn."

"I couldn't have said it better, Your Grace." With that, and a grand sweeping gesture with her full skirt, she preceded him into the elegant, overfurnished drawing room.

As Sam knew it would be, since this was the usual room to which he and his family and guests repaired following the evening's meal, the drawing room's sconces were lit and a cozy fire burned in the fireplace. Despite it being the calendar month of May, he'd ordered it knowing the cavernous rooms of the manor turned cool the moment they lost the day's ration of the sun's warmth.

He closed the doors behind them and then turned to her. Damned beautiful, she was. His gaze lit on the closed French doors. "Here," Sam said, unbuttoning and then shrugging out of his coat. "Put this around your shoulders. I want to step out onto the terrace."

"Your coat. How gallant of you." She accepted it and laughed with him at how it swallowed her small frame. But as she snuggled down into its depths, she sighed. "Mmm, so warm." She lifted her eyes to his, her expression sensual, inviting. "And it smells wonderfully of you, Your Grace. I find the mix of your particular scents very appealing."

Her voice, as much as her words, sent fire exploding through Sam's body. The things she said to him—but then he sobered. "Is that you talking? Or was that part of your undercover personality?"

She smiled some secretive, enigmatic female smile that made Sam's knees rubbery. "It was me. Make no mistake, you're quite a delight for the senses, Your Grace."

Sam exhaled raggedly. He'd almost had his body talked back into a dormant state, but not anymore. No, now it stood at proud and throbbing attention. "Air," Sam said, barely able to walk to the French doors and throw them wide. "We need good, cold air. Lots of it. Now."

Once outside on the terrace, and facing away from her,

he planted his hands at his waist and breathed in great drafts of the flower-scented night air. He knew Yancey had followed him when she appeared at his side. Such a tiny presence to exert such a force on him. Backlit by the fire in the fireplace and the lamps behind her, her child-sized hands held his coat in place by its lapels. She said nothing and seemed merely to be enjoying the outdoors as much as he was enjoying her.

His body fairly hummed. Sam couldn't take his eyes off her profile. Each time he'd looked at her over the course of the past three days, he'd felt as if some huge unseen fist were squeezing his heart, but not in an entirely unpleasant way. He'd never felt like this before, not even with Sarah. Probably especially not with Sarah.

So what was this—this desperate urge to lock Yancey away in the tower and stand guard himself at the door? From what enemy or monster did he think to protect her? All of them, he supposed. It was most disconcerting, this physical pain that scared him and excited him at the same time. He wanted to possess her one moment and then set her free to thrive the next. He couldn't put a name for this feeling inside him, but if it was love, then he wanted no part of it. Surely, it would only get worse and then would weaken and kill him.

"Look at that moon. So bright and startling," she said suddenly, breaking into his thoughts. "As if you could reach out and pluck it from the sky. You can't see the stars this clearly in Chicago. It's sad, really. I think they get lost among the buildings there and the noise."

How wistful she sounded. Sam's heart ached for her, and he suddenly saw her as a woman with hopes and desires. Hopefully, some of those desires were for him. Smiling at his own play on words, and warming toward her to the point of fearing he was utterly besotted, he fondly noted how the moon shone fully in her face. She was luminous. So beautiful. And he wanted her so badly. Standing there with his feet apart, Sam purposely locked his hands together behind his back to keep from shocking her by grabbing her to him. "It's the same way in London. The sky, I mean, and it getting lost."

She nodded. "I recall. I like it here much better. It's very beautiful."

"Yes," he said softly, his yearning gaze still fixed on her face, "I think so, too." Much more of this, a more objective part of Sam's mind noted for him, and he would find himself engaging in his favorite fantasy of late. In it, he saw himself scooping her up into his arms and, in a heated rush, carrying her up that wide sweep of stairs that led to his bedroom. Once there, he would—

Yancey suddenly turned toward him. "Why did you bring me out here, Sam?"

"For the privacy." Well, the moment had arrived. He reached a hand into his trousers pocket and couldn't believe how tense he felt. "And to give you this." He pulled out a small black velvet ring box. "I thought, under the circumstances, that you should have it."

Irritated that his heart should be pounding and his palms sweating like that of some silly young swain, Sam held the box out to her . . . much as if it were his heart.

"I don't want it," Yancey said, shaking her head, refusing to take it.

Instantly insulted, Sam became stubborn. "What do you mean, you don't want it? Of course you do."

Shaking her head, Yancey eyed the box warily and then him suspiciously. "No I don't. What is it?"

"See? You don't even know what it is."

She poked her nose a little bit closer to the box and really stared at it. "Then tell me."

Sam exhaled his irritation. "It's a poisonous viper whose bite will strike you dead in less than a minute."

Undaunted, she poked a finger at the box. "Well, it's an awfully little one, then, if it fits in there."

"Little but potent. Much like you. Now, take it." Again he urged the box on her.

But again, fisting her hands at her sides, she refused it. "I said I don't want it."

Giving up, cursing under his breath, Sam opened the dratted ring box himself, showed her its contents, and felt completely gratified by her gasp of appreciation. Back on his game, he plucked the impressive diamond ring out of its velvet bed, snapped the box closed, tucked it back in his pocket, and held the ring out to her. "Take it. Please."

But she wouldn't. Already, she was backing up. "Sam, have you lost your mind? You can't give me a ring like that."

He advanced on her. "I'm not giving it to you. It's a family heirloom. I mean only for you to wear it while you're posing as my wife."

Looking suddenly unsure of herself, vulnerable somehow, as if he'd hurt her, she looked down and away from him. "I don't want to wear it," she said quietly.

"But I want you to." Sam heard how petulant he sounded. This was not the warm and tender scene he'd envisioned. But then, nothing ever went how he believed it might where Yancey was concerned. "There's no need to attach any significance to this act. I'm offering it only for expedient reasons having to do with your employment with me."

She swung her attention back to him, looking stubborn herself or perhaps angry. "How romantic."

Sam gestured his helplessness. "I strove for romantic to begin with. And you rejected that. This is very simple, Yancey. As the wife of a duke, you would be expected to have jewelry and to wear it. I simply thought it would forestall any questions, that sort of thing. Now give me your hand."

Unbelievably, she still wouldn't, putting both of them behind her back. "No."

She was going to drive him insane. But sudden amusement had Sam chuckling. "Yancey, what do you want me to do? I can't see us in a wrestling match. Or is it that you want me to go down on one knee and do this?"

She pulled a face, her bottom lip poking out to show she'd taken offense. "No. Of course not. Don't be silly. Why would I want you to do that? We're not really married. We're not getting married, either. And I don't care what anyone thinks. I don't want the ring. And you can't make me wear it just because you're the duke and my employer and I'm posing as your wife. So there."

His eyebrows arched, Sam just stood there, waiting for her to run out of denials. At last, into the quiet, he asked,

"Why are you so afraid of marriage, Yancey? It won't kill you."

A look of pure pain, one that pinched her nostrils and furrowed her brow, crossed her face and then was gone. "My experience says different, Sam."

"Your experience?" Sam's knees stiffened with shock. "Are you telling me that you're already married?"

"No. Hardly." Then she surprised him by stepping up and plucking the ring out of his hand. "Oh, give it to me. I'll put it on and wear it. But only as long as you understand that it doesn't mean anything."

"Certainly. Not a thing," Sam lied, smiling as she put the ring onto her left third finger. It slid perfectly into place. The diamond, almost the size of her knuckle, overpowered her tiny hand . . . but looked very right there.

Apparently pleased despite herself, she waggled her fingers . . . a purely feminine gesture . . . and then held her hand out and surveyed it from all angles. Then she looked up into his eyes and realized she'd been caught. She dropped her hand to her side and lifted her chin, giving him a good snubbing. Sam laughed softly at her antics, feeling warm, tender, angry, defeated, hopeful, completely lost to her. Christ, he was doomed.

Yancey turned to him. "I'm sorry I was so rude just now. I misunderstood your intentions," she said, sounding as if she'd rather be branded with a hot poker than have to apologize for something.

Determined to enjoy this moment, Sam crossed his arms over his chest, arched his eyebrows, and said nothing.

"Oh, all right, Sam, the ring is beautiful. And you were right. A married woman, a duchess, would have a ring like this." She held her hand out again and smiled. Then she frowned. "What do I say to your mother and Roderick about it? Obviously, I wasn't wearing it earlier when I met them."

"I doubt if Roderick got as far as staring at your fingers. And it was my mother's idea. The ring, I mean."

A look of pure surprise claimed her features. "Your mother's idea?"

Sam nodded. "Where did you think I was all afternoon after we came back inside?"

"You said you were going to your study. To do the accounts."

"And I did. Then I thought about everything and went up to my mother's rooms, shooed all her maids out, as well as Mrs. Edgars, and told her the truth. All of it. I thought she deserved that."

"Oh, good for you, Sam. Certainly, she deserves the truth. But how did she take it?"

Sam exhaled sadly. "My mother has buried her husband, his parents, her own parents, and one of her sons. She took it in stride, except for Roderick's part in all this, assuming he has one. And I think he does."

"As do I. But that poor woman. I mean your mother. Still, I think there's a lot you're not telling me, Sam. I saw her faint, remember, at the mere sight of me."

"Rest assured you have the same effect on me."

Finally . . . a laugh from her. "Be serious."

"I am. Of course, Mother was very sad about Sarah and very angry with me for not telling her before now about Sarah's, well, illness. She's also thrilled with your being a Pinkerton. All very high drama to her. But most especially, she's absolutely horrified that she sent you those letters by mistake."

Yancey nodded. "That's quite a mix of news and emotions to deal with for one woman. No wonder she's taken to her bed." Pensive of expression, Yancey spoke as if only thinking aloud. "Well, I can question her tomorrow. That's soon enough with Roderick out of the house." She focused on Sam. "The letters. Did you ask her what the trouble was that she alluded to in them?"

He grinned, watching Yancey's beautifully delicate face for her reaction to this bit of news. "You'll appreciate it after our discussion this afternoon regarding children. Or *our* lack thereof."

She shook her head. "I don't understand."

"You will. Grandchildren."

"Grandchildren?" Yancey echoed.

"Exactly. Distraught over Geoffrey's demise, over losing one son, she suddenly wished to be surrounded by a large family. And that means children. Or to her, grandchildren. She then realized that I was her only hope for producing the same. And here I stubbornly refused to discuss my wife, from whom I'd told her only that I was estranged. Well, she thought me silly and stubborn. And she feared, if left to my own devices, she'd never have grandchildren and, besides that, the duchy needs an heir. So she took it upon herself to orchestrate events."

Yancey looked shocked, as he knew she would be. "Dear God, Sam." She was all but sputtering. "Look at what her letters have set in motion."

"I am all too aware. But never underestimate the power of a mother who wishes to dandle on her knee the heir to the hereditary title."

Yancey startled him by clutching at his sleeve. "Stop right there. If you don't produce an heir, Sam . . . who inherits Stonebridge?"

"I know what you're thinking, so you won't be surprised to know that it's Roderick, will you?"

She frowned. "No, I'm not surprised, not in the least." Releasing her hold on his shirtsleeve, she gestured for him to continue. "But go on, then. Your mother . . .?"

"I feel certain you will appreciate this, too, Yancey. She hired a London investigator and sent him to America to contact my wife."

"Just as I suspected. My Englishman."

Sam nodded—and labored under the growing conviction that he was merely verifying for her things she already suspected. "But instead, of course, and as you are too fully aware, he found you. Apparently the man was a bit bumbling, and not as good as you Pinkertons."

And for that, Sam was eternally grateful because the man had brought Yancey into his life. Jealously, wishing he could do it for her, he watched her running a finger over her mouth as she thought things out. "Not so bumbling, Sam. He was good. Very good. He found my address, didn't he?"

"True. But is that so hard to do?"

She shrugged. "It's not a secret, where I live. But neither is my address readily available. I like to think this private investigator she hired had to do more than a little snooping to find it." Suddenly her expression blanked and she stared up at him as if she'd just seen a ghost. "Oh, Sam. Oh no."

Sam tensed, ready to hear anything. "What is it? What's wrong?"

"Your mother . . . did she tell her *sister* that she was going to hire a man to find your wife?"

Frowning, he shrugged. "I suppose. She tells Aunt Jane everything." Then he understood, and dread washed over him. "Then Roderick knew."

"Yes. Roderick knew. And no doubt he made good use of that information. I think it's entirely conceivable, Sam, that Roderick acted on what your innocent mother divulged to her sister."

Emotion drained from Sam. "My poor mother. I don't know how much more truth she can take. She will never forgive herself."

"But she couldn't know, Sam. No more than you or I could."

"I know that. But it won't matter to her." Sam hung his head, shaking it at the thought of such treachery. Then, feeling dull, perhaps lifeless, he took up the subject again. "Then you think Roderick had an agent in Chicago?"

"No. It's worse than that. I think it's more likely that he paid the same one your mother hired and sent to America to keep him informed as well of his, shall we say, findings."

Outrage and anger seized Sam. "I'll choke the very *life* out of Roderick. How dare he plot against my mother? He can plot against me all he wants. I can take care of myself. But my mother is another thing. Entirely defenseless, she is. A paragon of motherhood and virtue."

Yancey said nothing. She merely stared soberly up at him . . . waiting for him to calm down, Sam finally realized. He exhaled, rubbed his forehead, and shook his head. "Sorry. You were saying you believe Roderick orchestrated a double cross?"

"Yes. That, and more, of course."

By *more* she meant the murder of his wife, for one thing. Sam now believed that the poor unfortunate woman killed in Chicago *was* Sarah. Why it would be necessary to kill her, he couldn't think. But Yancey also meant the subsequent attempt on her own life. Sam stared out into the moonlit darkness. "That would certainly explain why things started going badly for you at about the same time letters from my mother began arriving, wouldn't it?"

"Very likely, yes. It would also explain the same man coming after me who went after Sarah. That much we know. In both cases, he was English and the descriptions matched."

"*Damned* diabolical, Yancey." Righteously angry, Sam sought her gaze. "I cannot fathom such evil. And within my own family. My own blood. How could he kill one of his own?"

Yancey didn't answer him. Sam slowly became aware that a change had come over her face. She looked . . . wounded somehow. Sam put a hand out to her and started to speak, to ask her what was wrong, but she shrank away from his touch and said, "It happens more often than you'd realize, Sam. And in the best of families. In my work, I've learned that motivations behind even the most despicable of acts are all too . . . human. Such things as greed. Envy. Jealousy—"

"But they lead to monstrous acts, Yancey. Dear God, my brother and my wife." Filled with sadness, Sam shook his head. "Call it what you want, but it *is* evil because how, otherwise, am I to understand how someone could murder their own family? How? I will never understand it. What could possibly be worth it? What?"

Upset as he was, Sam at first thought nothing of Yancey's silence. But as he calmed down, he recalled the looks of pain on her face he'd noticed twice already in the last hour.

He turned to her, putting his hand on her arm. "You're awfully quiet, Yancey. Is something wrong?"

Yancey exhaled, turning away from Sam. Moving woodenly and feeling stiff all over, she stepped over to the low railing that girded the terrace. She closed her eyes, trying to blank her mind. But it wouldn't allow her to do so.

"Yancey?"

She turned her head slowly, only enough to speak to him over her shoulder. "Please, Sam, just . . . give me a moment. I need only a moment."

"I don't know what's wrong, Yancey. But . . . just . . . I'll be right here. Waiting for you."

She wanted to offer a thank-you, but the words wouldn't come. Instead, her throat threatened to close and her eyes filled with tears. Silently, she begged it to leave her be, this sudden and overwhelming impulse that swelled within her and told her she must finally speak aloud her guilty deed. With every fiber in her being, she did not want to do this. Yancey fisted her hands, resisting, refusing.

No. She couldn't do this. She'd told no one, not even Mr. Pinkerton, of her deep, dark secret, one that ate at her soul and deviled her sleep. What would Mr. Pinkerton say? she'd feared. Would he fire her? Lose faith in her? Turn his face away from her? She couldn't bear disappointing him. He expected such exemplary behavior from his agents. He hired only the best. And he thought her the best. And so, for eight long years, she'd lived with her secret and the guilt and the fear of being found out.

Why couldn't she go on doing so now? Why?

Her answer was a tightening inside her chest that said she must speak or her heart would explode with the weight of it. Yancey's features contorted with her agony. No. She couldn't. She'd sooner die. But the urge was too strong. A small, quiet voice in her mind said this man, Samuel Isaac Treyhorne, the Duke of Somerset, was the one she needed to tell. He needed to hear it, to be saved by it, the voice told her, every bit as much as she needed to confess it.

Yancey closed her eyes and raised her head to the night. Then it was true . . . she had to do this thing. On her exhalation, she hung her head, feeling nothing, steeling herself. Only by thinking of Sam, of putting him above herself, could Yancey turn around and face him. When she did, she saw him there . . . in the moonlight that silvered his black hair and cast his face in shadows. He took a step toward her, and she saw in his face his concern and his worry . . . and what might be his love for her.

Then this was doubly dreadful. Finally, and at long last . . . love. But too late. Because now she might be forced to kill it in order, somehow and in ways she had yet to understand, to save Sam.

Standing there on the flagstone terrace, on a clear and starry night, feeling suddenly cold despite his coat around her shoulders, and certain that her heart was not even beating, Yancey spoke. "Sam, just a bit ago we were talking about how someone could kill a family member. You called it evil. And perhaps it is. I don't know." Yancey drew in a deep and much needed breath before continuing. "You need to know— No, I feel a need to tell you that I . . . killed my father."

There. The words were out. She exhaled a gust of guilt and now felt her heart pounding, her blood racing. Sam said nothing. He didn't move. He only stared at her. Yancey, though, felt a tremendous burden lift from her soul, a feeling much like a bird taking flight. She felt so light, as if she could spread her arms wide and soar.

But still, Sam said nothing. And his silence brought her back to earth.

Yancey sobered. "Did you hear me, Sam? I said I—"

"I heard you." His expression matched the flatness in his voice. "Don't say it again. Please."

She stood there, alone now with her guilt and her grief. Not for her father. The man did not deserve it. The world was a better place because he was dead. She had no regrets. What she feared was Sam. What was he thinking right now? What would he do? What would he say? Dread once again washed through Yancey. She swallowed and was surprised that it hurt. She put a hand to her throat. Though she felt no lump, it was there. Sorrow was its name. Only when she wiped at her eyes did she become aware of the tears that streamed down her face.

"Why, Yancey?" Sam asked. "What happened?"

She stared at him, not knowing how to begin. She inhaled deeply of the cool night air and exhaled slowly. "All my life,

Sam, that man was cruel. Mean. He drank. Gambled. Hit my mother. Hit me. I grew up fearing him and hating him. He'd disappear for weeks, months, at a time. We didn't know where he was, and I didn't care. We had a hard life, my mother and I. But things were better when he was gone. We got by the best way we could on the farm. But then he'd come back. He always did. When I was thirteen, he came back for good."

She breathed in again, this time through her pinched nostrils. Her heart felt like a stone in her chest. Sam said nothing. He didn't move. He could have been made out of the same stone as her heart. "For five long years after that, we endured him. I would stay out of his way as best I could. But Mama took the brunt of his anger. Then one day . . . I came upon him, Sam. He was beating my mother. With his fists. Just beating her to death." Yancey sobbed and covered her mouth with her hand, wanting to hold back the remembered terror.

"Oh, Yancey. You poor, dear thing." Sam rushed to her and suddenly he was holding her and her head was against his chest. She felt his heart beating under her cheek, and she was clinging to him, crying, unable to stop the torrent of words or the rush of horror. "He kept hitting her and hitting her, Sam. What was I supposed to do? I was only eighteen. I didn't know what to do. I pulled on him, begged him to stop. But he wouldn't. He pushed me away, shoved me down. My mother was already on the floor, Sam. Dying. Bleeding. My mother. Oh God, my mother, Sam."

"It's all right, Yancey, it's all right, I'm holding you now, it's all right, you did what you had to do, it's all right." He just kept saying it over and over. "Shhh. You don't have to talk about it anymore. It's all gone now. Done. He can't hurt you anymore."

But Yancey shook her head, her breath coming in ragged sobs and gulps. "I had begged her to leave, Sam, I had. When he wasn't there, I told her we could leave the farm and get away from him. But she wouldn't. She couldn't, Sam. Where were we going to go? What were we going to do? She didn't know anything but the farm. We worked it together, my mother and I. But *he* always came back when he figured there was money from our small harvest. And then that one time . . . she wouldn't give it to him, Sam. She said no, that the money was for *me*. For *me* to go away and to get out. Oh, God, Sam, she died because of me. Because of *me*."

"No, Yancey, that's not true. You poor thing. God, no. You mustn't believe that. You were strong and brave and you did what you had to do."

"No." She spit the word out, pulling back, angry, hard, her hands fisted around Sam's shirtsleeves. She stared up into his face, a part of her brain noting that his expression was as ragged as her emotions. "I threw it at him, Sam." Yancey felt the hate inside her pull her lips back from her teeth. "The money. He wanted the money, so I *threw* it at him and begged him to take it and leave us alone."

"Dear God, Yancey, what you had to go through. No one should have to endure it."

But she wouldn't be comforted. "I begged him. I just wanted him gone. And I wanted him to leave my mother alone. But he wouldn't, Sam. Do you hear me? He wouldn't. I had to kill him to get him to stop. I shot him with his own gun. I pulled it out of his holster and shot him and shot him and shot him. I couldn't make myself stop."

Finally, she collapsed against the warm solidness that was Sam's body, holding on to him, knowing that if she didn't, she would drown. "I couldn't stop myself, Sam, until there were no . . . more . . . bullets."

Sam clutched her to him. "Oh, God, Yancey, that's enough. Please don't do this. I love you. No one will ever hurt you again. I won't let them, I swear it." He was kissing her hair, her forehead, stroking her back, and holding her so very close. Yancey stilled, listening to him, at last hearing him. "I love you. Oh, God, Yancey. Don't do this to yourself. You had no choice. He would have killed you next. Don't you know that? He would have killed you next."

Drenched in her own tears and fiercely hugging Sam, Yancey blinked and thought about that. On some level, one she hadn't ever allowed to have much of a voice, she had always known it was true, that she would have been next.

But she'd never been able to convince herself of that. And now here Sam was telling her the same thing. Maybe it was true, then, that she'd done the only thing she could. Still . . . the man had been her father. You weren't supposed to hate your father. Or kill him. But, sometimes, some men, well, they just deserved it.

She would never feel otherwise, she realized. She wouldn't. She would always believe that he got exactly what he deserved. Still, even with the stain of sin on her soul, Yancey suddenly felt calmer, more whole, more alive, much as if her confession had cleansed her soul.

But she had more to tell Sam. Quietly, and around hiccoughs, she said, "I buried them both. Together. I didn't want him anywhere near her. Not even in death. But do you know that she always loved him? Always. Can you imagine that? She *loved* him. He beat the life out of her, but she loved him. So I buried him next to her. And then I took the money, and I packed my clothes, and I left. I went to Chicago and made my own way until I came to Mr. Pinkerton and he hired me. He gave me a chance."

"I'm glad he did, Yancey. And I'm glad you're alive." Sam pulled her away from him, holding her out by her arms, leaning over so he could look into her eyes. "Do you hear me? I love you, and I'm glad you're alive." His words washed over her like a benediction, leaving her weak. "I'm glad you left, and I'm glad you kept yourself alive because I don't think I can live without you."

"Sam, you—"

"No. Listen to me. I have to say this. For all my life, I've been waiting for you. And you alone. I didn't know it then, but I know it now. And now it's as if I always knew, always wondered if you'd ever come, if you'd ever show up. I wondered if I would know you if you did. And then . . . there you were. In my house. Standing there and looking out the window. And from that first moment that I saw you . . . I knew. I just knew."

"Sam—"

"I know I said I would let you go when the time came. But I'm afraid I lied. I don't think I can. I don't know how all this is going to end up, Yancey, but if I don't have you, then I have nothing and there is no life. Not for me. I don't know if my wife is still alive in that asylum. And, God forgive me, I don't care. She is beyond my help. Poor Sarah has been dead for many, many years, though she's lived. And I've been dead in more ways than she ever was. But only until there was you, Yancey. I love you. I don't know what I can offer you. Or if you even want me or want to stay, or could ever stay. But all that I am, everything that I have, I lay at your feet, Yancey. I love you."

Standing there, his hands gripping her arms, Yancey realized that at some point his coat had slipped from her shoulders and she was cold. His expression was fierce with the strong emotions that lurked just under his skin. She'd suspected as much of him, that he was like a deep river, calm on the surface but roiling underneath with currents no one could see. "Yancey?"

The sound of his voice sparked her into speaking. Very calmly, she said, "I'm cold, Sam. I want to go inside."

She'd surprised him with that. He blinked and pulled back, though still holding on to her arms. "You want to go inside?"

"Yes. But that's not all."

"Then, what? Anything. Tell me."

He was so handsome. Such warm gray eyes. That stubborn jaw. Those high cheekbones. And his loving heart. How could she ever have thought him a villain? Yancey smiled at him. She'd never felt more calm or sure of herself than she did at this moment. She was like a new being, one with no hurts or scars. Whole. Good. Clean. Or perhaps it was that she was merely drained, emptied of all emotion. She didn't know. And she didn't care. Tonight, she wanted only one thing, and that was to be filled back up. And it was Sam she wanted to fill her.

At last, her thoughts ordered, she spoke. "I want to go inside with you. And I want you to make love to me, Sam."

His eyes widened and his grip on her arms tightened.

"I want you to carry me up those wide steps and take me to your bed," Yancey told him in a matter-of-fact voice. "I want you to love me. And I want to stay with you all night. In your bed. I want to sleep with you and see the sun come up with you. I want this for tonight, Sam, because I can't promise you anything more than that . . . or beyond that."

# Chapter Nineteen

She'd given him everything he wanted. She'd allowed him to place his coat again around her shoulders. She'd walked quietly with him back into the drawing room, had waited while he closed the doors, and then had crossed the drawing room with him. At the foot of the stairs, she had turned to him. And Sam had picked her up, holding her in his arms, as she wrapped her arms around his neck, her face nestled against his shoulder. Wordlessly, he had climbed the sweep of stairs. She weighed nothing. Even to himself, he seemed more to float upward than to take the steps one at a time. Her love carried him, he knew, in a much more real sense than he had her.

They'd encountered no one on their way to his room. And Sam was especially glad tonight that he had no valet, no one standing there to be shocked or embarrassed when he entered the room carrying Yancey. He felt certain that had they seen another person, the magic spell that wove itself around them would have been irretrievably broken. They both would have come to their senses, and she would have asked to be put down. And then she would have left him. But nothing like that happened. And so it was that they found themselves standing in Sam's bedroom, beside his bed, and facing each other.

Sam worried. She was so impossibly small and fragile. She wanted this to happen. He knew that. She'd even been the one to say so. But still, he feared that this wasn't the right time. Not the best moment. She'd been through so much. But on another level, a physical one, he feared he would crush her under him or bruise her . . . or otherwise hurt her. Not intentionally. Never intentionally. But the act of loving could be less than gentle. He started to speak his fears, even opening his mouth—

"No." She put her fingers over his lips. "Don't speak. Please."

Looking into her eyes, holding her gaze, Sam clasped her fingers and kissed her palm . . . softly, gently. He watched her face, saw her mouth open, heard her breathing quicken. Her green eyes glazed with desire. Sam slowly straightened her arm and kissed the inside of her wrist. A tiny moan escaped her. With nipping, biting kisses, he pulled her ever so slowly to him as he worked his way to the hollow of her elbow. He kissed deeply of her there, his other arm going around her waist.

She'd told him not to speak, but he couldn't stop the words that, for him, were as much a part of lovemaking as was his lover's touch. "I want you, Yancey. As I've never wanted anyone before."

"Oh, Sam. You are so good to me." She cupped his face with her free hand, her eyes shining. Then she moved her fingers until they were against his lips. And again he kissed them. She surprised him by taking her fingers to her mouth and wetting them with her kiss. Then she put them back against his lips. Her expression, as she captured his gaze, pulsed with a passion all its own. "I want you, too. In all ways. I will deny you nothing. I have no defenses where you are concerned, Sam. I stand naked before you."

"Not quite yet," he remarked, his body exploding with a rush of desire. He pulled her to him, kissing her mouth, plundering it, taking from it the life she gave him. He'd meant to go slowly their first time together. He'd meant to seduce her, to know every part of her body, to feed his hunger for her. But the things she said, the way she looked at him, the very feel of her in his arms, would not allow for tenderness. His body wanted only to know hers. He wanted to feel himself inside her, pushing against her, his strokes—

Yancey was unbuttoning his shirt. Sam broke their kiss and lifted his shirt over his head, shrugging out of it and throwing it to the floor.

"Oh, Sam, you're magnificent. Look at this chest." Thoroughly enjoying herself, her face alight with delight, she ran her small hands expertly over him, exciting him beyond measure.

"I love this hair here. So dark. So crisp." She splayed her fingers, the diamond on her finger flashing with her every movement. "I've been dying to get my hands on you." She raised the green eyes of a temptress to him and affected a pout. "It teases me, you know, peeking out of your shirts."

"Bad chest hair," Sam said, thoroughly enchanted with her, yet frowning as if he were scolding a dog. He was relieved to see nothing in her face or her manner of the broken little girl she'd been downstairs. So damned relieved.

Yancey chuckled, capturing his attention as she planted a quick kiss on his chest. Then, she turned around, her back to him, and said, "Undo me, please."

Never a man to question a woman's orders, and in a fever of desire, Sam started on the row of tiny buttons. As he did, Yancey began unpinning her hair. Button after button came undone. More and more of her thick, lustrous auburn hair fell down her back and over his hands. So soft. Like her skin. Sam had the buttons undone to her waist before he realized that she wore nothing underneath the dress. The realization took his breath, and then had him releasing it in a slow, sensual exhalation.

Her flawless, smooth skin was exposed to his eyes. At last.

Her arms were at her sides. Sam held on to them and bent to kiss his way down her spine. She wriggled at the sensations and, moaning, arched her back. Shirtless, about to bulge out of his pants, Sam squatted behind her on his haunches. He wanted the remainder of those damn buttons to come loose. Now. He worked them, almost beyond control, silently cursing each one and threatening to tear the fabric away from her.

But then . . . the dress fell away from her, pooling at her ankles and leaving her, like him, unclothed from the waist up.

Every male instinct within him begged him to turn her around. He wanted to see her breasts, wanted to taste her flesh, and take her nipples in his mouth. Wanted to flick his tongue against each one until they were hard buds and she could no longer stand on her own. And he would do that. But first he untied her crinolines with a slow pull of the satin bow that held them in place. These garments too went the way of the dress. Sam damn near lost consciousness . . . Yancey also had on no bloomers, no smallclothes of any kind.

"My God, Yancey, you are so beautiful."

She turned her head, her movement swinging her long hair across her back, and peered at him over her shoulder. Her eyes slanted sensually. "I'm so glad you think so. Robin was horrified."

"Poor Robin. But, oh, I think so. I very much think so. You are beautiful," he quickly assured her, grinning, feeling his blood rush wildly through his veins. Though he throbbed with need for her, he couldn't reach out to touch her. He couldn't move. She was that exquisite. A thing of beauty to be enjoyed. Squatting there behind her, his weight on the balls of his feet, Sam ran a hand over his mouth and chin and feasted his eyes on her perfect little heart-shaped bottom. If he could have sculpted one as an example of feminine perfection, it would have been this one, hers. Peaches-and-cream skin covered taut, firm muscle. "You are an absolute work of art, Yancey."

She still peered at him over her shoulder. "Are you an art lover, Sam?"

She was going to drive him mad. Sam nodded, finally catching enough of his breath so that he was again capable of moving. He wrapped an arm gently around her unbearably tiny waist and tugged her back to him. "I am the world's foremost lover of art. As of this moment."

Her chuckling response ended as a tiny gasp . . . Sam was

kissing the small of her back. He smoothed his free hand over her firm buttocks. She dug her nails into his arm that he'd wrapped around her waist. A satyr's grin claimed Sam's mouth. Her body felt and tasted just as he knew she would. He wondered only if the rest of her tasted like this warm, rich cream of her back.

Coming to his feet and directing her movements with his hands, Sam turned her until she faced him. The sight of her staggered him. He raised his eyebrows in an invitation for her to step out of the cloud of her clothing enveloping her ankles. She did so, also slipping out of her shoes, with Sam holding her hand as if they were preparing to dance a rather risqué minuet.

Then, she stood before him fully naked, unashamed, unabashed. Now Sam's heart all but stopped. Her hair had fallen over her shoulders and hung almost to her waist. Peeking through the long curling dark auburn tresses were her breasts, each one a milky-white, perfectly shaped handful topped with a rosy pink nipple. High and firm. Overcome, he had to remind himself to breathe.

Her figure itself was the stuff of romantic poems. A narrow waist and gently flaring hips that showed a hint of the bones underneath. Her smooth, flat belly boasted a dark round mole to one side of her navel. Sam's first impression was that of a tiny moon orbiting the sun. Then, the auburn vee at the juncture of her rounded thighs captured his attention and held him riveted.

"Sam, I feel I should tell you that, well, you're not my . . . first."

Still holding her hand, still very much under her spell, Sam looked into her green eyes . . . and smiled. "Good. Then that means I don't have to explain everything to you. Or worry that you'll be frightened by the sight of an aroused man." Her face colored prettily and she lowered her gaze, causing her hair to fall forward and hide her face. Sam sobered. "I'm sorry. Was I crude?"

Still not looking at him, she shook her head. Her hair danced with the motion. "No. It's just that you're an exceptional man, Sam Treyhorne. Most men would—"

"Uh-uh." She raised her head, showing him widened, worried eyes. Sam tenderly tucked her hair behind her ears. "If I were most men, Yancey, then I wouldn't be exceptional, would I? And you're not my first, either. I hope that doesn't diminish me in any way in *your* eyes?"

Her smile became an imp's grin. "Not at all. I'm glad, too, because I would hate to have to walk you through this."

Sam laughed outright, tugging her to him. "Come here, you."

Unexpectedly, she put a hand against his bare chest and resisted him. "No. I don't want to be the only one with no clothes on. Take off your pants."

Amused, he released her and arched his eyebrows. "Yes, ma'am."

Yancey made a face at her own expense. "I'm sorry. Being a Pinkerton made me bossy."

"You misunderstand. I wasn't complaining. And I like a woman who knows her mind." Sam slipped out of his shoes and tugged, one at a time, at his stockings. Then, barefooted and bare-chested, he put his hands to his trousers' opening.

Yancey surprised him by stepping up and brushing his hands away. "Oh, no. No, no. Allow me."

Sam gestured widely. "Please. Do as you wish."

"And we both know what you wish, don't we?" She pursed her mouth primly.

"I can only hope so."

Yancey rolled her eyes and expertly worked his buttons. As she did, she grinned up at him and then almost sent him to his knees when she, without warning, captured one of his hard, flat nipples in her mouth. Gasping, his eyes closing almost of their own will, Sam had to grab her arms and hold on as she swirled her tongue around and around over the sensitive bud there. From the touch of her fingers against his skin, he realized that she'd worked all the buttons and was even now slowly lowering his trousers, along with his smallclothes, down his hips.

In only moments, he would be naked and proudly jutting, free of restraint.

Blessedly, she released his nipple, but only so she could

kiss her way down his chest and belly as she took his pants ever lower. In a fever of wanting to be inside her, Sam gripped her shoulders and then caressed her arms. "Oh, evil woman," he growled, his voice guttural.

She took her mouth away from his skin only long enough to ask, in a husky whisper, "Do you want me to stop?"

"Yes. Tomorrow."

"Now who's evil?" she quipped, kneeling gracefully in front of him and going down on her slender haunches to help him step out of his pants. When he did, she tossed them aside and met what was now just above her face level. "Oh, Sam. Look at you. I feel I should applaud."

He looked down at himself. "It wouldn't be the first time. But . . . if you must."

She smacked playfully at his thigh. "Conceited man."

Shaking her head and laughing, she pulled herself up to her knees and held him by his hips. "On second thought, I have a better idea."

She then lavished her attention on the most sensitive part of Sam's entire body. Gently holding her head, and groaning at the exquisite torture of her mouth on him, he had to tense every muscle in his body just so he could remain standing. Sam's only lucid thought was that the Spanish Inquisition had never devised a torture as cruel as this one. He could stand no more, literally or figuratively. Already hating himself, Sam pulled back and away from Yancey and helped her to her feet. She smiled at him . . . just smiled.

"Yancey, you . . ." He could say no more. He lifted her up under her arms and she clung to him, wrapping her legs around his waist.

Kissing her, caressing her back, and stroking her hair all in a fevered rush, Sam worked them over to the bed and managed to brace himself with a hand and a knee against the mattress. Yancey let go of him and was now on her back, stretched out suggestively, her pose leaving nothing to the imagination.

Sam's breath caught. He could contain himself no longer. He slid off the bed and knelt beside it, lifting her legs and pulling her to him. The instant his tongue found her center, she gasped, and he heard her clutching at the bedding. "Oh, Sam, oh Sam, oh my . . ." A sound of need, of compelling desire followed. But no more words . . . only mewling gasps that urged him on. She rotated her hips slowly and seductively against his mouth and arched her back.

Sam continued his loving ministrations, eagerly awaiting the moment when she would still . . . and tense. And then, it was there. Feeling himself stiffen even more in response to her pleasure, Sam flicked his tongue against her bud with a steady pressure that had Yancey's muscles rippling and jerking in a spasmodic rhythm. She cried out, and he held her hips firmly, helping her ride the crest of her release. Her body opened to him, rewarding him with a rush of warmth and wetness. He sipped and sipped of her until she was drained and begging him for surcease.

Almost out of his mind now with his need for her, Sam could wait no more. He came to his feet and leaned over her. Her knees bent, Yancey raised her arms to him. "Oh, Sam, you make me so happy."

"Good. Because I love you, Yancey."

She smiled, warm and genuine. "Come to me, Sam."

That wasn't exactly the answer he needed . . . he'd hoped she'd say she loved him, too . . . but, under the circumstances, it was the exact answer he wanted. Needing no further encouragement, Sam positioned himself at the side of the bed and pulled Yancey to him. He entered her in a smooth, slow, slide that left both of them gasping with the exquisite pleasure of their coupling. When he was fully sheathed in her, Sam held still, his eyes closed, just savoring the moment.

She was as he'd known she would be. Hot. Slick. And tight around him. Opening his eyes, meeting Yancey's inviting green eyes, he held her hips. She wrapped her legs around his waist. And perhaps sensing what was to come, Yancey clutched wide-eyed at the bedding. She was wise to do so, because this first time was not one for finesse. The need was too great. Sam was helpless to stop his body from seeking its pleasure. It instantly found its rhythm with her and pounded against her, wanting its release, seeking her center, wanting to take her there with him. All too soon, Sam felt himself tighten, felt his member swell . . . and heard Yancey make that guttural sound at the back of her throat that told him she was near.

He forced a slower pace on himself, waiting for her, pushing into her, sliding out of her, then back in, penetrating his fullness into her enveloping depths. Then she moaned and stilled as she had done when he'd held her in his mouth. Excited beyond imagining, Sam quickened his pace. Yancey matched him stroke for stroke. She was absolutely exhilarating. Such wanton abandon. Sam leaned further over her, and Yancey gripped his arms. The pleasure was unbearable. He must have relief. He must. Driven wild, Sam took them to the height of the loving precipice, and then held them there, suspended . . . carrying them finally over into the chasm of pleasure realized.

Done, empty, sated, happy, Sam fell atop Yancey, bracing his elbows on the bed to hold his weight off her. He tried only to breathe as he watched her face. Her eyes were closed, her mouth was open, and her cheeks were colored a dark pink from their sexual exertion. And she had never been more beautiful. Sam smoothed a hand over the satin-slick sheen of wetness on her ribs.

She opened her eyes and smiled at him, weakly putting her arms around his neck. He hadn't lied, he told himself. He would never let her go. She belonged to him. To Stonebridge. To England. She was truly the Duchess of Somerset. And he would have her. No matter what it took. No matter what he had to do, where he had to go . . . he would keep her. And God help any man who ever, ever tried to hurt her. Because he, Samuel Isaac Treyhorne, the Twelfth Duke of Somerset, would kill him. Or be killed trying.

Yancey awoke that next morning to find herself part of a tangle of arms and legs and sheets. She felt so deliciously sore and wonderfully lethargic. And decadently naked. Last night Sam had used her body in pleasurable ways she would never have thought possible. Wicked, wicked man. She smiled, relishing now the feel of his warm muscled chest under her cheek. This was heaven. Lying pressed to his side, her head nestled at the juncture of his shoulder and his chest, she had apparently draped an arm and a leg over him sometime during the night. He, in turn, lay on his back and had an arm around her. He was fast asleep. His even breathing told her that much.

Seized with a sudden desire to lovingly study his every feature, Yancey ever so carefully, so as not to awaken him, raised her head. Her heart full, her eyes those of a lover, she feasted on the sight he made. His strong neck, his skin so taut. She eased her hand up his chest and touched his throat. Surprising her, and halting her movements, was the huge diamond ring on her left hand. Then it came to her. *Oh, of course.* Sam had pressed it on her last night. Smiling, shaking her head at the memory of how she had resisted him over wearing it, she gave in again to her desire to touch him and to study him.

After pushing her hair back from her face, she ever so slowly edged a finger up to his jaw and felt of the beard stubble there. Sam's mouth twitched and, without waking, he brushed at his jaw where she'd touched it. Grinning, biting down on her bottom lip, Yancey pulled her head back, out of his way. She waited for him to settle again into a deep sleep. Then her grin changed to a smile for all the good things in her heart. This man was such an answer to all her prayers.

Her smile faded. An answer to her prayers? She didn't remember praying for a man to love. Ever. If anything, she'd prayed that one didn't come along . . . ever. And yet, here he was. So, didn't that make him more of a complication in her life, rather than the answer to anything? She frowned. Probably so. But right at this moment he didn't feel like a complication. Or seem like one. Yet he was, and she knew it. He was also a heartache waiting to happen. Yancey exhaled sadly and rested her hand against his chest, propping her chin atop it as she stared at him, so close and warm and sleeping.

Suddenly, she wanted to cry. What was she going to do about him? He'd been so wonderful to her with her awful confession. For the first time, the memory of her deed didn't overwhelm her. Perhaps telling him had set her on the road to healing that wound. It certainly seemed so. But he'd been wonderful in every other way, too. Such a gentleman he'd been at supper. He'd made her laugh. And that was hard to do. He'd made her feel whole and welcome. That was even harder to do.

Then he'd told her—and more than once—that he loved her. She hadn't been able to say it back. For one thing, that word held such permanence in its four little letters. He'd also told her that he wouldn't let her go. But he would. She knew that. She also knew what he meant when he said it. Not that he'd physically stop her. He wouldn't. What he meant was he wouldn't want her to go. She shied away from the realization that maybe she wouldn't want to go, either.

No, that couldn't be right. That wasn't what she was feeling. Yancey quickly conjured up the men from her past. There weren't many, only three. They were good men, too, and not a one of them had wanted her to go, either. But she always had. One of them, Spence Caulfield, a deputy sheriff out in Wyoming, where one of her cases had taken her, had said that he loved her and had tried to hold her with that. She'd cared about him, of course. But she'd still left. It had been easy to do, which had told her everything she needed to know.

But now, with Sam? *Oh, Sam.* Yancey sighed, moving her hand only enough to allow her to plant a tender kiss on his rib. Overcome, she laid her cheek against him, where she'd kissed him. So solid and warm. She wasn't so sure she wanted to go. Or that she could. He loved her, and she hated that he did. Because she feared she loved him, too. Could she do it? she wondered. Could she give her unconditional love to a man forever and marry him and give him children and be happy with that?

She blinked, pursing her lips and staring at the tangle of sheet that covered them. She didn't know if a life of domesticity would be enough for her. She was too used to using her mind and living by her wits. It would be hard to settle for anything less. Not that Sam was a mindless imbecile who wouldn't excite her and challenge her. He would. But the thing of it was she loved her career.

She'd worked hard at it and had built up quite the reputation as a top agent. That meant a lot to her. Marrying and living in England—or even America—would end all that. Mr. Pinkerton did not encourage his female agents to marry. Nor did he encourage them to stay on once they did. But every married one that Yancey knew of had quit because her husband had insisted on it, and not Mr. Pinkerton. Yancey didn't want to be one of those women. She knew how she and the remaining female agents disparaged their sisters for leaving, and how they'd assured themselves they were better off without a husband and children.

That brought Yancey back to her original question. Would settling down and giving up the excitement of the job be fulfilling enough for her? Did she even want a family? A husband and children? And what about a lifetime spent in England among the nobility and in London for half the year? Could she be happy making social calls all day and abiding by strict rules of etiquette? Would she miss the danger, the excitement, of a new case, the delicious subterfuge of donning a new disguise?

*Or getting shot at and chased and living on the edge and never having a home or anyone to come home to?*

Yancey frowned. Where had that come from? But she knew. Her darned old heart, the fickle thing. But speaking of her work, what would Mr. Pinkerton say if she were to quit, if she were to send him a letter of resignation? She couldn't even begin to imagine how disappointed he would be. Then, in her mind, she heard him saying, that day in his office when he'd told her she was coming to England, that the duke would probably end up wishing she were the woman he'd married. Yancey smiled. Truer words had never been spoken.

Sam loved her. Sighing with the contentment of that truth, she hugged Sam to her, snuggling in next to him as close as she could get without actually crawling under his skin. As soon as she was settled, though, her heart—or was it her mind?—had an observation it felt compelled to make. What Mr. Pinkerton—or even she—hadn't considered that day, this ornery part of her self commented, was . . . would she come to wish she were the woman Sam had married?

*Oh, I don't know,* Yancey fussed, frowning. Why did she have to think about this now? Couldn't she just enjoy their warm, loving nest for a little bit longer? Sometimes she hated her overactive mind. It just never gave up. She felt certain, Yancey fussed, that if she dwelled on this long enough, she would ruin her mood and the coming day . . . and would end up wanting to scream.

At that exact second, a scream shattered the morning quiet.

# Chapter Twenty

Shocked, Yancey heard the scream echo in her head. But had she only imagined it? She could only wonder because it didn't seem possible that such a sound could invade her morning, not while she was so happily snuggled with Sam.

But in the same instant as she thought that, Sam jerked awake and struggled against the bed's heavy covers and Yancey's weight atop him. "What was that?" he demanded, his voice husky, his features frowning. "I thought I heard a scream. Did I dream it?"

Dread washed over Yancey, stiffening her muscles. "Dear God, Sam," she cried out, a sense of urgency seizing her. She shoved away from the warm protection of Sam's body. "I thought I'd only imagined it. But if you heard it, then it *was* a real scream. A woman's scream."

Behind her, she felt the mattress shift and then Sam grabbed her arm. "Where do you think you're going?"

Instead of fighting his hold on her, which would only delay things, Yancey met his gaze, seeing the steel in his gray eyes. "Let me go. I think the scream came from my bedroom. I have to go see—"

"No. Whatever is happening in there was meant for you. I'm going, and *you* will stay here."

Before he could move, Yancey clutched at his hand on

her arm, now holding him in place. "I'm the Pinkerton here, Sam. You let go of me. *I'm* going."

He narrowed his eyes at her, apparently measuring her stubbornness and resolve . . . and arriving at the correct conclusion. "We'll go together."

She could have screamed herself. Yancey let go of Sam, but he didn't release her. "Fine, then," she hissed. "But we need to go *now,* Sam. We're wasting time arguing. Someone could be dying as we speak."

"Quite possibly. And we could be, also, if we go haring in there naked and unarmed, Yancey."

She looked down at them both, confirmed her forgotten nakedness for herself, and his, as well. "Good point. We'll get dressed. Do you keep a gun in here? Mine's in my room."

"Yes, I do."

"Where is it, Sam?"

He raised his eyebrows. "A valiant effort, Yancey. But I see your trick, and so I won't tell you."

Damn his quick-wittedness. Yancey gritted her teeth. "I work alone, Sam."

"Not this time."

A cry of frustration erupted from her. "All right, all right. Just let's go now before there's no need." Still he didn't release her. Yancey fisted her free hand and raised it threateningly. "If you don't let go of me, Sam, right now, I fully intend to—"

"Don't even try it, Yancey." His fierce, challenging expression backed up his warning.

Yancey was frantic with awareness of each passing second. "Sam, I will not tolerate your misplaced romantic and manly sentiments. If you don't release me this instant, I'll be forced to render you unconscious."

He looked her up and down in such a way that she felt the mouse to his lion. "I don't think you can."

In truth, she didn't, either. She lowered her fist and resorted to another, more compelling argument. "You're keeping me from doing the job you hired me to do, Sam."

"Then you're fired, Yancey. You now have no job to perform."

She ignored that. "Do you not care about what might be going on in the next room, Sam? Someone could be dying. For God's sake, man, where's your concern?"

His expression was fierce. "My concern is for you alone."

"Oh, for pity's sake." Yancey reared back again, cocking her arm to smack him in the jaw—right at the point she knew from experience would drop a full-grown man in his tracks. Well, most full-grown men.

But Sam handily captured her other wrist. Now he held both of her arms. "We'll go together, and I'm going in first."

Yancey went limp with defeat and said, sourly, "As you wish. However, you may as well order up a bath and breakfast and a carriage for a leisurely ride before we go investigate. Because whatever has occurred in there is already over and done with."

"Then we need to go see what has already happened, don't we?" With that, Sam finally released his hold on her and swung his legs over his side of the bed.

Knowing this was a race—one she meant to win—Yancey scooted off the bed and quickly searched the floor for a suitable article of last night's discarded clothing. Her gown and crinolines would never do. She found what she wanted at the foot of the bed. Sam's shirt. Plucking it up and fussing her way into it, she took a quick, deep breath of frustration which only worsened things when her senses were invaded by the man's intoxicating scent that lingered in the shirt's folds. Fighting against its effect on her, and shoving the shirt's sleeves up her arms, then rolling them over and over, she hastily looked around for its owner.

Already in his pants, and with them buttoned, he was stalking toward his dresser. She glanced from it to the man and quickly put two and two together. *The gun. He's going to get the gun.* In only a moment he would have it and would leave her behind. Galvanized by urgency, she raced to cut him off, darted by him, evaded his lunge to grab her, ignored his "Damn you, Yancey!" and beat him there. Knowing he was on her heels, she yanked open a drawer and cried out in triumph when she saw the weapon resting atop his neatly folded handkerchiefs. Grabbing it up, triumphant, she turned around—and ran smack into Sam's solid bare chest. A startled yelp escaped her.

He plucked the Colt out of her hand and smiled grimly at her. "Thank you."

Yancey held out her hand and all but stomped her foot. "Give me that blasted gun this instant."

He held it up and out of her reach. "I will not. As we agreed that I'm going in first, I'll need the gun."

"Oh, really?" She crossed her arms under her breasts. "And what do I do, unarmed as I will be and behind you, should someone come through *that* door?"

She stabbed a pointing finger at the door that opened onto the hall. Sam glared at it and then her. Undaunted, she raised her eyebrows, awaiting his answer. Looking furious, he said, "What do you suggest we do, then? We can't both hold the gun."

"I agree. All right, keep the gun. But we'll both go by way of the other door, out through the hall, and enter from there. That should surprise whoever might be in my bedroom. If our villain is still about, he'll want to get away. And when he does, he will have to go past us."

Sam firmed his lips. "I would have thought of that . . . the other door, I mean."

"Of course you would have." Sarcasm dripped from her remark. She shook her head. "This is exactly why I never work with a partner. All this arguing and these delays. I think our villain has now had enough time to have escaped as far as Lakeheath-on-Somerset."

Vexation still ruled Sam's features. "Oh, do you? Allow me to point out, Miss Pinkerton Agent, that I am not the one who was the delay. *You* are the one who argued with me when I would have got up and—"

"*I* was the delay? *I* kept you from your job? Me?" Yancey held her arms out, allowing him a chance to see for himself the picture she made. There she stood, one-third his size and in his shirt, the sleeves of which had hung more than a foot past the tips of her fingers before she rolled them up and the tail of which hung down past her calves. "With my tremendous bulk, I held you down and delayed you?"

He squared his jaw and a muscle there jumped. "All right, then, I was the delay. Now if that's all, let's go." He whipped around, again facing the dressing room door. The man took two long, determined strides in that direction before Yancey discreetly cleared her throat. Sam stopped, did an about-face, and stalked toward the door to the hallway. "This way," he announced forcefully.

Exhaling, thinking their behavior had taken on the overtones of a theatrical farce, and that the scream had surely been that of an off-stage actress, Yancey followed after him and instructed, "When you get to that door, Sam, don't just open it and stand there, exposed. Open it and then stay to one side, against the wall. Wait to see if anyone rushes in or shoots at you. It stands to reason that our villain could be standing there waiting for you."

Sam kept walking. "I assure you that I have every bit as diabolical a bent of mind as the best of villains, Yancey. After all, you will recall that I too lived out in the wilds of America, and I know full well how to use this gun and how to defend myself."

"I, of course, believe you."

He stopped short and jerked around to stare angrily down at her. "Good. And I thought you also believed our villain to be as far as Lakeheath-on-Somerset."

She nodded. "I do. I think by now he's even had time to be breakfasting, perhaps, at the tavern."

Sam narrowed his eyes and glared. Yancey raised her eyebrows and smiled. It was true. She did believe that whatever the damage was in her bedroom, it was already done and the villain was far removed from the scene. After all, the markers for an ongoing life-or-death struggle weren't there. No sounds of crashing and banging about of furniture. No further screams. No shots fired. And no moans or cries for help from a wounded victim.

A wounded victim. The very notion frightened her—if she put Sam's face on that bleeding person.

"I wish you'd put on a shirt," she said suddenly, frowning, her gaze roving over his beautiful musculature under the smooth skin of his bare chest.

"A shirt? What the devil for?"

Yancey's mouth turned down with the mere thought of him lying wounded and bleeding. "So you won't look so . . . so exposed."

"Good God, Yancey, it's a bit late for prudish modesty, wouldn't you say?"

"Modesty be hanged. I was thinking of a bullet. Look at you." She cut her hand up and down his length. "You look so . . . fragile, Sam. I hate it."

Sam's expression became a soft smile. He squeezed her arm affectionately. "Thank you. It means everything to me that you care. But a shirt won't stop a bullet, Yancey, if that's what awaits me."

Yancey's heart all but stopped beating. "Don't say things like that, Sam. Don't. Just be careful. Please."

"I will. I promise you I will." With that, he turned around, again intent on the door ahead of them.

Right behind him, focused on his broad shoulders and suffering terribly, Yancey knew she could not allow his amateur intentions to be his undoing. Certainly he was a big, smart man with a weapon of his own. But he needed her instincts and her experience whether he would admit it or not. And, for her part, she needed him alive.

This could not be worse, she knew, this caring for him so. Loving Sam had made her cautious. And this caution, she knew, was exactly why Mr. Pinkerton frowned on his agents having families. She'd thought his a repressive attitude. But now, she understood her boss fully. She wanted to live for Sam, but she would die trying to protect him. At once cautious and rash. A potentially deadly mixture for an agent.

Just then, Sam put a hand out, urging her to get behind him. Yancey quickly complied as Sam leaned a shoulder against the wall, his gun in his right hand. He reached out with his left to jerk the door open. With much high drama, the well-oiled door instantly swung wide and then slowed before hitting the opposite wall. Yancey held her breath, waiting. Nothing happened. No one charged in. No shots were fired. No knife came sailing through the doorway.

Sam, leading with his gun—and with Yancey admiring his technique—snatched a quick look out into the hall. Then he looked over his shoulder at her. "No one's there. You ready?"

She nodded that she was. Sam winked at her . . . and in a flash Yancey realized that only a moment ago she'd admitted to herself that she loved him. Before she could do more than stare up into his devastatingly handsome face and be stunned by the depths of her feelings for him, Sam pushed away from the wall and incautiously stepped into the open doorway, essentially framing himself there as he grinned at her and held his free hand out, wanting her to take it.

"Sam! No!" Terrified for him, Yancey grabbed his hand with both of hers and pulled with all her strength, finally gaining his cooperation in allowing her to pull him out of harm's way.

"What the devil are you do—"

"Anyone could have been on the other side of that door and against the wall, Sam, just as we were in here." She threw herself into his embrace, fiercely hugging him, her arms wrapped tightly around his waist, her cheek against his beating heart. "Are you just trying to get yourself killed?"

His arms encircled her. "Yancey, what has got into you? Are you telling me that we should stay in this room for the remainder of our lives because there *might* possibly be someone on the other side of this door who wishes us harm?"

"Yes," was her emotion-filled reply. He was so warm, so alive, and his heart beat steadily in his chest.

"Nothing is going to happen to me. Yancey, look at me." She felt him tugging at her, his efforts hampered by the gun he held in his hand. Still, she complied, pulling back only enough to look up at him, at his sweet, precious face. "What is *really* wrong with you?"

Her expression crumpled. "Everything." She rested her forehead against the warm skin of his bare chest. "Oh, Sam, this is awful. Just plain awful. I love you. And I hate that I do."

Sam tensed, then tugged at her again. Yancey looked up at him. He was staring down at her, and his eyes were wide with wonder and amusement. "You love me and you hate that you do? While I'm thrilled to know that—the part about you loving me, at any rate—your timing could not be worse, my love."

Yancey let him go. "I know. It just ruins everything. My whole life, Sam. Everything."

He gestured with both hands, actually waving the gun about. Yancey saw her chance and grabbed it from him.

"What the—?" Sam sputtered. "Come back here, you little vixen. Give me that gun."

Ignoring his cry of protest and evading his grasp, Yancey darted around him and ran out into the hall, turning right and holding the gun two-fisted out in front of her. But what she saw there, nothing could have prepared her to see. Shocked, gasping, she dropped her pose and stood with her gun hand down at her side. "Oh . . . my . . . God."

Sam came charging right behind her and snatched the gun from her unresisting hand. "Aha!" But when she had no response, he straightened up and gripped her elbow. "Yancey?"

Feeling numb, as if she were drowning in a cold, swift current, Yancey looked up at him but pointed down the hall. "Look."

Shifting his weight and turning a bit, he did . . . he looked. Then he too dropped his gun hand to his side. "What in God's name has happened here?"

What, indeed. Standing just outside the open door to Yancey's bedroom was the stalwart Scotty . . . with the uniformed and limp body of Mrs. Edgars, the housekeeper, held in his arms. The woman's arms were flung wide and her head lolled drunkenly.

Muttering an oath, Sam started forward, toward his butler. But Yancey snaked a hand out, grabbing his arm and pulling him back. "No. Sam, wait."

"Yancey, don't be ridiculous. It's Scotty."

"I can see that. But the truth remains that you *don't* know what has happened here." She quickly assessed the evidence before her. No blood. No weapon in sight. No scratches on Scotty. And Mrs. Edgars's bun wasn't even the least bit mussed. No struggle, then.

"Yancey, I hardly think—Dear God! Nana!"

Yancey saw her at the same moment Sam did. A draining weakness invaded her, making jelly out of her muscles. She grabbed in earnest at Sam's solidity and hung on. "Oh, Sam. Oh, my God, no."

This could not be. Yancey refused to believe it. It just couldn't be. And yet it was. Her Grace Nana, of all people, had exited Yancey's bedroom. She stood there in the hallway. Milling around her ankles and her trailing skirts were the ever-present Mary, Jane, and Alice, the white cats, and Mr. Marples, the terrier. Though the three cats appeared unaffected, the dog's ears and tail drooped unhappily.

The front of Nana's dress was covered in blood. In her hand was a sharp knife of the kind readily available in the manor's kitchen.

"You'd best come quickly, Samuel, Sarah," the very ancient little lady announced calmly, shaking her doddering little head. "Poor Roderick is in there." She pointed an age-gnarled finger at the open door to Yancey's bedroom. "I'm afraid he's taken a knife to the back."

No more than an hour later, dressed now and with his mind an aggrieved mishmash of emotions, Sam was in his study. His loaded gun lay atop his desk, within easy reach. He was pitched forward in his desk chair. With his elbows atop his knees, he scrubbed his hands over his beard-stubbled jaw and concentrated only on breathing. He looked up to see Yancey still at the cabinet that sported his crystal liquor service and private stock. She was pouring them both a much-deserved drink.

Sam watched her every movement as if each gesture of hers was the only thing keeping his heart beating. In some ways, they were. He freely admitted to himself that he needed her warm, competent presence and her closeness. Otherwise, he would die. He was sure of it. Yet he had accomplished many important tasks this morning, and on his own. He now reviewed them for himself in order to make certain that he had attended to every person and detail. First of all, he had turned Nana over to her shocked and distressed maid. And Mrs. Edgars had been helped away to her room by Robin and an entire contingent of clucking maids.

Two stalwart men Sam trusted, gardeners both, had been summoned and charged with the removal of Roderick's body to a downstairs drawing room. Upstairs maids worked now to right Yancey's bedroom and scrub away the blood. And others would be cleaning Roderick up before he was placed in a simple coffin even now being constructed at Sam's further orders. Only then had Sam, with great reluctance and a heavy heart, awakened his mother to tell her of this newest family tragedy. The dear woman was in shock and her maids were attending to her every need.

An errant part of Sam's mind wondered just how many maids he *did* employ.

But Roderick . . . thus trussed and nailed down would accompany Sam's mother back to her sister's. *Poor Aunt Jane. This will certainly kill her.* Sam's frown was a grimace of guilt—guilt for not accompanying his mother to his aunt's. But how could he leave his household at the mercy of a murderer who might strike again and whose identity they did not know? Sam shook his head. No, he couldn't leave now. His duty was clearly here.

Just then, Yancey moved away from the cabinet, her actions drawing Sam's attention back to the moment. She approached him, her practiced steps not allowing a drop of liquor to spill from the two squat but brimming tumblers she held. Sam stared at her in admiration. Dressed in a belted blue skirt and stylish white blouse, and with her hair pulled back at her neck and held in a ribbon, she looked the innocent girl until one took into account the gun she had tucked into her waistband. *No more unpleasant surprises,* she'd said earlier. *And no more polite pretending. This is war.*

She stopped in front of him. "Here you go. Drink up."

As if she were a doctor and the whisky medicine, Sam took the glass from her and helped himself to a healthy dose of the rich, warming liquor. He then watched her sip at her own portion as she seated herself in the leather-upholstered chair he'd pulled around from in front of his desk for her. He wanted her close. In fact, her skirt-covered knees all but touched his.

Feeling very warm toward her, yet numb about everything else, Sam smiled at her, and she returned it. "You are the strongest person I know, Yancey. Made of iron. Very steady."

She raised her glass in a salute to him. "Thank you. You're very kind." She sat forward, her expression a mask of compassion. "And you? How are you? Are you feeling any stronger yet, Sam?"

Greatly embarrassed, he couldn't quite hold her gaze. "I believe so. I've, well, I've never lost consciousness like that before."

Yancey patted his knee. "Many people do at the sight of blood, Sam. And especially if it's splattered on one's beloved nana, who happens also to be holding a large knife. I myself thought surely I'd follow you to the floor when I saw her like that."

"You're kind to say so. But thank *God* she hadn't been injured in any way." His strong emotion had him seeking Yancey's wonderful understanding eyes.

"Nor was she wrong about Roderick's being dead. I can safely say he most certainly was . . . but only just."

Curious about that since he'd been consoling his mother while Yancey had dressed, told the staff she was a Pinkerton, and then questioned everyone present—she'd also, in the interest of safety, banished every uninvolved servant but Scotty to his or her room—Sam asked, "How did you make that determination, about the time of the murder?"

"The evidence. His blood was still bright red. And the, uh, body—I'm so sorry, Sam, I don't mean to be callous."

"You're not. But perhaps I'm the hard one. I have no love lost for Roderick. He was a despicable man, and I feel nothing. Only shock. And sorrow for my aunt."

"Yes. This will be awful for her."

Sam nodded, remembering the emotional and chaotic scene upstairs with his mother when he'd broken the news to her. "Mother's maids are packing her belongings now so she can go to Aunt Jane straightaway and take Roderick with her. But please go on. You were telling me how you made your determination that the murder had just happened."

Yancey took a breath and continued. "The blood was still trickling and the, uh, body was still warm. And there were no other rather ghastly changes evident that occur after death, none of which I suspect you'd want me to delineate for you."

Sam held up a staying hand. "Thank you. I don't think I've had enough to drink yet to hear any of that."

"I thought not." Yancey's expression softened, and she made a tsking sound. "Your poor nana, pulling the knife out like that and trying by herself to turn Roderick over. Bless her."

"She's such a frail thing, Yancey. Do you really think she could have pulled that knife out?"

"I wouldn't have thought so, yet Mrs. Edgars says that the knife was on the bed and Her Grace Nana, alone in the room, was trying to turn Roderick over."

Sam nodded. "No wonder poor Mrs. Edgars screamed and fainted."

"Yet she hardly seems the type, does she? I do wonder, though, Sam, if your nana was actually alone in that room before Mrs. Edgars came in."

"You mean Nana startled the murderer, don't you? And then he fled unseen by her but before Mrs. Edgars happened in?"

"You've been doing some thinking, haven't you? Yes, I think both of those are possibilities. But Mrs. Edgars didn't just happen in. She was checking up on Robin, she says, looking to see if the girl was about her duties." Yancey frowned skeptically. "She does a lot of checking up, doesn't she? Not very trusting of her staff, I'd say. But, at any rate, there Nana was. When I questioned her, she said she'd been seeking a place to hide from Scotty in one of their games of hide-and-seek. And what she found was a murder . . . but no murderer."

Sam shook his head. "I have to confess that I feared the doddering old dear did, in one of her more deluded moments, actually kill Roderick and perhaps even Geoffrey months ago by some subtler method."

"Understandable suspicion, but no. She doesn't have the presence of mind for something subtle or sustained. Or the strength for this knife attack." Yancey frowned pensively. "Or the height, actually. I'm thinking of the depth and the angle of the knife's plunge."

Sam could only stare at this most remarkable of women. How she excited him on every level. "You are amazing, do you know that?"

She smiled prettily, a delicate flush staining her cheeks. "Not amazing at all. Merely well trained and amply experienced."

"Well, thank God and Mr. Pinkerton, then. Now, what about Scotty? Although I hate to believe it, certainly had Roderick gone to your room to do you harm and Scotty encountered him, I believe he would be capable."

"I agree, but Mrs. Edgars says Scotty wasn't there. Just her and Nana. He must have come in moments later because your housekeeper awoke in his arms, remember. But even so, I don't suspect Scotty. For one thing, he would have had no need of a weapon."

"That's true. Scotty could merely have pinched Roderick's head off, had he chosen to do so. But I can vouch that Scotty is nothing if not honest. If he'd killed Roderick, I believe he would have simply said so."

"Well, there you have it," Yancey said brightly. "Two suspects eliminated. You're getting very good at this, Sam."

"I've had a bit of practice of late."

Her expression sobered. "Oh, I'm so sorry. My remark was unthinking."

Sam smiled his forgiveness and shook his head. "Think nothing of it. The truth is I'd best be getting good at this, what with my family dropping around me like flies. But with Roderick dead, Yancey, we're fresh out of villains."

She shrugged. "Maybe not. He may still be *your* villain—and someone else's for some unrelated reason that got him killed."

Frowning, Sam felt numb inside. "I see what you mean.

But . . . murder. And for whatever reason. I can't imagine. It boggles the mind, Yancey."

"It does—if you're not used to dealing with such treachery on a daily basis."

"As you are, you mean?"

"Yes." She looked down at her whisky and then up at him. "I worry sometimes that I will become hard and that life will mean nothing to me. Or death, I should say."

Sam gripped her hand. "That's not the woman I held in my arms last night, Yancey. You have such a good heart. And you've had your share of suffering. I discovered that last evening, as well."

Her smile was bittersweet. "You're a kind man, Sam Treyhorne."

"But up to my neck in troubles." He sat back, running a hand through his hair. "There are implications well beyond Stonebridge and even all of Somerset. Roderick's murder will cause a huge scandal and gossip. That's bad enough, especially for my mother who cares about these things. But I fear Scotland Yard will look upon me unfavorably since I stood to gain so much by Roderick's death. I mean his duchy and title."

Yancey raised her eyebrows. "I hadn't thought of that." A look of fierce protectiveness claimed her features. "But Scotland Yard won't be a problem for long, I assure you. I'd like to see them even intimate that you were involved in any way. I stand ready to be your alibi."

Sam smiled at her outrage on his behalf. How endearing.

Then she eyed him over the rim of her whisky glass as she took a sip. "You weren't involved, were you?"

Sam sat up sharply. "You suspect *me*? But you just said you are my alibi.' "

She shrugged, her face alight with her teasing grin. "I am, but I *had* to ask. It's what you pay me to do."

"Is it? Well, then, you're fired."

She shook her head. "You can't fire me again, Sam. You already did once this morning."

He thought about that and then remembered. "I did, didn't

I? Well, it was under exceptional circumstances. Consider yourself rehired."

"Thank you. I will."

"Well, then, all things considered, what do we do now?"

"We? Not *we,* Sam. This is possibly a new case, one not related to my reasons for being here in the first place. That being so, I—and I alone—will conduct my interviews of everyone in this household. Then I will expand my investigation to Roderick's last hours, starting with where he went last night and whom he saw. And why he did."

"But we know where he was and who he was with. He told us."

"Yes, he did. But I'd like to find out for myself if it's true. Remember, he said he would not be back until midday. Rather bright and early for him to be back here, then, don't you think? And what *was* he doing in my bedroom? All very curious, if you ask me. Roderick certainly had his secrets and it will be my job to uncover what they were."

Just then, they were interrupted by a knock on the door.

# Chapter Twenty-one

Sam exchanged a look with Yancey. Without a word passing between them, he set his drink down, and she did the same with hers. He picked up his gun, and she pulled hers out of her waistband. They both secured their weapons in their laps . . . primed and ready, but out of view of whoever was at the door. Only then did Sam call out, "Come in."

The door opened and in stepped Mrs. Edgars. Behind her was Scotty, his new hat, as always now, perched atop his big head and he himself seemingly as unmoved as ever, despite the morning's events. Of course, Sam had to admit, tragedy was becoming the usual fare at Stonebridge. At any rate, Scotty had escorted the housekeeper here. Taking his job as policeman seriously, he was.

The middle-aged housekeeper's expression was every bit as severe as her demeanor. Her thin lips pursed, she dipped a somewhat less than deferential curtsy. Sam mentally excused her behavior, though, thinking that no doubt she was angry over the staff being shut up and not able to perform their duties under her direction. Add to that her moral disapproval of his and Yancey's drinking this early in the day. Compounding their sin were the two glasses sitting directly on the wood of the desk, where they could leave rings. How many times had she complained to him of this habit?

Eyeing the woman now, Sam recalled his past complaints to his mother regarding his housekeeper. Mrs. Edgars was very proprietary in her attitude toward him and his belongings, he'd said. But that attitude, his mother had assured him, was why his brother Geoffrey had hired the woman in the first place. Mrs. Edgars cared as much for the occupants of Stonebridge manor as she did for every item that occupied it. And you couldn't buy such loyalty as that, his mother had concluded.

"I'm sorry to interrupt, Your Grace," Mrs. Edgars said now, shooting a withering glance Scotty's way. "I didn't wish to do so at this moment, in your time of sorrow. Yet Scotty insisted that I do. Left to my own devices, I assure you I would have held off—"

"I understand, Mrs. Edgars. What is it?" Sam was in no mood for long explanations. "If Scotty thought it important enough to interrupt, then it is."

The housekeeper, clearly insulted, pursed her lips and held her hand out. All but crumpled in her white-knuckled grip was a letter. "Very well, then. It's a letter, Your Grace. It's only just arrived."

"Special courier," Scotty added, his expression as blank as ever.

"Special courier?" A start of surprise flitted through Sam. He looked to Yancey, thinking to gauge her reaction to this, but encountered only her profile. Her green eyes, narrowed like a cat's, were riveted to the housekeeper's face. Sam's heart thumped a warning. Barely moving his head, he subtly looked back and forth between the two women. Mrs. Edgars was giving Yancey as good as she got in the way of antagonistic looks.

With his gun still gripped in his right, hidden, hand, Sam held his left hand out to his housekeeper, waggling his fingers. "I take it the thing's not addressed to you, Mrs. Edgars, or you wouldn't be in here. So let's have it, then. Come on. Hand it over."

He was purposely and uncharacteristically brusque with her, hoping for a telling or unthinking response. Obviously Yancey harbored suspicions or at least a healthy dislike for his housekeeper. Sam had never liked the woman, either. He found himself wondering exactly why Geoffrey had hired her fifteen years ago when, as a young man of twenty, he'd inherited the title upon their father's death.

But the woman disappointed. Her expression severe, her entire demeanor disapproving, she nevertheless obediently walked toward Sam . . . yet kept her eyes on Yancey, even as she held the letter out to Sam. "Here it is, Your Grace. But it's addressed to *Miss Calhoun*. And it's from Scotland Yard."

The door closed behind Scotty and Mrs. Edgars. Only then did Yancey allow herself to look Sam's way. She saw his frowning, considering gaze. "What, Sam?"

"I saw that look you had on your face. You suspect Mrs. Edgars of something, don't you?"

She nodded. "I had the distinct impression that had Scotty not known about the letter's delivery, we never would have seen it."

"Hmm." Sam frowned, rubbing at his bottom lip. Then he pointed at her. "But it's not like you to be as obvious as you were in that look you sent her. Which tells me that you wanted her to know that you have your doubts about her. Am I right?"

The man was too smart by half. "Yes. But it's nothing I can put my finger on. All I can say is she hasn't liked me from the moment I set foot inside Stonebridge. And I'm certain that finding out that I'm an impostor, and a Pinkerton as well, sent here to snoop through her business doesn't sit well with her."

"Her business? How's any of this her business?"

"It's not. But I believe that's how she sees it. Think about it. She's in charge of the day-to-day running of Stonebridge, as well as of everyone who is employed here. And she has been for many years—long before you came home, as you told me. So my suspecting any of her charges is a slight to her ability. Add to that she wasn't told at the outset who I am. She probably feels tricked or like a fool. No one likes that."

"True. I didn't like it, either. But that's not all you think because you said you don't believe she would have given us this letter." He held it in his hand and waved it at her. "You suspect her of something, don't you?"

Yancey shrugged dismissively, purposely playing her cards close to her chest. She suspected Mrs. Edgars of plenty . . . but she had no proof and wasn't about to involve Sam until she knew something definite. "Not suspect, really. She could just be insulted at being tailed by Scotty and at being treated as a suspect. After all, she said only that she wouldn't have interrupted us *at this time* to bring it to our attention."

"Now you're defending her."

"I'm not. I'm trying to be fair."

"Have it your way." Sam narrowed his eyes at her. "But did you see how tightly she was holding this letter? Her knuckles were bone-white. What do you make of that? Simple insult?"

"Perhaps."

"Oh, fine. Keep your detective's thoughts to yourself." Yancey bit back a grin at his frowning countenance. "Here." He held the letter out to her. "It's addressed to you."

He handed it to her, stood up, and stalked over to the tall, narrow window that was open to the day's warmth. Yancey smiled affectionately at his giving her his back. He wanted to play detective with her. A dangerous game that was, and one she wasn't about to allow.

She laid her gun on the desktop and opened the letter. Pinkerton letterhead. She swallowed, instantly recognizing the handwriting. Mr. Pinkerton's own. Her heart pounded with dread and anticipation—anticipation of the answers to their questions that hopefully would be contained within the report, and dread for what they could mean for Sam.

She looked up at him, standing there so stiffly. "Sam?" He turned around, his face haggard and his jaw beard-stubbled. Yancey's heart went out to him. The poor man had been through so much already. "It's from Mr. Pinkerton."

"I supposed as much," he said, exhaling. "So read it to me. What does he have to say?"

Still seated but turned in his direction, Yancey read quickly and silently, her dread overtaking her anticipation. She looked up from the letter, hoping her sympathy for him was evident in her expression. "Oh, Sam, there's news here of Sarah. I am so sorry."

He pressed his lips together and looked down at the carpet. "Then this other Sarah, the one who was killed, was my wife?"

Yancey wanted to go to him, to hold him. But she couldn't seem to move and didn't really know if she should. "Yes. There'd been a recent switch in doctors, Sam. Apparently they were less than scrupulous and easily bribed into turning her out so she'd be vulnerable."

Sam scrubbed a hand over his face. "That poor creature." He lowered his hand, revealing to Yancey the raw expression on his face. "How frightened she must have been. When lucid, she was very much a child."

Yancey's heart ached. She could only imagine Sarah's confusion and terror. "What those doctors did wasn't your fault, Sam. You were faced with an awful situation back then, and you did the best you could by her."

He shook his head. "I wish I could believe that. And perhaps you're right. But I still blame myself. I should have visited more often, asked more questions of the doctors. But I—"

"Sam, the administration of the hospital is not the same as when you admitted her. You couldn't have known."

But Sam wasn't ready yet to forgive himself. "Sarah was ten years older than I, Yancey. And I never loved her. I never did."

Yancey's heart beat dully. She felt hollow, very fragile, as if she could break. Sam looked much the same way. "You don't have to tell me this, Sam."

"Yes I do. If I'm to have any chance at all with you, Yancey, any chance at happiness, I want you to know this."

She was afraid she would shatter and fall to the floor. The diamond ring on her finger was suddenly too heavy for her hand. She felt very much the impostor that she was. A numbing coldness crept into the back of her throat, but inhaling for courage, she said, "Then go on. I'll listen."

Looking everywhere but at her, much as if he couldn't bear to see judgment in her eyes, he began. "I'm as bad as Roderick, Yancey. I married Sarah for her money and nothing else. Yet she loved me, by all indications, and I—" He stopped, swinging his tortured gaze Yancey's way.

She felt numb. "What is it, Sam? Tell me."

His gray eyes were bloodshot and rounded with emotion. "I sometimes wonder if because of that, because I didn't love her and she loved me . . . I wonder if I drove her mad."

Yancey's heart tore. "Oh, Sam, you poor thing, no. You've been holding all that inside? Oh, you poor, dear man." She tossed the letter on the desk and went to him, throwing her arms around him. Sam immediately crushed her to him, burying his face in her neck. His breathing was troubled, rapid and heavy, and he felt too warm, as if intense emotion had heated him through and through. Desperate to heal him, somehow knowing this was her only chance to get through to him, Yancey spoke rapidly, telling him what was in her heart.

"Sam, you mustn't think that. You mustn't. No matter your reasons for marrying her, I'm sure you were good to her. Good heavens, Sam, the things you've told me about her and how hard you tried? She was ill, Sam. You didn't do that. Look how good you are with Nana and Scotty and your mother and everyone else around you, including me. You couldn't be more kind, Sam. And that's all I need to know."

She pulled back from him and cupped his emotion-ravaged face in her hands. "You're a good man, Sam. A good man. And I love you. Do you think I could if you weren't? Do you?" Overcome, he simply shook his head no. Yancey chuckled. "There. You see? You agree with me. You are wonderful."

His grin was fleeting. He nodded but refused to meet her gaze, though Yancey tried to trap it. Sam cupped her hands in his, kissed each of her palms in turn, then released her and stepped back. He sniffed and swiped a finger under his nose. His behavior told Yancey he was striving for equilibrium, for recovery. "I suppose you could be right."

She clasped her hands together tightly to keep from reaching for him again. She wanted so very much to hold and comfort him, but her woman's instincts told her she mustn't. His pride would only suffer for her continued sympathy. So she stood there, so close yet so far away, and forced a bright smile to her face. "You may suppose all you want, my dear man, but I know. And I'm a good detective with excellent instincts. So you have to believe me."

Giving him no time to gainsay her, Yancey picked up his whisky and handed it to him. Sam took it and drank it back. He set the emptied glass back on his desk and pointed to the letter from Mr. Pinkerton. "We should see what else he has to say."

Yancey nodded and picked up the report. She read quickly, relating to Sam aloud as she went. "Let's see, Mr. Pinkerton goes on here to say that the Englishman I killed knew Thomas Almont—a train robber who had nothing to do with your case—from a previous trip to Chicago." Yancey looked up at Sam. "Your poor mother didn't do much investigating of the man's reputation before she hired him. Apparently he was a less than honest private detective."

"Mother didn't investigate at all. She wouldn't know how to begin. She told me he came recommended by a friend of hers whom she wouldn't name but who had past need of his services and discretion."

"I see." Thinking that the upper classes certainly had their intrigues, Yancey returned to the letter, reading a few lines silently. "Oh, look here. Now it's all coming together. Apparently my Englishman—named John Bartholomew, it turns out—and Thomas Almont, the train robber, had actually met in the past in a saloon and became boon companions. And met up yet *again* several months ago at the, uh, house of ill repute where Clara works. You remember Clara? Yes, well, at any rate, evidently she told Mr. Pinkerton all this. So the two chums met up again there, had a conversation, and Thomas Almont happened to tell this Englishman about me. And that was when my Englishman realized he had another Sarah Calhoun in the same city. He had to wonder if he'd killed the correct one."

She again looked up at Sam. "I'm sorry. That was crass. Are you all right?" Sam nodded, and she continued reading. "That's when this man evidently began following me." She sought Sam's eyes. "Do you believe that? Some detective I am. I was being followed and didn't know it."

Sam smiled at her. "I think you're the best detective who ever lived."

Loving warmth suffused throughout Yancey. "You're just saying that because you love me."

"I do love you. But it remains true: you are the best detective who ever lived."

Suddenly shy, she took up the report again and poked a finger at the next paragraph. "Oh, Sam, I was right. The Englishman I killed *was* the same one who bribed the doctors at the asylum. Mr. Pinkerton turned them over to the police and they confessed, even describing him and saying the man who'd paid them to turn Sarah out was English. Ha."

Suddenly remembering the implications of all this to Sam, she looked up to see how he was faring. He'd crossed his arms and was frowning, giving the impression of listening and sorting facts. "I wonder that the doctors didn't allow your John Bartholomew to simply slip inside the asylum to . . . do his dirty work. It would have been more easily covered up. I would certainly have never known anything but what they told me. Nor would the police."

Yancey considered that a moment, trying to reason it out. Then she believed she had it. "That makes perfect sense, Sam—except for the fact that Sarah was not a run-of-the-mill patient. She was prominent, a duchess, and you had money. You could have made tremendous trouble for them. But this way, as Mr. Pinkerton says, they tried to convince him that she escaped and the rest was a tragedy. God's will."

Sam snorted. "Black-hearted bastards. The police and God can deal with them. But what about Roderick? Is there anything in there about him?"

Yancey sorted the pages of the letter. "Not so far. But there is another page here. Let me see if it sheds some light on that." She read silently and then looked up at Sam. "Oh, Sam, yes. Mr. Pinkerton writes that Clara told the agents that Thomas Almont, who was her sweetheart, said his friend Mr. Bartholomew had bragged last autumn that he was pulling a double-cross on a duchess who'd secretly hired him to find her daughter-in-law. He says the woman's nephew, a *duke,* paid him to send the woman a false report, which he did, including my address to throw her off. His own bit of genius, no doubt. And then he was paid to . . . kill the real duchess."

Sam covered his face with his hands and breathed raggedly. Finally, he lowered them and exhaled. "Why in God's name would he want Sarah dead? What threat was she to him?"

"I don't know, Sam," Yancey said quietly, although she had her suspicions on that score, as well. Jealousy. Ambition. Gambling debts. She thought about the baby Sarah had been carrying. A legitimate heir would be a threat to a man trying to eliminate all the heirs to a fortune that he saw as a quick fix to his problems, wouldn't it? She wondered again if she should tell Sam about the baby. But decided that no, not today. Today was fraught with too much sorrow already. Later, perhaps another day, when he was stronger, she would tell him.

But then she decided that one quick question was needed. "Sam, tell me, how long before you left for England had you had Sarah committed?"

"About a year. Why? Is that important?"

She shrugged. "No. I'm just trying to leave no stone unturned."

A year. Yancey could hardly believe that Sam would demand his conjugal rights of an insane woman. The child was not Sam's. Not an heir to Somerset at all. There'd been no need to kill Sarah and thereby the baby. But the much sadder truth was that Sarah had been terribly misused by either another inmate or someone on the staff. What awful knowledge. Sick to her soul, Yancey fought to keep her emotions off her face.

She watched as Sam took the few steps over to his desk and, turning, leaned against it, crossing his legs at the ankles and bracing his hands to either side of him. He now faced Yancey. "It's all so casually evil, Yancey. And, as you said, chance. Luck. Good intentions on my mother's part. Hard to take in all at once. But that's it, isn't it—all our answers?"

She hated to remind him, but . . . "Except for who killed Roderick. And why."

Sam exhaled sharply, looking away from her and shaking his head. "I'd already forgotten about Roderick. And after this letter, I can hardly say I care who did it. Bravo for them."

"I know you don't mean that. And you'd best care. The killer could still be in your home. And we don't know what his . . . or her . . . motivation is. Or who might be next."

Sam exploded. "Christ Almighty, Yancey. If it's not you or my mother or Nana, then it has to be one of my staff. There's no one else left. I give them everything, you know. Pay them more than the going rate. Give them more suits of clothes than is required. Feed them better. Furnish their rooms above standard. Give them liberal time off. And for what in return? Good service and loyalty. Is that so much to ask—that they don't go around killing off my family?"

These questions didn't require answers, so Yancey wisely said nothing.

Sam eyed her angrily, then exhaled gustily and seemed to settle down. "I'm sorry. Go on. What do we do now?"

"I begin my individual questioning of your staff. But Sam, I'm sorry that I'm the one who must expose all these awful plots and dark motivations to you."

"I appreciate that, Yancey. I'd much rather you be the one telling me all this as opposed to being the one killed by all this plotting. The fact remains that Roderick was in your room for no good reason. And it's my guess that the knife plunged into his back was originally meant for you." Sam stopped talking. His breathing sounded labored. "My God, it all but stops my heart just to talk about such a possibility, Yancey." He held a hand out to her. "Come here."

She went willingly. Standing between Sam's legs, she hugged him fiercely, lowering her head to rest it on his shoulder. She'd never felt so warmed and protected, so safe. God, how she loved him.

Sam kissed the top of her head and held her tightly. "When all of this is done, Yancey, what are you doing to do?"

She stilled. She knew what he meant, but she didn't have an answer for him, not one he'd like or even one she liked. So she chose to act as if she'd misunderstood him. "Why, report back to Mr. Pinkerton. Thank him for dropping the review of my past cases. Thank him for his timely letter. And let him know what's happened here."

Pressed so close to Sam that she could feel his heart beat under her hand, Yancey waited for his response. He said nothing but kissed the top of her head again and held her tightly. She felt she could go on forever like this . . . holding Sam and knowing he loved her and that she loved him. Why couldn't it be enough? And who was to say it wasn't?

Yancey frowned, thinking about that and feeling she was moving closer to some truth she needed to realize . . . a glimmer . . . a tiny light in her heart getting brighter, telling her—

The door to the study suddenly opened. Gasping, Yancey broke away from Sam, reaching around him for her gun. Sam just as quickly grabbed his up. Along with him, and in one motion, she cocked hers and whipped around, aiming her gun, as Sam did his, at—

Mrs. Edgars. Gasping her shock, the woman pulled up short, her dark little eyes rounded as she put a hand to her chest, over her heart. "Dear God, don't shoot. I am so sorry. I only came to tell you that Her Grace, your mother, is in her rooms and asking for you, sir. She sent me to get you. Her carriage is being readied, as you know, and she says she wishes to discuss with you what she should tell her sister."

Sam pulled his gun up, released the hammer, and held the Colt down at his side. Shaking his head, no doubt trying to recover from the fright they'd just had, he instructed, "Tell my mother I will attend her momentarily."

Yancey had lowered her gun, too, but gave the woman no quarter. Mrs. Edgars seemed awfully calm and collected for someone with two guns trained on her. Her reaction was more that of someone who'd turned a corner and accidentally bumped into another person she hadn't expected would be there. But at least this time, she hadn't screamed and fainted.

Had Mrs. Edgars been listening outside the door? Yancey wondered. Had she been there this whole time? Obviously she'd shaken Scotty somehow. And could her intention now be to separate Sam from her with this story of his mother asking for him? If she were right, Yancey believed, then Sam would be in no danger because Mrs. Edgars, for whatever reason, wanted her, Yancey, alone. Yancey's instincts said so. It was she Mrs. Edgars wanted. Not Sam.

Well, that was fine with her, Yancey thought, pronouncing herself ready. Right now, given that they'd started their day with a murder, she was also ready to suspect even the little dog, Mr. Marples, and his tormentors, the cats Mary, Alice, and Jane, of treachery.

Sam dismissed the woman and she left, closing the door behind her. He immediately turned to Yancey. "What do you think?"

She eyed the door and then looked up at Sam. "I think you should go see about your mother."

"And what are you going to do, my beloved Pinkerton?" He pulled her to him for a deep, lingering kiss that raced Yancey's blood through her veins and weakened her knees.

When he finally released her, she held on to his shirt and tried to regain her balance and her breathing. "Don't do that, Sam, when I'm holding a gun. It's liable to go off, darling."

"It's not the only thing," he said archly, tucking his Colt into his waistband.

Frowning, Yancey teased, "Be careful placing that gun there, my love. Really."

He winked at her. "I know what I'm doing."

She curtsied. "I can vouch for that, Your Grace."

Chuckling, he swaggered over to the closed door of the office. Though she thoroughly enjoyed his performance, Yancey eyed him soberly, worrying. But by the time he had his hand on the knob and turned to her, she had her teasing expression back in place. But it faded in light of the look

Sam sent her. A wealth of emotions shone from his wonderful gray eyes. A world of love and gratitude and understanding . . . all sent her way from his heart. All she had to do was reach out and take it, it suggested.

Sam cleared his throat, ending the quiet moment of communion between them. "Thank you, Yancey, for everything you've done and for everything you're going to do. This would be impossible without you."

Warmed to her toes, and embarrassed, Yancey said, quietly, "You're welcome."

Sam nodded, still holding her gaze. "When all this is over, I'll mourn, Yancey."

He meant for Sarah. Yancey felt tears prick at her eyes. She couldn't have loved him more than she did at this moment. "I know you will, Sam." Then she thought of the baby. "So will I."

Sam cleared his throat and became all business. "Now, where did you say you'd be?"

"I didn't. But I need to question your staff. Someone may have seen or heard something. Whom should I question first?"

Sam nodded. "I have an answer for you. But first let me say that you are to take your gun, be very careful, and trust no one."

What a darling man. "Do you realize, Sam, that you are beginning to sound like me?"

He ducked his chin in acknowledgment. "Your good influence, no doubt. Now, may I suggest you start with the kitchen staff? I'll need Scotty for a bit, to help with Mother . . . and Roderick. But then I'll tell Scotty to be at your disposal. He can fetch the staff to you. Why don't you use the dining room? Hopefully, you can quickly eliminate the cooks—despite their ready access to sharp kitchen knives—so that we may have a meal sometime today."

"How practical of you. Then the kitchen staff it is." Perfect. Yancey had her own plans for what she intended to do, but she wasn't telling him. "Now, I don't expect to be interrupted by you, Sam, while I am talking to your staff behind closed doors. They won't speak up in front of you, I daresay." Before he could protest, she waved a dismissive hand at him. "See about your mother and, by all means, keep your nana at your side. Oh, one last thing? If I may avail myself of your writing materials? I need to make a log of answers."

"Yancey." His gray eyes caressed her face. "What's mine is yours. You'll find everything you need in my desk. Take whatever you desire."

"Thank you, Your Grace." He was such a kind, generous . . . and easily duped . . . man.

# Chapter Twenty-two

Alone now, Yancey strode purposefully through Stonebridge manor. She regretted having to lie to Sam, but it couldn't be helped. *Hang the kitchen staff* was her opinion. *And the rest of the staff, too. Let them all stay where they are.* Though confined to their rooms, they were also safe and, more importantly, not in her way. She hadn't thought it a necessary step to begin with, sending them to their rooms . . . at least, not so far as isolating a suspect went.

After all, no one was guarding them upstairs in their rooms. So, if any of them were guilty, he or she could easily enough have slipped away. But not a one of them would feel the need . . . because not a one of them was guilty. Yancey thought she knew who was, though. And that was the one she sought. If this went well, then the master of Stonebridge and his staff would not miss their noonday meal. She hoped only that she would be among the living at that time and could join them at the table.

Yancey moved as silently as possible in and out of each room on the first floor. The conservatory. No. The front parlor. No. Looking, always looking. No need to check the study. She and Sam had just been in there, so her prey wouldn't be. And she wasn't in the dining room, either. Yancey stood there, thinking and staring at the ornate centerpiece in the middle of the impossibly long table. Where next?

The drawing room. She exited the dining room and went back down the hall toward what was, with the exception of Sam's bedroom, perhaps her favorite room in the manor. As she walked, though alert for any sudden noise or movement, she smiled a diabolical smile. Wasn't it interesting that she knew where every single person inside the manor house was . . . except one?

Sam, his nana, and her nurse, Mrs. Convers, were with the dowager duchess, as were the mourning woman's army of personal maids. The dowager had vouched for each of them and had insisted that they remain with her. Yancey wanted no trouble from Sam's indomitable and distraught mother and had quickly consented to that arrangement—as long as they stayed in her suite. But the remainder of the staff, including Robin now, was sequestered. And Scotty, soon freed by Sam, would lumber slowly up the interminable stairs, up to the highest reaches of the house, a sort of fourth floor under the manor's eaves, to retrieve for Yancey some hapless soul for her ostensibly to question.

By her best estimate, she had about thirty minutes before Scotty got back with a servant in tow. He'd find the dining room empty and would—no doubt, still holding the arm of the poor wretch he'd brought with him, if she knew her man—go find Sam and alert him that she was missing. She didn't want it to go that far, so she had to move quickly.

Mrs. Edgars couldn't have disappeared into thin air. And although Yancey was exercising every precaution, she didn't really believe the woman was actually hiding. What good would that do her? She couldn't stay crouched behind a door or piece of furniture forever. Ridiculous notion. In truth, and well Yancey knew it, all the housekeeper had to do was go about her business and say nothing—and she would get away with murder. The biggest mistake most murderers made was they told someone and left themselves vulnerable. In her employment as a Pinkerton, Yancey had had to figure out whom the suspected robber or murderer might have told of their crime, then disguise herself and go question them.

Simple but effective. However, in this case that wasn't

possible. The murderess already knew Yancey was a Pinkerton. The murderess probably also figured that Yancey knew she'd killed Roderick. And the murderess also knew she had an eyewitness—Her Grace Nana. A very unstable situation, at best—one that caused Yancey great distress.

Still, because her search of the rooms was proving fruitless, Yancey supposed the woman could have guiltily slipped away, now that Scotty wasn't dogging her every step. In fact, Yancey had given the housekeeper free run of the manor to see if she would leave. But she hadn't. Not that she was innocent. It was more likely that the woman knew she might escape the house, but given that the manor sat up on a hill, she would have been visible from any window. But if she did escape everyone's notice, she wouldn't have got far on foot. She would need a horse or a carriage and team to make good her escape.

Yancey was willing to bet that the housekeeper didn't have the authority to order one herself. And even if she did, the men were busy preparing the coach and carriages for the dowager and her entourage. Yancey found it hard to believe they would abandon those efforts to take orders from the housekeeper. At the very least, the stablemen would have questioned her or sent word to the manor for verification that her request was approved.

So, essentially, though the woman had freedom to move about the manor, the scene of the crime, she was also held prisoner here by her very secondary social status. She wouldn't leave. She couldn't. But she would make Yancey seek her out. So this was a game of cat and mouse. Right now, though, not knowing where the woman was, Yancey felt more like the mouse than the cat. Or the fox, she quickly reminded herself.

Yancey had her gun in her hand and her arm down at her side. She wasn't nearly as concerned for herself, or even Sam—a strong, capable man—as she was for Her Grace Nana. Yancey worried that, despite her warning to Sam to keep his nana with him, the old dear would slip away from the emotional crowd gathered there. That could be tragic because Her Grace Nana was the most vulnerable one of them all. She had seen Mrs. Edgars kill Roderick, Yancey was certain of it. Though the ancient woman didn't recall it at the moment, it was only a matter of time before her fog cleared—and well Mrs. Edgars would know that, too. Yancey couldn't bear the thought of Her Grace Nana being attacked by the knife-wielding housekeeper.

Just the thought of such a scene halted Yancey and left her weak. She held on to the wall a moment and concentrated on taking deep, calming breaths. She had to remind herself that it wasn't going to happen, not if she had anything to do with it. And she did. She had everything to do with it. There. Yancey let go of the wall and stood under her own power. She tested her legs and her resolve. Steady as a rock. Smiling grimly, she set off again for the drawing room, which was just ahead.

Thinking of Mrs. Edgars, Yancey wondered what could possibly be driving the woman to kill Sam's family. Yancey realized she didn't know enough about her to even hazard a guess. But she sincerely hoped she didn't have to kill the housekeeper. All she wanted was answers from her. Then she would have her locked away somewhere until Sam could get the authorities here to take her away. England had an excellent court system. As far as Yancey was concerned, it was up to them to try her and punish her.

It sounded all neat and orderly to her, but the reality was, and well Yancey knew it, that the woman most likely would not want to be captured, knowing the fate that awaited her. Yancey sighed. That meant a life-or-death struggle. Yancey pulled a face. *Not another one.* For her, the two deaths already on her soul were weighty enough. But still, she didn't rule out violence. She hated it, but never pretended that the potential for it didn't exist. To do so could only get her killed. And when it came to killing or being killed . . . well, she'd twice over proven that her will to live was firmly intact.

At this point in her thinking, she stealthily approached the drawing room. Curious that the doors would be open. They weren't normally. But there could be any number of innocent reasons for that. Or guilty ones. From the safety of the doorway, Yancey began quietly looking around. Her trained gaze considered each piece of furniture and every corner. Any nook or cranny that could hide a person the size of Mrs. Edgars warranted Yancey's attention. But nothing she saw gave her alarm. Too bad the woman couldn't have been simply sitting in here, perhaps with tea prepared, and waiting for Yancey so they could have a nice chat about what had happened.

*Wouldn't that be lovely?* Yes, but not likely. Yancey entered the room, thinking, *Drat.* Did the woman mean to make her search the second floor for her? Yancey didn't relish that prospect one bit. She thought of the long, mirrored ballroom, the many dressing rooms for the ladies, the billiards room for the gentlemen, and shook her head. All manner of rooms unfamiliar to her. Less certain ground. But the next places she had to look.

As she turned to leave, her gaze fell on the French doors leading out onto the terrace. They too were open. Of course, she'd seen that the instant she'd walked into the room. But *the very fact of their being open* hadn't struck her as important until now. Standing there, frowning, she concentrated on what she could see of the out-of-doors. A beautiful May day. Sunshine. A warm breeze. Birds chirping. A butterfly flitting hither and yon over the many flower pots. A perfectly innocent day, by all accounts.

Why would these doors be open if no one was in here to enjoy the air? Was this a trap? Or was it a trail, a clue, provided by her quarry? A way of directing her steps? Yancey suddenly felt certain of it. With each step she took toward the open doors, her heart rate picked up. This, then, was her old, familiar instinct kicking in. It happened every time she got close to the villain or the answers. Instead of scaring her, it reassured her that the end was near.

Yancey stepped out onto the terrace and looked around. Of course, no gardeners swarmed over the place today. Her orders. She'd wanted nothing and no one between her and her quarry. No one to be used as a shield or to inadvertently stop a bullet not meant for him. So where was she supposed to go from here? No obvious clues presented themselves.

Yancey worried her bottom lip with her teeth as she narrowed her eyes.

Her gaze lit on the high hedges that formed the maze. No. Not even if she saw Mrs. Edgars dart in there would she follow. Logic told her that wouldn't be necessary or even smart because all she would have to do, in that eventuality, was wait. The woman would have to exit at some point.

But again, no Mrs. Edgars. Yancey tensed her hand around her gun and took a slow, considering walk of the sun-dappled terrace's entire perimeter while she kept her gaze trained on the grounds. Nothing was amiss. No darting movements. No black-clad woman standing out in a field, waving a hanky and calling out to her. Yancey grunted her amusement at her own dark humor. If only something so obvious would happen. But the only movement she saw was that of birds and butterflies and breeze-fanned tops of the trees. Concluding her stroll on the right side of the terrace, Yancey turned back around and thought to look up.

Her heart all but stopped. "Good Lord!" She put a hand to her heart and realized her mouth had dropped open. "I should have known," she said aloud but quietly. "The tower."

There she was. Mrs. Edgars, dressed all in black. She was sitting in the high, high window of the room at the top of the ancient tower. She wasn't waving at Yancey, though. Instead, as if nothing were amiss, her hands were in her lap and her feet dangled outside in the air. From this distance, Yancey couldn't see the housekeeper's expression, but the woman's head was angled in such a way that Yancey knew her prey had spotted her.

The woman meant to jump. She meant to kill herself. Sudden and unaccustomed panic seized Yancey. She couldn't think what to do or how to stop the woman. She feared that if she called out to her or even so much as looked away, Mrs. Edgars would jump. Fear for the woman, and fear for herself for having to witness such a scene, held Yancey riveted to the spot, staring up at the housekeeper. Should she get Sam? Was there time to seek help? Or . . . should she just let the murdering woman jump? No. Yancey quickly dismissed that. Such a cold, hard thought. She refused to allow such a notion to claim her heart. She had to do something.

Suddenly the seconds seemed to be flying by, faster and faster. But then Yancey realized something else—something disturbing. Maybe Mrs. Edgars didn't mean to jump at all. Couldn't this be a ruse to have Yancey running up the narrow, winding stairwell, thinking only to stop her from jumping? After all, how hard would it be for Mrs. Edgars to wait until she heard Yancey on the stairs and then simply climb back inside and attack her the moment she entered the room?

Not hard at all. In fact, brilliant. But what the woman hadn't counted on was Yancey's realizing all that. Mrs. Edgars had underestimated the craftiness of the Fox. So it was professional pride and the thought of a fight with a worthy opponent that freed Yancey from her moment's panic and spurred her into decisive action. More than anything, she wanted her opponent to see exactly what she was doing and to know that she was coming.

Yancey leaned over the terrace's low railing. The drop to the soft ground was negligible. That decided, she tucked her gun into her waistband, hiked up her skirt, sat down atop the wide railing, swung her legs over, and pushed off.

Sam had accomplished quite a bit in a very short amount of time. He'd left his study and gone immediately in search of Scotty. Finding him in the butler's pantry, Sam had given him his orders. But they weren't the ones Yancey had wanted him to relay. No, they were instead Sam's own for the man. He'd told him to go the dowager's rooms and keep her and Nana and every single maid from leaving it. Scotty had merely nodded, turned around, and headed for the servants' stairs. But Sam knew he understood and would be effective.

Effective? Sam snorted a chuckle. Why, Scotty would corral that entire room full of women into one corner, if he had to, and stand in front of them glowering and with his arms crossed. And there they'd stay until Sam came to tell him otherwise. No amount of arguing or complaining on the part of the women would sway the silent butler, either. The wonderful thing about Scotty's granitelike state of mind was he wasn't the least bit impressed or intimidated by anyone. Sam knew that not even his mother would be able to move the man—and that was exactly what Sam was counting on.

For him to be effective in what he intended to do, he needed first to be certain that his loved ones were safe. At least those two loved ones would be. The other one—namely, a little hellion named Yancey—wasn't. But Sam was about to rectify that, too.

Fussing silently to himself as he left the pantry off the dining room and came around the corner, which put him at one end of the long hallway that ran the width of the central building of the manor, Sam spotted Yancey at the other end and stopped cold. Her back was to him and she appeared intent on making a search of the downstairs. Sam arched an eyebrow. So he was right. The Pinkerton agent had her gun, but no writing materials in her hand. And if she meant to make her way to the dining room, then she should be facing him . . . which she wasn't.

Feeling smug because he'd correctly guessed her intentions, Sam stood with his feet apart and his arms crossed over his chest. He watched her turn to her left and face the open doors of the drawing room. He could just see her profile, no more than the back of her head and skirt, as she evidently looked around that room. He wondered if he should make himself known to her and then confront her. He thought not. All that would do was start an argument he probably wouldn't win. And from where he was standing, she didn't appear to be in any danger. But if he heard any signs of a struggle, he could be in the room in a matter of seconds.

Satisfied, he told himself he could wait . . . at least until she came out of the drawing room. And then he would allow her to see him and to explain herself.

*A man faints one time and then docilely takes orders from a woman one-third his size,* Sam fumed, *and she thinks him both weak and mentally dull.* Had it been anyone else, he would have been angry and insulted. But this was Yancey and he loved her and found her wanting to protect him at all costs endearing—not to mention infuriating and hair-raising. Certainly, his male pride had taken a trouncing today, but that didn't mean he intended to compound his inadequacies any further by being stupid.

In a nutshell, he hadn't been taken in—not in the least—by Yancey's pretty little speech about needing writing materials to make a log or by her benign plan to question his entire staff. She meant to send him on his merry little way, none the wiser, and then go after Mrs. Edgars herself. Did she think he hadn't realized that she suspected his housekeeper—no, actually his brother's housekeeper? He'd seen clearly enough the look that had passed between the two women.

That was exactly the moment when he'd known what she intended to do. And that was when he had come up with his plan to stop her. And now here he was, about to outfox a professional Pinkerton agent and reclaim his pride. Once he'd had it out with her, he'd turn her over to Scotty and go on his own to confront Mrs. Edgars. This was his fight.

So all he had to do was wait for Yancey to exit the drawing room. He stood there, grinning. Waiting. After a few seconds, his grin faded. It became a frown. Then he became impatient and, finally, curious. *What the devil is she doing? Why is she taking so long to look around in there?* He considered the size of the room and her curiosity and concluded that maybe it hadn't been all that long. He'd wait a bit more.

Then he wondered if it would make a bigger point with her if he went to stand in the room's doorway and startled her when she turned around. Wouldn't that prove to her that she wasn't infallible—that she could be surprised? Then he remembered that gun in her hand and that she was on the trail of a villain. In that frame of mind, she was more likely to shoot him than fuss at him, should he surprise her.

So Sam stayed where he was. He uncrossed his arms and planted his hands at his waist. He shifted his weight from one foot to the other. He looked behind him in the hallway. Empty, of course. With the lawn and formal gardens off to his right, he faced forward again and watched the drawing room doors. No sign of Yancey. Not a sound, either. No raised voices. No crashing noises. *Was the woman napping?* Perplexed, Sam scratched at his head, wondering what he should do.

Then he wondered if maybe Yancey had spotted him out of the corner of her eye and was smugly waiting for him to enter the drawing room so she could show him that he wasn't as smart as he thought he was. That could be. But would she play such games with him, given that they were in dire straits? Sam's conscience was quick to point out to him that he was doing exactly what he'd just accused Yancey of. He was standing here, playing a game, much like Nana and Scotty's hide-and-seek.

Well, that did it. Stung again, Sam set himself in motion. This was nonsense. A straightforward approach was called for here. He would confront the woman and tell her that if there was any sleuthing to be done in his home, then he would, by God, be in on it. And he would not listen to any arguments from her. If he had to, he would again fire her. Sam turned into the drawing room, a pointing, accusing finger already raised and his argument already forming on his lips. But, to his great shock, the room was empty. "What the devil—?"

He looked all around, not knowing what to think. "Yancey?" No answer. His patience with her evaporated. "Yancey? Where are you? I find it hard to believe that, at a time like this, you are actually hiding behind the furniture. Come out this instant."

She didn't. Angry and frowning mightily to prove it, Sam stalked around the room, looking for her. He stopped, standing in the middle of the room, thinking and rubbing his hand over his stubbled jaw. This made no sense. He'd seen her come into this very room. And he hadn't looked away long enough for her to have escaped his notice.

A bird chirped loudly.

Startled, Sam whipped around, seeing it take wing from the balustrade. Was she out there? He sprinted out onto the terrace and quickly looked around. Nothing. She was nowhere. Gone. Vanished into thin air. Ridiculous. That did not happen. Looking this way and that, searching, hoping, he caught a movement from the corner of his eye, off to his left—and his heart came close to stopping. *Dear God, there she is.*

She was entering the door to the tower.

"Now, why the devil is she going in there?" Another movement fluttered at the edge of his vision . . . Sam looked up and gasped. Shock stiffened his knees and left him staring helplessly. "No."

He could hardly believe what he was seeing. There at the very top, and seated on the ledge of the high window, acting for all the world as if nothing were amiss, was Mrs. Edgars.

Sam took only a few precious seconds to put it all together. Yancey had done the same thing he'd just done, he reasoned. Entered this room, looked around, found it empty, stepped outside onto the terrace, again looked around, and then had caught sight of the woman sitting on the ledge. And now she meant to go up there and confront the housekeeper before the woman could jump.

*If* she meant to jump. Sam's next thought was this could be a trap on Mrs. Edgars's part. Then he knew in his heart: if he'd thought of that, so had Yancey. She was purposely, and foolishly, placing herself in great danger.

That was all he needed to realize. Sam leaped up on the railing, vaulted over it, hit the ground, and ran after Yancey. His heart pounded with his fear that she would get to the top of the narrow, winding stairs before he could catch her. He'd never forgive himself if he were too late.

# Chapter Twenty-three

One step at a time. One hard, bare stone step at a time. Creeping sideways up the winding, twisting, narrow confines of the ancient spiral that was the tower, Yancey led with her left hand along the rough wall at her back. In her right hand was her gun. At least it was cool in here, and that was good because she was in a hot sweat. Her senses attuned to the danger ahead, she kept her gaze ever upward, watching for Mrs. Edgars. The woman could decide at any moment to attack and, since Yancey had a ways to go before she even approached the tower room, the element of surprise was on the housekeeper's side. She could have a knife and could come shrieking around the next spiral at any second. Or, like Yancey, she could have a gun.

Yancey exhaled, though her tight chest made it difficult to do so. She already regretted that she'd taken the bait and entered the tower. It only now occurred to her that, just as she'd reasoned with the maze, she could simply have sat on the terrace and waited the woman out. Yancey winced. No, she didn't think she had the nerve to simply sit there and wait to see what Mrs. Edgars's choice was. She only had two. She would either jump or climb back inside. Even eventually, had she chosen the latter, she would have come out of the tower. Or she could stay in here and starve to death. Or die of thirst.

Yancey shied away from those images, focusing instead on another possibility—the one that told her she had no choice but to climb these steps. What if the woman simply waited until nightfall and came down out of the tower and reentered the house, intent on killing them all? Of course, they could post guards, but it hardly seemed fair to use as sentinels some untrained stablehand or an innocent page. And neither Sam nor Scotty could do it alone. Why put them in harm's way when she, a trained Pinkerton agent, was here and on the job? Sam had hired her to solve this. And solve it she would. No sense in allowing the woman to escape their notice.

That idea alone gave Yancey the shivers. Just as did the image her scared mind insisted on showing her, that of Mrs. Edgars charging her. Should the woman attack, Yancey knew she was too far up just to turn and run. She couldn't. That would make her a perfectly helpless target for a raging, demented woman with a big knife. Of course, she could just shoot the woman, Yancey assured herself, should Mrs. Edgars charge her. But the question was: would she have time? And would it be wise, given how bullets that missed their target would most likely ricochet off these walls?

*These thick, thick walls.* Like being sealed inside a stone mausoleum. *No.* Yancey closed her eyes and gulped in several deep breaths, assuring herself that there was air to be had. The only openings for fresh air were infrequently placed and extremely narrow portals. No doubt ancient archers had positioned themselves along these very steps so as to rain a deadly hail of arrows down on the enemy. Although she couldn't see how they'd had room to draw a bow. Not a big one, anyway. Because, had she stood in the middle of a step and stretched her arms out to either side to touch the walls, she could not have completely extended either arm before she met stone-cold resistance. It was that narrow.

And very scary. Eerily silent, too. Yancey began to wish the woman *would* charge her. Anything to break the tension.

At that second, a rock-hard arm whipped around her waist

and a big hand clamped down over her mouth. Yancey damned near passed out. Shock seized her as she was literally lifted off her feet. In less than a second, there she was—effectively trussed and gagged and held tight against the man behind her. Though she could barely draw in a breath and though she stared helplessly ahead, her senses frozen and her bones melting, she managed not to squeeze the trigger on her gun or even to drop it.

"Shhh, Yancey, it's me," her assailant whispered in her ear.

Yancey tensed with recognition, lost her temper, and kicked back as hard as she could, connecting with Sam's shin. His satisfying—to her—"Oof!" of surprise and pain had him letting go of her as quickly as he'd grabbed her. When he did, Yancey fell forward in a heap, catching herself with her left hand as she helplessly scrambled forward in a crouching run that had her two steps up before she could stop herself.

When she did, she jerked around, took the two steps down to Sam—who leaned against the wall, holding his right leg bent and rubbing his shin, a pretty helpless posture, really—and smacked his arm soundly. He grimaced, biting back a protest and frowning at her.

"What in the hell are you doing here?" she hissed, shaking his arm and dividing her gaze between him and the upward spiral of the twisting stairs around which a very demented woman—surely curious, at the very least—could come charging. "Why aren't you in your mother's room, Sam?"

His glare alone should have melted her gun. "Because I am not five years old to be sent to my mother's room. Why aren't you in the dining room?"

Well, he had her there. "Because," Yancey said, letting go of him. That wasn't much of an explanation. Sam's raised eyebrows said he agreed. Yancey stuck her gun in her waistband and changed the subject. "Do you know that Mrs. Edgars is sitting up there in the window? I think she means to jump."

"At the very least, she means to jump," Sam whispered stridently, letting go of his leg and standing now on his own two feet. "I saw you come running in here and then saw her up there and feared this could be a trap."

"Which is why we're whispering, Sam." Yancey pointed back down the way he'd come, toward the bottom of the tower. "Now, go on. Get out of here. I can take care of this by myself."

The stubborn man crossed his arms over his broad chest and said, "No."

Yancey firmed her lips—a dangerous sign to anyone who knew her well. "I work alone."

"We've had this conversation." He stood there like a rock. Solid. Determined. Immovable.

But . . . he was lower on the stairs than she was. Giving no warning as to her intentions, Yancey simply turned around, making a darting run up the stairs. She was about one up on him before the back of her skirt was grabbed and she was again yanked backward and hauled up against Sam.

"Dammit, Sam," she gritted out, hissing and squirming in his grip as he turned them around in the stairwell. In their struggle, Yancey's gun dislodged and went clattering back down the stairs. Along with Sam, she froze, staring after it as it disappeared around the curve of the worn-smooth steps. "Look at that. You put me down and stop this nonsense. That woman up there is a killer."

"I am fully aware of that. And you are now unarmed. So . . ." He finished his sentence by lowering Yancey to her feet and letting her go.

Blinking, she stood there for one disoriented second, and then realized what he'd done. She now faced downward, and he was behind her. Yancey spun around and, sure enough, she saw Sam disappearing around the next bend. Frustrated with him, she charged up three narrow steps and did the only thing she could think to do. She grabbed the back of Sam's waistband and hung on for all she was worth . . . which turned out to be about ten cents, maybe, because she barely even slowed him down.

Determined, and desperate to protect the man she loved, she stiffened her entire body in a straight line and dragged her feet. Her boot-toes edged against the riser of the next step and held tight. Yancey had just effectively made an anchor of herself. The resistance of her weight finally, effectively stopped Sam . . . and lowered his pants a good couple of inches.

Cussing, tugging at her grip on him, and trying hard to surge forward, all while hanging on to the wall and trying desperately to keep his pants up, Sam conceded the battle. His back to her, he stopped resisting and held his hands up. "All right, all right. This isn't working. I give up. You can let go now."

"Ha." That was too easy, and she wasn't about to fall for such a play. The second she let go, he would bound up those steps again, and well she knew it. "Not on your life, Sam Treyhorne. Which is exactly what I'm trying to save." She stared at his behind. "Or your sweet ass, at any rate."

The sound of disgust he made told her he was unmoved by her sentiment. He planted his hands at his waist and tried to turn enough to see her . . . but Yancey tensed, a clear sign that she meant to yank his pants down farther should he try anything untoward. He froze. "I said I give up." His voice was a hoarse hiss of sound. "What the hell do you suggest we do, Yancey? We can't stay like this the rest of our lives."

"Say you'll go back down and let me handle this."

"Don't be ridiculous. You don't even have a weapon now. Besides, I am more than twice your size. And look—" He produced his gun from the front of his waistband and held it up, waggling it for her to see before replacing it in the front of his trousers. "I have a weapon, should I need it. And Mrs. Edgars is *my* housekeeper, and I will deal with her."

Yancey's arms were getting tired. "You hired me to do that."

"Well, I certainly didn't count on this, did I? So . . . you're fired."

"I am not."

"I can fire you if I so choose. Now tell me, do you really intend to pull my pants down?"

"To the ground, Sam." She was having trouble keeping her grip and it was making her feel grim. "If need be, my love, to the ground. And then we'll see how fast you can get up these steps having to hop like a rabbit."

"I have absolutely no intention of doing something so undignified. Now let go."

"No." Every muscle in her body ached with the strain.

Sam lost his temper, no longer bothering to keep his voice down. "Yancey, by now Mrs. Edgars could have already jumped, her body been discovered and hauled away and buried and the funeral over. We *must* solve this impasse."

His voice echoed and ricocheted up and down the hollow spiral of the tower.

"I'm fully aware of that, Sam," Yancey shouted back. She felt Sam give an experimental push forward. She renewed her grip and pulled down hard. The twelfth Duke of Somerset's trousers now rode around his hips, almost to his legs. "But," Yancey assured the stubborn man, "you'll still be standing here with your pants around your ankles and with me latched onto them . . . Your Grace."

Sam muttered a particularly foul oath and then declared, "That's enough." He then did the one thing Yancey had feared he'd think of. He backed down one step, causing her to lose her toehold and therefore her tension. The second she squawked and felt her body give, Sam reached around behind him and grabbed her hands up together. "Aha!" he cried triumphantly, forcing Yancey's grip off his pants and hauling her upright.

In one swift move, with Yancey protesting and struggling, though ineffectually against his size and strength, Sam very neatly clutched both of her wrists with one hand and pulled his pants up with the other. "What do you think of *that,* Miss Pinkerton?"

Yancey looked past Sam and stilled, sobering dramatically. "Sam," she said, speaking slowly and deliberately, "behind you."

He eyed her dubiously, but then shook his head. "No. I assure you I am not going to fall for that old trick, my dear. Geoffrey used to try that one all the time when we were boys. Tell me some scary monster was behind me."

With her hands being held above her head by Sam, Yancey faced toward the tower room, and divided her wide-eyed gaze between Sam and the stairs behind him. Her mouth went dry. "And when you turned around, Sam, was he ever telling the truth? Was someone there?"

Perhaps it was something in her voice, Yancey didn't know. Or maybe it was the look on her face. But Sam sobered and stilled. "She's right behind me, isn't she?"

Her heart pounding, Yancey nodded. "Yes. She is."

Almost conversationally, Sam said, "What's she doing?"

Yancey spared the madwoman a glance. "Just standing there."

"Lovely. Any weapons that you can see?"

"A gun."

"Well," Sam commented, mock cheerfully.

Yancey eyed the unmoving woman again and then looked up at the man she loved more than she loved anyone else in the entire world. "It's been my experience, Sam, honey, that things get interesting at about this point."

He nodded, being very congenial. "I can see how they would. Any suggestions?"

"You could probably let go of my hands before they go numb. That would be a good start."

He looked from her face to her hands and then met her gaze again. "Oh. Sorry. Of course." He released his grip on her.

"Nice and easy now." Yancey lowered her arms. "No sudden moves," she coached Sam. "Don't turn around and look at her. That might set her off."

"And we don't want to do that."

"No, we don't," Yancey said, her gaze now slipping to Mrs. Edgars, whose black eyes shone with an oily glaze. The woman had clearly snapped and gone completely around the bend. "Don't move, Sam, I need you to cover me," Yancey said quietly, edging her left hand, since her right was in Mrs. Edgars's line of sight, toward Sam's waistband.

Yancey saw in his eyes that he meant to question her, but she gave a serious but subtle shake of her head, mouthing *No.* His features contorted by a look of fear, Sam mouthed back *I love you.* And Yancey winked at him.

Absolutely terrified, though—one single mistake in judgment now could get them both killed—Yancey inhaled and exhaled very slowly. God alone knew what would set the woman off . . . or when. Yancey flicked her gaze the woman's way again. And wanted to die. She was right behind Sam. Right behind him. Maybe two steps up from him. Dear God, the man's entire broad back and precious head were exposed to the gun Mrs. Edgars held pointed at him. If he so much as moved one inch, some instinct told Yancey . . . just one inch . . .

Sam suddenly shifted his weight, and Yancey froze. His gray eyes had a look in them that scared her terribly. He meant to do something brave and stupid. "Yancey," he said very softly, "I can't let—"

"No." She felt certain she would cry. He was going to do it. Already he was slowly bringing his hand toward his gun. "Sam, honey, no," Yancey pleaded quietly, desperately. He would be dead before he could get turned around with it. Tears spilled over and coursed down her cheeks as she got her hand closed around the grip on Sam's Colt before his could. But then he closed his hand over hers, holding them both there. She never looked away from him. "Please, baby. This is what I do for a living."

He smiled down into her face. "Well, you're fired. Forever."

Just then, behind Sam, Mrs. Edgars spoke. "I had to do it. I had to."

A jet of fear shot through Yancey and widened her eyes. Sam's features hardened, as did his grip on her hand. Over his shoulder he barked out, "Why?"

"Because he lied to me. He told me if I helped him, he'd make me his overseer of both Glenmore and Somerset. He was poor. Had no money. Was about to lose his precious estate. But he lied to me, and then he laughed at me."

Then it was true. The gambling debts. All of this sadness was over money and greed and pride. Yancey felt suspended in time, as if her heart weren't even beating, as she listened to Sam question his housekeeper. She hoped he realized that when she was done talking, she would start shooting.

"What happened to my brother, Mrs. Edgars?" Sam's grip on her hand tightened painfully. Yancey bit down on the inside of her cheek and held on.

"I gave him a medicine that killed him. For the heart."

"There was nothing wrong with Geoffrey's heart."

She cackled. "There was after that. It was easy. He was having trouble sleeping. Had his own gambling debts to worry about. So I got him something for sleep—we were in London, it was easy to buy—and I slipped the other drug in his sleeping powder. He took it right down with water. Just like a baby."

Yancey watched helplessly as Sam's face drained of color. He closed his eyes and exhaled slowly. Then he opened them and said, still over his shoulder, still with his back to the murdering woman, "Why didn't you kill me, Mrs. Edgars?"

"You were next. I wanted you here a while so no one would suspect another death so soon. But then *she* arrived—"

"Leave her out of this. Tell me about Roderick, the man who was going to make you mistress of the combined duchies. Why did you kill him?"

"He was trying to stop me from killing her!" Greatly agitated now, Mrs. Edgars narrowed her eyes on Yancey.

Yancey felt chilled, much as she would if a poisonous snake had her in its sights. "Roderick meant to *stop* you from killing me?"

"Yes." And she hated that he had. It was there in her malevolent gaze.

This was a revelation. Yancey didn't have to ask the woman why she wanted to kill her. She knew. Last night, she and Sam's cousin had believed she, Yancey, was the actual Duchess of Somerset returned from America, reunited with Sam, and ready to produce heirs that would complicate their dreams of grandeur. But why Roderick should stop her—

"He said you didn't need to die anymore. But I didn't believe him, and I couldn't let you have babies." Spittle foamed at the corners of Mrs. Edgars's mouth. "I couldn't. But you weren't in your room. You were in his bed and—"

"What happened, Mrs. Edgars?" Sam interrupted. "Did my cousin just come home early and surprise you?"

The woman directed her gaze and her gun to Sam's back. Yancey's knees weakened . . . but she held on to his gun, even when he moved his hands to grip her arms and hold her close to him.

"Yes. He laughed and told me he didn't need me," Mrs. Edgars all but shouted, her voice echoing like Sam's had moments ago. "He said he was going to tell the authorities that I had killed the duke on my own. He said they'd believe him, too, because he was a peer and I was nobody. He said I'd spend my life in prison. I won't do that."

Yancey could only exchange a look with Sam. What could they say? Mrs. Edgars was right. Roderick would have been believed over Mrs. Edgars.

"But what changed, Mrs. Edgars? Why did Roderick no longer need me and Miss Calhoun dead?"

"Because last night he found himself a wife. No Englishwoman of the nobility would have him. You know that. But he and the Duke of Yarborough got the man's ward, a rich German niece, to consent to marry him." Mrs. Edgars's expression became a snarl. "The Duke of Yarborough is as bad a man as your cousin. They don't care how they use a woman as long as she's rich. And this one's ugly and old, past her prime. A spinster. But her dowry would have saved his precious Glenmore. That was all he cared about. Not me and my plans. But I showed him. He can't use me like that. Nobody uses me. And now it's your turn to find that out."

The moment was here. There was no sense arguing that Sam or she hadn't used the woman at all. Fright seized Yancey. She wet her lips and shifted her weight, hoping to communicate the urgency to Sam. But his attention was riveted behind Yancey, back down the stairs. She couldn't see what or who—

"Now, Scotty!" Sam yelled.

*Scotty?* That was all she had time to think before Sam shoved her aside and down, following after her, crashing into her and sending her to the cold, hard steps. His weight atop her knocked the breath out of her. Yancey banged her head against the wall and her ears rang. Shots were ringing out from all sides, it seemed. She thought she heard Mrs. Edgars scream and Scotty—where had Scotty come from?—grunt as if in pain. Then Yancey realized that somehow she had Sam's gun in her hand, that he had lifted his weight off her, and was up on his knees—

But then, sickeningly, he toppled limply and fell atop her, only to immediately roll off her. Frantic, screaming, Yancey reached for him, grabbing his shirt. "Sam? Sam?"

But he was slippery and her hand slid off him. Yancey's mind wouldn't comprehend what she was seeing. Numb, she held her hand up. It was red. Blood. Sam's blood? Had she shot Sam? She looked stupidly at the gun. And then looked up from where she sat in a heap with her back to the inside curve of the wall. Scotty was lying like a broken doll off to her left. Blood covered his chest.

"Scotty?" Yancey wondered where that child's voice had come from. Then she realized it was hers. Numb, feeling as if every movement were accomplished only with great effort, Yancey turned her head the other way. There stood Mrs. Edgars. She had her back to the wall and one foot on one step and her other on the next one down. She had blood on her, too. But, her arm trembling, she was raising it and pointing her gun at Yancey. Yancey stared at the woman and then at the gun in her hand.

Something in her mind clicked. A familiar memory. She said, quite simply, "Oh," and raised the gun, aiming at Mrs. Edgars. She fired one shot and caught the woman neatly between the eyes. In a daze, Yancey watched the woman slide down the wall and just sit there.

"You're an awfully good shot, dear," an ancient-sounding little voice said. "I find that a very helpful trait for a duchess to have."

Yancey slowly rotated her head to her left again. There stood Her Grace Nana. Suddenly so very, very tired for some reason, Yancey smiled at the elderly woman. "Thank you."

Yancey then passed out.

# Epilogue

**NOVEMBER 1878, STONEBRIDGE MANOR**

The Duchess of Somerset, dressed regally yet warmly, stood at one of the two long windows in her sitting room. Her expression serious, she tilted the letter she read toward the day's light outside, the better to make out the writing. Coming to a place where she could stop, she glanced up and saw that outside a gentle snow had begun to fall. Her reflection in the window showed her she had a delighted smile on her face. By tomorrow morning, the grounds would be coated in a mantle of white.

Then her frown returned. Oh, dear, tomorrow her mother-in-law and her sister, the dowager Duchess of Glenmore, were supposed to come for a visit. Now they might not be able to, if the snow kept up. Well, if she knew Rosamond Sparrow Treyhorne, nothing could keep her from visiting her grandchild. She might have chosen to live with her sister, but they were only a two-days' drive away at Glenmore and were frequent, and welcome, visitors at Stonebridge.

Behind her, a burning log in the fireplace snapped and popped, drawing the duchess's gaze there. She saw Robin brushing and hanging her gowns in an armoire. Everything was as it should be. Satisfied, the duchess went back to her letter, her quick mind absorbing all the pertinent facts.

"Begging your pardon, Your Grace. But will that be all?"

The duchess looked up, smiling at her lady's maid. Very polished now and sure of herself, Robin hardly looked like the same raw girl who, eighteen months ago, had been frightened by Rosamond's maids. "Yes. Thank you. Where is the duke?"

Robin sighed. "He's in the nursery again, Your Grace."

The duchess sighed as well. "Tell me he's not watching Eugenia sleeping? He'll wake her, and she'll be a little dragon princess all afternoon."

Robin giggled. "He pulls up a chair and sits right by her cradle, he does. Just sits and watches her. Makes her nurses quite testy. But he's ever so very much in love with her, he is."

And this pleased the duchess tremendously. "Yes. He's like a child himself with her. I do believe, however, he runs Scotty and Her Grace Nana a good race on who will spoil her the most."

"Oh, I think it's Scotty, hands down, Your Grace. I've never seen the like of such a big man to be so gentle with a little one, and the baby not even a year old yet."

At that moment, the door from the hallway opened and in walked the very handsome Duke of Somerset and Glenmore, a good man much loved by his wife and all those around him . . . except for his new valet, Carrouthers, who could not get the duke to submit to his ministrations without a pitched battle.

The duchess very quickly held her letter down at her side, away from the duke's notice.

"And here you are, Yancey, my love," he said. "I've just been in the nursery. Eugenia looks more and more like her beautiful mother every day."

"Yet she has your eyes. And your stubborn chin."

"Yes," he said proudly, in danger of popping his buttons off his vest. "I think we're in for it with her. Oh, and you missed it, dear. Eugenia rolled over."

He smiled at his wife, and her heart began to beat as if for the very first time. It happened every time she saw him.

"She's nine months old, sweetheart. She's been doing that for many months now."

"Yes, but she's the best at it I've ever seen." The duke nodded at Robin when she curtsied. "Hello, Robin, old girl."

"Your Grace." Robin quickly left the room, closing the door quietly behind her.

Sam watched the maid do so, and then turned to his wife. "She flees from me."

"You frighten her."

"I do? What do I do to frighten her?"

"You speak to her. You really aren't the usual thing in a duke, you know."

His grin was a sly one. "Yes. I know. That's your American influence at fault." Coming to stand behind Yancey, he wrapped his arms around her waist, holding her close and tight. "I haven't seen you all day. Where have you been keeping yourself, my love?"

Yancey leaned her head back against Sam's warm muscled chest. This man was her world. "I've been about. You are the dreary one, locking yourself away in your study all day."

"The dratted accounts, my love. Double the accounts now. And Mother's and Aunt Jane's bills were in the lot. They're not the most frugal of women." He brushed aside her hair and nibbled at her earlobe. "And then there were tenant petitioners all afternoon. By the way, I think my new secretary has his eye on your Robin."

Oh, this was good news. "Michael does? Really? Robin blushes to her roots if anyone even says his name around her."

"I'll be sure to tell him."

"You will not."

"I will. Oh, and a contingent even came in this afternoon from Lakeheath-on-Somerset. About the yearly Christmas pageant."

"Dear God."

"That's the spirit, dear." He gently turned Yancey around to face him. She could—and fully intended to—spend the rest of her life staring into his gray eyes. "I hear you received a letter today." Teasing her, he clutched at her wrist and held up her hand. "And what's this? Is it from Mr. Pinkerton?"

Yancey stared at her husband. "Yes, it is. And no, you can't."

Sam's expression fell. "No, I can't what? I don't know what you're talking about."

"You do. And you can't."

"Why not?"

Yancey crossed her arms and stared up at her vexed husband. "Because you faint at the sight of blood. And darling, I don't like to bring up bad times, but I thought you were dead that day in the tower."

He grumbled his irritation. "And I could have been, too, if I'd rolled down all those steps. Thank God for Scotty's quick thinking."

Yancey bit the inside of her cheek to keep from laughing. "Yes, wounded though he was, he managed to stop you."

"I could have been wounded, too."

Yancey nodded, putting her hands on his arms, which he'd now crossed over his chest. She leaned into him and raised her face for a kiss. "I know, sweetheart. But I thank God every day that you weren't."

"Scotty gets to go with you, doesn't he?"

Yancey sighed. "We've been through this, Sam. Yes, he does. He always goes with me." She thought to distract him. "Come on, let's go see if Eugenia is awake. We can bundle her up and take her out to see the snow."

"You're changing the subject, Yancey."

Taking her husband's hand, Yancey turned to head for the closed door to the sitting room that was now hers and Sam's together. She much preferred his suite of rooms to her prior ones when she'd arrived here undercover for Mr. Pinkerton. "Yes, I am changing the subject."

When she passed a low table in the room she dropped the letter there. Sam snatched it up, reading it as she led him out of the room. "Where's he sending you this time? Not before Christmas, I hope?"

"Yes. Before Christmas. And he wants me to go to London—"

"London? At this time of year? Is the man mad? The roads will be treacherous. Yancey, my love, when we married and you accepted Mr. Pinkerton's proposal that you become his foremost detective in England, I must say I never once thought about what it would mean to our family life, your keeping your career. While I have the utmost respect for you, dear, and your abilities, you are also my wife and—"

"Would you like to go with me?" Yancey opened the door to the hallway and turned to see Sam's face light up.

"Really? Do you mean it? And Eugenia? We have to take Eugenia." He pulled the letter up to read it. "Good heavens, stolen artwork from America has shown up in London? Splendid. That shouldn't involve any bloodshed. We'll open the house there. And take Nana. She loves London."

"Of course." Yancey's heart brimmed with love and joy. She could never have pictured an ending like this to events that began eighteen months ago as a marriage masquerade.